Praise

Leadership requires a distinct vision, which has to be translated into action, and actions, which can be emulated. Through this book, Dr. Sandeep Arora, methodically puts across the essence of this trait as it has taken shape over the years and sums it up with great observations on recent trends, on a lighter note.

Dr. Ashok Chitkara, Chancellor and Dr. Madhu Chitkara, Vice-Chancellor, Chitkara University, Punjab, India

Leadership has been defined in many ways and Leadership existed from the dawn of the civilization. Is Leadership cultural? Is Leadership a value? Is it gender specific? Is it earned or commanded and is Leadership a trait you are born with? Do leaders drive a specific agenda due to the influence of the social context in which they operate?

One can get a perspective of the above and many other questions which are in the reader's mind. Dr. Sandeep, in his book has come out with vivid details of different leaders, their leadership styles and in different cultural contexts and periods. The author is not concluding on any one style of leadership and leaves it to the reader to build his perspectives after going through different leaderships, styles in different cultural context and time-period.

A book worth reading for all the corporate leaders to broaden their horizon on leadership and styles.

Mr Venkatram Vasantwada, CEO, SEED

Nicely bejeweled by self-compiled and quoted verses, the book makes a great evolutionary reading of society as led by empires, armed forces, executives and of course the era changers -writers, poets, musicians, and the entertainers. Great reading on the world as it came up over the years.

Ashu Shukla, Dy. Inspector General of Police, CRPF, Jamshedpur

Leadership has definitely transformed civilizations over the ages, sometimes for the better and many-a-times for the worse, but so far only time has unravelled this. Often the changes have been puerile or even hilarious. The corporate world too, has had its share of such theatrical impact. Dr. Sandeep Arora has come up with a tell-all-tale on such transformations, which will be thought-provoking for corporate leaders.

Mr Alok k Sinha, Managing Director, International, Capita Software

Leadership.... Over the Years
Society & Nations......
Between the Ears!!

Dr. SANDEEP ARORA

Arrowsand Group

ZORBA BOOKS

ZORBA BOOKS

Publishing Services in India by Zorba Books, 2019

Website: www.zorbabooks.com
Email: info@zorbabooks.com

Copyright © Sandeep Arora

Print book ISBN - 978-93-88497-78-7
E-book ISBN - 978-93-88497-79-4

Zorba Books Pvt. Ltd.(opc)
Gurgaon, INDIA

In dedication to
Father,
All BITians, All those impacting me at any time of life
And
Aryan
In special dedication to
Global Autism Societies

Contents

Socio poilitical
visions over the
years

Profiles

II. Emerging Leadership Styles
(Between the Ears..........!!)

III. Afterthoughts

Prologue

Leadership as a trait, has evolved over the centuries, with physical strength and endurance being the prime capabilities during early stages of human development amidst difficult natural conditions and hostile primitive rival groups, to grand leaderships by kings and their generals to great dynasties and kingdom, requiring charisma, power, scheming and influence over the masses and warrior skills, to the later Army and military Generals of France, United Kingdoms, Russia and other countries, tasked with the toughest of the tasks to be carried out in the roughest of terrains, with an aptitude for thinking of and being party to great technological developments in automotives, armed vehicles, ammunitions and telecommunications, which became a must for an astute and precise military warfare in the 20th Century World war theatres.

Military developments in 20th Century warfare, generated entrepreneurial and managerial leadership post World war, wherein industrial production of consumer goods ensured that many heroes in this domain emerged leading the industrialization and technological advances for an easy human life. (

Social leadership has been a very important part of human development, with great thinkers, philosophers and religious preachers ensuring that the human face of all leadership activities became more visible through practices, culture, religion, arts, music and mutual acceptability. Iconic country leaders have emerged over the years, exhibiting this great sense of poise and fine balance of aptitude for social welfare, far sightedness, eye for development, excellence and flair for stimulating innovation, entrepreneurship and management to take the societies forward. Those who have shown even a slight imbalance in the above mix of attitudes, have made some erratic decisions and taken the society astray over the years for a brief period. Even great industrialists have worked for entrepreneurial success with service to society in mind, while some others have definitely not.

A stage has emerged in the 21st Century, wherein entrepreneurship practices have become more innovative, with trends of outsourcing, acquisitions and mergers throwing up great examples, wherein leadership traits have become even more intriguing, not just requiring a desire for business growth, but an attitude at offering simplified solutions as great entrepreneurship ideas, be it Business process outsourcing, IT solutions, analytic solutions, research outsourcing or business development solutions. The opportunity for leadership have multiplied and it is the skill to look out for simple ideas and make them large is what is defining leadership in the present century.

Further in the new age of equal opportunities for both gendres, leadership skill set definition paradigm has already evolved extensively, with concepts of time management, prioritization, effective communication, delegation and above all leadership impact and personal charisma being equaly available to both men and women to acquire leadership roles, and work place ease of work for both men and women being facilitated through various regulations, leadership is now more defined by the state of mind rather than a show of both physical and mental prowess.

As recurrently put across by various thoughts, what counts greatest in this age and the next, evolving too fast, it will be agility to learn and adapt, generate ideas and solutions, and thinking beyond the physically visible world into the abstract, hidden, prospective and outside this world, that will mark the frontiers of leadership traits for the next millennium.

Dr Sandeep Arora
Sand_orbbd@rediffmail.com
Sandeep.arora@chitkara.edu.in
09501105659/09316314667

1.

Leadership: Initial Traits

Braving the Odds and Coming Up Trumps

As human race evolved, slowly settling down at various locations on the globe, the relative competencies in taking adverse situations head on by themselves started taking shape as deciding benchmarks in establishing leaders amongst the herd.

Quick Decision Makers as Earliest Leaders

Lots of odds cropped up in the daily ways of life, wherein human mettle was put to test as to the mental acumen, presence of mind, decision-making and agility in execution and other traits that helped an individual or a group to avoid or escape a potential fatal threat by a beast or a savage. Be it, feeling the extreme pangs of hunger and taking a decision as to what was worth putting into mouth and how, or taking on the mighty natural men with ferocious and animal spirits, or trying to revive a seriously ill group member with all possible ways, or putting up a plan to beat the big cats and other beasts from ravaging the group's peace, fast decision makers were more readily and expectedly accepted in leadership roles.

How surprising it is that at that level of evolution, there was a distinct sense of attachment to one';s own kith and kins, and also surprisingly extending to the group, which actually were formed by way of having the same set of enemies and adversities to deal with, and a parallel sense of competition, hatred, emotions and fierceness against the groups assumed as rivals.

The goals were thus centered around a sense of evading opponents and coming up trumps at all means and the management skills were all but based on a single trait-*the spirit to conquer*, resist, attack and physical strength.

As the mutual acceptance for each other within the group increased and the group sizes increased with the realization of possibility of mutual help by recognition of different sets of talents in different individuals, which could be put to use for mutual and group welfare, the acceptable leadership qualities started acquiring new dimensions. Ability to take a larger group along, ability to convince and an evidence of having a sense of larger welfare of the group, ability to advise as to the upcoming dangers and ability to generate a new found sense of group and community happiness repeatedly, were some of the traits gradually sought for in acceptance of a leader. This also involved generation of newer social traits that included sense of giving, sense of forgiving, sense of dancing and rejoicing with others.

((i) Reference picture on page 146)

Thus the first leaders could be listed as follows:

1. The persons with good capacity to hunt
2. Those with agility to save themselves and others from beasts
3. Those who could enjoye the rain fearlessly
4. Those who could make a bed atop a high tree top
5. Finally, the invisible almighty was assumed as the *Supreme Leader* in all difficulties.

Nirakar (Formless), yet *Sarvman* (Omnipresent)- *The Supreme Lord,* later named *Shiva, Jesus, Mohammed, Gurunanak, ...and by many more names.* Today, although the society has taken jiant leap in every sphere including health management, due to inevitability of death, we still have to reach out to *the Lord and Supreme Leader,* as the last resort. So, in praise we start for *the Lord,*

Om Ganeshay Namah

2.

Community as the first functional unit

The Early community Leadership

Context:

Communities were gradually formed by symbolic, monosyllable or fluent oral and physical communication, and bonding started happening with a sense of humanity, positiveness and respect for some supernatural forces that ensured safety and happiness. Apart from the physical prowess and ability to fight and protect, emergence of traits, which could enforce discipline, uniform civil code and positive virtues in the community, were gradually recognized as the desired pillar of leadership virtues in addition to the physical and tactical prowess.

As time passed the sense of community rejoicing, sharing and happiness became more prominent factor in binding the group together, helping develop more vocal expressions in the form of songs, theatre and more refined physical expression and dance that could regale others. On the other hand community enjoyment in excess developed its own pitfalls with many in the group not able to establish a limit for themselves and going overboard and trampling on other's toes many a times, creating ruffle and tension within the groups and getting labeled as trouble mongers, rabble rousers and good for nothing in the contemporary dialect in the races existing across the globe. They were naturally deemed as unfit leaders.

रात के काले रंग में जब
आग ने अपने पीले रंग लुटाये,
अपनों की आवाज, पैरों की थपथपाहट ने,
खामोशी और खौफ के मंजर हटाए,
अलाव के इर्द गिर्द, समां बंधता गया
इसके इशारों में, उसके जोश में
कुनबा बनता, फूलता, पनपता गया!

Gradually a pattern of specialization and division of work started emerging, with some tending to food collection, others taking care of shelter, some others showing good skills at food preparation or making the food more palatable, others proving to be good at draping the community, another group at entertaining or retailing, and above all a group for protecting. There came the need for someone to Marshalall the human resources for the mentioned rolls, to define and identify schedule of activities, time of work and time for relaxation and time for community enjoyment. Thus a primary image of a leader, who had the impact, the acceptability, convincing power and the forcefulness to get the instructions implemented, emerged.

((ii) Reference picture on page 146)

Peculiarly, an emotion of respectful compliance to senior members in the group also emerged, and those entering the third phase and twilight of their life were expected as leaders on basis of their experience to handle diverse situations and ability to build up consensus. It was in case of emergencies due to demise of the senior most member that the selection of leader started taking place on the basis of cumulative merit.

Gradually the size of the group became important factor in survival with a situation whereinnormally an attack by a larger

5

group led to total or partial annihilation with men mostly being casualties and women and kids being taken over as slaves by attacking group.

Thus a second phase of organization buildup started taking shape with focus on maximum numbers, warfare training, and development of advanced attack and defense gears and buildup of community boundaries or walls with bolsters.

Religion and cognizance of a supernatural existence varied from groups and tribes, with those more at the mercy of regular natural calamities, requiring more strong emotional and spiritual healing offered by belief in the existence of a superpower who could be summoned to tide over extreme grief during the loss of a beloved community member. Thus in those communities witnessing greater catastrophes, religion started emerging as a bonding force, with the religious leaders stressing the need for a regular lifestyle, importance of empathy to others, control of emotions, ego, hatred and anger and inculcating virtues. Thus concepts of bad and good virtues started getting clearly defined, and helping communities to align inherently to a lifestyle, which could bring them together in case of emergencies. Thus leadership style here underlined the importance of uniform discipline, civil code and positive virtues, which could make the community more united, strong and peak at the time of external attacks.

The fact that Social and community living could be made more harmonious by way of a disciplined and noninterfering life was realized by many senior common members in a community and understood and taken up well by many rulers and generals and therein the concept of a uniform religion based concept of social life was taken up by many communities. Even the generals or the kings subscribed to the religious way of life and observed ceremonious obeisance to the supreme force and the associated practices as recommended by the respective preachers. The compassionate and considerate way of living led to further human evolution with the focus changing from continuous conquer and acquisition to sustenance, increasing human bondage, mutual happiness and exploration of the esoteric and reveling in art, music, poetry and other expression forms.

खुदा की खुदाई

मुष्किल–कुषाई से सजाया जहाँ उसने,

हौले हौले कौम को लगाया बसने।

कुछ दिन गुजरे अच्छे

हर शख़्सियत में ख़्वाब थे जहीन और सच्चे

फिर कुछ दर्द उछले, कुछ किस्से और कुछ अदावत,

बस्ती के बांषिदों में हुई मुखालफित।

सारे रिष्ते सारे नाते हुए जार जार,

इंसानी खुषबू हुई बेजार–जार।

एक ही मंजर आया नजर,

खुदा की रेहमत में था ऐसा असर।

खुद के गरूर पे हुआ शरमसार,

एक खुदा की खुदाई पे ही हुआ जब ऐतबार।

Use of positive and negative Reinforcements as required traits for leadership

Compassion for others created the sensitization towards well being of others, first for the people within the same tribe or community. The physically strong leader of the herd condescended to let go excess resources in the form of food, hunt, agriproduce and even women to others less stronger in the group. Thus emerged the first pattern of daily lifestyle or social living. Thus individual family units comprising a man, woman and kids,

7

were given social recognition. Men in the community were ruled to enjoy their companionship with their wives, and then expected reciprocally to take care of the needs of the family, and further also of the community, including mandatorily required being a part of the armed combat unit as and when the threat or the need to attack arose. For the same the need for reinforcing discipline was identified, and this started as reinforcement of a habit of a daily socially acceptable lifestyle. Arrangements were made to increase daily synchronization including morning alarm, hooting, afternoon lunch and siesta announcements and war training and activities, to ensure that the group created could remain cohesive for a very long period to sustain geographical, climatic, ethnic, racial, rival, medical and other catastrophes.

With the importance of uniformity and discipline established for maintaining and protecting the community, lifestyle habits and behavior patterns which disturbed community unity and stability and overall strength to take on external threat, were regularly identified and commented upon as unwanted, and in some cases punishments, starting from smaller ones and even extending up to capital punishments, were established. On the other hand useful values were recognized and appreciated with reward systems, initially in the form of free or additional eateries or as advanced designation and associated paraphernalia, or embellishments on costumes.

खुद की खींच कर, आग को समेट कर जीना सीखा

उजली सुबह, सियाह रात का सलीका सीखा।

उठने बैठने के हुए अर्थ हजार

हर बात का मर्म जहीन उसने सीखा

खुद की खिदमत में न जाऊं खुदाई भूल

उसकी रहनुमाई को पूजना सीखा,

कुछ कायदे कानून, कुछ तौर तरीके,

सबको आदाब देना और कुछ लेना सीखा

Emergence of agricultural sustainance and barter system

One fine day, the tribes understood that, plants giving them fruits, leaves and roots for eating could be grown by sowing and cultivating methods starting from seeds and other parts. Thus the concept of cultivation came in first in small quantity on small piece of land with keen observation by groups each day as to the growth of the plant and origination of research as to what factors led to more productivity and more refined varieties. Side by side, recognition of precious things (whether eatables, defense goods or ornamental) and their comparable valuation started with some things accepted as more valuable and others as less valuable on a scale. This led to a barter system with small quantities of a more valuable item being exchanged for large quantities of an item supposed to be lower on the value scale.

((iii) Reference picture on page 147)

Things acquired positions on the value chain on the basis of efforts in acquiring or availability, the more hard to acquire being higher up the value chain ladder. Land became an important possession for sustaining continuous requirement of food by agriculture or by cattle raising. The strongmen, warriors and kings acquired land by excursions, and conquering. The merciful kings doled away the wins into the dependents in a wise and equitable manner, while the shrewd and doughty ones kept more with themselves and just threw away petty areas for the dependents, helps and soldiers to fight and divide amongst themselves. The less strong landowners depended on the king or the generals to help them protect their land and exchanged protection by bartering away items higher up the value chain.

Barter system and cultivation practices initiated initial land and turf wars and tiffs which could be labeled as initial matters of discord which could culminate into smaller or severe verbal or physical duos, fisticuffs, mortal combats or generate group fights which could even lead to division in a community.

जमीन की कीमत

तूफानी रात और कड़कती धूप में

कभी हवाओं को पकड़ना, कभी गिरना सीखा

उठना, बैठना, भागना

हक, हिम्मत, हौसले से होगा हासिल, हमने सीखा,

जब खिली पहली कोम्पल, जब निकला पहला दाना

जमीन की कीमत, उसका बढ़पन सीखा

The creation of value chain, on the other hand, motivated a group of people in various communities, to devise items which had a higher value in the chain and exchange them and gain a higher barter or return value within their own community for their own welfare. This created the first clan of businessmen in different communities. Items that were high on the value chain were cloth items, stones, warfare items and food items. With the invention of leather and increase in the leather quotient in the trendy and fashion or regal clothing, these items attained prime spots in the value chain.

Moral corruption, terrorizing and coercion also creeped in as negative social character wherein the powerful would scare the others into exchange of valuables else face loss of things dear to them. The moral quotient of a community could historically be deduced to be linked to the moral and social conduct of the leader or king of the community. Thus the Mongols under Taimur Lane or the Ottomans with lascivious, corrupt and brutal leaders, were highly savage and immoral in their conduct whether within the community or when on conquering or plundering spree.

Till date, the social, political and public administration is evaluated for its leadership on the basis of a proper balance and control on the ethical ways of administration and presence or absence of elements of moral or physical corruption. Society has evolved to have a system where it give power to some people to get administered and then reciprocally also demonstrates the power to bring down those in power, if they show extreme imbalance of ethics and moral corruption. In fact, the more such powers are vested in the society, the more is a society considered evolved.

Of late however things have started taking interesting turn, where many concepts in socio-political or personal lives, earlier looked at in clear black and white, are being accepted with tint of grey. Thus the national man-made disasters, the many railways over bridge collapse, the Himalayan Kedarnath catastrophe, and the international ones as cited in documents including Panama papers and Wikileaks, have become momentary topics of heated glamorous televised debates in one-upmanship, wherein the conclusions often thin out and disappear in judgemental incrimination, accepting the thing as "Whatever happened..................". But yes, the things are evolving fast.

3.

Global Ethnocultural settlements

As the groups of nomads changed to settlements and then transformed themselves into tribes and further to small states and then a geographical civilization, the leaders developed distinct community lifestyles, community languages and sociocultural norms within their community, to ensure homogeneity within the group and ensure noninterference and mixing by intruders.

Still, climate changes, basic necessities and food forced many groups to migrate and mix with different geographical groups, wherein final geographical races were defined, as evident in the case of Indo-European and Afro Europian regions.

बड़ी कौम, बड़ा कारवां, बड़ी रियासत, बड़ी बसाहट

बढ़ता गया फैलाव,

कोई पूरब बसा, कोई पश्चिम,

कोई उतर तो कोई दक्षिण,

कुछ ने बसाया खुद को ऊरल के पहाड़ों में

कुछ ने ग्रीस के किनारे पकड़े

कुछ बसे ब्रितानी किनारे पर

और कुछ नील की घाटियों में

हर कौम में कुछ कौम निकली सयानी की

जिनकी कोशिश रही काफिले को सजाने की
हर कौम में कुछ कौम रही बेदर्द परवानों की
जिनकी कोशिश रही काफिले को गिराने की
नाम जुदा हम दे दें ऐसी हस्तियों का
पर होता एक है अंजाम सारी बस्तियों का।

Many great conquerors showed exemplary leadership traits and shaped movements of one race into another geographical area and creating entirely new modern races. Thus kurgans of the Indo European race mixed with palesigans in Greece and created modern day Greeks. Some Afro Asian semitic and Indo Heddite speakers also moved and mixed with people of the local palesigans. The Indo Heddites also moved into the Arabian peninsula and mixed with locals. Globally, the earliest ethnic communities that occupied different geographical areas on the globe included:

Settlements around Modern Day Russia:

The Proto-Uralic People settled before 4000 BC and inhabited area around Ural Mountain Range in modern Russia. Their culture later spread west, serving as a predecessor to Finnish and Estonian cultures, and they then migrated south to form the Magyar nation (future Hungarians). Proto-Uralic language may not be a sub-branch of Proto-Indo-European, but possibly the head of its own language family. The Finnic People settled by 4000 BC, after breaking off from the Proto-Uralic group, becoming primary inhabitants of the heart of modern Russia (the highly populated NW region surrounding Moscow). By 3000 BC, the Finnic culture spread to the Gulf of Finland and splintered to the NW and SW, and permanently divided into separate "nations", such as Slavs and Baltic peoples, settling on the east shores of the Gulf of Finland, while original Finnic people settled into modern Finland. By this period, the Proto-Baltic-Slavs become a distinct ethnogroup (shared culture & language), a sub-branch of Proto-Indo-European language & culture andcentered around modern Lithuania, they became ancestors to both Baltic (modern Lithuanians and Latvians) and Slav nations.By 2000 BC, a group of Finnic people splinterd toward the NW, becoming ancestors to modern Estonians while continuing westward, south of the Gulf of Finland. By 1000 BC, Magyar tribe splintered from Proto-Uralic group in Ural Mountains (modern Russia), migrating south of Ural Mountain range, north of the Caspian Sea, and eventually migrating to modern Hungary, becoming the modern Hungarians.

By 1000 BC, the Proto-Baltic-Slav culture & language spread south into modern Ukraine, evolving into a new culture/language known as Slavic, giving birth to the Slav people, the forefathers of most Eastern Europeans and becoming the primary ancestors to Russians, Belarusians, Ukrainians, Poles, former Yugoslavians, and partial ancestors to Bulgarians, Romanians and Albanians.By 1000 BC, Scythians, originating in modern Iran, spread to southern Russian and Ukraine, as a sub-branch of Indo-Iranian peoples, another sub-branch of Proto-Indo-Europeans which migrated east of the Ural Mountains (Asian side) in modern Russia.

((iv) Reference picture on page 147)

Settlements around Modern Day Germany:

The Germanic People settled by 3000 - 750 BC after Proto-German language branched off from Proto-Indo-European around 3000 BC in modern Scandinavia, giving birth to the Germanic "nation" (ethnogroup). Germans became the ancestors to all Scandinavians (except Finnish), as well as Germans. Germanic people later migrated to the mainland (modern Germany), becoming a separate ethnogroup from their Scandinavian relatives to the north.By 1500 BC, the Thracian culture & language splintered from Proto-Indo-European, resulting in Thracian ethno group and the ancient Thrace, covering SE Balkan peninsula, which rivaled Greek city-states for superiority, and along with Slavs, became a primary ancestor of the modern Romanians.

Settlements around Modern Day Greece:

By 1500 BC, the ancient Greek culture and language branched off from Proto-Indo-European on southern Balkan Peninsula, forming the Greek ethnogroup (Greeks). By 1450 BC, Greeks conquered island of Crete, ending Minoan Civilization and island of Cyprus in 1125 BC ensuring that both islands were permanently assimilated into Greek culture & genetic lines. Greece gradually Became Europe's Most Sophisticated Civilization,due to proximity to advanced civilizations to the east, such as Hiddites in modern Turkey, Phoenicians in modern Syria & the Egyptians. Geography & fertile lands around Mediterranean Sea's eastern shores brought large & diverse cultures into contact, where they interacted through trade, learning from one another & pushing each other toward greater progression. Greece went through the Dark Ages between 1100 - 750 BC due to war/invasion & possibly famine, whereby the Greeks reverted from sophisticated city-states to small villages, with art, government, academics, trade, farming, etc. all regressing substantially. Minoan culture and people established themselves by 2700 - 1450 BC, as a highly advanced society on island of Crete, engaged in manufacturing & trade and a community that upheld equal distribution of wealth & equal rights for women. They were later conquered by Greeks by 1450 BC.

Settlements around Modern Day Britain and Europe:

By 1300 - 1000 BC, inhabitants in central Europe became banded together under a fairly unified culture/language known as "Celtic", a branch of Proto-Indo-European language/culture to form the Celt "nation", which would grew to cover much of Europe by 400 BC and became a major genetic contributor to many modern Europeans.

Settlements around Modern Day Italy:

By 800 BC, a group of people from outside of Europe (likely Anatolia - modern Turkey) became primary inhabitants of Italian peninsula, concentrated in central region (modern Rome), and become known as Etruscans, after 800 BC, and later intermix with Celts from the north & Greek settlers from the south to form the Italians of the Roman Empire. By 300 BC, the Illyrian language became a distinct sub-branch of Proto-Indo-European, distinguishing Illyrians as new ethno group, becoming ancestors to modern Albanians.

These geographical and ethnocultural settlements have helped in defining the spirit of the nation, defining national boundaries, and shaping the globe. The massive jingoistic spirit on display during Football or Cricket World Cups and Olympics is in fact this spirit of ethnocultural bonding and brotherhood, evident as hysteric love for one's own, which is definitely the required trait for a healthy Global order.

4.

Rise of Kings, Kingdoms, Sultans and Sultanate

The Kings as the Supreme humans and single Command

As the group size increased further, depending on the geographical compulsion, similarity of food habits, appearance, acceptance of chief and other heads, and other conditions, kingdoms were born, with large groups of normal families extending their support to a group of warriors to depend on them for protection and in return providing all facilities, support and luxuries and exalting them to state of a superior human being or king, who was recognized as someone who could protect a large piece of land and create and enjoy the maximum usefulness of the resources in that area, and was also recognised as someone who could create the desired harmony in a very large group of diverse people.

The kings of that era worked mainly on establishing a protected territory and the dependents automatically settled around in the territory and surviving by way of skills that they had dedicated in the service of king and his men, or by virtue of acquiring land in different sizes, which later indicated their status, as a larger area meant a larger farm yield and a greater barter capacity. Thus the landowners acquired a distinct status in the kingdom, superior to those that did not own. This led to further indirect dependence of these landless members and their family on the king and his warriors, through these landlords or landowners.

महाराजा

हजारों में एक वह बहादुर था

परवरिष पक्की, इरादा पक्का, मंजिल का सच्चा था

जिसे मेहनत का जोर सिखाया गया था,

गिर के उठ के गिर के संभालना बताया गया था

मीलों की दूरी जो कर लेता तय

चट्टानों को तोड़ उठता प्रलय

अस्त्र ले शस्त्र से प्रहार करे विषाल

डरे न किसी खौफ से न अपने लहू का मलाल

ऐसे ही वीरों ने दिषा दी समाजों को

इन्हीं में सजाया सुलगते उलझते वीरानों को

टीला, कबीला, गाँव, कसबा फिर शहर की बसाहटें

आबाद हुई कई ऐसी इंसानी सलतनतें

कई हुए राजा, कई बने राजा,

हुए मशहूर दिलों के बस के सिर्फ कुछ महाराजा।

Conquering leadership was typical during the evolution of civilization and formation, expansion and rearrangements of Roman, Greek, Mongolian dynasties in Europe, which had a huge impact on all the continents one by one by virtue of their conquering spirits and marauding habits. The conquering leaders were either aspiring or ruling kings or generals, and in some phase of history, simple strong, defiant and spirited persons who sometimes despite having great leadership skills, preferred their own independent way of life rising to conquer only when challenged to do so or only when enticed by extreme sense of adventure. These characters earned the sobriquet Bogatyr or Baghatur (Mongolian title), indicating a chivalrous, knight, warrior or a strong personality.

The king varied in the way he ruled. While some were great connoisseur of human values, life, art, music and literature given to virtuous ways of leadership and administration, the others were prone to wanton, hedonistic and bullying ways, and misused their exalted status to extort, armtwist and exploit their dependents.

Learning by experience and wisdom shared by elders, the kingdoms developed their own ruling value systems, which stood out in ensuring that such empires could withstand the push and pulls for a considerable length of time.

Thus, on one side of the spectrum, the history has examples of Julius Caeser, King David, Charlmagne, Chandragupta Maurya, Akbar and others, who were fundamental in establishing and strengthening a definite value system along with the administrative activities and enriching human life by way of promoting diverse social, community, human creativity and spirituality, and establishing an appreciation system for excellence by way of awards. On the other side of the spectrum were kings and their army who gained name and fame for their savagery.

The kings further exhibited styles, which involved either a group decision, or a single firm say on everything. Thus autocracy, aristocracy, and later on beaurocracy emerged as the righteous, or more often of the self-righteous centres of power. The World order we see today, has been shaped and reshaped by events where the general public at some point of time, have exalted some people taking them to the level of God, and paradoxically, the same public has again downsized the same revered few, within some days or years. Thus, kings rose out of succession or through other processes, but to retain the exalted status and remain on the throne, the kings or the admistrators have had to walk this tightrope of balance between charisma, deeds and concern for his masses.

5.

Leadership and Administration of the Kingdoms

CONTEXT:

With the rise of the Kingdoms, allocation of roles happened, with hierarchical decentralization and division of labour, and a clearcut differentiation between peacetime and wartime activities. Administrative planning was strengthened by defining and streamliningthe collection or the tax system, as a price for protection and for creation of public utilities.

At a time when, the civilisations had just established some social, religious, defense and other systems and settled down, with no formal training in basic management aspects including planning, sourcing, staffing, execution etc, leadership traits were more intuitive and often based on Emotional quotient (EQ). Thus how much thought a king would give to making his subjects comfortable was less of a logically calculated decision and more of a distant support sufficient to maintain loyalty to army.

As most important expected trait for leadership in a king was raw power and towering force, it was also assumed that, the subjects should definitely be able to survive in an average condition and supply the king with the best available resources. Of course the fighters were maintained in a better way with nutricious food and other supplies to keep them in good shape. In general, these fighters were able to deliver some facilities to their kins, or sometimes extended by the king. The generals and others next in command in the hierarchy also enjoyed some perks. Thus the system of collection started with hunt and supply of meat by the subjects to the King and his fighters or army, and this changed to supply of crops, as civilisations changed to agricultural methods. Later on informal presentations by the subjects in the honour of the king and to please him, started including a diverse variety of things from clothes to merchandise to fight gears to weapons and wide variety of services including helping him in daily chores.

Greek, Roman and the earliest Indus valley civilisations incorporated the initial element of planned social administration and for the same somewhere included the concept of tax collection for social facilities and administration, and gradualy other civilisations picked up the idea.

Initiation of Tax system

The collection or the tax system initially operating in an irregular, and as and when basis, led to severe discontent in the dependents during episodes of sudden collection. The other factors causing discontent included pressurization by men sent for collection and their unfair demands in some cases. Thus some kings developed a detailed thought on the same and initiated regular, small consistent collection that factored the financial status of the dependent for the percentage of collections, and started employing trained men rather than warriors themselves who were sensitized to the nature of the job and public dealing. Also with the need arising for cross verification of finance and produce declaration by individuals, whether landowners or landless dependents, which in some cases were found false, a proper audit, accounts and revenue department came into existence.

Tax collection, still mainly for maintenance of war force and protection of the kingdom, was further thought upon by some kings, and converted into a planned activity for a quarterly, half yearly or annual period.

The king had to maintain a force of warriors, which in the later stages, started comprising a fleet of horses, sometimes elephants, organized artillery in further later stages, weaponry, and still later, firearms and their cartridges and explosives. The dependents provided support in the form of preparation of all the above items as well as arranging materials for fabrication of the same and manually doing it. Further, the fighters, who could be used either as defense personnel, attackers, invaders, and mercenaries, and sometimes also as looters, had to be provided a regular, nutritious and stimulating diet. Some of this could be generated from king's own land and resources but still a large amount could be done only with the help of the dependents, both the landowners and the landless dependents by way of their lands, resources or the skills that they possessed. Further to this, the kings started levying a collection which earlier was in the form of farm grain production from landowners, manual labor from unskilled dependents and free items of use produced by skilled workers, and also free skilled services from them in the form of stitching, fabrication of protective gears, armaments and explosives and creation of barracks for warriors, providing saloon facilities, toiletries and prepared food items which later started including wines and wine preparations.

Thus how a king justifiably applied the tax system and how it could be correlated to the protection provided, determined content in the leadership, although, fear of detachment from the kingdom and straying into dangerous territories sometimes made the discontent irrelevant and seem trifle. Further some kings developed the positive leadership style by distributing goodies to dependents in good times and organizing festivities and fairs. Others went further and provided free medical camps.

((v) Reference picture on page 148)

Once a uniform annual tax collection system was created, some kings realized that judicious use of surplus collection in peacetime would further exalt their status amongst the ruled. Thus a thought was given to planning and creation of budget heads of expenditure and departments to oversee the same, bringing into existence the ministries for public administration, bringing defense, wartime activities and security as one of the constituent ministries. Thus defense and wartime security and war force did not remain as the sole priority area and public administration gained an upper hand in budget expenditure and supervision.

Corruption, and leadership in handling Corruption

Corruption crept in when the distribution of goodies was through middlemen, who sometimes did not, or only partially deliver the same to final beneficiary. To this a king responsed by creating a stamp of receiving and receipt system, wherein thumb or finger expression on a bamboo or fresh wood cross section was obtained to mark delivery. In some cases the king himself distributed the largesse or ordered the prime minister or landowners to do in their respective areas. Thus a vigilance department was thought of and gradually created, initially as the King's Secrecy and Informer network which oversaw effective execution of kings orders.

Over the centuries, civilizations, societies and political systems have shown stability or unstability based on this finer balance of scupulus ruling and ruled relationship, where the rulers have to make sure that they are able to exhibit the required skills and ensure protection of dependants, maintain land and resource surplus, ensure judicious distribution and enhance growth. Self centred autocracies and even corrupt democracies have come down crashing over the years and in contrast judicious monarchies and communist or socialist societies have stood tall and constant for years. The case histories of Bhutan, Thailand, China, and Egypt, Libya and Iraq have been stark examples in contrast.

6.

Leadership in Massive Battles

CONTEXT:

The dust gradually settled down in various parts of Europe and the rest of the world, culminating in creation of new world order, with repeated imperial confrontations between civilisations, empires and kingdoms in the British island, the Mediterranian region, the Indo Chinese regions and the Persian Gulf for the expansion of respective empires. But this happened only through centuries of aggression, machinations, regional aspirations, geographical challenges, interlaced with emergence of different religious and social thoughts & processes, many a times inciting the conflicts. Many leadership styles can be clearly identified for these periods, which could leave their definite imprint by manging these diversedimensions.

रियासतों का बढ़ता गया गरूर
सल्तनतों के किस्से हुए मशहूर
जमीनें जीती, दरिया जीते
खड़े हुए कई किले बदस्तूर शानो शौकत हुई, खुशामद हुई
रस्मों रिवायत का हुआ दस्तूर
बन्दे और बंदगी ने बढ़ाया उनका खुमार ऐसा
हकूमत हर शख्स, हर ख्वाहिश, हर चीज, इनायत में हो
बढ़ता ही गया ऐसा सुरूर।

Some of the earliest kings who enjoyed a great and exalted respect by way of their physical, leadership, organizational and judicious prowess included, King Philip, Hannibal, the Great, Chandragupt Maurya, Ashoka, Akbar, Harsha Wardhana, Alexander, Charlemagne, Caesar, Otto and Constantine, King Alfred. Others demanded respect by their ferociousness and included the likes of, Changez Khan, Muslim Caliph Omar and others.

As the kingdoms and empires tried to organize themselves, the conflicts over boundary disputes created extensive churning over the extent of empires and the organizational skills of their leaders were put to full test in prolonged and overstretched periodic wars between adjacent kingdoms lasting from one rule to another. Following wars are particularly remarkable.

The Roman Empire and its Expanse

Romans engaged themselves in many battles to establish their supremacy far and wide, exchanging swords with Carthage in 260 BC in 1st Punic War, then defeating them in Naval battle 20 years later, conquering the Etruscan city Veil and then Tarquinia, Etruscan, and then destroying it as a civilization, declaring war on Samnites, winning the second and third war fiercely with characteristic maniple based army structure or legions and acquiring the mightiest fighting force status in the ancient world, and then overpowering gauls, establishing the mighty Roman empire from North to South, the whole of Italian peninsula.

The major challenge presented against the Romans was by Hannibal, who developed deterrent to Roman naval power with vessels designed by Archimedes, but was ultimately defeated by Africanus Major in the 2nd Punic War around 200 BC and then the Romans further overpowered Macedonian King Philip

V and by 140 BC Rome conquered Greece and by 133 BC – The whole Mediterranean region was under Roman control, which was extended later to Syria and also to Jeruselam by Pompey, who formed the first great triumvariate with Julius Caeser and Crassus. Soon Julius Caeser subdued mutual revolts by Pompey and gauls and became the greatest Mediteranian emperor, "The Imperator", and further extended his kingdom to Egypt and won over Queen Cleopatra, being ultimately killed by sabotage by Roman senate. The next triumvariate of Mark Antonyq, Octavius, and Aemilius Lepidus again maintained the glory of the Roman Empire which was extended by Augustas upto Balkans by the 30th AD, and later by Trajan upto Mesopotamia by 110 AD and then with conquer of Syria by Constantine by 330 AD.

The Roman Triumvariate

Context:

The first examples of the combined leaderships-Internal and external confrontations in the build up to The Great Roman Empire Lessons in modern business strategy, leadership and management:

Together, the Roman Triumvariate of Caesar, Crassus and Pompey created an indefatigable administration model far and wide in Europe, Middle East and African shores. It was the first example of a mutualy understood trifurcation of responsibilities to ensure sustainable success and common goal of keeping the Roman Empire flag flying high. To efficiently manage the vast expanse, with delegated responsibilities, without advanced communication technologies available today, must have required remarkable strategic planning, impeccable mutual communication and strategic camaraderie.

The Roman civilization was initiated by Romulus in Central Italy around 800 BC. Gradually starting as a beautiful Hill city, and developing into a large monarchy ruled by the Etruscans. By 500 BC, the Romans entered into conquering spree, revolting against the Etruscans and establishing the Roman Republic, entering into battles with the Latins, through the Pyrrhic Wars with the Greek, the Punic wars with the Carthage in the Spain and then also with the Gauls in and around the British isles.

With the formation of first combined or group leadership, the First Triumvariate consisting of the unparalleled machismo and warfare skills and acumen of Caesar, Crassus and Pompey, the Roman Republic had established its expanse to include the Mesopotamia, the Egypt, majority of Europe and the regions in Greece by the 50th BC. Caesar, in a very short but glorious stint eventually won over Queen Cleopatra from Egypt and became the emperor, but became victim of the greatespionage led by Octavius, Antony Lepidus who formed the Second Triumvariate to rule the Great Roman Republic. Ultimately Octavius took over as the sole emperor acquiring the title of Augustus and paving the way for the roman Empire with the end of Roman Republic by the 23rd BC and continuing till his death till 14th AD.

The Empire was later led by various Dynasties including, the Claudia Dynasty, represented by Tiberius, Claudius, Nero and Caligula, overseeing ethnic clashes between the Romans and the Christians. It was followed by Flavian Dynasty, during which expansion upto Wales happened, and with Trajan as an outstanding emperor of the period the empire expanded with the conquering of Mesopotamia by 116 AD. With an intermittent period seeing spread of plague epidemic, emperor Aurelius marked his stint in the 160 AD century. By 250AD, the difficulties in keeping the vast roman empire together were visible with constant affront by the barbarians, the Persian revolts and freedom, which culminated in the Tetrarchy with Diocletian

Augustus, Maximian Augustus and two junior emperors taking care of the eastern and western halves, until the emergence of Constantine as the emperor who was able to revive some glory with center around Constantinople in Turkey. After the golden Constantine era the Roman glory was lost again having to withdraw from Great Britain, attack by Huns and Vandals by 480 AD, until finally the Western Roman Empire degraded fully and only the Eastern Empire continued, embracing Christianity as the principle religion, adopting Greek as the official language for administration and army use due to its capital being stationed at Constantine, modern day Istanbual, with former name as Byzantium, and proximity to Greece, and also following Roman-Hallenistic culture with Greek influence. For the same reason it also came to be known as the Byzantine Roman Empire with Theodosius, Justinian I and Heraclius as the other great rulers after Constantine, and maintained its regions around Rome, the Mediterranean costal cities in Africa, including Egypt and modern day Turkey and Greece. The Byzantine Empire got initiated in 610 AD with Heraclius defeating Persian forces, and later by 627 AD, Persia was conquered by Byzantine forces. The Jerusalem cross is retrieved from the Persians, who stole the relic in 614. Heraclius reigned until his death in 641.

After the origination of Islam in Medina Arabia, in 622 AD, further expansion and spread of the Islamic religion far and wide by 640 by Moslem Caliph Omar, and subsequent prolonged religious conflicts between Moslems and Christianity, in the form of the Crusades (11th-12th century) Europe witnessed reorganization in the form of fall of the Byzantium and Ottoman empires (15th century). Byzantine Emperor Leo the Isaurian, who reigned until 741, proved to be tough resistance to the Arab attacks and attempts on Byzantine empire, after the first attack in 677 AD on Constantine, he bounced back in the second attack in 717 AD, where he first used the famous "Greek Fire", a powerful fire ammunition fired from Ship mounted bronze tubes containing liquid mixture of sulfur, naphtha and quicklime, also arranged all along the walls of Constantinople. Thus he was able to integrate Constantinople, Greece and Asia Minor in Byzantine Empire, which continued upto 12th Century.

The Eastern Roman empire was better off financialy and was also able to fend off attackers by way of satisfying them with Gold and valuables, as in the case of Theodosius keeping Atilla, the Hun, off for along time by the same method. The Huns were later also used as merceneries by the Byzantines after the death of Atilla. The Eastern Empire continued upto the 1450AD with intermittent blows in the form of loss of some far east territories and Egypt and Syria to Muslims during Byzantine-Sasanin Wars around 7th century AD, and then during the Macedonian Empire, with loss of Asia Minor to the Seljuk Turks around 1100 AD and finally Constantinople fallingl to Ottoman Turks in 1453 AD.

The rise of the United Kingdom

Context:

Vikings, Normans, Danes and Anglo Saxons, came as frequent invaders into the British islands, marauding the original Celtic settlers, and then many of them gradually settled in Britain and Europe, shaping its heterogenous composition. With such a diverse array of settlers and frequent flow of settlers between British island and France, it was but expected that future rulers would engage in prolonged wars of annexation of grounds, which is much evident in the well known history of French - Britannia mutual annexation wars.

In the ancient Britannica around 1500 BC, the inhabitantsincludedthe Celtics from France and other European areas supposedly mixed with the local people. The Romans repeatedly returned with intent to annex Britannica around

55 BC with Caesar as the charisamatic emperor at the time but could make some inroads only under the leadership of Claudius around 43 BC.They settled and created the scenic cities of the present day England with majestic forts characteristic of Roman Empireincluding Manchester,Lincoln, Winchester, Bath, York, Chester, Leicester, Colchester, Lancaster, Exter etc, and also parts of Wales.The Saxons and the Angles from northern countries, particularly Germany and Denmark, then entered around 5 BC first as invaders and then as migrants who settled around and together marked the creation of Anglo Saxon Heptarchy. Mercia, Sussex, Northumbria, Essex, Anglia,Wessex and Kent came up as beautiful cities at this time, demarcating the seven kingdoms.

Saxon Britain 600-900 AD

The Saxon Britain was not a silent period, with a mandatory and foregone unwritten rule that an emperor or his descendants would have to strive to keep their powers intact, which normally could be simply deciphered as being ready to exhort any one in sight for a fight, and then give a strong fight, show the capacity to take the battles to successful culmination, and acquire land, treasure, slaves and much more for the army and his citizens. The Anglo Saxon period was in fact not a very long and a stable period, as there were hectic changes on the throne, as if a game of musical chair, with each of the king constantly on job of waging wars and conquering to keep his candidature for retaining the seat intact, as even their fathers could not promise them an infinite legacy. In case some better adept and equipped relative or distant relative projected his claim, it was a matter of proving the best claim by way of a fight, either a small hedging or a full scale war and showing appropriate support and generalship. This was evident even in the not so impactful neighborhood adventures and conquers.

Two kingdoms came out strong during the period, the Mercia and the Northumbrians.King Offa, stood out amongst the various kings between 750-800 AD. The initial years established Northumbrians way above the Mercia in the 7th century, with Mercia playing second fiddle, a role, which reversed by the next century. Offa, the most powerful and well known of the Mercian kings,ruled between 750-800 AD, was amercurial personality and a fiercewarrior, and overpowered Sussex, Anglia, and Wessex, proclaiming himself King of the English.

Offa caused to be built the earthwork that still bears his name, Offa's Dyke, which stretches the 150 mile length of the Welsh border. Begun in the 780's, the purpose of the dyke seems to have been as a fortified frontier barrier, much as Hadrian's Wall some six centuries previous. In most places the ditch was 25 feet from the bottom of the cut to the top of the bank, with wood or stone walling on top of that. The work involved has been compared to the building of the Great Pyramid. This gives us some idea of the power wielded by Offa. It seems that the dyke was not permanently manned, relying instead on the warning given by a series of beacons.

The Mercians could not sustain dominance in Britannica for long after Offa's death around 820 AD, first being threatened and challenged strongly by the Wessex led by Egbert, and then constant raids and threats by the Danes attacking the east cost and the Norwegians attacking the north through Ireland and Scotland and attack by the Vikings. Normandy was thus established by the Danes, under the great king Canute, in the French region, who overpowered the king Edmund II the Anglo Saxon King. Canute was followed by king William II and till date Britain is ruled by descendents of Williams II.

Together with Normandy, the Dane rule continued with French as the official language till 1360s when the Hundred Year's war started. William was succeeded by Henry I, Henry II,

Edward I, Edward II and then Edward III, all having to be constantly on war for sustaining or expanding the empire and internal strife, particularly with Scottish resistance being most prominent and not annexing to the rule of Normans. The 100-year War between France and Britannia started during the reign of Edward III particularly to annex Normandy and nearby areas. Henry IV, the nephew of Edward III, and his son Henry V further took forward the war with Henry V being successful at the great battle of Agincourt giving a major blow to French in around 1415 AD. Henry VI although was not much adept and inclined at art of War and hence lost major areas by the famous resistance of John of Arc, a 17 year old war head in France who stood out for her mettle in the Hundred Year's War.

The War of Roses started between the followers of Henry VI (Red Roses) and the followers of Edward IV (White Rose) trying to install their respective leader. Edward IV ultimately ruled for a small period being ultimately again replaced by the Henrys, Henry VI and Henry VII (Henry Tudor) and finaly by Henry VIII the, the most famous king till date, who was the first to take over the Wales and become King of Wales and then also Ireland, taking over as King of Ireland too.

The French Dynasties and the Gaulls

Context:

The Great Merovingian and Carolingian Dynasties of Franceemerged as the mighty empires in that era, setting up standards in administration, rule and religion. This period concurred with the dominance of Gauls in North Western Europe, with whom France has a long history of interaction. Charlemagne emerged as one of the greatest ruler and administrator, and is still known for the initial tenets of local and public administration and ruling a remarkable kingdom.

In the early part of the period, the Roman province of Gaul giave way to the Frankish kingdoms, led for some 250 years by the Merovingian kings. Even under the Merovingians, the region remained recognizably Roman, preserving Roman administrative structures and language, with ever-greater importance as the nobility converted, founding large numbers of monasteries. The network of churches and monasteries built in the Merovingian period provided Charlemagne with an administrative infrastructure that allowed him to create his great empire in the ninth century.

Charlemagne's descendants, known as the Carolingians, ruled the region until almost the end of the period. Metalwork remained an important art form throughout the period. Highly accomplished examples of ivory carving and manuscript painting emerged under Carolingian rule. Though relatively few survive, many stone buildings -particularly in the form of churches, monasteries, and palaces-were built.

The Merovingian dynasty was founded by Clovis in 500 AD by integrating most of France and Belgium and aligning it as Western Catholic Christianity. The dynasty however lost the relevance intermittently, by way of mutual struggle between the sons of Clovis. During this period, various tribes active in Europe, the Franks, Alemans, Thuringians, and Saxons, indulged in mutual wars, with extreme turbulence in the area called as Germania, with mutual strife taking place also on the basis of religious allegiance to Christianity. With the French and some other tribes having affiliated to the Christiann faith, the other tribes, collectively called as pagans, largely comprising of fierce warriors Germanics and Thuringians, had another reason to go for each other's blood, that was allegiance to Christianity. The Meruvingian dynasty, although not being able to hold its forte in most of these regions, was able however to maintain its territory in France, and after emergence of Martel, Pepin and finaly Charlmagne, was able to regain its initial glory during establishment by Clovis.

The Meruvingian dynasty reestablished itself under Pepin in around 687 AD with centre in Belgium and Rhine, being later succeeded by son Martel forming a strong alliance with Church and expanding into Germany, further consolidated during the times of Pepin, the short, by way of wars titled the Battle of Poitiers or the Battle of Tours, and also stopping at the same time the muslim incursion with the arrival of Arabs in the Iberian peninsula between 710 to 732 AD. With the anointment of Pepin, the short, as a divinely sanctioned king by St Boniface, the Meruvingian Dynasty became the Carolingian Dynasty as each ruler had to have support of the church to rule. At that time the extent of Roman Empire included central Europe, northern Italy and central Italy and areas under French.After Pepin, Charlmagne initiated a revival period of learning called "Reinessance" under Benedict Alcuin, opened schools and administered through Counts of different areas who were in turn supervised by Charlmagne's court representatives.

Charlemagne conquered various areas in Germany, Austria, Switzerland, building castles everywhere and formed his capital at Aachenin 772 AD and also a Palace Chapel similar to San Vitale in 792 AD. Following this, various French monasteries published many single volume Bibles on old and new testaments. Charlemagne was crowned "Emperor and Augustus"in 800 AD by Pope Leo III to increase the status of Pope as well as the king, but after his death in 814, his son could not keep the empire intact and devided the empire into 3 regions between his sons who could not hold on because of mutual rivalry and raids by Hungarians, muslims and Scandinavians. With the division of Carolingian empire into Francia occidentalis, Francia media and Francia orientalis by 843 AD between Charles bald, Lothar and Louis II, there was further degradation. But parallelly a system of well planned, self contained, city like monasteries with an abbey church, dormitory, library, Infirmary, guesthouse, all within, takes shape as per Saint Gall plan.

After 909 AD, whenWilliam I the Pious, Duke of Aquitaine, donated land in Burgundy for the building of a Benedictine monastery, named Cluny dedicated to saints Peter and Paul, the monasteriescame directly under the control of the Papal See and by 910, the total number of such monasteries started multiplying and reached sixty-seven by 1049. The phase indicated comprehensive external influence in the form of European church and politics, making France look a lot subdued and less strong. Further subjugation came through the Treaty of Saint-Clair-sur-Epte between Charles the Simple, king of the Franks, and Rollo (Hrolf), Viking leader of the Normans, in 911, in the form of concession of Normandy to Vikings. France regained its prestige after ascendance of Hugues Capet in 987 AD, and formation of Capetian dynasty which remained dominant until 1328, with its capital at Paris, which became an important centre of administration in Europe.

Parallely, the Germanics transitioned their image from the hard warrior pagans, loyal to their individual chieftains, to the faithful Christians under the leadership of Otto I in the 1000 AD, who was instrumental in reestablishing the glory of Roman Empire as the Holy Roman Empire. Germanic artisans however made a mark in metal carvings, decorated weapons, portable luxury objects with rich surface patterns and colourful inlays.

Confrontations between the Chinese and Mongol Dynasties

The First Mongolian Dynasty Xiangnou (200 BC to 100 AD) led by the first ruler Toumen, was involved in boundary clashes with the first Dynasty in China, the Quin Dynasty, which in the process to prevent the Xiangnou attackers from crossing Gobi deserts in the north into the Yellow river plains, completed the construction of Great Wall of China at a breathtaking pace.

The next Chinese dynasty, Han Dynasty continued its confrontation with the Xiangnou Dynasty, but the ruler Gao had to give in against Wen, the emperor of Xiangnou dynasty and sign a marriage alliance, which entitled Mongols of all territories north of Great Wall of China. Wen and his warriors troubled China for about 70 years entering deep into the Chinese territory but finally met their match in the next Chinese emperor Wu who forced them to retreat.

Such disputes continued with both empires holding forts turn by turn, with the Xiangnou empire extending deep upto Huang Ho river in Chinese territory at one time and then with the advent of Eastern Han Dynasty having to retreat back to Central Mongol and the Steppes in Alps, and gradualy the Xiangnou empire getting divided into Northern and Southern Xiangnou empires, with the northern empire later becoming today's Kazakhasthan and Siberia. The Southern Dynasty was gradualy replaced by the rebel powers, the Xianbei around 100 AD which lasted upto the 300 AD and it was majorly ruled by Tanshihuai, who was able to take the empire well within northern China upto the Yangtse river with the Chinese Eastern Han dynasty acutely fragmenting, and the resulting in utter chaos in the region.

Tuoba fraction of the Xianbei tribe ruled the Chinese northern lands late till the start of 5th Century AD and then another fraction Ruran tribe under Mugylu ruled the areas. At that time the extent of the Ruran empire included Mongolia, North eastern China and Ganshu, Southern Siberia, eastern Kazakhastan, Xianjiang in China in the period 350-500 AD. Later the subjects of Ruran empire, the Turks revolted in what is called as the Blacksmith rebellion under Buman and formed the Turkic Khanganate which existed between 550 to 800 AD. The Chinese Qui, Sui and then Tang dynasties constantly tried to defeat them and Tang dynasty was able to overcome them, and they were ultimately replaced by the Uyghur khanganate under Bayanchur as leader, who were in fact the subjects of Turkic Khanganate and finally by the khitan or Khitan Liao Dynasty led by Ambagyan, which extended into the 10th and 11th century.

Finally the Mongol Khanganate fragmented into many tribes Shiwei, Khamag etc which fought between each other and were interfered too much by the Chinese dynasties. They had some powerful leaders like Khabul khan, but not many and until his great grandson Temujin who was later christened as the great Changiz Khan/Jangiz Khan, under whom the Mongol empire gained a glory far and wide in Asia, central Siberia much of China and Europe, and even in India.

The Persian Dynasty and The Arabs: Two thoughts

Persian Empire refers to any of a series of imperial dynasties centered in Persia (modern–day Iran). Achaemenid Empire with king Cyrus the Great was established first in 550 BC and included Median, Lydian and Babylonian empires. It had a grand splendor, but was later conquered by Alexander the Great. Several later dynasties claimed to be heirs of the Achaemenids. These included the Parthian Empire, the Hellenistic Seleucid Empire, and then the Sassanian Empire, which ruled until mid 7th century AD followed by the Samanid and Saffarid dynastiesthat ruled for sometime.Zoroastrianism was the main religion of ancient Persia. With a brief interlude, interrupted by the Arab Muslim conquest of Persia in 651 AD, when establishment of the larger Islamic Caliphate happened, and later by the Mongol invasion, and thus Islam as a religion established influence over Persia. Safavids and Afsharidsa series of Islamic–notably Shiite–dynasties then ruled Persia, followed intermittently by Zand dynasty, keeping themselves independent of the Arab/ Turkic Sunni Caliphates, who became Persia's classical rival, similar to pagan Romans and Christian Byzantines before. The Pahlavi dynasty was the last dynastic rule and after its downfall, a theocratic Shiite government is in rule.

7.

Leadership through Religion

In the early part of the period upto 1000 AD, central Europe was inhabited by various tribes, either pagan or newly Christian. By 1000, the region became majorly the heartland of the Holy Roman Empire, a loose confederation of territory ruled by a Christian dynasty aspiring to the greatness of Roman and Byzantine imperial power.

With Central Europe going through a great churning, The Great Roman Empire having been curtailed due to Britain having carved its separate entity, Europe was mainly characterized with pagan or newly Christian tribes of various origins, including some French, German and others. The Roman Papal Church had lost some of its grandeur and power in Central Europe and was subordinated by the Eastern Roman emperors. In 590 ADPope Gregory, originally a Benedictine, created a fusion of the Roman papacy with Benedictine monasticism to form the Latin church, which served to counteract the subordination of the Roman popes to Eastern emperors and reestablish its lost glory. St. Gregory the Great was inspired by the theological philosophy of Ambrose of Milan, and Jerome of HIPPO. In 599–600 ADPope Gregory categorically emphasized his principle that the images in diocese not be destroyed and preserved, as they were useful for educating the illiterate. He communicated the same to many Bishops including Bishop Serenus of Marseille. The Latin Church concept gained more reputation during the Byzantine civilization initiating by 610 AD with Heraclius becoming Emperor in Constantinople during threat by Persian Empire over Byzantine civilization, and followed with periods of Diocletian, Constantine or Justinian.By 700 AD theBenedictine missionaries completed the conversion of England begun by St. Gregory the Great. The Benedictine principles and Latin Church received constant support and pull by the the Franks, who asserted their dominance throughout central and western Europe, established palaces for their kings, with an invincible reputation of their armies being able to halt the advances of Islamic forces into Europe and styled themselves as true torchbearers of the Christian faith and special sanction of the pope.By 955 AD, with John XII becoming pope at the age of eighteen and ruling for nine years, the title of pope and halo of Church saw a decline in the early-medieval period. Local lords establish control over churches and monasteries which were managed by unqualified persons with majority of priests being illiterate and living with concubines, majority of them also being sons of powerful Roman families.

The Holy Roman Empire: Leadership by Church

After crowning of king Otto in Germany in 936 AD, Germany gained strength in Europe with Otto I following the policy of close alliance with the Church and at the same time making a strong conquering impact in the region. King Otto I, Duke of Saxony and King of Germans was further crowned emperor by Pope John XII in 962 AD and led the revival of Roman empire in the west and reestablished it as the Holy Roman Empire which persisted till the 1806 AD. Otto I further added to the glory of the Holy Roman Empire by dedicating new imperial churches, the prominent of them being the Magdeburg Church in Saxony in 968 AD, which were significant by way of having special structures "the Westwork" attached to the entrance wall, with attached galleries for Imperial appearances. Such churches became missionary bases for conversion of western pagans to the Holy Church, with Mauritius being an important Patron City Saint for these churches. Otto II brought a symbolic alliance between the Byzantine Empire and the Holy Ottonian Roman Empire by marrying Byzantine princes Theophano in 972 AD. The German and Ottovian contribution to the Holy Roman Empire continued in the next generation too with Mathilde, the granddaughter of Otto I patronizing art and religion by contributing 3 huge bejeweled processional crosses, and a golden statue of Virgin, which still remain the earliest available grand German sculptures.

Thus religion and administration have gone hand in hand in many countries and even have been successful at that, viz., the Holy Roman Empire, the Persian and later the Iranian Theocracies in the world. Such administrations enjoyed special background support in the form of religious patronage, and thus an easy acceptance with an element of sobriety attached to the administrative work that subdued some arrogance of power.

8.

Leaders in War Strategies .... and their relevance in modern management strategies

CONTEXT:

War strategies and their importance became much evident over the years with great commanders making huge impact with their conquering styles.

The present day marketing and management strategies often take the shape and resemble war like situations, wherein, rules are made, forgotten, overlooked, redesigned and product launch and promotion manouveres and strategies bear stark resemblance to war strategies, combining offence, defence, aversion, enticing and all overt and covert operations.

As the feeling of being exalted set in amongst many kings, and having accomplished all their basic motives of achieving power, status, luxuries and nuptial settlements at will, some kings, with a decorated upbringing, and a philosophical bent of mind gave more thought to paying back the love and respect received by way of creating better public utilities for dependents, and thereby opening up tax collection for public use. Having come to a decision on various areas chalked out for development, appropriate supervision and time frame for completion was deemed necessary and thereby the realization that delegation would be the most ideal thing to ensure equal priority to all areas earmarked, and thus ministry came into being. It was further understood that as an administrative head and a wartime leader, king should remain focused on management of wartime adventures and attack and defense and at the same time be kept updated of all administrative aspects through a Prime Minister, thus creating the historical post.

With the delegation of war and conflict management to generals, the focus on tactics and strategies used by these generals became important. The great military theorist Carl von Clausewitz described the connection between tactics and strategy as "Tactics being the art of using troops in battle, and strategy being the art of using battles to win the war."

As the size of warring forces increased, and the opposite sides tries to create a massive, mighty and tearing impact on each other, the importance of covering difficult terrains, crossing mighty rivers and delivering a stunning and speedy surprise blowplayed heavily on the minds of the generals while devising strategies. Thus fortification for prevention maneuvers in creating impact, and supply for sustaining the forces over rough terrains became crucial factors in the strategy in the 17th and 18th Century. This led to parallel advancements in military and ammunition technology.

Military strategy gradually got integrated with national policy or "grand strategy," ensuring proper utilization of the entire military, technological, economic, and political resources for successful conflicts. By the 19th and 20th century, emergence of mass ideologies, vast conscript armies, global alliances, have greatly affected the war tactics over time along with rapid technological advancements.

War strategy also became important with the realization that the location of the group could also play a part in protection of the group, which had taken the shape of a tribe by now. Thus location on one side of the river, in a mountain valley, beside a hill base, or even atop a steep hill proved to be an important strategic asset. Gradually the war strategy got more intricate with planning also focusing on the layers of defense standing behind each other in case of an attack, thus making sure that not all members were uselessly injured or killed in an attack without appropriately harming the opponent. Thus concept of small platoons and platoon heads took shape and a unified command who could marshal these platoons in an effective manner.

Thus departmentalization or decentralization started acquiring a prominent hierarchical structure and division of labour started taking place, with assigned teams for cooking, nursing, entertainment, war, internal peace and social management, health, infrastructure and other areas taking up their tasks individually.

What was the expected role and quality combinations for a military leader in such cases?

1. He necessarily had to be of an impressive built, with a deep impressive voice, a thirst for combat.

2. He was able to incite the battalion into action, make them go for the kill and acquire the organization goal as their own goal and fight till death.

Wars were the prime movers of most activities upto the early 20th Century. Now, in the aftermath of the nuclear blasts during the IInd World War, and ensuing realization of restraint by all, as the civilization, has moved into the 21st Century, war strategies and tactics are often recalled and reflected to effectively manage global business positioning and success. Great leaders through the times have used many tactical and strategic principles. While Confederate general Nathan Bedford Forrest had but one: "Get there first with the most men", others have many principles for the strategy. Some of the most commonly cited tenets of the War Strategiescomprise:

The objective: Whether it is for accession, annexation, expansion, protection, seclusion, dominance, subversion or survival). The objective should be to win a war without waging a battle, or in case a battle is must, it should be with minimum loss of soldiers on both sides. Cities should never be attacked as the first strategy and objective.

The element of Surprise: Surprise, considered as a very important tool for creating a mighty impact of the offensive, is to be clearly thought upon as to its timing, extent, the element of surprise and backup plan in case of spilling of plans due to sabotage.

The offensive: What could be the most productive method for a productive offensive, which could create the desired impact in achiving the above objective/s.

Security: Keeping both the ends secured while launching an offensive, is as important and critical as the offensive itself, as a disconcerted effort offering loopholes is certain to spoil the chances and even be counter productive, detrimental, self destructive and colossal.

Economy of force: Minimum force-maximum impact and appropriate hierarchy of force to manage frontal, second line and core offensives and defence, cordoning, hedging and support and serve activities need to be appropriately economized to be sufficiently ready to counter prolonged offensives or defense.

Mass: A minimum mass or number is critical for ensuring appropriate defense or an impactful offense, which may be simple, multipronged or multi directional.

Unity of command: When in the middle of a war, whether on an offensive or in defence, the command should be emphatic, crystal clear, highy exhorting, goading, pushing, setting emotions afire, and stearing actions into immediate massive actions. Duplicacy, difference, multiplicity and confusion in command, is sure to diffuse the energy, offensive and direction and be self-destructive.

and

Manoeuvre: Finaly, how the maneuver or the blow is delivered, and its ability to divide, subvert, destroy or open the opposition, is very critical for the overall success of the operation.

Most of the above factors may be interdependent determinants in success or failure of an operation. The same principles are equally applicable in these times of business competitiveness and intense marketing blitz.

Sun Wu, later known as Sun Tzu: After receiving the tittle of master- Tzu, spent many years helping the Chinese military, and after retirement, compiled his thoughts in a thirteen chapter book "The Art of War", which has influencedvarious thoughts on military strategies and tactics and is still studied today, to understand how to wage war, army position, enemy's movements, use of spies, making a good General, and more.

Sun Tzu's book contains thirteen critical chapters. In present day management, the inherent thoughts are very relevant.

1. Estimates: An effective pre war strategy takes care of to the point and accurate estimation of distance, quantity, time, maneuver, combination/s and impact required and the objectives. It also makes accurate estimation of one's own strength and its use.

For the present day manager, it interprets as, "An effective product launch should be based on to the point estimates of demand, competitive pricing and correct placement".

2. Waging War: Waging awaris a critical decision and may go right or wrong depending on the losses incurred for the outcome achieved. The time may also make a great impact on the outcome.

3. Offensive Strategy: When declaring a war, the offensive strategy has to be impeccablen and perfectly planned as a wrong offense may leave an army on the backfoot and defence and sometimes defenseless.

    Product launch strategy emulates the offensive strategy in a war, and a slightly wayward strategy, may make the launch fall flat.

4. Disposition: How the army is diployed and positioned as a unit at the time of offense, carries a great impact on success.

    As a unit, a company's marketing, sales and operations unit should be on the same page during launch

5. Energy: A general has to make sure that he is able to actuate the last soldier to the same energy and passion so that cumulative strike causes maximum impact.

6. Weakness and Strengths: A correct assessment of strengths to use the best of them definitely makes success more achievable. In today's business parlance this refers to deciding the best combination for the business portfolio.

7. Manoeuvre: Manoeuvres have to be overpowering, with elements of surprise, power and awe to the enemy. In today's markting parlance, maneuvers are relevant in market penetration and launch.

8/9.   The Nine Variables and The Nine Varieties of Ground: A war is affected by the nine variables, as mentioned, and the same have to be managed.

10.   Marches: The marches of the front, middle, back and last lines and units may stave off the enemy forces and exhaust them out fighting one level after the other.

11.   Terrain:A unit must be well aware of the terrain that has to be encountered for the offense, and prepare to composition and arrangement of the army accordingly.

12.   Attack by Fire: Fire and use of firepower has become indispensable to all wars and the ferocity and positioning makes the difference to shatter the enemy's sytems. In business parlance an innovative and unique product gets the required fire power which can ensure great market penetrability.

13.   Employment of Secret Agents: Preemptive asesments of enemy's strategies to execute counter attacks is ensured by effective espionage and counterinsurgency operations.

In modern business terminologies, business and competitive analysis/intelligence serves the same purpose to ensure that the company's product scores over the competitor, by dint of complete knowledge about the other products.

The strategy of masquerading adds to the above strategies, and suggests attacking the enemy when five times his strength, dividing him if he doubles his strength, disrupting him and not allowing to get together, engaging him if equally matched, be capable of eluding him if in all respects unequal.This strategy may also be quoted as that of deception, acting incapable when capable, acting inactive when active, make appear distant, when near, luring enemy with a bait, acting disarranged and striking immediately with a three pronged attack when he is preparing, angeringinsulting, enraging, irritating and confusing him. If the enemy is obstinate and prone to anger, and enrage him, so that he will be irritated and confused, without a plan he will attack recklessly.

Victory may be predicted, if some basic tacts were ensured:

1. It is important to know when to wage or defend a war and when not to do so to ensure one comes out victorious.

2. Whether one has a large or a small force at one's disposal, how to use the same effectively creating maximum impact, ensures chances of being victorious.

3. Unity in the ranks, appropriate camaraderie, bonhomie, vivaciousness and unityof purpose ensures victory.

4. It is important to be prudent in majking decisions on the movements, strength and capacity of the enemy and adopt a wait and watch policy rather than jumping into the ring unprepared.

5. A king who gives the purpose and objectives to his generals, who are able and not interfered with is sure to be victorious.

6. If a Know the enemy and know yourself, in a hundred battles you will never be in peril.

Some unique and principle war strategies over the years

The Mass Strategy

Context:

Napolean first used scale of military enrolment as a war strategy model, wherein just the massive numbers or strength and size of the army could create a sense of terror, horror, awe and abdication by the opponents.

Once countries like France realized the constant threat by neighboring invasions, it was Napolean in the 18th Century who came up with spirit of nationalism, and consequent mass self motivated enrolment or recruitment in the army in the form of Universal male Conscription, that motivated the soldiers with a politicized spirit of defending their nation and cause. Thus, France's army, counting to more than 1,000,000, changed from a defensive to an offensive force by a remarkable force consisting of soldiers with high morale, discipline and sense of sacrifice for their cause, led by equally remarkable officers, which conducted command orders in an unaristocratic manner and as a sense of service to nation. This spirit of nationalism as a war strategy developed, matured in the 19th century and was at full show in the 20th century during the World Wars. Thus, with a sense of nationalism, the armed forces started representing an institutional structure and a respected citizen's service where recruitment was open to anybody wearing pride for the nation on his/her sleeves.

Leaders integrating new warfare in the army

Song Dynasty in China developed the gunpowder technology, which was taken over and adapted magnificently by the Ottoman Empire, who became known for the fiercest use of gunpowder and armed mercenaries. Other dynasties followed including the Safavids in Persia, Ahmad Ghazi in Ethiopian War in 1530s, Mughal Empire in India and then the European Armies during the Italian War in the 16th Century. Thus the armored cavalry was replaced by professional standing armies with coming together of smaller medieval city-states into larger states.

Leaders integrating industrial technology in warfare

Other war leaders, as in the massive Prussian defeat of the French forces in 1870-71, integrated the industrial advances into their war strategies to make the fight effective and successful. Thus the industrial revolution in the 19th Century bolstered the war strategies in many ways, including start of a successful rail transport system, the distant communication wizard-telegraph system and initiation of many industries that could produce on a mass scale the arms and ammunitions, including advanced, stronger, rapidly reloadable, easily serviceable with interchangeable parts, rifle barreled guns and canons with exploding shells. The industrial technology also revolutionized mass production of ammunitions, so that ready stock was available and transported to far off war sites in short time, giving appropriate back up support of ammunition and services supply to the army. The warships were also integrated with new industrial advances including iron hulls and multiple engines. Thus the army which was good at logistics by use of mass transport by rail network, and effective distant communication by wireless, naturally stood out superior, as also seen in case of US civil war, in which Sherman and the team from West Point Technology, including Grant and others, and his forces from Northwere able to subjugate the Confederate Officers Corps from the South at Atlanta.

The Blitzkrieg Strategies

Giulio Douhet (1869-1930), Billy Mitchell, Henry ("Hap") ARNOLD, and Hugh Trenchard (1873-1956) advocated use of airpower in all conflicts with a conviction that air power alone could win wars, by striking and strategic bombing on cities, industries, and lines of communication and supply that became characteristic of the allied strategy during World War II. The other World War I development was that of motorized armored vehicles such as the tank. B. H. Liddell Hart (1895-1970), Charles de Gaulle (1890-1970), and J. F. C. Fuller (1878-1966) advocated the use of the motorized armored vehicle, the tank, as the new cavalry of the modern age.

A third wave of industrial revolution gave sturdy motorized tanks, which could barge into anything, shelling grenades through their cannons, prominent during the Blitzkreig strategy employed by Germans during World War I, helped by air power by way of planes, which could go and strike deep into army territory, and finally, a navy supporting the offensive by way of aircraft carriers, as shown by Japan during the Pearl Harbor attacks in 1941. While some European countries like Britain and France developed superior navy power with advanced metallurgy and designs often using it economically as small force against less industrialized Chinese army during Opium Wars,US using steam powered fleet in Edo Bay and forcing Japan to open up trade Channels, Ottoman Janissaries became famous for most effective and fierce use of gunpowder, and those superior in something could overpower or inflict major damage to others, and gain socio-political upper hand.

There were a few exceptions where despite a non-industrialized armed fleet, some countries could protract their fight against the opponent and being even able to prevent being overpowered, as in the case of Frontier Wars in the 1800s in South Africa, or in Afghanistan, wherein the small armies proved to be effective against the larger ones by way of better terrain acquaintance, guerilla warfareor by other methods.

Total war as the new hallmark decimation and war leadership strategy

The overwhelming forces created by industrialized technologies, greatly increased the war making capacities of the countries, and combined with the use of maximum resources from within the country, including production, transportation, communication and manpower, were commandeered by the government into supplying the large scale requirements of the army to produce mass scale destruction and devastation in another country, well inside the boundaries causing civilian casualties in much larger capacity. Thus, total wars brought civilians into the line of fire, targeting civilian bases, and emotionally crippling the ability to wage war by massive killing of civilians. Total Wars were played out in detail during the World Wars where the Allied and the Axial Forces caused severe damage to civic facilities in each other cities. Thus total civilian deaths amounted to around 30 millions during World War II and military deaths to 15 millions. Also, most of warring states ended with large-scale destruction, weaker socioeconomic conditions and poverty.

Eisenhower as the first Global strategic leader in World War II

Context:

The pre and post World War II era is about the Allied military Forces and the Rest, The second wave of struggle for Acquisition, expansion and wars propelled by Advanced military and destruction capacities, Culminating in World Wars.

An effective and successful maneuver mixes effective ways to deploy troops to obtain offensive, mass, and surprise. This was sharply evident during World War II when the Allied forces defeated Germany by a direct offensive against the European continent, when led by Gen. Dwight D. Eisenhower, they first massed their forces in England, and with accurate intelligence on the German force placements, deceived Germans on the entry point to Europe and plundered the Axis forces by the Operation Overlord.

Nuclear Bomb, Manhattan project and the catastrophe as the final assault

Context:

The Manhattan Project for the creation of nuclear Bomb was the next level in Total Wars: Men central to the nuclear Decision build up-President of USA Harry Truman, Secretary of State of USA James Byrnes, General Douglas McArthur as proponents and Gen Dwight Eisenhower and Henry Stimson, Secretary of War showing reservations.

In 1940, after getting informed about Nuclear research by Nazi Germany, the U.S. government began funding its own atomic weapons development program, taking clue from a group of refugee American scientists from fascist regimes in Europe, and put it under the joint responsibility of the Office of Scientific Research and Development and the War Department after the U.S. entry into World War II. The construction of the vast facilities for the same was delegated to the U.S. Army Corps of Engineers. As the site facility was built up at Manhattan, the engineering corps' district as a top-secret project, it was codenamed "The Manhattan Project ".The key materials for nuclear fission–uranium-235 and plutonium (Pu-239) were produced after sometime and taken to Los Alamos, New Mexico, and the final project was initiated to turn these materials into a workable atomic bomb, and early on the morning of July 16, 1945, the first successful test explosion was done at the Trinity test site at Alamogordo, New Mexico. This was the first test of an atomic device–a plutonium bomb–and the leader of the team was J. Robert Oppenheimer.

During the World War, when the Allied forces had brought the Germans on heels in Europe by the successful operation Overlord, the instigation for practical use of the nuclear bomb first came in the form of Japanese blunt refusal to cave in to the Allied demand for surrender as per the Potsdam Declarationand threat of "prompt and utter destruction" if they refused, and rather severe retaliatory action by the Japanese army in April to July 1945, causing heavy, major and unprecedented casualties to the Allied forces. President Truman pondered and with the thought of making a massive impact to bring the war to a quick end and to prevent expected 1 million casualties in case of prolonged war operations "Downfall" against Japan, decided to use the atomic bomb in the hope that it will not only end the war, but also put the U.S. in a dominant position and affect the course of the postwar world. For the decision, he did not heed to reservations of Secretary of War Henry Stimson, General Dwight Eisenhower, of the Manhattan Project scientists, and rather rested faith in proponents James Byrnes, Truman's secretary of state and the reasoning of Gen Douglas McArthur, and gave a go ahead after entering into the Quebek agreement with United Kingdom for the same. Thus about 9,000-pound uranium-235 bomb "Little Boy" aboard a modified B-29 bomber nicknamed *Enola Gay* (after the mother of its pilot, Colonel Paul Tibbets) was dropped by parachute at 8:15 in the morning on Hiroshima, exploding 2,000 feet above,creating impact of 12-15,000 tons of TNT, destroying five square miles of the city, a manufacturing center of some 350,000 people located about 500 miles from Tokyo.

Another plutonium bomb "Fat Man" weighing nearly 10,000 pounds and for a 22-kiloton blast was dropped on August 9 1945 on Nagasaki by Major Charles Sweeney aboard B-29 bomber, *Bockscar*, starting from Pacific coast US base Tinian, foregoing primary target Kokura due to heavy clouds, destroying 2.6 square miles of the valley surrounded by hills. The required impact was created by these bombings- killing about 1,30,000 people, mostly citizens, and causing morbidity to many- on Japan, which shuddered to think of a repeat and Emperor Hirohito announced surrender on August 15 1945 and signed the agreement on September 2 on US battleship Missouri in Tokyo bay.

Over the years war strategies have greatly evolved as seen in the prpolonged Iran Iraq Wars, the gulf Wars, the Iraq invasion of Kuwait and resulting action by Allied Forces, use of missiles extensively and lately use of drones by US for the final avenge of 9/11 attacks. It may however be noted that war strategies have been largely influenced by the geopolitical and socioeconomic impact expected as a measurable outcome.

9.

The Swashbuckling War Generals

CONTEXT:

Delegation, Staunch nationalism by the second Rank- The Generals, Ministries and Prime Ministers

The second in command in any organization has a great responsibility. The person concerned has to be steadfastly behind the leader, keep the rest of the unit united and fighting fit, and at the same time, he has to abstain from overdoing his role. He has to ensure that he listens and gets the commands carried out in the best possible way. For any of his thoughts or ideas he should first get the same vetted by the leader. The earliest organisations were the tribal war units, then the armies and the military.

Carrying out this role of understanding the writ of the leader whether told or untold, whether expressed or unexpressed, explicitly clear or implicit and to be read between the lines, demands exceptional self discipline and restrain. To top it all, the General concerned has to have an individual personality of his own, being independently able to motivate, goad and inspire his team towards the assigned goal.

The world has been witness to some exceptionaly extraordinary show of this commandership, resilience, restraint, dedicatedness, steadfastness and ferocity all mixed together in equal proportions to give us Generals like Leonidas, General Hannibal, Scipio Africanus, Suleiman, Trang Hung dao, Vo Nguen Diap, Gen Manstein, Gen Rommel, Gen Hari Singh Nalwa, Gen Patton, Gen Mc Arthur, Gen Eisenhower and many others.

As survival of the earliest community groups depended on how well it could retaliate as a team to the perpetrators, the role of the general became crucial, in bringing the team together, building it up as a force to reckon with, making all the guns fire alike at the same time and sustaining the energy of the team till the dead end. History has been witness to some of the finest generals who have tested their mettle against storm, hoaned themselves to startling discipline and acumen and led their men to jaw dropping victories.

Three generals Leonidas, Miltiades and Themistocles stood out in the Athenian and Spartan army who prevented Persian intrusion between 500-350 BC. While Leonidas was a mountain fighter, proving a great force in the Battle of Thermophyle mountain pass, Themistocles proved his might at the naval battle of Salamis and Miltiades is known for the battle of Marathon. All the three prevented the Persian dominance and preserved the European civilization.

Who can but forget the great King Philip II and then his son Alexander, the Great, who were successful first in establishing Macedonian control over whole of the Greece, and then stretch the Macedonian kingdom from Ionian Sea upto India by the 300th BC!!

कठिन राहों के वोह मुसाफिर निकले
जहाँ न थी कोई राह, वहाँ भी कर गुजर निकले
था होश में एक जूनून,
था जोश में पूरा सुकून
रहूँ पीछे किसी के, यह मेरी फितरत नहीं

मंजिलें अपनी, मेरी आदत, मेरा यकीन,

चीर के बियाबानों को, लाऊंगा तस्वीर ऐसी

तोड़ पर्वत, झरने उतारूँ, ताबीर ऐसी

जोश अपना, औरों में भर के

उठते गुबार और आंधरियां समेट के

जब मैदानों में लहराते थे शमशीर

करते थे मुकम्मिल हर फतेह की तस्वीर

करके हर हुक्म की तामील, वोह कुछ शहसवार

नाम बना गए अपना मैदाने जंग में हर बार

Such generals laid down the first golden rules for manpower, resource, strategic management and planning to execute herculean tasks marvelously. In many a sense, they established the first tenets of effective management of minimal resources to its full potential and maximum efficacy. Their working strategy was very simple- clear vision, staunch and 'till death do us part" dedicatedness and honesty to their tasks. The more illustrious of them all need mention.

Hannibal:

Hannibal Barka will forever be remembered as the man who brought Rome to its knees, despite having every advantage, numbers, terrain, better equipped, excellent naval support and supplies. Using a team of merceneries, who had to be tamed to prevent them fighting against each other, he traveled through Spain, France, and the Alps to reach Rome, winning almost every battle with opposition from his homeland and without naval support. If only he could have brought siege weapons across the Alps then history would replace the Roman Empire with the Carthagien Empire.

General Hannibal defeated the Romans in three major battles during the Second Punic War, mainly by his ability to integrate his troops, who came from all over Spain and Carthage, together as one fiercely aggressive fighting force, equivalent to that seen for Spartans.

His eventual defeat by Scipio Africanus, a determined Roman general was possible only after Scipio spent a prolonged and expensive time studying and learning Hannibal's tactics. Hannibal may not have expanded the Empire of Carthage the way Alexander the Great did for Macedonia buthe is the one who first exemplified military leadership, exhorting the mercenaries into a devastating military aggressive force.

Scipio Africanus led the Roman Empire expansion across the Europe, first conquering Carthage in Greece and then other parts and regions of Africa, by the 200 BC. Marcus Agrippa was another Roman general, who brought fame to Caesar Augusts, the Octavian and helped expansion of Roman Empire by 30th century BC.

Julius Caesar: The king and the General

Very few generals can boast of having won so many pitched battles at such damning odds. He was a brilliant tactician, able to make effective use of his troops to achieve various and often-unorthodox tactical advantages, and was known to marshal the Roman Legionary into a conquering force. He was also equally able to wage and win a civil war against powerful generals with an army of equal discipline and greater numbers. Only a brilliant man could establish himself in power by civil war, while acting within the socio-political constraints of Rome to preserve his popularity and establish his supremacy.

Julius Caesar conquered Gaul, being christened the destroyer of tribes, killing 500,000 Germans who tried to cross the roman border. He also conquered modern day France, Belgium, the Netherlands and England, West Spain, Morocco, Algeria and Tunisia and defeated Pompey to expand Roman Empire.

Khalid Bin Walid

The man responsible to sustain and stabilize the Arab world by his martial skills, discipline, morality and truthfulness to the cause of spreading Islam across the globe and prevent it from extinction was Khalid. His military skills are exemplified by his ability to marshal small forces into major victory against the mighty Roman, Persian or other army, leading from the front. Because of his indefatigability, he was christened as the man who carried the "Sword of Allah".

King David, Israel

A patriarch of three western religions Arab Jews, Jordan and Palestine, killed giants, conquered his enemies, wrote songs, had the greatest kingdom that ever existed. He was a blessed king and it was assumed that God gave him rule over all beings, including Humans, Animals, Plants, the Wind and Demons.He was an ancestor to Messiah (Jesus Christ) and he foresaw and wrote prophetic about the messiah in the psalms (in Bible) as God's millennial king who would bring peace and prosperity to the world!

Generals in Contrast: King David & Genghis Khan

Gengis Khan

Who can forget Genghis Khan, who made a mark as a ferocious conqueror between the period 1162 –1227 AD. The story of Genghis is that of survival against all odds and of meteoric passion to overcome adversities. Son of a Mongol chieftain, he saw drastic changes in fortunes, when his family, was expelled and left to die on the desolate Mongolian plains by their clan after the death of his father. The tough warrior however survived the merciless plains and again regained his status gradually first as a leader of a few outcasts like himself, then as a leader of a clan, and finally as leader of his former clan and others, and finally as king of united Mongol steppes, after overpowering and killing anyone who got in his way, wherein even the Abbasid Islamic Empire couldn't stop them.

He invaded the Xi Xia of China, and fighting in a completely different terrain, facing stonewalls most of his people had never encountered, as well as a professional army, brought them to heels. Genghis Khan ruled the largest contiguous empire in the world to date: The Mongol Empire, covering almost all of Asia and some parts of Eastern Europe.

There have been many generals, who have risen to staggering heights, but many were defeated in battle, including Hannibal, some were replaced, a la Patton, who could not prevent their army to loose morale, some met an equaly thunderous rival, as in case of Alexander the Great, but the only way Genghis was truly defeated was by his death, due to which, the Mongols couldn't conquer Western Europe, which would have changed the history of the world, considering that Western Europe later on ruled most parts. He was able to ensure that his men were loyal, and he developed superior tactics, and was the one who was never replaced as the head of the Mongol army.

Saladin and Subutai

Saladin was one of the most charismatic Muslim leader in the Crusades between the European and the Muslim Mongol forces, known for the battles for Jerusalem at Ramala in 1187. Subutai was a prominent general under Changiz Khan, who was very successful at siege and adapt strategies in winning battles for Changiz.

Suleiman I and Memeid II were strong generals who took the Ottoman Turk empire to great heights by acquiring Constantinople and expand to Africa between 1450 to 1530 AD.

Tran Hung Dao

Whenever there is a discussion of war generalship, Tran Hung Dao's name is amongst the foremost. The Mongols were the strongest conquering force in the world at a time, but were matched teeth to teeth by a Vietnamese people's army lead by

Tran Hung Dao who commanded Dai Viet armies to Mongolian Invasions in 1285 and 1287. His victories over the mighty Mongol Yuan Dynasty under Kublai Khan are considerably the greatest military feats in world history with strategies of protracted people's war.He is supposed to bethe greatest general ever, and famous Vietnamese inspiration for generations.

Võ Nguyên Giáp

Võ Nguyên Giáp was a twentieth century Vietnames army general, who organized the small Vietnamese army as a frustrating force to reckon with which fizzled out the mighty powers of the capitalist empires - France and America. A man passionate about his countryside, his people, culture and love for life, he managed to prevent Vietnam being overpowered by mighty and advanced American and French Forces, with a steadfast and stubborn purpose that simply stated "I come from Vietnam, I love my country and I love the World where we are living! Protect it - Make love not War!", out lasting all others in whatever wars he faced and being crowned as the General who was never defeated, and lead a life as passionate as his wars, marking out 1911-2013 as a life period that inspired many within and outside Vietnam, even his opponents.

((vi) Reference picture on page 148)

Generals Equal in Character & Valour, but on Different Sides

Erich Von Manstein

Manstein was one of the most brilliantly strategic politically aware generalsunder Hitler, although not in consonance always with Hitler, often differing from Hitler, and not being in agreement to his ideas. The force behind the German Reich and Hitler was actually Manstein, probably the greatest strategic genius in WWII, who was able to take on the might of allied forces, defeat them in France, putting a stubborn resistance against Rusian forces marshaled by Zhukov, who could out maneuver him only due to massive difference in numbers-10:1. It would have been a different outlook if he was given a free hand by Hitler.

Erwin Johannes Eugen Rommel

The Desert Fox was a German field marshal of World War II and is known so because of his successes while he commanded the whole army troop at Africa for the German Reich or Axis, where the Axis could almost have won North African campaign. He is famously recalled as an excellent leader as well as great human being, making sure his army did not commit any war crimes. Under his command, the axis army, though small and badly outnumbered, was able to pull out remarkable victories, with far inferior forces and supplies at his disposal against the Allied Forces. American army has in fact incorporated specific strategies of Rommel as Desert Fox.

Many other Generals earned reputation during the World War II, including Hughes Wilson (Britain), General Patton (Cowboy General), General McArthur, Gen Eisenhover, Gen Bradley (America), Gen Lucian Truscott, K K Rokosovsky (Russia). Gen Stanislaw (Russia), General De Gaulle (The Free French Navy), Gen Mark W Clark, Gen McAuliffee, Gen Marshal Plan, Wladivlav Skidosky, Bernard Montgomery, Gen karl wihelm (Germany), and later, Harisingh Nalwa etc.

Many authors have written profoundly on famous World War II generals, including Raymond Callahan (Churchill and his Generals in World War II), Stephen R Taaffe ("Marshal and His

Commanders"), John Macdonald ("Great battles of World War II"), World war II (The Definitive Visual History), Thomas E Ricks ("The Generals"), Antony Weever ("The Second World War").

Famed Fighting groups who gained reputation during the World War II included The Black Watch (Scottish parachutist Regimen), The Royal Irish Fusiliers, The German Ju 87 Stuka Dive Bombers, The British Expeditionary Force, British royal Air Force Bombing Squadron, German Mountain Troops (Gerbigsjagers)

Many locations, witness to fierce fighting between Germans and Allied Forces during World War II, include, Dunkirk Beach, France, Dinant, Belgium, Meuse River Bridge, Narvik Norway, Stalingrad Antverp etc.

Gen Lee

Lee was a decent defensive general, but poor when on offense. His offensive campaigns basically destroyed the Army of Northern Virginia by bleeding it to death, but there are not many such victories boosting his profile. Also, the impact that he left was shortlived and the opponents, majorly he faught against the Union Armies, gained strength and retaliated leter, as in the case ofthe battle at Chancellorsville, where the opponentslater got their acts together to stop him at Gettysburg with heavy losses. He was ultimately outsmarted by a General with equal sense of intuition, fortitude and resilience and in Grant, he found that formidable foe, against whom he was forced to fight a skillful but ultimately losing campaign as he was not able to inflict a decisive defeat.

One fact that is often forgotten about Lee is that he was not the commander of the confederate forces in the Civil War. He commanded one army, and with that single army conducted the total defense of the CSA. He was not allowed any command over the total war strategy used by his country, and had no control over resources, troop movements, and logistics that go into winning a war. The fact that his country mismanaged resources, did not collaborate in a cohesive defense, and offered no means of production for a prolonged war, illustrates how important and effective Lee's tactics really were. While the union was able to focus their whole war strategy in concert against the south, Lee became the south as he won victory after victory against larger, better-equipped, better trained, and better-fed troops. No other commander on this list had to fight with such handicaps, and no other commander would have seen Lee's success if they had to. It's easy to say that since the confederacy lost.

Lee is overrated, and certainly isn't in the same class as the greatest of world history. Gettysburg was winnable, and likely the war with it due to the spectre of the peace democrats looming over the 1864 election. But due to mistakes by Lee and by his subordinates like Ewell and Hill, whose blunders he is as much responsible for as their triumphs, he was outmaneuvered by George Meade and lost both the battle and war decisively-the only war in which he was ever a major player.

10.

Military as the New Organizational Model for Army, Fostering Entrepreneurship and Management

CONTEXT:

The first case of Army under and owned by a state and not a king-with independent units, greater decentralization, yet federal spirit- the rise of British army as a strong, well structured, globaly allying state army, strategizing global restructuring in Europe, Africa, America, Australia and Indian Subcontinent, is a marvelous case study in itself. It has stood out as a phenomenal model everywhere else in he world, where democracy or the power of a people's representative state has been given due recognition. The military is supposed to act in a rationale way under orders from a hierarchy which follows the state's laid down instructions for use of force only as and when required, and readiness for a decisive attack and aggression against other state or aggressors on immediate basis as instructed. The military also distinguishes and prides itself in the fact that it is under a single command as it spreads out and silently stands by to protect the whole country.

Recent value addition to military as a massive and formidable organization over the years includes, also coming to the fore as a premiere organization in cases of internal strife within the country, taking charge as a primary component of Disaster management and Relief Force and in natural calamities.

Some trait common to all decorated and valiant Generals in Militaries across nations is the sense of deep love for duty, the assigned task & targets, abilty to stretch beyond limits when asked for, stickler for discipline, positive imagination and an eye that sees possibility in the toughest task. Be it the crisis of Sierra Leone, Gulf Wars, World Wars, Irish tussle, the Falklands, Congo, Serbia, or recently Syria, Afghanistan or other hotspots across the globe, the men in uniform stand anchored and brave the scorching dserts, dead cold clifts, dep sea targets or bushy and scary forests.

Thanks to the men in uniform, the civlisations saw development of major roads across small helmets, atop hills, stout and firm small or major bridges across streams and rivers, even well laid out areas which could be developed around for safe townships with the merit of proximity to the camps. What we talk today as new technologies, whether in telecommunication, telegraphy, audio video transmissions, water systems, construction tools, have in one way or the other passed through the tests after being put to grueling screen during military processes and use. To say the least, the only nuclear test to have ever happened, involved the team from defence to take it across and get delivered by the armed team.

Though there has been a flip side, with stories of military atrocities, armed men wreaking havoc during total wars, misuse and abuse of power and even instigating conflicts, but these traits can be taken in consonance with how the people in political, civil and other hierarchies of power have behaved and evolved in their thinking over the years. Society and the world have indeed been testimony to such unbridled military actions and have witnessed great devastations over the years, but yes, that is how the social traits of the society has evolved balancing the basal or even animal instincts.

The organization of an Army is based on a smallest unit of about 30-40 combat personnel headed by a leader, generally the Captain with assistance of Subedars, with further upward accumulation of Groups into larger units which may be Company, Batallion, Brigades, Divisions, Corps and Commands, as in the case of Indian Army, with the leadership role changing from executing or operational nature to strategizing, planning and policy making. Present day top military leaders have to integrate knowledge of international and domestic politics, internal affairs, emerging technologies and government coordination, apart from skills in man management, psychology, communication, administration and financial management of resources.

The key to military leadership is ideas, strategy, balance, calculated aggressiveness and ability to induce the required bon-homie within a combat unit to fire at the spur of the moment. Globally, various armies have made a mark succesfuly and some not so succesfuly, based on the type of mission imagined by their leaders and its righteousness.

It can be presumed that, somewhere, military as an organization played a great role in development and elaboration of advanced management tenets and techniques, wherein, team and employee motivation, team building, mission and goal setting, execution and success were defined and redefined over the years, and various success stories from wars across the globe, with specific cases on setting goals, organization of resources, assessment of execution strategy and actual execution have been taken up for study of management principles and methods.

Interestingly, apart from management principles, even entrepreneurship theories and enterprise itself has somewhere been fostered by the innovation requirements of the armies in tackling different war situations. Situations of crisis coming across the military or the armed forces, often demand ingenuity, innovation and problem solving skills and therein the spirit of entrepreneurship has helped further the growth of many an industries in the 20th Century parallel to major wars, including grand success stories of Oil, ammunition, automotive and many other industries.

The British Army

The British Army is the oldest military organization created by an ACT under an independent country and for the state, when it was mooted in the Bills of Rights in 1689, and enacted by the Act of Union by the British parliament in 1707 after union between England and Scotland, whereby it was ruled that parliamentary consent every 5 years was necessary to decide on the need and the size of the peacetime army to be maintained by the Crown. Its antecedent, the English Army, was otherwise the Royal Army, with direct allegiance to the emperor who had the absolute power to decide on the size of the peacetime army and the authority to use the state resources for its maintenance.

It was the first incorporation of a standing army, enacted by the state, and not at the sole command of the king, but under parliamentary jurisdiction. Prior to this, all the major empires, had a practice of raising temporary army for a particular expedition, with the help of the local influential nobles or heads, spread across different areas, who in turn even utilized the mercenaries and other elements for the specific task.

The appropriate transfer of administration and the judicious control of budgeting by the Parliament for maintenance of the army, took some time to happen afte the enactment of the Bills of Rights in 1707, when the purpose of incorporation was to ensure that, the army should act in support of the national requirement for Britain and not be affected or influenced by the local nobles or Royals who also happened to be member of Parliaments and could make use of the army more for local gains.

The structure of the British army, now under the Parliament, still remained similar to that of the Royal or the English army, with Scottish and Irish armies combined together. The War of Spanish Succession was the first assignment for this structure, and it included many regiments from all these three armies given a combined function. Initialy there was a difference in the ranks given to the officers of the three armies with those from the British army being specifically considered for specific ranks, a practice which later was made homogenous, along with allotment of Dragoon rank to the units on the basis of date of formation and not on the basis of joining the combined British army.

This first State owned Army or the military, was used effectively in the British expansion and control interests for establishing and maintaining its colonies, Protectorates and Dominions in Americas, Africa, India, Australia and other countries, making sure that it was able to counter the French interests in expansion in the Europe, during the wanning of the Spanish influence and the Wars of Spannish Succession, conquering the New france in North America during the Seven Year's wars. However, there were some setbacks too, the major being the loss of 13 constituent colonies during the American War of Independence, thus loosing North America, but still being able to retain Canada and Maritime.

When required, the Militarised British Army also formed first global alliance structure, combining with the Dutch and Prussian Armies for stopping the massive expansion drive undertaken by the Great French General Napolean Bonaparte, by the decisive win at Battle of Waterloo, led by Duke of Wellington and Field Marshal Von Bluchor in 1815.

The British Army however, also witnessed revolts in its ranks, when it could not hold on to its Protectorants, as in American War of Independence in 1812, when the American units protested against the high taxation policy for import of American goods into Britain. However, in other revolts, as in case of Irish War of Independence, the Army judiciously took support of political solution, and was able to supress the Irish rebellion in 1798, the Battle of Rorke's Drift in Africa in 1879 and the Mutiny in the Indian Army Unit of the British Army in 1857 led by Nawab Siraj Ud Daula. The British Army showed readiness for reforms through Cardell, Childer's and Haldern Reforms where the Army was appropriately restructured into the Territorial force, the Yeoman's Force, the Militia and the Voluntary Force.

The British Army allied globaly differently in different eras, collaborating with the Germans, Dutch and Prussians in the 19th Century to stall the march of French Gen napoleon Bonaparte, and then in the 20th Century, countering the German expansionist aggression, allying with France, by the the Gobal Entente Treaty, also involving America and even Russia, which had a secret pact with France to prevent Prussian dominance.

The British Army continued to show its global might and posessions, via colonisations in various continents, and also by forming specific regional expeditionary forces, namely the British Expeditionery Forces, sent to various European countries either for protection of British properties or for helping out allied forces from attacks, as in the case of France under attack by Germans at the start of 20th Century, or Mediterranian Expeditionery Forces sent to Ottoman to secure sea routes to counter Russia. In both World Wars I and II, British Army started as the main retaliatory force against the axis, but suffered major loss of count, nearly 8 lakh, of its army in grueling battles including the battle of Somme and the Battle of Pschendelle in World War I and then in Battle of Dunkirk in France while helping out France against German attacks. Bolstered by Supoort of America and then by the Canadian, New Zealand,

Australia and Indian Forces, and indirectly supported by Russia, it was successful in making conclusive acquistions first in Battle of El Amein in Africa and then in the D Day Battle at Normandy in France, and finaly against the Japanese Forces in Invasion of Burma in World War Ill.

The World wars changed the global acquisition and control strategy of the British. The army was further downsized and major colonies were granted freedom, including India, Pakistan, the frican and other Asian Colonies. Still British Army kept itsef in the position of a major balancing force in areas like Korea, Indonesia, Cyprus, Kenya and even in Germany as a special force, the British Army of Rhine to stall Russian advances. It maintained a big Brother position in Ireland from 1967 till 2007 to prevent internal conflicts and separation attempts, as Special Forces namely Royal Ulster Constabulary, Ulstar Defence Regiment and then as Royal Irish Regiment. It also intercepted release of Falkland Island from Argentinian Aggression. While decreasing global operations and size, the British Army kept modernsiing through Tank regiment, Chemical warfare facilities and Royal Air Force competencies, and is still a model Force in the world.

The Present British Army has had some famous Generals who have stood out amongst the crowds for their outstanding services. Some of them are, Sir James Rupart Everard, Chief of Defence Staff since 2017, who also serves ar NATO's Dy Supreme Allied Commander Europe, commissioned in 1983, served as Chief of Staff, deployed at UN Protection Force HQ, NATO Implementation Force IFOR, Commander of Queen's Royal lancers, awarded Order of the British Empire (OBE) in 2000, Commander of the Order of British Empire (CBE) in 2005.

Christopher Deverell, Chief of Defence Staff 2016-17, commissioned in 1979 in Royal Tank Regiment, KCB (Knight

Commander of the Bath), MBE (Member of Order of British Empire), ADC General is UK's joint Forces Command, and has commanded UK's Joint Chemical, Biological, radiation and Nuclear Regiment, and has played active role in The Troubles and Iraq War.Sir Richard Shirreff, Chief of Defence Staff, bestowed with Commander of the Order of British Empire (CBE), Companion of the Distinguished Services Order (DSO), Knight Commander of the Bath (KCB) served from 2011-2014, after having proved his mettle at various points in his professional life, that included serving with Royal Artillery in Germany and Northern Ireland, critical acclaim in Sierra Leone Civil Wars against the rebellions, association with NATO as Major General, Lt Gen International Security Assistance Force, in Afghanistan, and finally Chief of the General Staff till 2011.

Sir John Reith, Chief of Defence Staff in 2004-05, conferred with Officer and Commander of the OBE, Knight Commander of the Bath, started in the parachute regiment and rising through his ranks, handled all UK oversees operations in Iraq, Afghanistan, Balkans and Sierra Leone as Chief of the joint Operations and also as Deputy Supreme Allied Command Europe. Sir Rupart Antony Smith, CDS 1998-2000, KCB, DSO, OBE, QGM, has outstandingly served in the Gulf Wars and Bosnia Wars, for which he has been ordained with different merits and also served as Dy Supreme Allied Commander, Europe, and has authored the book "The Utility of Force". Sir Mike Jackson, CDS 2000, KCB, DSO, showed his mettle and commanding skills during the Bosnia war, in Sarajevo as Commander to UNPROFOR, Gen Officer Commanding Northern Ireland, NATO's Operation Allied Force, and Dy Supreme Allied Commander and Aide de Camp General to the Queen.

Sir Nickolas Patrick carter, KCB, CBE, DSO, ADC General, has been GoC 6th Division, Commander ISAF regional Command South, mainly served in Afghanistan, Bosnia and

Kosovo, Director General Land Warfare, main architect of Army 2020 vision for the army, Chief of General Staff and the next to be Chief of Defence Staff since June 2018. Other Generals, including David Ramsbotham, Gen Billiere, Gen Learmont, Gen Charles Baron, Gen Garry Johnson, Gen Luxemborg, Gen Michael Rose, Gen Roger Wheeler, Gen Michael Walker, Gen Alexander Harley, Gen Nick Parker, Gen Edward Jones and all others have stood the test of the times and kept the British Flag flying high, and even set the highest standards in administration, strategy, social contribution, philanthropy and makingthe impossible happen.

The Indian Army

The Indian Army comprised of 4 major Commands in the pre War era, namely Northern, Eastern, Western aand Southern, nd of Brigades headed by a British Commanding Officer, trained from Sandhurst Academy as King's Commissioned Officer, with each Brigade consisting of various Battalions or regiments headed by a Subedar major, the regiments in turn consisting of companies headed by Subedars and the Companies consisting of platoons headed by jemadars, who were usually Indian experienced soldiers commissioned as Viceroy Commissioned officers (VCOs) on the basis of their skill and experience. Indians who qualified to be trained at Sandhurst Academy came back as King's Commissioned Officer, and later with the formation of Indian Military Academy at Dehradoon, they graduated as King's Indian Commissioned Officers, being promoted maximum to the Brigade rank.

The Indian army was made to focus on policing Indian state, but with the initiation of World War II, they were sent to various international locations including France, Egypt, Libya, Sudan, Malaya, Abyssinia, Iraq, Burma etc. and forming a 25 lakh strong force dring the World War consisting of soldiers from diverse religion and sect. British also maintained separate Beitish Army Units, composed of British Soldiers, to counter incidences like the Indian Mutiny, and the last units of British Army to leave India and Pakistan after independence were the 1st and 2nd Battallion in 1948. During the World War, the Indian Army was reorganized into North Western Army, Southern Army, Eastern Army and the Central Command. By the end of World War, the above 4 divisions or Armies were again converted to Commands, and after Independence, the Northern Command moving to Pakistan as the Army Headquarters. The Army in India was the name for the Headquarter at Delhi and controlled the British Army Units in India as well as the Indian Army and consisted of Military Secretary's Branch, General Staff Branch, Adjutant General's Branch, Quarter-Master-General's Branch, Master-General of the Ordnance Branch, and the Engineer-in-Chief's Branch, headed by a Commander in Chief or the General.

Before the end of World war, the size of the Indian army was quite huge with 8 Lieutenant Generals, 30 Major Generals, 83 Brigadiers, 102 Colonels and 2375 other Officers, with a Principal Administrative Officer at the headquarters or the General Head Quareters (GHQ). After the end of War, the numbers were downsized to 2 Major Generals, 15 Brigadiers, 20 Colonels ans 729 Other Officers. To oversee partition and division of Army, the British created a special post, Supreme Commander and Field Marhal Achunileck was the first designate.

((vii) Reference picture on page 149)

Presently the Indian Army is organized in 7 Commands (Central at Lucknow, Northern at Udhampur, Western at Chandimandir, Southern at Pune, South Western at Jaipur, Eastern at Kolkatta, and Training Command at Shimla), each headed by a Gen Officer Commanding in Chief or The Lt General, with each command comprising of 2-more Corps and each Corp having a combination of various Divisions. A Division, headed by Gen Officer Commanding (GOC), may have 15000 combat personnel and 8000-support team, and may be categorized as RAPID Action, Mountain, Artillery, Infantry and Armoured Divisions, and each is further divided in Brigades with around 3000 combat personnel headed by a Brigadier, with each Brigade comprised of Batallions each of around 900 combat personnels and support staff headed by a Colonel, further composed of Companies of about 120 personnel headed by a Major, and further down the line Platoons headed by Captain with at least 32 personnels.

5 Independent armoured, 15 Artillery, 7 Infantry, 1 Parachute Brigades, 3 Air Defence and 4 Engineers Brigades also exist apart from those within Divisions, with two independent Air Defence Groups also forming integral part of Indian Army.

Era of organized Military overuse

On the flip side, some references have been made in various twxts about military overreach and overuse. One such detail is mentioned as under. The point is, power with responsibility and empathy is an essential tenet for leadership.

A historian's account of a thirteenth century traveller's description of Great Benin city in Africa says "The town seems to be very great. When you enter into it, you go into a great broad street, not paved, which seems to be seven or eight times broader than the Warmoes street in Amsterdam...The Kings palace is a collection of buildings which occupy as much space as the town of Harlem, and which is enclosed with walls. There are numerous apartments for the Prince's ministers and fine galleries, most of which are as big as those on the Exchange at Amsterdam. They are supported by wooden pillars encased with copper, where their victories are depicted, and which are carefully kept very clean. The town is composed of thirty main streets, very straight and 120 feet wide, apart from an infinity of small intersecting streets. The houses are close to one another, arranged in good order. These people are in no way inferior to the Dutch as regards cleanliness; they wash and scrub their houses so well that they are polished and shining like a looking glass."

Here is another account of the great Benin City regarding the city walls "They extend for some 16 000 kilometres in all, in a mosaic of more than 500 interconnected settlement boundaries. They cover 6500 square kilometres and were all dug by the Edo people. In all, they are four times longer than the Great Wall of China, and consumed a hundred times more material than the Great Pyramid of Cheops. They took an estimated 150 million hours of digging to construct, and are perhaps the largest single archaeological phenomenon on the planet.

Sadly, in 1897, Benin City was destroyed by British forces under Admiral Harry Rawson. The city was looted, blown up and burnt to the ground. A collection of the famous Benin Bronzes are now in the British Museum in London. Part of the 700 stolen bronzes by the British troops were sold back to Nigeria in 1972.

11.

Industrial Revolution: Innovation and Industrialization

हर शख़्स का कुछ हिस्सा होता था
हर शख़्स ही एक हिस्सा होता था
इंसानी सफर में,
मुझसे और तुमसे ही कारवां जुड़ता था
कुछ तुम मुझको दे देते थे
कुछ मैं तुमको था थमा देता
कुछ इस तरह से देना होता था
कुछ इस तरह से लेना होता था
पैसे की कुछ बात न थी,
जब दो दिल हों राजी, कोई और न मतलब होता था।
क्या चीज ये तुमने नयी बना दी है
एक मुश्किल आसान कर दी है,
शाबासी और ताररुफ से ही नया सा मंजर बनता था

This sums up the preindustrialisation efforts to provide succor and help to each other and society at large, when people contributed individualy in small ways to help and comfort each other in various ways. Industrialisation was given a small peg or fillip with the first test use of the "Spinning jenny or engine" in 1764, when James Hargreaves, coming up with the innovation to assist the textile merchants who were left hard pressed often not being able to manage the demand and supply system, as they were dependent totally on the whims and schedules of the cottage industry workers who provided them with the finished textile products from the raw material they provided by manually spinning the fibers at their homes with the help of some basic equipments provided by the merchants. This helped in a first instance where large scale production was improved upon by use of a machine with decreased manpower and enhanced efficiency. Industrialisation had taken its first baby steps.

The spinning jenny was further improved upon by Samuel Crompton as the "Spinning mule" and by the end of the 18th Century, there were around 20000 such machines all across Great Britain. It was further improved upon as "Power loom" by Edmund Cartwright, which further mechanized the spinning jenny and converted it into a full fledged machine.

आशा की किरण दिखते ही
उसे थाम के छलांग लगानी है,
यही सोच हर अविश्कार की,
हर खोज की कहानी है।।

Thus all innovations sprang from the innate urge to just catch on to some solution that could pull one out from a dire situation. The textile mechanization was helped by developments in the iron and steel industry, with Abraham Darby already having developed a cheaper and easier method to develop cast iron using coke fuel furnace as compared to charcoal fueled earlier furnace at the start of 18th Century, and later Henry Bessemer developing first inexpensive process for mass production of steel from Iron. Thus the, origination of iron and steel, gave a massive fillip to developments in the appliance, tool, machines, building, infrastructure and ship industry.

A preliminary steam engine was developed by Englishman Tomas Newcomen in 1712 for pumping out water from mines, and later a massive improvement by James Watt led to the discovery of a full fledged steam engine, which served as a milestone in the development of powered machinery, locomotives and ships, and there and behold, a full fledged industrial revolution had been sounded. Transportation gained speed across all means, by land or by sea, by development of advanced methods of smoother, durable and less muddy road construction as innovated by Engineer John McAdam from Scotland by 1820, development of first commercial steamboat in early 1800 in America by Robert Fulton which developed into a well established system of freight steamships running across the Atlantics by 1850. The railways designed by British Engineer Richard Trevithik in the early 1800s developed into a 6000 mile railroad track across Britain with first major Railway Stations at Liverpool and Manchester offering passenger train services with a fixed Time Table by 1830.

A few iron pieces, gave the first sense of power,

The smoke from the steam engine, like a beautiful shower

Hardly did they sound alarm bell of pollution,

But instead set the heartbeats roll at the visible solution,

As the locomotive pulled a load colossal,

Thousand thoughts jumped aloud,

We can ferry all, food, fuel and crowd!!

Industrialisation had woven its own magic,

When for the masses, it was charismatic,

But when for war, it was tragic.

Railways: keeping the Industrial revolution on Track

Heroes: James Watt, Murdoch, George Stephenson

These were the three men who improvised and improved upon the steam engine and bringing the locomotive into its final shape, which was able to provide a faster, powerful and new alternative to horse driven carriages with extremely limited ferrying capacity for limited distances. Railways, as they were laid out gradually offered ease of massive transport and mass public transit across the countries, as evident in the extensive rail line network that was built up in England by the end of 19th century and in 20th Century, which could even transfer goods and people through a steep slope.

Railways emerged initialy in 1600 as wooden carts driven on wooden rails or initialy pulled along a funicular system based on a pulley system, normaly established on a hill slope with the two carts balancing and moving in opposite direction, to transport load of coal from mines or passengers wherein it was a short distance very slow small level transport. Later wagonways, a series of wooden wagons hitched to each other, rolling with wooden wheels on wooden rails, and pulled by horses were successfully established by 1605 by Hunttingdon Beaumond in Wollaton, England and other places. The York Building Company established more waggonways and the Tanfield waggonways, which had greater efficiency of transferring 60 wagons driven by horses' acros 5 miles per hour. The first state owned waggonway; the Middleton Railways, became operational after Parliament enactment in 1758 between Middleton coal pits to Leeds for cheap transfer of coal. The Middleton Railways pioneered the use of steam engine Salamanca by 1805.

As Iron production and Iron industry evolved after 1760, the railways also changed with change of track fabrication. Thus iron Edge rail lines and tracks were used in many new rail lines such as Charnwood Forest Canal, Cromford Canal lines for coal and lime stone ferrying. After expiry of the steam engine patent by James Watt, whose idea taken up and improved upon by Murdoch, modifying the reciprocating engine wherein the steam instead of acting on the vaccum in the cylinder, directly acted on the piston. In the 1800, many innovators tried to develop various steam locomotives for the railways, the prominent ones were by William Murdoch, later by Richard Trevethik, who developed a steam engine wherein a flywheel was used to even out the piston force and move the locomotor on the Pennydaren Tram way in South Wales and later the first locomotive train tried on a circular track in Bloomsberry.

Finaly, it was by George Stephenson who developed the most acceptable model, also the flanged wheel locomotive and the first fully steam railways, the Stockton and Darlington railways and later the famous Liverpool and Manchester railways, the first fully organized railways system powered by steam locomotives. By 1815 passenger railways strted operating, such as Swansea and mumble Railways and Kilmarnok and Troon railways, but theat were still horse driven. George Stephenson finaly worked upon the steam locomotive and executed the first passenger feery railway line the Stackton and Darlington railway line as the first steam locomotive driven passenger railways. Later the Cantebury and Whitstation railways and the Liverpool and Manchester Railway lines became the first long distance lines in England by the 1830, and the Ohio and Baltimore railway line in USA, and by 1840, railway lines had been established across the globe including US, Belgium,France and other countries. By 1879 Germany had conducted trials for electric lines and tramlines, which became operational by 1890s along with formation of first London Undergrounds, electrified railway metro system in London, and by 1900, the Diesel engine was introduced.

In India, in 1845, Sir Jamsetjee Jejeebhoy, along with Hon. Jaganath Shunkerseth (known as Nana Shankarsheth), formed the Indian Railway Association. The first commercial train journey in India between Bombay and Thane on 16 April 1853 in a 14 carriage long train drawn by 3 locomotives named Sultan, Sindh and Sahib. It was around 21 miles in length and took approximately 45 minutes. By 1901, an early Railway Board was constituted, under the Department of Commerce and Industry with a government railway official serving as chairman, and a railway manager from England and an agent of one of the company railways as the other two members, with overall powers formally under Lord Curzon. At the time of independence in 1947, about 40 per cent of the railway lines went to Pakistan and new lines had to be constructed to connect important cities such as Jammu, and only a total of 42 separate railway systems, including 32 lines owned by the former Indian princely states existed covering a total of 55,000 km creating the Indian Railways System.

The railways the world over, have come up with some of the most marvelous and difficult engineering works and tracks on very difficult terrains. Lynton and Lynamouth Cliff Railway that climbs 500 ft on the cliff slope to connect the two twin towns in England. The Comber's and Toltec Track passes through the dangerous gorge and pass terrain in New Mexico, about 1000 ft high. The Georgetown Loop railroad passes through the hills of Colorado in USA with trenches below. The tracks for the Aso Minami rail route lie very close to the active volcano Aso in Japan. The Kuranda Scanner railway track passes at hair's breadth to the massive waterfalls in the Baron Gorge in Australia and at that height it scares the passengers to their depths. The

Devil's nose railway track traverses the most of the Andes in Ecuador at 9000ft height going upto the beaches. The Chennai Rameshwaram railway track in India is built mostly on the Indian ocean, with changing water levels, sea storms and cyclones testing the mettle of the railwaymen as well as the passenmgers.

Some enticingly beautiful and others strange and shocking wonders also catch attention, including, the 3 km long railway tracks through the lush green tree surrounded almost closed avenue named the The Tunnel of Love in Ukraine at Klevan, where the train provides wood to the fireboard factory. Contrastingly The Death Railway, a 450 km track along the hill slopes connecting Thailand and Burma, is notoriously known for the high numbers of deaths, 90000 workers and many prisoners, during construction related calamities. Also those catching attention include the Napier Gisborne Railway in Newzealand, with the railway track running across an air strip, and the Meklong Market Track in Thailand, with the train track being converted to busy market on either sides as soon as the train passes and winding up every time again!!!

((viii) Reference picture on page 150)

The development of railways, and the feeling that it created amongst the common masses, of possession of railway facility as a state, public, and also their own property, was a charisma in itself. As the railways grew in massive expanse, infrastructure and network across the globe in Europe, Americas, Asia and other continents, it offered a sense of liberty, liberation and exhilaration in the haves and have nots equally. A fast rail ride could be equaly stimulating the Lords, the Bards, the Byrons and the helots, and inspire many a life at the same time, allowing all to drift momentarily from the worldly business and associated pangs. The passion and zeal of some engineers, socialists and lawmakers, thus slowly gave shape to a magnanimous institution, which became a leadership model in itself all across the globe. It gave immense zeal of creativity to scores of planners, architects, engineers and builders during massive transformation of large areas of lands in various countries, erecting sprawling and fabulous structures of railway stations, yards and long tracks, that serve as lifeline, picnic spots as well as shelters with food for millions.

A leader leads by inspiration, and the railways globaly have inspired great engineering, marvelous architecture, awe inspiring human and manual labour and team work and great inputs from the world of arts and humanities. The management of day to day business in efficiently running the railways, encompasses and draws from diverse principles including those from the army, military, the industry as well as research, philanthropic, psychological and philosophical school of thoughts.

((ix) Reference picture on page 151)

Railways have been inspiration to many a great writers and literary works. To site a few, the lead Jude in Thomas Hardy's *Jude the Obscurer*, set in the 1850s, shows his great appreciation for the female lead Sue's choice for having a meeting on a railway staion, which rather more aptly represented a new town life, rather than in a cathedral, showing how the society took railways as the new idea of modernism and progress in the 19th century with railway boom establishing an efficient cross country network.

12.

The Oil Merchants

Entrepreneurs and Industries critical to War strategies

CONTEXT:

With the exploration of oil and the identification of various rigs across various states in USA in the end of 19th Century and beginning of 20th Century, and rise of demand of fuel oils in the automobile and airline industry and gradually in the airforce, oil and gas industries fuelled and made wars more fast, fatal and furious and and in reverse propelled by wars; these industries further turned the world economies round, helped America attain the super power status, and have been at the centre of contention and power struggle, strifes and wars across the globe and continents in the 20th Centur, till date.

Heroes/Oil Heroes: George H Bissel, James Townsend, John Austin, John D Rockefeller, Edward Doheny, Joseph Cullinan, and Henry Duterding.

Rapid industrialization happened with speedy developments in the iron and steel industry in the beginning of the 19th Century. Rapidly advancing railroads connectivity network across the countries, gave new dimensions to travel, industrial transport and military movements. With the discovery of oil as a new source of fuel, the 19th century was a period of great change spawning new construction materials, faster mass movements and fuel energy to live on.

George H. Bissell, a New York lawyer, and James Townsend, a New Haven businessman, became interested to develop oil found floating on water near Titusville, Pennsylvania, when it was certified by Dr. Benjamin Silliman of Yale University after analysis of a bottle of the oil as an excellent source of light. Bissell and several friends purchased land near Titusville, and associated Edwin L. Drake as surveyor to locate the oil there and William Smith, an expert salt driller, to supervise drilling operations. On August 27, 1859, oil was struck at a depth of sixty-nine feet, tapped at its source for the first time, using a drill. Thus, the first oil corporation, was created to develop oil near Titusville, Pennsylvania, and was known by the name of the Pennsylvania Rock Oil Company of Connecticut (later the Seneca Oil Company).

Whale oil, initially used as the fuel oil for quite sometimes as an illuminant, as medicine, and as grease for wagons and tools, gradually lost its relevance due to increase in price owing to the growing scarcity of that mammal. Following this, rock oil distillation from shale became gradually commonplace and became available as kerosene prior to the Industrial Revolution. Samuel Downer, Jr., an early entrepreneur, acquired the patent for "Kerosene" as a trade name in 1859 and became licensee for its usage. A model oil lamp was first introduced by John Austin, a New York merchant, that upgraded kerosene lamps. As oil production and refining increased, prices collapsed, which became characteristic of the industry.

John D. Rockefeller, who was a small time entrepreneur operating a commission partnership firm in Cleveland, with his excellent entrepreneurial instincts and organizational capacity, built a small oil refinery company in 1859 in partnership, which he soon bought out from his partner, expanded with an export office in New York city in 1866, and by 1867, incorporated the Standard Oil Company with his brother William, S. V. Harkness, and Henry M. Flagler. Rockefeller became a leading figure in the U.S. oil industry and Titusville and other towns in the area boomed because of the emergence of oil industries, expanding to areas near Drake well. Standard Oil Company further strengthened itself by buying out or combining with its competitors, uniting its capital and skill and becoming the dominant refinery in Pennysylvania. The Standard Oil Company integrated itself horizontally and vertically by acquiring pipelines from Pithole, Pennsylvania, to the nearest railroadwhich were set up by other organizations, ensuring cheap and efficient oil transfer. Other refineries also set up in the area and Cleveland became a refinery center. As the market became more competitive with decline in prices, the Standard Company had to further upscale and form alliances by 1871, for finding better alternatives and go a level higher in the refinery products, even employing experts like an industrial chemist, Hermann Frasch II, to remove sulfur from oil found at Lima, Ohio. Sulfur when removed made it easy for distillation of kerosene as well as removed the stink. The oil exports to European countries from Philadelphia, New York and Baltimore provided a huge benefit, and large number of companies came up in the eastern cities linked by rail and boat. Gradually Standard Oil Company initiated its operations in the Western States in the form of Pacific Coast Oil Company by 1900 to deal with the obstructions due to Civil War and by 1906 turned into Pacific Oil, which recently has been rechristened Chevron.

Apart from Cleveland, Pennsylvania, Los Angeles grew as another major centre for various Oil Companies, starting in 1892, when Edward L. Doheny located first well in 1892, increasing to twenty-five hundred wells and two hundred oil companies five years later, and seven integrated oil companies by 1900, when Standard entered California.

To overcome operating difficulties and manage taxation on other properties, Standard Oil Trust was created in 1882, with Standard Oil Company (New Jersey) in 1899 as the parent company and controlling member corporations by stock ownership. There were two other major corporations besides Standard Oil, the Union Oil Company and the Pure Oil Company, Ltd., created in 1895 by Pennsylvania producers, being the most important of all.

Beaumont, Texas, became the next, and ultimately the most prominent oil location in US, with the greatest gusher discovered in the most significant oil strikes by drillers in history in US on Spindletop mound. More than fifteen hundred oil companies came up one year after the Spindletop discovery, with the Gulf Oil Corporation, the Magnolia Petroleum Company, and the Texas Company, founded by the Pennsylvanian, Joseph S. ("Buckskin Joe") Cullinan (who organized several small companies), with only another half a dozen only surviving, but in the process, finishing off the monopoly of Standard Oil Company. Many other companies also joined at Beaumont including The Sun Oil Company, an Ohio-Indiana concern, also moving to the Beaumont area, with many others. By 1909, Oil production in the United States more than equaled that of the rest of the world combined with many other refineries coming up in Oklahoma, Louisiana, Arkansas, Colorado, and Kansas. Henry Deterding was another oil businessman operating from Holland, founding Royal Dutch Shell Group, who diversified his operations to California starting American Gasoline company apart from his British operations.

Due to some of the methods as used by Standard Oil, including securing preferential railroad rates and rebates on its shipments, influence legislatures and Congress, improper handling of labor, the Supreme Court in 1911 charged Standard Trust with monopolizing and restrcting trade, and ordered the trust dissolution into thirty-four companies. That the trust's share of the industry had declined from 33 to 13 percent the Court held to be of little consequence. The splitting-off of the Standard in 1911 thus promoted splitting companies to focus on vertical integration of operations from drilling to storing to marketing rather than focusing on one activity, and also ensured enough competitive balance in the oil business in the country.

Oil has played a major role in development of America as a world power. With the discovery of gasoline from crude oil and establishment of its utility as a fuel in internal combustion engines as well as in aeroplane industry, many entrepreneurs initiated business in the oil refinery chain in the 1900s, ranging from crude drilling, refinery, distillation, by product purification, transfer, pipelines, storage, distribution and other verticals. In fact America had to centralize the oil economy and regulations by creating the Fuel Administration, which made sure that America took care of the vast business opportunities as the major oil supplier to Allied Powers in World War I, and later in the post war period, carrying on the Fuel Administration, by the name of American Petroleum Institute (API). The API, along with the Secretary of Commerce Hoover and Secretary of State Evans Hughes, then laid out an extensive off shore oil exploration initiative in foreign land, fearing exhaustion of US oil sources and many firms further established operations in Southeast Asia, South America, Middle East areas. But some individuals, like Columbus Joiner still had a gut feeling that more was yet to come and carried a passionate exploration in the Eastern flatlands in Texas, ultimately striking a goldmine in the form of a massive 140000 acre area in Tyler, Texas in 1930, with a stock of approximately 5 billion barrels.

With a brief interlude of few years of economic depression after 1030s, the oil economy boomed again during the World

War II, stimulating extensive research and development for production of *tnt,* artificial rubber and other by products, which became an industry in themselves. Even Tetraethyl Lead industry boomed riding on the oil industry, used as an additive to gasoline for producing speed efficiency in aeroplanes.

Extensive studies have identified heavy losses in oil and natural gas, stocked below the oil, during exploration, transfer and storage as seen in the case of Texas and other stocks, as compiled by Wallace E Pratt. Further this was an additional pitfall for the oilfield owners of having the right of Capture along with ownership of Drilling area, as it entitled them to everything else lodged in the land even below the oil. Thus lot of natural gas was lost during rigging without taking care.

American economy got a massive push from the rise of the oil industry in the early first half of the 20th Century, peaking in the World Wars as the only major source, but with massive consumption in the World War II, about 5 billion barrels from American wells and 6 billions from the middle east and Venezuela, the stock considerably depleted in America, and presently it is now dependent on the import of oil for its energy requirements. Thus the foreign and domestic policy in America, as a superpower has hinged around balancing preservation of domestic stocks and procurement from other sources from various countries, as seen in various oil related international crisis in the post Wporld War Ii period after 1950s, whether the Iranian Crisis 1950-54, Suez crisis in 1956, Kuwait crisis 1990, or the balancing act between Israel and the OPEC nations.

The present stock of oil, and the alarming rate of use and depletion, has led to huge research and development

initiatives on green and clean energy from alternative sources, including, solar, wind, air and other sources and development of alternatrive automobile and aeroplane fuels. The future in automobiles, transportations and vehicles is of automated and electric vehicles, utilizing energy supplied by nuclear or solar plants, depending less on natural underground crude store. Oil and other industries have included alternative energy sources and development as one of the R and D domains and are doing extensive work on the same.

13.

Air power and the Air Force: Leading and Pushing Globalistion

Building up with Boeing, the leaders in war planes and Public planes

Heroes: Wright Brothers, Major Ramon Franco and Captain Julio Ruiz de Mequelei, William Boeing, Thomas Morse, Captain Charles E Yeager, Gonzalo, navigator Ruiz d'Alda and Pablo Rada, Charles Lindberg

Context: The aeroplane industry grew out of an initial seed of curiosity and wild imagination, fuelled by maverick passion, and as the trials flicked right one after the other, it stoked desire to go on building on small gains to make a marvelous flying machine, leading to development of monoplane, biplanes, multiple engines, and then the heavy logistics and traffic carriers. It also became relevant to the armed forces giving them strategic utility and command by way of massive destroys and escape capacity with fighter plane fleet. Thus a commercial and utility industry grew driven by the force of desire and requirements of the Air Forces of different countries, initialy invented out of maverick passion of experimentors by people like Wright Brothers who wanted to experiment as to how heavy bodies could be made to maintain their stable position by modification of wing structures and propelling force, thereby developing the first airplane.

Further enthusiasm was created by the pioneering flights undertaken by ace pilots and aviators including Franco, Julio, Gonzalo and finaly by Charles Lindberg who became an all time hero and cult figure, nick named the Lone Eagle, for his daunting solo transatlantic flight from New York to Paris. It was later taken up earnestly by various state and private organisations who developed various modifications for transport, carrier and flight planes, with Captain Chatrles E Yeager finaly breaking the supersonic barrier in 1947 for the fighter aircrafts, and thereafter, Air Forces in all major powers of the world have become the deciding factors in war outcomes with their speed, manouvers and destructive prowess.

After the thrilling first flight of Wright brothers, Orville and Wilbur, the two American engineers, inventors, aviators, who made the first controlled flight on an aircraft in 1903 in Carolina,often called as the flight of maverickidea,use of air fighters was initiated, starting with expeditions initialy in January 1922 byMajor Ramon Franco and Captain Julio Ruiz de Mequeleiz aboard a Spanish Air Force Dornier J Wal Plus Ultra, from Rio Tinto through Huelva in Southwest Spain to West Africa, flying to Brazil and finaly to Argentina through South Atlantic. It was a mark of respect to the great seafarer Columbus, who had taken on a similar course back in 1492. They were also accompanied by another copilot and a mechanic. It was an open cockpit aircraft bolstered with two Napier Lion engines, 4 blade propellers, and a Marconi AD6 telephone.

Charles Lindberg, American military officer, aviator, author, carried out the first official transatlantic flight from Long Island, New York to Paris in a first 33 hour long solo flight in 1927, making him a hero and being christened with nick names like Lone Eagle, Lucky Lindy and winning the Orteig Prize and the highest military honour the Medal of Honour.

Another 20 stage 25000 miles expedition flight was taken in 1928 by Franco with team including Gonzalo, navigator Ruiz d'Alda and Pablo Rada, from Cadiz in spain as an around the globe flight in a Spanish Dornier R4 Super Wal Numancia with 4 British 500hp Napier engines, but had to cut short due to technical snag.

Boeing, initialy starting as Pacific aero Products, with its B & W (Boeing and Westerwelt) Model 1 as a simple twin float sea plane in 1916, has gradualy grown into a huge organization, designing and manufacturing different categories of aircrafts and big airplanes in different categories. The company was initiated by the businessman William Boeing with MIT trained engineer George Westervelt, and became US army's and navy's backbone in fighter planes in 1920s and 1930s. It became a hallmark for innovation and invention, designing mould for shaping jet airliners, half of the World War II fighters, creating the Pan America fleet, and pioneering the pressurized airliner and jumbojets.

The nearest competitors Thomas Morse, the prime supplier of fighters to US Army Service, were outbid by Boeing in 1920 for supply of the stupendous fighter plane MB 3A, and then there was no stopping Boeing. Innovative ideas like having its own spruce forests to supply low cost wood for aeroplane frames in the initial years, and then developing a specialized steel tube frame manufacturing line setup using high temperature arc welding over traditional Oxyacetylene flame welding, in the later years, which helped change the earlier 180DH-4s into DH-4Ms, took Boeing to new heights. Other innovations included the FB-1 or the PW-9 models used by US navy and army respectively, with a tailhook, which were model 15 Biplanes. The improvements in this category were the army's P 12 or the navy's F4B, beating the rivals Curtiss and theit P-6 Hawks.

P-26 was the last fighter monoplane, and lost in competition to the closed cockpit, cantilever wing, retractable gear fighter aeroplanes from Germany, Italy Japan, Britain and USSR. It was nicknamed peashooter because of its too little firepower in the form of two rifle gauge guns, and slow speed.

Boeing started thinking about ferrying planes when it entered into the purpose built mail planes with Model 40, an open cockpit biplane carrying half ton of mails, for government contracts. The advanced verion M 80 was a trimotor biplane, for 12 passengers, with additional comforts including hot and cold water, earplugs and cushioned seats, at the same time forming its own fleet, the United AirLines, which converted into a passenger plane with a stewardess too. However, a small decision to make the Model 247 airliner only for their in house airline United Airlines, cost them dearly as they lost out a possible mega requirement of TWA Airlines, who got about 10000 DC 3, C 53 and C 47 models manufactured from Douglas. The small achievement during the design of this monoplane twin engine, all metal retractable gear aircraft was that it originated the instrument glareshield to eliminate reflections as an overhanging panel, now present in all planes. An airborne sabotage nitroglycerine bomb explosion in one of the M 247s in 1933 further damaged its reputation.

Boeing suffered heavily in the mid 1930s when the government policies suddenly cast question mark on an aircraft manufacturing company to also own an airlines, for which Boeing had to give away United airlines and its other ancilliaries including Pratt and Whitney, Chance Vought, Sikorsky, Kamilton Stanford and others, causing Bill Boeing's furious resignation and farewell to the aeroplane industry. But it came back strongly with gigantic public plane models including Model 314 Clipper, B-29, double-deck Stratoliner, eight-engine B-52 and the largest of them all, the 747.

The B 15, first built as 4 engine, long range heavy 850 HP, R 1830 radial bomber for US army to mount 2600hp liquid cooled kAllison V 3420, could not gain much, and was never mass produced. It procuced some specific features, like high lift wing that made the lines of Boeing fleet famous for. The model features continued in the next Boeing Model, the Model 314, the tandem engine bipliane Clipper, which was the largest flying boat at that time.

The era of super sonic planes was ushered in 1947 with Captain Charles E Yeager boomed at speed greater than sound on Bell XS 1 rocket powered research plane, showing why he was renowned as a military test pilot, and later winning the prestigious Collier Trophy parallel to Larry Bell, the industrialist and aerodynamist John Stack. The three with their strong advocacy for supersonic flights took the Air Force into adopting a fleet of Supersonic jet fighters, interceptors, supersonic jet bombers and transporters. Yeager is remembered parallel to Wright brothers and Charles Lindberg in aviation history.

14.

Leaders in War Espionage and Spying in Early and Late Cold War Eras

CONTEXT:

Business and Strategic intelligence, as is prevalent in today's commercial parlance, takes its roots to war espionage, as it became commonplace during the end of 19th Century and full blown by the mid 19th Century. As in war strategy, it is relevant that appropriate information be obtained of the market, competitors, pricing, product, packaging and branding strategies of all competitors, before making an effective and impactful product launch.

The secret agents gained in high currency in the pre and post World War II Era, when they were needed not only to assess the opponent moves but also constantly look out for new ideas or defence instrument which could be used or analysed for counter development by their bosses in respective countries. 20th Century saw rapid phases of discoveries exploration and development in civil and defence equipments and gadgets and their usage methods. The secret agents played multiple roles providing inputs to defence, research and development, industry and also many other stakeholders.

It can be said for sure that but for the charming, dark and murkier world of secret agents, double agents and the spies, the rapid global spread of technology and development would not have occurred.

Heroes: Joshua and Caleb, Sun-Tzu, Chanakya, Ninjas, Francis Walsingham, Thomas Phelippes, Edward Cardwell, William Melville, MO3, MO5, SSB, Evidenzbureau, and the great fictional James Bond era.

Events involving espionage are well documented with the Old Testament of the Christian Hebrew Bible, detailing Joshua and Caleb and the twelve spies adventuring in Promised Land. Chinese and Indian military strategists such as Sun-Tzu and Chanakya mention on deception and subversion. Chanakya's student Chandragupta Maurya, expertly made use of assassinations, spies and secret agents, during the rule and expansion of Maurya Empire, as detailed in Arthashastra. The Egyptians, the Greeks, the Romans, all had an exhaustive system for the intelligence system, as could be understood from Rahab and other texts. The Mongols used the espionage very effectively during conquests in Europe and Asia and the Japanese used Ninjas for feudal rivalries.

The initiation of proper classified dynastic intelligence service took place under King David IV of Georgia in the 12th century by the name *mstovaris*, where spies were involved in uncovering feudal conspiracies, conduct counter-intelligence against enemy spies and infiltrate key locations, e.g. castles, fortresses and palaces.

Francis Walsingham in the Elizabeth period in England introduced Modern espionage methods using cryptography and deciphering skills of Thomas Phelippes and expertise of Arthur Gregory in breaking and repairing seals to ensure that all clandestine correspondence of Marry, Queen of Scot to overthrow Queen Elizabeth were uncovered in time. At one time Walsingham had an espionage network spanning Mediterranian, Constantinople, Algiers and also involving Catholic exiles.

Classified government intelligence agencies came up in the 19th century evident as the Great Game, a phrase popularized by Rudyard Kipling in his book Kim, during which the British Empire and the Russian Empire rivaled each other for strategic gains throughout Central Asia, where the British used, a system of surveillance, intelligence and counterintelligence through the Indian Civil Service. The military attaches attached to the Embassy and diplomatic services in different nations served as the first official intelligence system to be used in England during Crimean Wars, providing open as well as clandestine information and operate spy rings.

The first permanent military intelligence service in 1850, the Evidenzbureau was utilized by Austrian military for information against Prussia and Russia and other countries wherein the agency was divided in different regions and reported to the Chief of Staff daily and weekly to the Emperor Franz Joseph. Later, the Topographical & Statistic Department T&SD came up as an internal organisation within the British War Office and later converted to the Military Intelligence Branch by Edward Cardwell to support army reforms and performed map making, statistical and strategic collation of military data and intelligence information. The French military initiated a military counter espionage service, which later discredited during the Dreyfus Affair leading to incarceration of a French Civil Officer for espionage for Germans. The German Army had a military intelligence unit reporting to German General Staff, Italy had the Ufficio Informazioni del Commando Supremo by 1900 and Russia had the Russian Military Intelligence under the Imperial Executive Headquarters.

The political turmoil that followed the Dreyfus Affair in France, led to the thought of having a separate Espionage services not under the military control, eg under the interior or internal ministry. Thus, the Deuxieme Bureaue was created in the 19th Century France as a separate Department for counter espionage. Integrated intelligence agencies run directly by governments were also established.

Global leaders in independent intelligence Organisations

The British government first started with MO3 and then MO5 services under William Melville, as the first independent Intelligence Services, after success of Melville against German counter espionage operations. The British Secret Service Bureau was founded in 1909 as the first independent and interdepartmental agency fully in control over all government espionage activities, by strong support from the Winston Churchill government. The SSB consisted 19 Military Intelligence units MI1 to MI 19 and it was a joint Department between the Admirality, the War Office and the Foreign office specifically for espionage operations against Imperial Germany, with Capt. Sir George Smith Cumming as the first Director, and later specialized into naval or foreign espionage section and army or internal counter espionage section by 1910 with Sir Venom Kell heading the internal division. The French did away with Deuxieme Bureaue and created an independent Surete Generale for order enforcement and public safety under Internal ministry. The Austrians started using Evidenzbureau more for internal security and countering the actions of Pan slavist movement from Serbia. The Russian Government established the Okhrana to detect internal political terrorism and revolutionary activities by left wing by using Agent provocateurs who penetrated into groups like Bolsheviks. Thus all these independent agencies carried out peacetime internal surveillance and information collection for prevention of insurgency apart from external espionage and counter espionage functions and had appropriate interaction between army, police and other agencies.

Soviet Russia initiated the separate intelligence organization with *Okhrana* in the late 1800s, which after transformation of characters through the various stages, including the communist CHEKA (1917-22), the OGPU (1922-34) and Stalin's NKVD (1934-54) was finally replaced by the KGB (Komitet Gosudarstvennoy Bezopasnosti) handling both domestic security and foreign intelligence. The KGB became a force to reckon with in Espionage During World War II, by the highly famous Manhattan Project, involving the infiltration of the America's nuclear weapons research program to obtain technical information including blueprints, with remarkable ease. FBI investigations in the late 1940s uncovered a chain of Soviet spies and paid informers within the US. The sentencing and electrocution of the couple Rosenbergs, convicted of espionage and colluding with KGB to pass on critical information, became a flashpoint, with different opinions and condemnation of the death penalty.

The Double Agents and the defectors

Philby, a high-ranking member of Britain's Secret Intelligence Service (or MI6) was actualy a double-agent for Moscow since the mid-1930s, and he along with Donald McLean and Guy Burgess, defected to the USSR and lived there until their deaths. Another incident shook the British intelligence, when Donald Profumo, a member of cabinet, came out a double agent for Moscow sharing information through a mistress. In 1954 Vladimir Petrov, a Soviet diplomat and KGB colonel proved to be a double agent for Australia, providing the government there with information about Soviet spies operating in Australia. Even after his settlement in Australia the Russia Australia ties were strained for quite a period.

Although military and state intelligence and counter intelligence still persist, and have been fortified with very highly

sofistigated Internet technology, spywares, spy softwares, deception, decoy and communication tools, another area has latched on to some tenets of spying; and that is business intelligence. Corporate and business decisions require lot of data on market rends and business sense is helped by intelligence data and support. Whether it s about automobile, telephony, luxury, or fixed assets, everyone seems to be more interested in what is happening on the other side of the fence.

15.

The Innovator, Entrepreneur, Industrialist Leaders

The New Global Economic, Industrial and Development Leadership IN 20th Century and Beyond

REPRESENTATIVE TOP 50 COMPANIES IN THE 20TH AND 21ST CENTURY

Over the years mammoth brands have been created by fascinating entrepreneurs with their acumen, innate urge to create, astute business sense and ability to adapt. Many tested initial failures, but continued with greater passion and came out shining. GM Motors, Ford, GE, Texas, AT & T Chevron, CBS, DuPont, Kodak, Union Carbide, Boeing, Coca Cola, Wyeth and many others from the yester years in the 20th Century; or Facebook, Oracle, Caterpilar, IBM, Pepsico, Philips, Boeing, bank of America, AT & T, Walmart and others of 21st Century, all have made it large for themselves led by a passionate and heady bunch of stunning leaders, who have seen opportunities through a glimmer of light and created conglomerate wonders through their infectious insatiable hunger for going that extra mile and taking others along.

It is relavant to go through the life of business leaders and their rise through the echelons, as they serve as text book learning cases giving insight on what to do and what not, and the ways to wriggle through slippery business rides.

The Industry Leaders in the 20th Century (Few of first 100)			The Industry Leaders in the 21st Century (Few of first 100)		
S No	Company	Revenue million $	S No	Company	Revenue million $
1	General Motors	24,295	1	Walmart	500000
2	Exxon Mobiles	14,929	2	Exxon Mobil	240000
3	Ford Motors	14,755	3	Berkshire Hathway	240000
4	GE	8448	4	Apple	230000
5	Intnl Business Machines	7197	5	United Health	200000
6	Chrystler	7052	6	McKesson	200000
7	Mobil	6624	7	CVS Health	180000
8	Texaco	5867	8	Amazon.com	180000
9	ITT industries	5474	9	AT&T	160000
10	Gulf Oil	4953	10	General Motors	160000
11	AT & T	4883	11	Ford Motor Co	155000
12	US Steel	4754	12	Amerisource Bergen	153000
13	Chevron Texaco	3825	13	Chevron	134000
14	LTV	3750	14	Cardinal Health	130000
15	DuPont	3655	15	Costco	130000
16	Shell Oil	3537	16	Verizon	126000
17	CBS	3509	17	Kroger	122000
18	Amoco	3469	18	General Electric	122000
19	General Telephone and Electronics	3262	19	Walgreen Boots	118000
20	GoodYear Tyre & Rubber	3215	20	J P Morgan	113000

21	RCA	3187	24	Bank of America	100264
22	Esmark	3107	27	Boeing	93392
24	Union Carbide	2933	28	Philips	91568
25	Bethlehem Steel	2927	29	Anthem	90039
26	Boeing	2834	30	Microsoft	89950
27	Eastman Kodak	2747	32	CitiGroup	87996
28	Proctor & Gamble	2707	34	IBM	79139
30	Rockwell Automation	2667	35	Dell Technologies	78660
31	Navistar Intnl	2652	37	Johnson & Johnson	76450
32	Kraft	2580	42	Proctor & Gamble	66217
33	General Dynamics	2508	45	Pepsico	63525
35	Conoco	2395	46	Intel	62761
36	UnitedTechnologies	2350	50	FedEx	60319
37	Firestone Tyre and Rubber	2278	54	Sysco	55371
38	Conoco Philips	2202	55	Dysney	55137
40	Armour	2153	58	HP	52056
41	Lockheed Martin	2074	65	Caterpillar	45462
46	General Foods	1893	67	Morgan Stanley	43642
51	Continental group	1780	70	Goldman Sachs Group	42254
52	International Paper	1777	75	Delta AirLines	41244
53	Burlinghton Industries	1764	76	Facebook	40653
54	Borden Chemical	1740	78	Merck	40122
56	Amaerican Can	1723	80	Tyson Foods	38260

60	Uniroyal	1553	82	Oracle	37728
63	ARMCO	1565	86	American Express	35583
65	Citgo Petroleum	1561	87	Coca Cola	35410
67	Alcoa	1545	89	Nike	34350
71	Xerox	1482	92	Exelon	33531
79	Coca Cola	1365	95	Conoco Philips	32584
82	American Standard	1307	98	Time Warner	31271
94	Wyeth	1193	100	USA A	30051

Then and Now: The Corporate Bigwigs in 1950s and Now & The Entrepreneur Heroes

GENERAL MOTORS:

Heroes: William C. Durant, Joseph Dort

General Motors, the No.1 car company in the US used to be the No.1 car company in the world. In 1955, GM had more than 50% of the American vehicle market and, between direct employees and those at suppliers, it was responsible for more than 3 million US jobs. GM has emerged from bad times, but has fewer people, and its US market share is less now. Making top vehicle brands -Buick, GMC, Cadillac, Chevrolet, Holden, JieFang, etc. with 20% stake in IMM and 96% in GM in Korea it is present in 37 countries with a number of joint ventures like FAW-GM in China, Ghandhara industries in Pakistan, General Motors India, etc. General Motors was capitalized as a holding company by William C. Durant in 1908, the pioneer of multibrand holding companies in US, acquiring Buick Motor Company, and other twenty companies including Oldsmobile, Cadillac, Oakland, now known as Pontiac, and McLaughlin of Canada. Durant thus modified his earlier carriage business Durant-Dort Carriage Company, in Flint since 1886 in partnership with Joseph Dort, producing over 100,000 carriages a year in Michigan and Canada. Its other subsidiaries include famous automotive component brands, including Euclid, Terex, Electromotive Diesel, Detroit Diesel engines, Allison aircraft and turbine engines, Frigidere freezers, Delco electronics, GNM defence motors, GMAC finance etc.

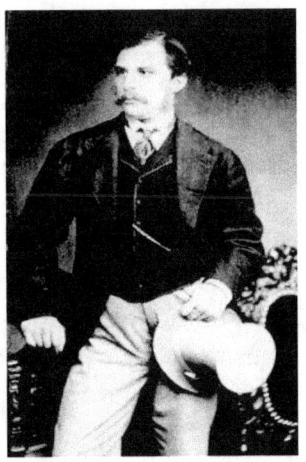

William Durant started with Cigar sales, formed Durant Dort carriages in partnership, then revitalised Cheverlot, and finaly formed Durant motors all through rivaling and giving tough competition to Henry Ford.

The cool, calculative investors-Durant, Walter Chrystler and J P Morgan

US STEEL

Heroes: J P Morgan and Elbert Gary

J P Morgan, belonging to the Morgan Group, symbolizes a great sense of business strategy, a master at collaborations, mergers, acquisitions and initiations.

US Steel was the largest company in its industry worldwide and was among the Fortune 50 in 1955. A large portion of the steel manufacturing business has moved offshore from USA, first to Japan and then China. Founded in early 1900s by J P Morgan and Elbert Gary by merging carnegi Steel Company, Federal Steel Company and National Steel Company, the company is second largest steel producer after Nucor Corporation and now operates under the name USX Corporation. During its initial years, it also acquired coal and iron business by acquisition of Northampton & Bath Railroad and Tennesse iron and Rail road company.

CHRYSLER

Heroes: Walter Chrystler:
A true dream story, the start of Chrystler as a railroad mechanic, who parallely cleared Mechanical degree from the International Correspondence School, Pennysylvania, becoming Works manager at the American Locomotive Company (ALCO) at Pittsburgh, then shifting to Buick motors as Works manager, and later offered Presidentship by William Durant of GM Motors at a stupendous salary and perk, shows the mettle and determined spirit of a man known and recognized as a hard core motor man. He finaly started his own enterprise, the Chrysler.

Chrysler, founded by Walter Chrystler in 1925, as redemption of Maxwell motor Company, and addition of Dodge Brothers and Fargo trucks, is one of the three car giants in US, now known as Fiat

Chrystler Austomobiles US with its Italian counterpart, benefitting from a very limited number of imports in US in the early 20ᵗʰ Century. It represents some of the massive brands, including JEEP, Plymouth, DeSoto and the RAM SUV/truck, also diversifying into Chrystler defense tanks, Chrystler Aircrafts-VZ-6, and radar antenna divisions during the war. The firm nearly went out of business during the 1980s recession and was rescued by the US government. It moved into Chapter 11 nearly two years ago.

Another piece of the Rockefeller trust, the Amoco company was merged into BP America and is now part of BP plc.

CBS CORPORATION

Heroe/s: Arthur Judson, William Paley, Frank Stanton
William Paley and Frank Stanton, stand out for their young and fresh entrepreneurship and leasdership in making a media business stand out as a great advertising medium.

Incorporated in 1927 as United Independent Broadcasters by talent agent Arthur Judson, changing to Columbia Phonograph Broadcasting Company after merging with Columbia Phonograph and record company, rechristened as Columbia Broadcasting System after being taken over William S Paley of La Palina Cigars, and finaly, as present CBS corporation after being taken over by Westinghouse Electric Corporation in 1997. As media has broken into more forms of delivery, including cable and Internet, CBS has grown smaller. The strategy that made CBS rival the leader in broadcasting, the Nationmal Broadcasting Corporation, was the dynamic and enterprising leadership by William Paley and his Chief Executive, Frank Stanton, President for the company, and together they made sure that the number of stations went beyond 100, and also the sponsored programs and the audience also substantially increased making it hugely popular broadcasting corporation.

GENERAL ELECTRIC-GE

Heroes: Thomas Edison, J P morgan

Thomas Edison himself best exemplifies a masterly combination of researcher, innovator and entrepreneur, and the stupendous stature of GE company is a strong testimony to this.

General Electric, formed in early 1900s by merger of the great Thomas Elva Edison's various enterprises, including the Edison General Electric, Edison Lamp, Edison Light Company and Edison machine works with Thomos Houston Electric companies, with J P Morgan, the leading banker, financier and corporate leader of 19th Century, playing again a major role as in the case of formation of US Steel Corporation, is one of the few companies that has grown significantly over the last five decades. It was largely an industrial firm in 1955, and now makes a large amount of its revenue and profits from financial services too and a diversified range of highly successful businesses including GE Power, GE Aviation, GE Additives, GE capital, GE Digital, GE Healthcare, GE lighting, GE renewable energy, GE transportation and others. It later on also initiated the Radio Corporation of America (RCA), spearheaded by Owen D Young, after acquiring the Marcohni Wireless Telegraph Company of America.

The inventor entrepreneurs-Graham Bell and Thomas Edison

AT&T TECHNOLOGIES

Heroe/s: Graham Bell: Innovator, entrepreneur rolled in one, pioneering a great start to a long distance communication invention and enterprise, how phrnomenal which has been, emerging and constantly influencing lives in more ways than one.

AT&T Technologies a division of AT & T handled the telephone company's R&D was spun out of AT&T completely in 1984. The American Telephone and Telegraph Company (AT and T) Company was initiated in 1885 by the great inventor Graham Bell who merged his earlier enterprise Bell Telephone Company into it to make it the largest phone company in the US, later initiating AT and T long lines, the largest netwotk across the nation, acquiring three diode vacume tube patents from Lee De Forest for signal amplification, acquiring Dobson Cellular and ;kk.jT-mobile, cable television assets TCI and Media one, continuing as a conglomerate till 1982 after which it went into acquiring spree and also splitting. AT&T has been dissolved and rebuilt since the government decided to break it into several pieces in 1984 because it was considered a monopoly. Most of the operating businesses have been reunited under the original brand and the company is primarily a provider of cellular, landline, and home entertainment.

IBM

Heroes: Thomas Watson Sr and Thomas Watson Jr

IBM, beginning in 1911 as the Tabulating-Recording company (CTR) was started by Charles Ranlett Flint by bringing together 4 novel inventions computing scale, dial recorder, Electric Tabulating machine, and time clock, and was renamed "International Business Machines" in 1924 by Thomas Watson, taking CTR to outstanding sales revenues with his experience from NCR and its President Patterson, from where he was removed, and retired after 40 yrs, when his son Thomas Watson

Jr carried on. IBM was primarily a provider of high end and expensive computing machines, and after 1950s diversified into artificial intelligence, Fortran language development, associating with NASA space missions, developing IBM 360, 370 and 380 mainframes which remined the top branda till 1980s with OS and VS1 operating softwares, IBM cloud services, console gaming systems and Playstation 3, and software technologies SPSS and Kenexa at the end of 20th Century. Over a period of 50 years it has added large software, IT consulting, and server businesses to become one of the world's largest tech companies, and invented the Floppy, hard disc drive, ATM, DRAM.

Thomas Watson institutionalized the word "Think" as the tag line for IBM, in an effort to motivate his team to go beyond, retaining it as a prime business atrategy in its innovative profile.

The technocrat entrepreneurs-Watsons and Hewlett –Packard

HEWLETT –PACKARD

Heroes: Dave Packard and Bill Hewlett
The HP story has been an inspiration story for many engineers worldwide, and has been recognized as the start of the Silicone valley story near Stanford. After graduating in engineering from

Stanford University, the two friend decided to tug along for discovering novel technologies for the world, and Bill took leave from GE and they settled down at a small rented house in Palo Alto in San Jos4e California, and initiated their developmental work in a small garage allowed by their land lady for use as their development lab. While Dave married his college sweet heart Lucile, Bill later married Flora, the family accommodating on two different floors in the same apartment and using their living room tables as office, with both wives accommodating enough to work on documentation in the evening. They initiated with small developments initially including, flush eye sensor, diathermy machine, telescope focusing ancilliary etc and made small money from some of them, ultimately hitting the track with an audio oscillator, which was picked up by Walt Disney group for use in their next film fantasia, thus giving them the first business push to register and launche HP, and the rest is well known, with path breaking products becoming the world's largest tech company based on revenue, in the 1940s and 1950s, concentrating on making professional and industrial testing tools. The company is now a major force in in personal computing and ancilliaries PCs, laptops, printers, servers, software, and IT consulting.

WALMART

Heroes: Sam Walton

Walmart, starting as a low price departmental Store in Bentonville Arkansas by Sam Walton in 1950, converting into the first Wal Mart Brand Store in 1962 in Rogers, and then expanding as a chain outside Arkansas by 1968, ultimately covering the different states in USA and becoming international in 1995 starting from stores at Canada, and presently operating 11000 stores in 28 countries, leaving behind rivals founded years earlier using intelligent product sourcing and low prices. Walmart is now the largest company in America, and its acquisitions include

Mohre Value, Hutcheson Shoes, Western Merchendise in US and offsore the Seiyo group in japan and the Metro in Germany. It has initiated specialized clubs like the Sam's Club and the first WalMart Super Store in Washingtom.

Walton stressed on customer satisfaction, calling him the ultimate boss who could fire the chairman by changing his prefrence, employee esteem and incorporating diverse business strategies for excellence.

((x) Reference picture on page 151)

FIRESTONE

Heroes: Harvey Firestone

Firestone was initiated in 1900 supplying pneumatic tyres for traditional vehicles in that area and then upgrading itself to large scale manufacturing of automobile tyres, becoming the the second largest tire company in the world in 1955, being at one point the exclusive supplier to Ford. The company was sold to Bridgestone of Japan in 1988. It exhibited a typical multidimensional horizontal and vertical integration, with establishment of rubber plantations in countries like Liberia in Africa, setting up Firestone integrated tyre service Centre at many places, establishing large plants near Los Angeles, England and Memphis, becoming a major Wartime contractor to America in World War II supplying artillery shells, rubberized military products and plastic helmet liners, and also diversifying into contract manufacture of MGM-5 missile system by 1960s. Gradually losing business strategy, it had to ultimately merge with Bridgestone Japan by mid 1980s.

Firestone, starting as a salesman for vanilla flavourings, lotions etc, developed a typical strategy, that it was always useful to sell to a big business, not necessarily meaning an established one but also including the one on road to development, when he found that it was easy to convince a bigger store to try the products for sale. By the same business sense Harvey judged it would be better to associate his new formed tire company with Ford, by helping them launch a new car tyre at a competitive price and grabbing a big order of 2000tires, and then staying along with Ford for 30 and more years.

TARGET

Target, initiating in 1902 as the Dayton Group as a Multistory building on the request of the Westminster Presbytarian Church, developed into the No.2 US retailer opening its first store by taking over the Goddfellow Departmental store and accommodating it in this building, as Dryton Dry Goods Company, at about the same time Wal-Mart did. It has never been able to match its larger rival's size but has still built a $65 billion a year business, and has incorporated other businesses, viz., J B Hudson jwellery, the Lipman's departmental store at Portland, Oregon, also initiating the insurance business, and gradualy changing from

The largest tire company in the world in 1955, Goodyear had large plants around the world. As competition from Japanese companies grew, the company went through several restructurings including a move into energy.

STANDARD OIL AND EXXON MOBIL

Heroe/s: John Rockfellar
Rockfellar, a great explorer and an astute businessman, championed the oil exploration as a brilliant pioneer, and with his associates, founded the first trust in the US based on oil exploration, products and distribution, which remained for a long time in the first quarter of 20th Century, as a leader in he oil industry, monopolising the oil business in more than one sense.

It was only after the formal legislation of the anti trust and monopoly laws in relevant industries that competetors could emerge out of Rockfellars and Standard's shadow.

Standard Oil of New Jersey was part of the original Standard Oil trust created by John Rockefeller. The company was merged into what eventually became Exxon Mobil.

Kroger was a relatively large chain fifty years ago but has aggressively grown through M&A and entry into the private label business.

Sears owes much of its size to the merger between K-Mart and Sears that created it in 2004. The two retail brands are not as successful as rivals like Wal-Mart but the company does operate at many locations.

United Parcel Services, the global mail and freight carrier used the growing movement to transport packages by air and a huge network of trucks to capture the lion's share of the industry and effectively helped ruin the profitability of the US Postal Service.

The Bank of America existed in 1955, but did not look anything like it does today. B of A was based almost exclusively in California in 1955. It is now a global bank with commercial, institutional, and investment banking arms. Two years ago, it bought Merrill Lynch and mortgage banking firm Countrywide.

THE CONGLOMERATES

Berkshire Hathaway

Berkshire Hathaway was initiated as a textile company by Oliver Chace in 1839 by the name of Valley Falls Company in Valley Falls Rhode Island, and later merged it with Berkshire Cotton Manufacturing Company in 1889 in Adams, Massachusetts, to form Berkshire Fine Spinning Associates, and later in 1955 merging it with Hathaway manufacturing Company formed by Horatio Hathaway in 1888, later establishing 15 plants with 12000 workers and over $120 millions as revenue and with headquarters at New Bradford.

However, due to phases of slow market growth, some of the plants closed down with major lay offs and considerable decrease in stock values off and on, which Warren Buffet closely keenly watched as a stock entrepreneurs and continuously bought major stocks of the company, and became major stakeholder pushing out others major investors like Stanton, even knowing well that the textile business was drastically falling. Side by side, he started investing in other businesses as insurance, by purchasing NIC (National Indemnity Company and acquiring equity shares in Government owned GEICO (Govt Employees Insurance Company), which is still the major revenue source for it for many other businesses. In 1985 it closed down its core business of textiles.

Presently the Berkshire Hathaway Group comprises Insurance, Finance, Manufacturing and retail, Utilities and Energy, Flight Services, Media, Real Estate and NonFinancial Services. The Insurance Group comprises about 70 domestic and foreign-based insurance companies, including GEICO, Gen Re, NRG group acquired from ING Group, and Berkshire hathaway Group engaged in Government Bonds, all engaged in either General insurance, reinsurance for property and casualities coverage, apart from life, accident and health, with a surplus status of about $50 Billions, rated as AAA or A++ by agencies like Standards and Poor's or A.M.Best.

Berkshire hathaway energy represents the energy arm of the group, with a subsidiary in UK, the Northern Powergrid, and is further likely to acquire Energy Future Holdings.

The Manufacturing Services and Retailing Group comprises of many companies, with Union Underwear Corp, Fruit of the Loom, Garan, Russell Corp, representing some of the Companies in Cloth Business, and H.H. Brown, Shoe Group, Acme Boots, Brooks Sports, Justin, Chippewa Boots, Nocona Boots, Tony Lama Boots as some of the Companies in Boots Business.

The Building Products Companies of the Hathaway Group include Acme Building Brands (Clay bricks, Concrete Blocks, cut limestones etc) based in Texas, Benjamine Moore and Co, New Jersey (Architectural coatings), Johns Manville (Fibre glass insulation products, pipe, ducts, etc), MiTek Inc (Engineered Connector products, engineering softeares and manufacturing machinery for building component industry), Shaw Industries, based in Georgia (World's largest Carpet manufacturer, also into laminate floorings), and Clayton Homes, to name some.

Hathaway entered Flight Service business with Flight Safety International Inc (FSI) at New York (High technology Pilot Training to aircraft operators by more than 4000 courses and 2000 instructors for operations spread in 167 countries. NetJets, providing fractional ownership for general aviation, offers a fleet of about 700 with more than 150 different types of aircrafts.

The Retail business includes Nebraska Furniture Mart, RC Wiley Home Furnishings, Star Furniture Company, Jordan's Furniture Inc etc in furnishings retail, CORT Business Services providing rental furniture, accessories etc, Ben Bridge Jeweler, a jewelery Chain Store and Helzberg Diamonds. The Pampered Chef, at Illinois, the largest kitchen tool designer and seller, See's candies, at California, selling boxed chocolates and confectionery products, Dairy Queen at Minnesota, and its associates Orange Julius.

The Media business comprises of Buffalo Evening News acquired in 1977, publishing Sunday edition, Buffalo Courier Express, as morning edition, Business Wires, a press release agency, BH Media Group, incorporating Omaha World Herald, Media General, publishing many newspapers across Nebraska, Iowa and other states. The Eagle and the Waco Tribune Herald, the Texas dailies, the Tulsa World, and the News and Record based at North carolina were also acquired.

The Real Estate business comprises of the Home Services of America, at Minnesota, offering real estate brokerage, mortagage loan originationa, title and closing services, home warranties, property and casualty insurance. Home Capital and Store Capital are the other arms in Real Estate business for Hathaway. Albecca, at Norcross Georgia was acquired in 2002 and designs, manufactures and distributes custom framing products, wood & metal mouldings, framing supplies, foamboards etc. CTB Intnl Corps, Milford, Indiana is involved in design, manufacture and distribution of systems used in grain industry, poultry, eggs etc.

In 2002, Berkshire acquired Albecca Inc. Albecca is headquartered in Norcross, Georgia, and primarily does business under the Larson-Juhl name. Albecca designs, manufactures and distributes custom framing products, including wood and metal molding, matboard, foamboard, glass, equipment and other framing supplies. Berkshire acquired CTB International Corp. in 2002. CTB, headquartered in Milford, Indiana, is a designer, manufacturer and marketer of systems used in the grain industry and in the production of poultry, hogs, and eggs. Products are produced in the United States and Europe and are sold primarily through a global network of independent dealers and distributors, with peak sales occurring in the second and third quarters. McLane acquired in 2003 caters to convenience stores, quick service retaurants, movie theatre complexes and others.

TTI and Marmon groups are also now a part of the Berkshire Group.

The Royal Dutch Shell Group

The group took shape in 1907 by merger of two majors, the Royal Dutch Petroleum Company, Netherland (August Kessler, Hugo Loudon and Henery Deterding) and the Shell Transport and Trading Company, UK (Markus Samuel and Samuel Samuel), to ensure competition with Standard Oil and worked by division of responsibility, with the manufacturing at Netherlands by Dutch Manufacturing partner and transportation and storage being managed by the Brtish arm, the Anglo Saxon Petroleum Company, based at London.

Shell was the main fuel supplier to the British Forces in World War I, Sole source of aviation fuel, and suffered some losses due to destruction of Romanian Production facilities. However it further expanded by acquiring the Mexican eagle Petroleum Company, formed Shell Max Group, and by 1920s, was world's leading oil Company supplying 11% of total crude supply. Between 1930 to 1975, it suffered in Mexican operations due to government tak overs, Dutch operations due to German invasion and Denmark operations due to ombing, but it recovered and it tied up with British Petroleum for UK marketing, to form Shell-Max and BP Company.

After having diversified into many groups Sheel decided in 2004 to create a single cspital structure The Royal Dutch Shell Group. It also entered into a Consortium Group that was awarded Iraqui Oil exploration Contracts in 2009, and included other groups like Exxon Mobil and Petronas for different Iraqui oil fields. It also entered into partnership with Cosan to diversify into Ethanol production, Energy generation, Fuel distribution and Sugar activities, selling off its LPG business. Further slimming activities and offloading its investments in many

Companies have been done by Shell off late and also additional diversification and acquisition activities, including purchase of BG group, and presently the Royal Dutch Shell Group stands as world's second largest non state oil company leaving behind Chevron Corporation.

Presently, The Royal Dutch Shell is known for its constant business model innovation and restructuring, acquiring and shedding continuously to balance and position itself magnificiently as a coherent and compact organisation, making sure that its vertically integrated Oil exploration, development, operations, distribution and sales business works efficiently, at the same time not giving away an inherent beautiful facet of business operations typical to Shell since ages-that of allowing maximum independence to its various arms in various countries to almost run themeselves as autonomous organisations. Thus it manages the upstream business-comprising exploration, recovery and infrastructure maintenance for these things-, the downstream business including manufacturing and distribution, shipping of oil products, and also acts as a provider of Technology and project execution to other companies. Apart from petroleum, the group has acquired sufficient capabilities in Natural Gas also and has appropriate verticaly integrated activities in the natural gas section too and is providing its expertise to others.

It has also ventured into other fields, viz., Arctic oil exploration and Floating Liquified natural Gas capacities (FLNG), in the process acquiring offshore floating Natural Gas recovery prowess in Australia, which is under review presently, the Kullug oil rig, and the Noble Discoverer Drill ship, however the project is under scrutiny owing to some major setbacks including Kullug breakdown and others.

THE EATON GROUP

Joseph Eaton, Henning O Taube and Viggo V Torbenson as the entrepreneurs, started the group as Torbensen Gear and Axle Co in New Jersey in 1911, which shifted to Ohio and was taken over by Republic Motor Truck Company. Eaton and Torbenson later left and formed the Eaton Axle Co in 1916, merging with Standard Parts, and later reacquired the Torbenson Axle Co back from Republic, and formed the Eaton Axle and Spring Company. It changed in 1932 to the Eaton Manufacturing Company, after number of auto part company acquisitions including Fuller manufacturing, Yale and Town Manufacturing Co, opening plants at Canada, and changing to Eaton Yale and Towne Inc and further acquiring Samuel Moore and Company, Kenway Systems and Cutler Hammer.

Eaton products include circuit breakers, switchgear, UPS systems, power distribution units, panelboards, loadcenters, motor controls, meters, sensors, relays and inverters, supplying to agriculture, construction, mining, forestry, utility, material handling, machine tools, molding, power generation, primary metals, and oil and gas sectors. It is a conglomerate manufacturer of mobile and industrial applications systems and components and the Hydraulics group also includes Eaton's Filtration, Golf Grip and Airflex industrial clutch and brake businesses and hydraulic, fuel, motion control, pneumatic systems and engines for aerospace industry.

Eaton Electrical has magnificiently enlarged with acquisition of Westinghouse electrical distribution and control product business and is now the mega distributor for branded "Eaton" or "Cutler-Hammer" along with Westinghouse products in commercial and industrial applications. It further acquired the electrical division of Delta plc and the manifacturing facilities for Delta's brands Holec, MEM, Tabula, Bill and Elek under the Eaton nameplate with IECglobal standards. It has also initiated a joint venture with Caterpillar Inc and its Intelligent Switchgear operations, and later joint venture with Powerware for cobranded Eaton Powerware UPS systems.

Eaton also made a success of data centre power distribution market, by acquiring Aphel Technologies Ltd, developing PowerExpert metering systems and PDUS, also co branding with Powerwre brands in the same market. It also acquired specific high branded products from Scneider and also expanded to Chinese market by acquiring Phoenixtec, a Taiwanese manufacturer.

The Majestic And Magical Fortune Top 100 Executives Over The Years:What They Said!!

CONTEXT

As industrialization happened, entrepreneurs emerged, establishing some of the finest names and brands in products, services and trade in the late 19thand through 20thCentury. Be it the oil industry, the airlines, the automobile, the electrical appliances, healthcare or the utilities, some of the brands have taken deep roots and stood the test of times over the years, shining brightly across the globe. The 20^h Century has been a transformative one for the world with repeated global realignments and restructuring taking place while the countries and their masses have toiled tirelessly to take themselves on the path to progress, well being and happiness, amidst paradoxically violent and turbulent times of World Wars and other man made dangerous crisisapart from the natural calamities that struck from time to time.

While it was a matter of taking the entrepreneurship plunge and innovation that guided the industry leaders in the early 20th Century, the focus and approach had to be shifted to *other aspects, including demand and supply management and quality of products, with competitive strategies and customer satisfaction taking the precedence in the later part of the 20th Century, as the number of players in each industry grew over the years, and as the global industrial scenario stands today, regulatory compliance, sustainability & environment and ease of delivery have come to define business strategies.*

Some companies have marvelously been able to restructure, realign and redefine themselves during all these years at a very competitive speed and have been able to keep themselves up there in the top 100 group as defined by various rankings, viz., Fortune 500 and others. Many outstanding CEOS and Presidents marvelously helmed and steered these Fortune companies over the years in the 20th Century, through rough weathers too, coming out trumps consistently. They gave vision, direction and the required momentum to the organization to achieve and maintain the success. Many of them have been remarkable and exemplary in whatever they have done and some are quoted here as heroes.

Heroes: Rex Tillerson(Exxon), Stephen Hemsley (United Health), Ellen Kullman (DuPont), Edward Woolard (DuPont), Leslie Moonves (CBS), Allan Mullaly (Boeing and Ford), Henry Ford II (HF II) (Ford Motors), John S Watson (Chevron)

Rex Tillerson, Chairman and CEO, Exxon Mobil Corporation, has steered Exxonn Mobil magnificiently in the decade that he has held the position, ensuring that the company has constantly ranked very high up over many years in the Fortune 100 List. Starting as an Engineer at Exxon in 1975, after graduating with B Sc Civil Engineering from Univ of Texas, taking care of Business Development in between, and acquiring role of Production Advisor to Exxonn Corporation by 1992 and later as Vice President Exxon Ventures and Exxon Neftcap taking care of Mobil business in CIS countries, he has the acquired present position in 2006.

As CEO of the largest private sector oil corporation in US as against state owned refinery corporations, he has his calculations for 2040, on his fingertips-a projected 35% increase in total energy requirement, 65% increase in CNG as energy alternative, oil energy occupying two thirds of the total energy resources- and appropriate energy and environment management and protection offeres earmarked, increasing energy efficiency by 10% and beyond and diversifying into greater component of renewable energy sources.

Stephen Hemsley, the former CEO, United Health Group, claims change has to be done when things are placed nicely and strongly, and are to be done every two or three years. Thus United Group had a large change over in the upper management and now the CEO is David Wichmann.

DuPont's former hugely successful CEO, Ellen Kullman is always proud of the fact that she could use her engineering education to be apt at problem solving. She quotes how as an engineer she uses the basic principle of influence of heat, light and water as a solution to any thing. Heat, as she says, may be interpreted as the inner intensity and focus that is required to generate idea and solution for a problem. Light represents transparency; wherein one has to be open to suggestions, ideas and criticism and able to accept that one may be wrong too. Water represents the investment or nurturing that an idea has to be provided to make it effective and efficacious, and may be in the form of time and resources. Ellen kullman, described the experience of being able to tide over the periods of economic and financial slowdown, as being possible because of the ability to build up a strong team. Kullman, looked at cut down in employee strength as a window of opportunity, with new spin offs from Du Pont coming forward to absorb these lay offs.

Edward Woolard, the earlier CEO prior to Kullman, effectively conceptualized, executed and oversaw major dosnsizing and restructuring of the DuPont group, wherein the Group actually improved upon its earnings by 65% and increase in its stock value by 160%.

Leslie Roy Moonves, one of the longest serving and popular CEOs, served at CBS upto 2018 having taken charge in 2003 as Chairman and CEO, started after graduation in science in 1971, taking up small roles in TV series, until he shifted to creative affairs at Lorimar TV in 1985, becoming President in 1990, joining Warner Brothers as President and Ceo by 1993 and finaly at CBS. Moonves has earned a reputation for involving and enjoying himself in all capacities in TV and radio creative, production and business affairs and having a very precise feel of what the audiences or customers are looking for.

Ford Motors have been able to turnaround and maintain its position in Fortune top 100 list, thanks to CEOs like Allan Mulally, who worked on aspects like Brand revival, shedding unprofitable subsidiaries including Jaguar and Land Rover, and bringinging down the number of Ford variants from 95 tp 16 prominrnt ones and managing them well. He emphasizes an 11 points management style, which are:

- People first
- Everyone is included
- Compelling vision, comprehensive strategy and relentless implementation
- Clear performance goals
- One plan

- Facts and data
- Everyone knows the plan, the status and the areas that need special attention
- Propose a plan, positive, "find-a-way" attitude
- Respect, listen, help and appreciate each other
- Emotional resilience — trust the process
- Have fun — enjoy the journey and each other.

To many in the automotive industry, it was difficult to imagine Mulally as CEO in the automotive industry in Ford, with his stupendous reputation in the airline industry having served Boeing for many years as Sr Vice President and with additional CEO duties in the Airplane Development, Tomlin Space and Defence Systems and also in Boeing Commercial Airplanes and was due for anointment as CEO after Phil Condit, having earlier joined Boeing in 1969 after Degree in aeronautical Engineering from Kansas and being very instrumental in the later developments of the series 727, 737, 747, 757, 767 and 777 and the design of cockpit. Mulally has been listed in 2009 in the The Time 100 and in 2011 in the Chief Executive as the most successful CEO.

Ford Motors was helmed by Henry Ford II (HF II), after he joined in 1943 leaving his naval job and gradualy took over the Presidency between 1045 to 1965, to resurrect the business, which was being proposed by then president Franklin Roosvelt to be taken over by the state. Ford showed the tough decision making as called for, removing the then boss Henry Bennett and putting in charge John Bugas with a team of Ernest Breeche and lewis Crusoe from General Motors and Bendix Corporation which helped him in appropriate decision making. He also put in place a team of 10 Whiz Kids selected from the Armed Air Forces Statistics Department, and some of them including

Robert McNamara went on to assume Presidential roles. He also initiated the process wherein Ford Motors became publicly traded Company during that period, also unsuccesfuly trying to acquire Ferrari, and in the process succesfuly launching the Ford GT 40 which performed excellently at many racing circuits including Le Mans

John S Watson has steered Chevron since 2009 as CEO, having joined in 1980 and serving in various capacities including Chevron Financial Analyst, Chevron Manager of Intvestor Relations, Chevron GM Strategic Planning Mergers and Acquisitions, Chevron VP, Strategy and Development and others.

Doug McMillan, the present CEO of Walmart, has effortlessly steered Walmart since 2014 aligning the stores, the distribution and logistics channels and digital commerce, and taken the Walmart mission "Spend Less, Live Better" marvelously forward in an impeccable style. Doug has carried the cornerstone legacy of WalMart- Geting a bargain from wholesalers and passing on the savings to customers and generating profits through volume.

16.

Political Mass Leadership Over the Centuries

Socialism, Communism, Democracy as new Leadership models through 18th to 20th Centuries.

and

Political Populism and its destiny: Swinging public opinion

CONTEXT:

By the middle of 20th Century, many countries opted for self governance rather than being administered by monarchies, aristocracy, or colonial rules, taking up different patterns of thoughts for determining the way forward in adopting a government system, leveraging individual interests, control by the government, social justice and equality of status and obligaton to the nation. Thus various thoughts emerged, including, Socialism, Communism, Democracy as new Leadership catchphrases for governance with Military as the New Defense and Administrative support system, all of them having taken roots during various significant national revolutions bringing the welfare of the proletariat to the centre as the focus of policy making. A major drift in the leadership model was towards a rule by the commoners, with major political turnarounds and emergence of new public leaders. It is somewhere strange, that artistic expressions in the form of prose, verse and music became more popular, and in some ways made the people rally around for socio-political or economic reasons, and brought about massive revolutions.

Over the years, there have been mass uprisings against the administrative misrule, since as early as historicaly recorded, as in the case of Plaebian or Helot or Athenian revoltions in the Greece, the Servilian or Gladiator revoluts, or the Illyrian and Arminius revolts in the Roman Empire, all being armed rebellions, all in the pre Christ period. In the post Christ periods too, there were major revolts, significantly the Jewish revolts against the Roman Empire, the Vietanamese or other revolts aginst the Han Dynasty of China, the Samaritans against the Byzantine Roman Empire, or the Celtic and gauls against the Roman Empire or Saxons against Charlemagne. Other parts also witnessed major revolts, viz., the uprisings against the Umayyad Caliphate in Egypt, Iran and Iraq and establishment of saffarid Dynasty in Iran. Significan revolts in the era after 1000 AD included the Serb and Bulgarian revolts against the Byzantine Roman Empire, the Scottish war of Independence in the form of continuous small revolts, the uprisings and Granada and Portugese wars against Spanish rule. The revolutions by citizens started in the form of peasant revolutions in the England, Hungary, Slovania, the German peasant and the Swedish peasant revolutions against the Danes.

Large-scale revolutions marking significant historical events included The Glorious Revolution in England, the American Revolution in 1775-1783, the French revolution in 1789-1799 making a great social impact with the uprising of the bourgioisie, followed by the Russian, Spain and Portugese revolutions for constitutional monarchies in 1820s.

Socialism and communism as a concept motivated many such revolutions where the proletariat expressed their anguish *over unequitable disctribution of resources and facilities where the bourgeoisie benefitted extensively and the proletariats had to survive in poverty. Socialism and communism, and the immensely prominent leaders associated with these movements in the industrialization era, can thus be assumed to be major forces that were influential in changing the shape of the socity, nation and world through the 19ᵗʰ and 20ᵗʰ Century to make it as it is today.*

Heroes: Rousseau, Louis Blanc, Phillip Bounarotti, Karl Marx, Fredrich Engels, Bolshevik, Max Weber, Edward Benistein, Lenin, Stalin, Mao Zedong,

The concept of Communism and socialism, as coined by Karl Marx, was meant to ensure common ownership by a community of all wealth, property and enterprises, rather than giving individual liberty for capitalism at will. Their have been differences over issues, including the type of resources, property and wealth that should be controlled by the state and the extent to which the state should exercise the control, dividing the socialist on one hand into the centralist or the staunch communist, favouring complete control of the state over everything, and the decentralist or the soft socilists on the other hand, who whould rather let the local group or community decide on the ownership and control. The communists and socialists are in opposition to capitalism, which allows free market, individual choices in the ways as to how the property has to be distributed and allows private ownership, whereas the socialists believe that capitalism causes unfair accumulation of resources and wealth in the hands of a few, labeled the bourgheoise, causing misery to others, the proletariat. The earliest fierce proponents of staunch socialism were Thomas Moore, who in his novel Utopia, imagined a society, wherein there was no private property and equal distribution of resources, and French aristocrat Claude Henry Saint simon, who propogated that historically, the society should undertake transformation in various stages, and as industrialization was gaining ground, feudalism had to give way to socialism, as it was the workers and proletariat who had the knowledge to use industrial processes for social economy, who should be deciding the distribution of resources and wealth.

The concept was taken up vividly by various proletariat groups, either as an armed protest and revolution, or a peaceful resistance in many countries across the globe in the 1800s. Although it was a concept meant for reducing the impact of selective capitalism by the bourghioese and the exploitation of the poor working class or the proletariat in the industrialised countries, it gained more roots in countries which were more poverty ridden and with minimum industrialization having happened by the end of 19th Century. Thus Russia caught on to the concept with vengeance with the establishment of the Soviet Union in 1917 with Bolshevic revolution, and ensured that the concept helped the nation keep together and prevent much stratification by wealth, also covertly promoting communism in other European countries.

However, various countries which adopted communism, modified the governance methods to add various other features apart from true communism, as in the case of China, which initiated as Government of Republic of China (ROC) in 1912 after fall of Quing Dynasty, and gradually adapted the tenets of communism because of various proletariat movements, until in 1949, the Communists gained full control of the government and demarcation of mainland China and Taiwanese China. The mainland China governed by Peoples Republic of China, had to withstand further armed and violent communist movements, the severest of them being from the Red Army conceived during the era of Mao Zedong, who pushed China into a state of slow economy when his visionary and grand movements *"The Great Leap Forward"* meant for abrupt but instant industrialization, and then the Cultural Revolution" resulting in more violence, anarchy and damage rather than a socialistic economy, and it was only after the 1978, with Zing Jaopiang and the next government that the Marxism and communist principles were implemented in a systematic manner, and gradualy since the last two decades, China has emerged as a global economic superpower adapting the communist principles with selective capitalism and other ideas to have a mixed economy.

Reference to communism and its idea of equitable distribution and common wealth of the community and egalitarianism is evident through early writers, notably "The Republic" by Pluto, *"The City of the Sun"* by Tomasso Campanella in 1601, Rousseau's *"The Social Contract"* which was hugely influential in the French Revolution, the ideas being also made popular by later writings of Louis Blanc and Pierre Leroux and Phillip Bounarotti, whose "Conspiracy for Equality" greatly influenced the Communist league and draft manifesto by Karl Marx in Germany and Friedrich Engels, who with Marx published books highlighting these thoughts in "Conditions of working Class in England in 1840s", *"Manifesto of the Communist Party"* (1948), and also forming association of socialist and communists *"First International"*, stressing the point that "Condition for free development of each was free development of all". The communist and Marxist idea gained ground through events like the Paris commune in France by the end of 19th Century, but there emerged different thoughts, with some theorists like Max Weber and Edward Benistein advocating a nonviolent and legal course of action by the proletariat to gain their rights, while the others including Vladimir Lenin stressing on aggressive overthrow of the bourgioese.

Since the early 1900s, communism evolved influenced by major events including formation of Communist government in the Soviet Socialist Republic, further adaptation during rapid industrialization in Stalin's period in Russia, formation of Commintern, an international face of all communist parties across the world, largely influenced by Russia, a second aggressive rising of the communist and socialist thoughts and the era of Adolf Hitler in Germany. Formation of the First Popular Front as the global face of the Commintern and Soviet communism and severe purging of anti Stalin policies happened in the 1920s and 1930s, later giving way to to a peace proposing front, in opposition to the fascist ideas and the Second popular Front stood out as the anti imperialistic face of communists across the world, where led by Stalin, a united call was given by the communists to stand against the facist forces of Hitler and the Axis and stand by national interest.

Communism gained in governance in many European countries pushed by Soviet communists and the Chinese Red Guards in the Early cold war period against the interests and liking of the allied or NATO associates, but in the late Cold War period, the communists governments in various countries fell down in popularity, with even Chinese Red Guard's interests not merging with Soviet communists.

Many upheavals and revolutionary movements, often rising out of class struggle and often socialist in theme, made use of popular phrases and slogans to enthuse, stir and mobilise masses to stand up and express a united opinion on the prevailing conditions and their desire to change for better. Almost each such movement has been initiated using a single slogan wich has caught the fancy of the masses like fire, ignited a common passion and brought them around. *"Eat the Rich"* was such a slogan which resulted in a massive French social turn around. *"Proletariat of the world, Unite"* has been a major Marxist slogan bringing about mass movements across the globe.

Populist rhetoric have been since ages catching the whims and fancy of masses by their shear capacity of mass and massive appeal to the population in an area leading to historic movements and bringing in dramatic, sometimes catastrophic, and often cathartic changes in societies or systems for the better and sometimes for the worse.

As early as possible, Julious Caesar symbolized populism along with Caesar Augusta in the fact that they could mobilize masses by shear motivation and bringing in historic changes within their life spans or even after their death. After these classical populist movements, the early Populist movements were represented by German Peasant's war in the 16th and 17th century and then the English Civil War in 1660s which were more protestant driven in nature or anabaptistic and ideated peasants and artisans to read holy books themselves and were against overloardship of Holy Roman Emperor Charles V and Ferdinand

Many populist movements have been agrarian in origin or appealing to the farming society, viz., the Eastern European Green Society movement, The Nardoniki movement in Russia, or that lead by the US Peoples Party in US.

The Latin American Populistic movements have been more of movements based on strong Personalities who have overridden emotions during change from agrarian to induatrialised nationalism using growing low middle class urban industrial workforce and their issues, whether it is about Peron in Argentina, Vergas in Brazil, Aprismo in Peru, Cardenas in Mexico, Velasco Ibarra in Ecuador or later Goulart and Brizola or Fernando Collor in Brazil, Carlos Menem in Argentina or Hugo Chavez in Venezuela. The movements have also sometimes been to oppose the US hegemony and interference in Pan Amerric, as evident in such movements being covertly supported by US, eg., the Coup de etat in Goutemala, the Coup de etat in Brazil and the assassination of populist leaders in Columbia, viz., Jorge Gaitan.

Some important Populistic slogans have been

- Abolish the Wage system (World Socialist movements): Socialist Parties

- A fair days wage or a fair days work: US workers unions

- Arbeit Macht Frei (Work will set you free): Nazi movements

- Asalkan Bukan Umno Anything but UMNO –United Malays National Organisation- Used by barisan nasional Coalition and came to power in 1850s and still ruling.

- Better Red than dead: An anticommunist Slogan

- Black is beautiful: Afro American movement in US

- Come and take it: Battle of Gonzalez

- Chavez Vive: la Patria Sigue: Long live Chavez in Venezuela after his death

- Drill Baby Drill: Slogan used by Republican Party to increase Oil Production

- Each for all and All for Each: Tariff Reform League 1905

- Eat the rich: By Rosseau

- Erinn go Brach: Ireland Forever

- God made Adam and Eve: not Adam and Steve: An anti gay slogan used by Christians opposing Homosexuality

- Enna Enna Tesera 9114-the ordinance that says the king will not interfere with the working)

- Heins ins reich: Adolf Hitler to include all states within the Nazi region or the Reich-including Austria, Sundtland and others that led to World war II

- Hey, Hey LBJ, how many kids you kill today: During Vietnam War against Lyndon B Johnson of America

- It's Scotland's oil: By Scotland nationalist Party for Scotland freedom
- Jadam das Seine: To each his own/Justice for Everyone/ Eveyone gets what he deserves-Nazi slogan during World war also used earlier by Prussia and rome
- Jai jawan Jai Kissan
- Jai Jawan, jai kisan and Jai Vigyan: Atal Bihari Bajpayee
- Liberte, Egalite, Trayernite: During French Revolution and others in France
- Ma, maati, manush: Mamta Banerjee, Trinamool Congress
- Maggie, Maggie, Maggie: Out, Out, Out: Against Margaret Thatcher
- Not a step back: Soviet anti Nazi slgan
- Proletariat of the World: Unite: A Marx Slogan
- Stay the Course: Bush during Iraq War
- Serve the People: Maoist Slogan
- Remember Pearl harbor; To remember American Patriotism
- Remember Maine: Amaerican Spanish War
- Digital India
- Make in India
- Beti bachaom beti Padhao
- Roti Kapda Aur Makan
- Ham Do Hamare do
- Do boond Jindagi ke
- Aao School Chale Hum

17.

Industrial Growth and Counter Stimulus during Post War Fatigue

Post World War II America, having come out as the global leader and winner over the forces of evil in the world, witnessed rising living standards, increased opportunities, and a newly emerging American culture confidently reflecting the accrued glory in all aspects of life. Although the period is looked back as the most exemplary one of glory and growth and appreciation of government policies in USA, a critical analysis shows the other side too.

Various leaders in US including past president Obama and others have in their speeches extolled post World War stimulus for growth through the GI Bill and deficit finance spending, including increased focus on education and creating craving in the population to increase their economic status, that ultimately led to economic boom in the next 10 years. This was a corroboration of the fact that government policies were necessary for the economic stimulus, which actually helped America for first 10 years after the war, but the growth continued despite discontinuation of government support.

Many Nobel laureates including Paul Krugman, Paul Samuelson and Gunnar Myrdal highlighted the possibility that as the war would end, there would be a massive spurt in unemployment with about 20 million military forces being relieved from war duties, and a stupendous economic turmoil due to steep downturn in spending power of unemployed persons having been put off from military deployement, which would ultimately spiral into a frightening spree of mutual and social violence. It was expected that aggregate demand created by government's indirect stimulus for large scale spending by general public by large scale military employement, would drastically fall after the World War ended. But instead although spending showed a decrease from 55% GDP to 16%, bur real consumption increased by 22% with durables showing doubled spending. This was by increase by 223% in gross private investments, wherein many manufacturers of armaments turning their manufacturing facility into consumer goods manufacturing facility, viz., typewriters, toasters etc. This showed a massive shift from wartime economy to peacetime economy with resources going from public to private, with unemployement rate just rising by a small amount from 1.9-3.9%.

The reason for the resurgence and boom in post war American economy is pinned down to the change from command and edict economy to consumer economy. In edict economy most manufacturing facilities were converted to facilities for manufacturing ammunitions whose prices were controlled by edict by various government institutes like Office of Price Administration, the War Production Board, the Office of Civil requirements, and War Manpower Commission. Thus many manufacturers did not prefer entering into the manufacturing economy. After the war, when the command economy gave way to peacetime consumer economy with end of government control by edict or by price control, the shortage of public use items vanished as more manufacturing facilities were released earlier functioning as government armament manufacturing facility, and changed into commodity items manufacturing units, and quality of items increased as there was more private manufacturing competition.

Post War Europe:

Post World War II Europe was left a devastated area with a crippled economic structure, thousands left homeless and industry infrastructure destroyed. The UK spent heavily on purchase of war ships and air carriers from USA during war, spending above 400 million on the same and pushing more than 50% of its labor into war production, which were left jobless post the war. The Labour Party came to power on the premise of vast losses occurring during the War and what they argued as self-destructive policies of Winston Churchill. But the sudden withdrawal of Land Lease agreement initiated in 1941, by America dealt a serious blow to the actual implementation of internal policies by the Labour party and even the Anglo American Loan provided by US was majorly used to help UK tide over its international responsibilities rather than working on internal resurgence. Thus various tightrope fiscal measures including bread rationing and others had to be employed by the Clement Atlee government to maintain some respectability of the Sterling.

When the war ended, however, the command economy by government by edict and by ceiling price was dismantled. By the end of 1946, direct government allocation of resources—by edict, price controls, and rationing schemes—was essentially eliminated, By decrease in govt control, the resources that were earlier used for government supply were directed for production of consumer goods and still a large number of demands remain unfulfilled by short supply and thus elimination of controls actually led to an extended period of economic growth.

((xi) Reference picture on page 152)

Post War USSR

Post World War II, the population of Soviet Union decreased by about 309 million with about 10 million deaths as combat deaths and 20 million due to deaths in Nazi concentration camps in Germany, forced derogatory labour conditions in labour camps in Germany, famine and epidemics in Russia and other reasons. Post War, Russia focused on industrial rebuilding more as compared to agricultural revival and the same was evident by 1960 as doubling of coal and steel output as compared to 1920 with a parallel scarcity of food. The Russian rebuilding efforts were by utilization of the resources from the annexed east European countries during ousting of Nazi Army by the red Army and formation of the Soviet Socialist Republic, also referred as the Eastern Block countries, which were reciprocally helped by Russia to rebuild themselves post War. In contrast, there were the Western Block countries, including UK and France, which were majorly helped by USA to rebuild themselves. Thus there came a definite demarcated separation between the Eastern and Western European countries, named the Iron Curtain, with the countries on either side aligning to USA or Russia.

(i) Reference picture from page 2

(ii) Reference picture from page 5

(iii) Reference picture from page 9

(iv) Reference picture from page 14

(v) Reference picture from page 23

Erich Von Manstein, Võ Nguyên Giáp, Erwin Johannes Eugen Rommel

(vi) Reference picture from page 65

(vii) Reference picture from page 78

(viii) Reference picture from page 87

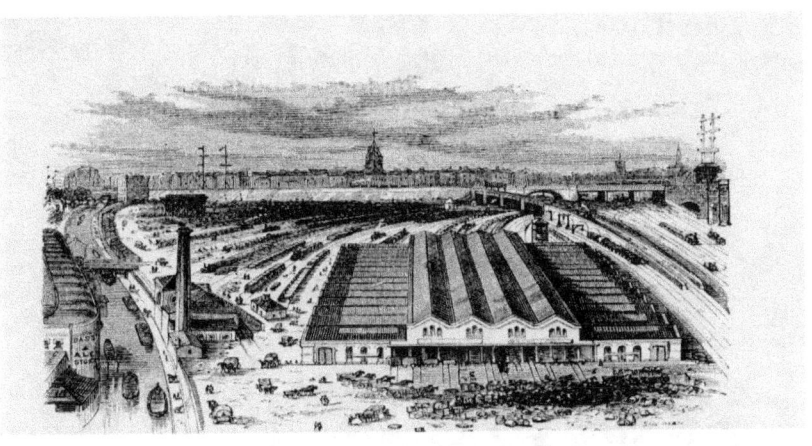

A typical railway station, yard and track complex in the England of 19th Century

(ix) Reference picture from page 88

The Flamboyant Trio-Walton, Firestone, Ford

(x) Reference picture from page 118

(xi) Reference picture from page 144

(xii) Reference picture from page 201

कोई तो सूद चुकाए, कोई तो जिम्मा ले
इस इंकिलाब का, जो आज तक उधार सा है।

Dharmveer Bharti, Kaifi Azmi, Faiz Ahmed Faiz

(xiii) Reference picture from page 203

(xiv) Reference picture from page 212

(xv) Reference picture from page 214

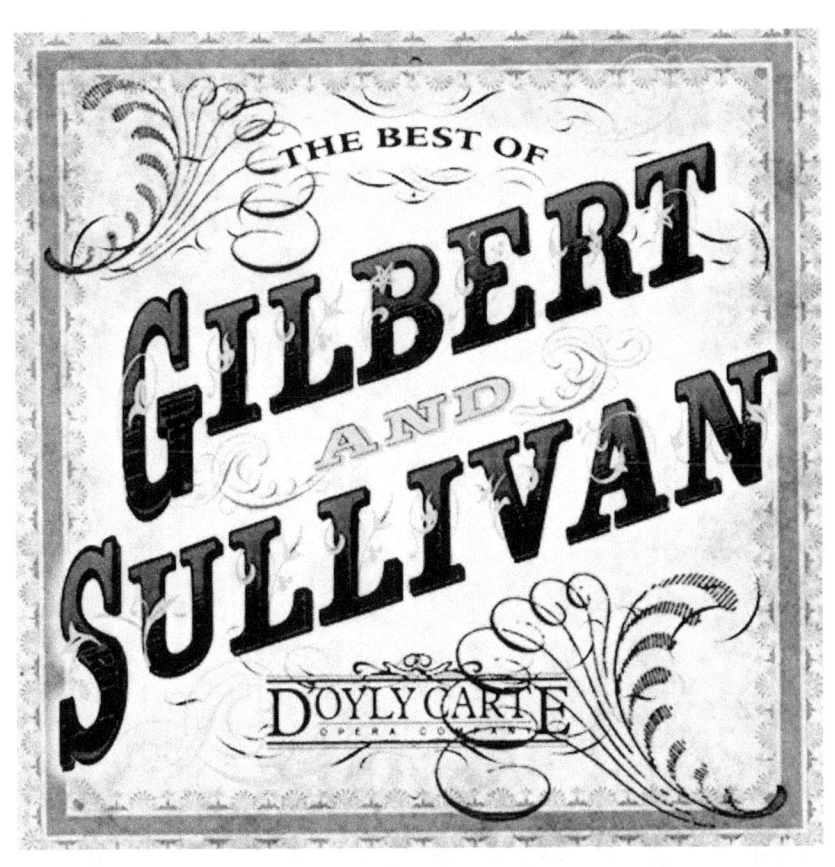

(xvi) Reference picture from page 219

Pop culture making a mark at the beginning of 20th Century
The Broadways theatres, then and recent

(xvi) Reference picture from page 219

(xviii) Reference picture from page 221

(xix) Reference picture from page 222

The Starblazers of metallic
Dire Straits, Mark Knopfler, Eagles, Duran Duran, The
Police, and later, The Guns & Roses

(xx) Reference picture from page 222

(xxi) Reference picture from page 223

(xxii) Reference picture from page 223

ERIC CLAPTON, MADONNA, BOYZ II MEN….
Individual styles…..Hearthrob of millions

(xxii) Reference picture from page 223

Britney Spears, Lady Gaga, Christina Aguilera, Katty Perry, the 21st Century material girls…..truly in League with Madonna…………..charisma, visuals, voice, melody, feet tapping music and a crazy generation…………..

(xxiii) Reference picture from page 223

(xxiii) Reference picture from page 223

Michael Jackson: The King of Pop: 3rd All Time Greats after The Beatles and Elvis Presley

(xxiv) Reference picture from page 224

(xxv) Reference picture from page 224

(xxvi) Reference picture from page 230

(xxvii) Reference picture from page 244

**Chandresh Nigam, Chaitanya Dalmia,
Ramdeo Aggarwal, Chandrakant Sampat:
Different personalities Different investment philosophy**

**Parag Parikh, Ashish dhawan, Sanjay bakshi,
Samir Arora: Different money management strokes**

(xxviii) Reference picture from page 281

**Rakesh Jhunjhunwala, Ridham Desai,
Aswath damodaran, Ramesh damani:
To each his own**

(xxix) Reference picture from page 283

THE IT GIANTS: Ratan TATA

THE IT GIANTS: AZEEM PREMJEE

THE IT GIANTS: SHIV NADAR, NARAYAN MURTHY

THE IT WIZ KIDS: GANESH NATRAJAN, SAJAN PILLAI, KESHAV MURUGESH

INDIAN IT: THE MEN WHO MATTER:
NANDAN NILEKANI, SHREEDHAR VEMBO,
MOHAN KIRANE, PRADEEP ERINJERY

(xxx) Reference picture from page 290

(xxxi) Reference picture from page 352

18.

Leadership in Social Progress, Public Welfare & Promoting Art & Culture

CONTEXT:

Over the Centuries, many a great leaders dedicated a quantitative time in imagining and creating a beautiful and comfortable world for their people, be it in the towns, houses, surroundings and facilities, and also making sure that appropriate harmonious relations between communities were created by way of constant upward shift in the level of human interaction through books, religion, art, music and thetre, which provided the required coherence for human bonding amidst a constantly changing and volatile geopolitical equation. Some kings majestically stand out for making this happen by their will and valour, including, Roman king Constantine, King Menes, King Leo, King Constantine V, French King Charlmagne, King Lothar, King Alfred the Gtreat in Englandand King Otto III in the first millennium by 1000 AD.

Mnay a great writers and performing artists have made the world a beautiful place by their literary and creative contributions including Virgil, Horace, and Ovid.

Many exemplary leaders engaged in improving Quality of life through improved systems of Medicine and health research, Creation and trading of lifestyle goods, Academic and religious books, and movements and impetus to Industrialisation, through different Periods including Medieval Europe, The Early Middle Ages (500 - 1000 AD) and later in different geographical regions.

After the fall of the Roman Empire the Nobles of Europe came to power with the help of the Roman Catholic Popes. This lasted for a thousand years (until about 1,450 AD) then the power of the cities and reformers became stronger and stronger. This resulted in the slow dismantling of Kingdoms, Counties, Duchies and increase in the power of the Roman Catholic Church.

The people who suffered during this long period under the joke of the Church and the Warlike Kings, Counts and Dukes became more and more independent with the help of the Cities. From the 14th century onwards most cities were fortified all over Europe to defend the citizens against Warlike Nobles. Finally came the time of progress in architecture, art, trade and science and the first form of democracy was introduced in 1462 AD.

Constantine was a ruler or rather a conqueror and emperor who could see the beauty in other things too apart from his strength of expansion and of overpowering the resistance. Thus he would think about the need for religion in a peaceful community and thus gave recognition to Christian Church. He would also think about the mental deprivation in the barbarous gladiator games, which ended with a winner on one side and mortality on the other, and thus decided to do away with them as a show of strength. He was able to unite Rome into a large empire and establish Constantinople at as far a place as Turkey. By 356 AD, Rome had built 28 libraries, 10 basilicas, 11 public baths, 2 amphitheaters, 3 theaters, 2 circuses, 19 aqueducts, 11 squares, and 1,352 fountains. This process of creation of well managed cities started as back as 312 BC, when Appius Claudius Caecus built the first Roman road from Rome south to near Naples, named the Via Appia and then the first aqueduct into Rome, the Aqua Appia and then by 272 BC a second aqueduct, the Anio Vetus, built by subsequent Roman emperors. Also the practice of freedom of self decision was initiated long back by 287 BC through The *Lex Hortensia*, the constitution for plebiscites and referenda voted on by the entire electorate, accepting it as a the status of law.

Leadership in creativity and public welfare was also visible in way back historic period in Egypt when a unified kingdom was founded in Egypt in 3150 BC by King, Menes, leading to a series of dynasties that ruled Egypt for the next three millennia. Egyptian culture flourished during this long period and remained distinctively Egyptian in its religion, arts and language and customs. The first two ruling dynasties of a unified Egypt set the stage for the Old Kingdom period, *c.* 2700–2200 BC., which constructed many pyramids, most notably the Third Dynasty pyramid of Djoser and the Fourth Dynasty Giza pyramid.

Many later day painters, particularly Victor Vasnetsov, and chronicles including Gallician-Volhynian chronicles have elaborated on these by way of Bylina poems and paintings. The famous ones include Popovich, Dobryna Nikitichand, Llya Muromets.

Leaders Promoting Academic Splendor

Roman literature in Latin, still is a permanent record of the culture of ancient Rome. Some of the earliest historical epics, give an extensive record about the early military history of Rome followed by (as the Republic expanded) literary works based on poetry, comedies, histories and tragedies. Latin literature show a very strong influence of earlier Greek authors and also took many inputs from the traditions particularly from the extraordinary and sensitive Greek literature. Few works remain of Early and Old

Latin, although a few of the plays of Plautus and Terence have come down to us.

The "Golden Age of Roman Literature" is usually considered to cover the period from about the start of the 1st Century BCE up to the mid-1st Century CE with plays by Platus and Terence. Although the start of Roman literature was in the Greek Lyric form, Catullus and some authors naturalized the Greek lyric verse forms into Latin in their expressive poetry. Other authors who mesmerized the generation by their expertise in the Golden age were Vergil, by his epic poetry, Horace by his satires and odes and Ovid by his elegiac couplets. After an intermittent period of eloquent, sometimes bombastic, poetry of Seneca the Younger and Lucan Pliny, the Younger and Juvenal raised the standards to bring out classical literature in the form of letters and powerful satires, in the Silver age between first and secondcentury AD. Two Roman novels have made their mark by their outstanding presentation, the *"Satyricon"* of Gaius Petronius and *"The Golden Ass"* (or *"Metamorphoses"*) of Lucius Apuleius, which served as the torchbearers for the classical prose form. After the mid-2nd Century, the Roman literature was not able to keep upto its reputation and was not recognizable and in fact was labeled as too ordinary. Thus the main authors in earlier Roman literature, and their styles included, Catullus, by his lyrics and eleggys, Vergil, by his epic and didactic literature, Horace, by his lyrics and satires, Ovid, for his didactic and elegiac poems, Seneca the younger, the tragic playwright and satirist, and Lucan for his epic writings.

In 575–591 AD another major mile stone ten volume book the Historia Francorum was written by Gregory of Tours, on the architecture style of the Franks. The book is an extensive description of the much of the French architecture at that time, the craftsmanship of his generation.

The trend to symbolize Church and religion by using ornate items started by 650 AD, when Saint Eligius, bishop of Noyon and renowned metalworker, created a cross of gold and jewels with very fine metalwork, which generated quite a repute as personal jewelry and ecclesiastical objects for posession. The Christian Churches, buildings, monasteries and objects were patronized in different ways in different periods. Thus Sixth- and seventh-century patrons stimulated portable metal objects and personal adornments, the ninth- and tenth-century emperors decided to replicate the splendors of Christian Rome by promoting building of stone churches and monasteries, the illumination of sumptuous books, and the casting of bronze sculptures in a revival of ancient technique. The Church was further venerated in 735 AD by Venerable Bede, an Anglo-Saxon Benedictine scholar, who wrote the History of the English Church and People in Latin, which became the best historical writing of medieval history.

By 750 AD, two books came to light, the first giving major push to prolonged poetic expression, as the first great English epic poem, Beowulf, in Old English, an anonymous and untitled work, exemplifying early medieval society in England and Old Testament Law. Another book, which represented early-medieval art by Irish monks, was the Book of Kells, a Gospel book of decorative art.

The Iconoclastic movement around 740 AD was a significant movement advocating renouncing the paganistic icon worship of images of Christ or saints as Christ could not be captured trough human imagery and art, and had support from Byzantine Emperor Leo the Isaurian, and further by his son Constantine V who rules until 775. The Libri Carolini (the Caroline Books) were published in 790–792 AD by Charlemagne's court responding to the Iconoclastic controversy by propogating limiting of images to decorative or mnemonic uses, opposing Pope Gregory's venerable claim that images can be used to teach the ignorant, but at the same time not advising on destruction of images. The Iconoclast controversy ended in the ninth century with a new

Byzantine spirituality that acknowledged the contemplation of icons for helping ascendance from the material to the immaterial.

King Charlemagne in France was a major driving force in the period to initiate major cultural revival, when he started in 795 AD withcommissioning the scribe Dagulf to create a small Book of Psalms (Paris, Louvre; Vienna, National Library) for Hadrian I, to be offered as a package of diplomatic gifts. The book with elegant ivory covers, use of gold and costly purple and blue pigments, still stands out as the first effort at textual dissemination of the holy message of the of the Psalms. This book was part of the Grand Plan of Charlemagne to highlight ecclesiastical and educational upliftment and peaceful coexistence, and for the same he took personal interest in large-scale production and distribution of newly copied and corrected Latin texts. By 805 AD at Aachen, Charlemagne had initiated revival of classical culture, founding schools, hosting learned scholars in his court, including Alcuin of York, encouraging artists to reinvigorate Greco-Roman traditions, initiating lavish manuscript books, copies of sacred and classical texts, and initiating a fashion trend, which continued for generation. Some Carolingian books have gem-encrusted covers, purple-dyed pages, text written in gold and silver inks, and miniature illustrations executed in a lively, confident style. Court workshops also produce cast bronze figures, ivory carvings, and treasury objects that incorporate precious metals, gemstones, and antique cameos.

855–869 AD King Lothair II, great-grandson of Charlemagne, commissions the engraving of a large rock crystal. Some four inches in diameter, the rock crystal, now in the British Museum, is carved with eight detailed scenes from the Old Testament story of Susanna.

871 AD King Alfred the Great, of England, established himself as leader, who built up constructs a system of government

and education which unified the smaller Anglo-Saxon states in the ninth and tenth centuries, brought about the codification of English law, revived the efficacy of local government and the reorganization of the army, promoting Anglo-Saxon literacy and national culture. King Alfred the Great (reigned 871-900), translated many works from Latin, especially in the areas of religion, history and philosophy. This was the foundation of the written national language. The first translated works included The Pastor's Book, containing ideals for a pastor, with which Alfred as a secular ruler identified. He also translated Baede 's Church History and other historical accounts. In addition, Alfred compiled medical information, annals, chronicles, and information for law books. His works lacked originality, and were more instructive and educational than artistic and beautiful.

In 10th century AD Hrotsvitha, a nun at Gandersheim abbey in Saxony, completed secular and religious poems, plays, and epics noteworthy for their highly sophisticated Latin.

Around 1000 AD Emperor Otto III commissioned a sumptuous gospel book illustrated with miniatures notable for their linear expressiveness and debt to Byzantine models (Munich, Bayerische Staatsbibliothek). Other Ottonian commissions include magnificent altar frontals, treasury objects, and architectural sculpture. Ottonian artists expand the gestural language and narrative potential of many-figured scenes, experiment with ways to express emotion, and bring both weight and grace to depictions of the human form.

Aggression And Hatred Against Education, Reading And Books In The 13[Th] To 18[Th] Century

Around 642 AD The Moslem Caliph Omar from Damascus ordered that all the books in the library of Alexandria in Egypt should be destroyed because, as he said "they will either contradict the Koran, in which case they are heresy, or they will agree with it, so they are superfluous." Therefore, the books and scrolls were taken out of the library and distributed as fuel to the many bathhouses of the city. So enormous was the volume of literature that it took six months for it all to be burnt to ashes heating the saunas of the conquerors.

African continent was at one time host to large collections of books on as diverse areas as Medical, literary, religion, philosophy, social contexts, and others. The African towns and cities, particularly Benin, the Mauritian cities, Timbaktu, Mali and others, there were huge libraries with massive collection of books. The cities were subject to constant plunders by various raiders, and emperors in the period between 7th to 16 th century and then by the organMany old West African families have private library collections that go back hundreds of years. The Mauritanian cities of Chinguetti and Oudane have a total of 3,450 hand written mediaeval books. There may be another 6,000 books still surviving in the other city of Walata. Some date back to the 8th century AD. There are 11,000 books in private collections in Niger.

Finally, in Timbuktu, Mali, there are about 700,000 surviving books. They are written in Mande, Suqi, Fulani, Timbuctu, and Sudani. The contents of the manuscripts include math, medicine, poetry, law and astronomy. This work was the first encyclopedia in the 14th century before the Europeans got the idea later in the 18th century, 4 centuries later.

A collection of one thousand six hundred books was considered a small library for a West African scholar of the 16th century. Professor Ahmed Baba of Timbuktu is recorded as saying that he had the smallest library of any of his friends – he had only 1600 volumes.

Concerning these old manuscripts, Michael Palin, in his TV series Sahara, said the imam of Timbuktu "has a collection of scientific texts that clearly show the planets circling the sun. They date back hundreds of years . . . Its convincing evidence that the scholars of Timbuktu knew a lot more than their counterparts in Europe. In the fifteenth century in Timbuktu the mathematicians knew about the rotation of the planets, knew about the details of the eclipse, they knew things which we had to wait for 150 almost 200 years to know in Europe when Galileo and Copernicus came up with these same calculations and were given a very hard time for it.

The old Malian capital of Niani had a 14th century building called the Hall of Audience. It was an surmounted by a dome, adorned with arabesques of striking colours. The windows of an upper floor were plated with wood and framed in silver; those of a lower floor were plated with wood, framed in gold.

Leadership With Pen: The Global Wordsmiths

context:

Writers who led the literature front in the later part of 18ᵗʰ Century and earlier part of 19ᵗʰ Century. Leaders creating impact with political, social and intense emotional writings (18ᵗʰ Century)

This was a great era of prolific writings by English writers, as the generation who felt, witnessed and expressed rapid historical dynamics, as well as changes in the sociocultural behaviours in the society, and poured out their personal pangs and emotions of longing into long prose and verses, which became milestones for literary discussions, wonderings, analysis, societies and study.

Lord Byron, Emily Bronte (*Wuthering Heights*), Charlotte Bronte (*Jane Eyre*), Anne Bront, Jane Auston (*Pride and*

Prejudice), Sarah Adams (*Hymns*), Elizabeth Barrett Browning, made a strong impact both by their novels and poems.

While Lord Byron wrote poignant expressions of the changed geopolitical situation in his poem "*By the rivers of Babylon we sat downand wept*", he wrote pensively in his poem "*This day I turn thirty six*", full of melancholy and reminiscent of his life and times of love, that would become a thing of past, and the gradual fading of the desires. Lord Byron also showed his extremely softer side in *The Tear*, when he cited different emotions a single tear could denote. His major poem is considered *An Epsitle to Augusts*, which was dedicated to his sisiter, with whom she cherished a passionate relation that even he could not ascribe as a simple brother sister story, reminiscing all the good time they spent together and lamenting his later life wasted away from her.

Byron's writings were affected by his own wanton life, sexual escapades, passion, being spoilt, exploited and infatuated by old ladies, and then engaging himself with mistresses while settling in Italy. His cantos, *Childe Harold and The Prisoner of Chillon, lament of Tasso, Prophecy of Dante, Mezzeppa* and others, and later dramas like *The Two Foscari*, somewhere reflected his own conflicts and also motivated out of his extensive travels across Europe and the thoughts generated during travel. It was evident, as in the case of Prisoner of Chillon, based on the underground imprisonment of Bonevard, a leading protestant hero in France and Geneva, by Duke, or in the case of Lament of Lasso, the writer, who again expressed his thoughts during imprisonment, which Byron elaborated in his work. Thus he was a prolific writer in emotions and in political movements.

Emily Bronte, was intense as a writer in her extraordinary novel Wuthering heights, which details the passionate love of Hathcliffe for Catherine, in a haunting tale of relations, so much so with a vengeance even after her death, filmed classicaly in films including that by Wlliam Wyler back in 1939 (Lawrence Oliver and Merl Oberon) and later by others, praised and reviled both by later day authors including Graham Greene for the efforts to recreate the magick of Yorkshire moors, that had a strong impact on Emily Bronte and her novel.

Emily narrated poems *Anticipation and A Day Dream* with an ability to create magic of hope and imagination, maintaining romance and idea as the driving force and theme.

Jane Austen, born in England and educated properly, started with humerous collecions as Juvenilla, and later came out with gems including *Pride and Prejudice, Sense and Sensibility and Morthanger Abbey* (Susan), which reflected her ability to dwell upon the two flip sides of any fact or matter and ponder over and look at he same with a sense of detatchment and humour. She set her own style and class of followers. It was also evident in her poems, *I have A Pain in My Head, A mock panegyric to a friend* and others.

A poet and a writer, who made immense impact on the social and political culture was Sarah Adams Flower, again borne to an influential parents, well read, and an author who based her works on diverse topics, including those for children (*Flock at the Fountain and other catechism* based on English church), conflicts between Christianity and heathenism (*Vivia perpetua*), contributing effectively to the Unitarian academic groyup of English ministery, and standing parallel to authors like William Wordsworth and Charles Dickense, who led the movement of expanding human thoughts on matters other than love, lust and materialistic things and advanced learning on child emotions and development through writings and use of such writings. Her feminism, professionalism, social, and her unconventional lifestyle, all propogated Unitarianism, a prominent ideology of the 19th century.

21ˢᵀ CENTURY BESTSELLER WRITERS

Over the years, many writers have stood out in their times. In the 21ˢᵗ century, writers have adopted stories from the real life, as in case of Paula Hawkins, with her riveting thriller *The Girl on the Train* (in 2015), also adopted into a movie, with a plot based on domestic violence, and drug abuse. Jezz Butterworth, coming out with Ferryman (2017), adopted into thetre, first on Royal Court Theatre, then by Gielgud Theatre and subsequently procduced by Bernanrd Jacobs Theatre, has been adopted from the real life disappearance of uncle of one of the actors. Dab Brown has continued with his series of drama and intrigue with his latest novel *Origin* (2017) after *Angels and Demons, The Da Vinci Code, The Lost Symbol and Inferno.* Stephen king, continuing with his crime novels, came out with *Mr Mercedes* (2014), his 66ᵗʰ book, winning Edgards Award and Goodreads Choice Awards. Donna Tartt, took her time after starting in 2002, to publish a masterpiece, *The Goldflinch,* based on the first person account of a terror explosion survivor, who recounts, how he survived after being wrecked as he lost his mother in the Dutch explosion, sticking on to a masterpiece ahanded over to him, his criminal escapades in brokering fake masterpieces, and then his conversion. The novel won Donna Tartt critical acclaim from various quarters, including Kirkus Reviews, Booklist, The NewYork Times, The vanity Fair and finaly bagging the Pulitzer price for fiction in 2014.

John Grisham continued with his criminal thrillers and legal crime thrillers, with *The Racketeers* (2012), based on the criminal protagonists in 1920s America, taking his stock further after the stupendous earlier novels and film adaptations of *The Firm, The Chamber, The Client, A Painted House, The Pellican Brief and others.* Gillian Schelber Fynn, another American thriller writer, and editor for Television's Entertainment Weekly, came out with three novels, *Sharp Objects, Dark places and finaly with Gone*

Girl, a story about two laid down writer couples, where the wife vanishes, adopted into a successful movie by same name. E L James and her *Fifty Shades of Gray* and other series, based on the erotic romance and relationships between a college graduate and a business magnate, made a thunderous appearance in the fiction segment, setting selling records for Vinatage Books and as a moneyspinner as film series for Universal Studios, but not with a positive critical accalaim.

Many authors who made significant writings in diverse areas in past 2 decades pssed out in the decade, including the widely appreciated, loved and OBE ordained Patrick LeighFermor, a war veteran, scholar, and looked up as real life James Bond, who published a lot of travel novels based on his travels.

Leadership With Pen: The Indian Writers, and How They Inspired, Led, and Changed a Generation

Context: After a generation of nationalit writers actuating the masses during freedom struggle in the run up to independence, including Bankim Chandra Chaterjee, tilak, Ravindra Nath Taigore and others, the next generation developed upon the post independence positiveness, hope, correction of social order, nature and other issues. Also, as living conditions improved by the 1970s, emotions and expression of love caught the fancy of many a writers. The Delhi sultanats of course had left behind a legacy of *shero- shayari,* which remained a principal source of bringing people together as a sharing community on various occasions. Stalwarts in all the above forms made a tremendous impact on the Indian lower and upper middle working class, giving them hope, patience, outlet for emotions and sense of creativity as they endured religiously through their daily chores building the nation along. If we look back, we can recall the period 1960-1990 as the era of slow, leasure paced and *"content in their small little way"* society, being able to enjoy the content, expressions and pathos in the writer's texts, prose, verses and shayari. Many of these writings also framed the tempo of various films and Indian film industry as scripts, songs, screen plays, and again left impressions on society in a big way on and off.

No doubt they were great leaders, leading masses in learning and improving on social conduct and pathos. They refined the social mindset and sensitized it to many things!!

Suryakant Tripathi "Nirala"

सूर्यकांतत्रिपाठी "निराला"

Known fondly as Kavi Nirala, he showed astounding hold on Hindi as a language, expressing pious devotion in *"Veena vadini... "*, deep sense of duty, respect and passion for motherland in *"Matra vandana..." and "De main karoon varan..."* and profound hope in *"Abhi na hoga mera ant..."*.

वर दे वीणा वादिनी वर दे !

वरदे, वीणावादिनिवरदे !
प्रियस्वतंत्र-रवअमृत-मंत्रनव
भारतमें भर दे !

काटअंध-उरकेबंधन-स्तर
बहाजननि, ज्योतिर्मय निर्झर;
कलुष-भेद-तम हर प्रकाश भर
जगमगजग कर दे !

नवगति, नवलय, ताल-छंदनव
नवलकंठ, नवजलद-मन्द्ररव;
नवनभकेनवविहग-वृंदको
नवपर, नवस्वर दे !

वर दे, वीणावादिनि वर दे ।

Oh Goddess of knowledge, inspire us all with new zeal, passion, new voice through your light of wisdom, so that there is ever flowing enthusiasm to work towards good of the society!!

मातृवंदना

नर जीवन के स्वार्थ सकल
बलि हों तेरे चरणों पर, माँ
मेरे श्रमसिंचित सब फल ।

जीवन के रथ पर चढ़कर
सदा मृत्यु पथ पर बढ़कर
महाकाल के खरतर शर सह
सकूँ, मुझे तू कर दृढ़ तर;

बाधाएँ आएँ तनपर
देखूँ तुझे नयन मन भर
मुझे देख तू सजल दृगों से
अपलक, उरकेशतदल पर;
क्लेदयुक्त, अपनातनदूंगा
मुक्त करूंगा तुझे अटल
तेरे चरणों पर दे कर बलि
सकल श्रेय श्रमसंचित फल

190

To you, my pious land, I submit myself and all men capable, to untirilingly work, toil and sacrifice to make and keep you free, irrespective of whatever calamities come in the way... ...

दे, मैं करूँ वरण

दे, मैं करूँ वरण
जननि, दुखहरणपद-राग-रंजितमरण।

भीरुता के बँधे पाश सब छिन्न हों,
मार्ग के रोध विश्वास से भिन्न हों,
आज्ञा, जननि, दिवस-निशिकरूँ अनुसरण।
लांछनाइंधन, हृदय-तलजलेअनल,
भक्ति-नत-नयनमैं चलूँ अविरत सबल
पार कर जीवन-प्रलोभन समुपकरण।

अभी न होगा मेरा अन्त

अभी न होगा मेरा अन्त
अभी-अभी ही तो आया है
मेरे वन में मृदुल वसन्त-
अभी न होगा मेरा अन्त

हरे-हरेयेपात,
डालियाँ, कलियाँ कोमल गात!
मैं ही अपना स्वप्न-मृदुल-कर
फेरूँगा निद्रित कलियों पर
जगा एक प्रत्यूष मनोहर

191

द्वार दिखा दूँगा फिर उनको
है मेरे वे जहाँ अनन्त-
अभी न होगा मेरा अन्त।

मेरे जीवन का यह है जब प्रथम चरण,
इसमें कहाँ मृत्यु?
है जीवन ही जीवन
अभी पड़ा है आगे सारा यौवन
स्वर्ण-किरण कल्लोलों पर बहतारे, बालक-मन!!

I see for me a long time to come, having just started, feeling full of youth, and a lot to come, and yes I will spread around this positiveness, making many young saplings to flower, and spreading smiles around.

What a positive composition....motivating....goading to positive actions....

RABINDRA NATH TAGORE

Tagore, born in 1861, was an incredible combination of talents and repertoire, a poet, novelist, short-story writer, essayist, playwright, educationist, spiritualist, lyricist, composer and singer, way ahead his time, honoured with the Nobel Prize for Literature in 1913, as a first non-European, and his *Gitanjali: An Anthology of Poems,* is a collection of various things small and crucial, pensive and celebratory. Some of his major works include stories, poems and reflections, viz, *The Homecoming, Fireflies, Still Heart, The Kiss, Lord of my Life, Tumi Sandhyar Meghmala,* which are soulful and reverberate with feelings. Others show his reflections on mortality and the truth, viz., *Last curtain, Death, Old and New, Parting words, Sail away.*

Others include his famous thoughts on a free nation, rights and humanity as reflected in Freedom, Where the mind is....

OUR MEETING

Two of us once met, where the streams of life and death had stopped

Where time stood still. Today it is so far and away

Now I am sailing alone, My boat is rocking in the storm

I now remember again, How once we met

At the end of the world, Where Taking your hand in my hand

I kept looking at the sky, We had no words

And didn't know how our time passed, That day I had realized in my heart of hearts

Where end the meanings of our words, How music rises from the core of the universe

How the pining woods blossom into flowers, These we realized when both of us wept

In endless pleasure, and descended the heaven.

True expressions of soulful love, bonding and unison of thoughts.....the Master expresses it simply and tersely put. No more or superfluous words needed for expression!!

THE DOG

Every morning this dog, very attached to me,
Quietly keeps sitting near my seat
Till touching its head, I recognize its company.
This recognition gives it so much joy
Pure delight ripples through its entire body.

Among all dumb creatures, It is the only living being
That has seen the whole man
Beyond what is good or bad in him, It has seen
For his love it can sacrifice its life
It can love him too for the sake of love alone
For it is he who shows the way, To the vast world pulsating
with life.
When I see its deep devotion, The offer of its whole being
I fail to understand, By its sheer instinct
What truth it has discovered in man, By its silent anxious
piteous looks
It cannot communicate what it understands,
But it has succeeded in conveying to me
Among the whole creation, What is the true status of man.

Again an expression of great understanding of feelings of bonding and selfless love by the Master, enlivened through this small description of this amall silent interaction between the Master and the Dog. Truly, a canine can teach a lot of lessons in this undemanding readiness to show abundance of emotions, irrespective of what his master stands for in this world.

SENSES

Deliverance is not for me in renunciation.
I feel the embrace of freedom in a thousand bonds of delight.
Thou ever pourest for me the fresh draught of thy wine of
various

colours and fragrance, filling this earthen vessel to the brim.
My world will light its hundred different lamps with thy flame
and place them before the altar of thy temple.
No, I will never shut the doors of my senses.
The delights of sight and hearing and touch will bear thy
delight.
Yes, all my illusions will burn into illumination of joy,
and all my desires ripen into fruits of love.

Rabindranath, in his own way tries to counter the call for
renunciation and controlling the senses, holding forth his way of
achieving the same by dealing with and interacting in all things
small, sweet and soulful, ensuring that delight of sharing love
and spread cheer was not lost till the last breath!!

FREEDOM

Freedom from fear is the freedom
I claim for you my motherland!
Freedom from the burden of the ages, bending your head,
breaking your back, blinding your eyes to the beckoning
call of the future;
Freedom from the shackles of slumber wherewith
you fasten yourself in night's stillness,
mistrusting the star that speaks of truth's adventurous paths;
freedom from the anarchy of destiny
whole sails are weakly yielded to the blind uncertain winds,
and the helm to a hand ever rigid and cold as death.

Freedom from the insult of dwelling in a puppet's world,
where movements are started through brainless wires,
repeated through mindless habits,
where figures wait with patience and obedience for the
master of show,
to be stirred into a mimicry of life.

WHERE THE MIND....

Where the mind is without fear and the head is held high;
Where knowledge is free;
Where the world has not been broken up into fragments by
narrow domestic walls;
Where words come out from the depth of truth;
Where tireless striving stretches its arms towards perfection:
Where the clear stream of reason has not lost
its way into the dreary desert sand of dead habit;
Where the mind is lead forward by
thee into ever-widening thought and action–
Into that heaven of freedom, my Father, let my country awake.

The superlative poem, titled 'Where the Mind is Without Fear', talks about the boundless power of human knowledge, valour of standing by the truth, and the essence of true freedom. This was Tagore's way of expressing his thoughts on the need for independence, the possible shape that an independent Indian socity could be given and the desire to ensure that every man could achieve true independence of fearless thoughts, good deeds and dedication to the nation.

MAHADEVI VERMA

महादेवी वर्मा

Mahadevi Verma, borne to an illustrious father, who was a renowned educationist at a senior college in Indore, and to a very religious mother, took to creativity with words at a very early age. In a post independence India, the smell of everyday freedom in evrything small is very beutifuly expressed in her innumerable small poems dedicated to small things in and around the nature, as a bird, a lamp, sunlight, clouds. Very beautifuly expressed these poems opened up the sensitivity towards innumerable day to day small pleasures that the mankind could be thankful about, and that is what she did, instilling happiness in millions, the haves, the have nots, the kids, young and old alike. That was not a mean thing in a newly independent India slowly making efforts to economicaly stand on its own. At the same time, she could be very thoughtful and patriotic as seen in many of the poems that were written in pre independence and even post independence period, where she could goad people into patriotic service by her prose and verse. Just sample the small representative ones, as under.

दीन भारत वर्ष

सिरमौर सा तुझको रचा था, विश्व में करतार ने,
आकृष्ट था सबको किया, तेरे, मधुरव्यवहार ने।
नवशिष्य तेरे मध्य भारत, नित्य आते थे चले,
जैसे सुमन कीगंध से, अलिवृन्द आ-आकरमिले।
वह युग कहाँ अब खो गया वे देव वे देवीनहीं,
ऐसी परीक्षा भाग्य ने, किस देश की ली थी कहीं।
जिस कुंज वन में कोकिला के, गान सुनते थे भले,
रव है उलूकों का वहाँ, क्या भाग्य हैं अपनेजले।
अवतार प्रभु लेते रहे, अवतार ले फिर आइए,
इस दीन भारतवर्ष को, फिर पुण्य भूमि बनाइए।

*Lamenting the loss of greatness of India as a country standing
tall in righteousness and deeds, the poetess expreeses the wish
that India will stand up again as the true inspiring nation, as it
comes out from the shackles of British rule.*

मस्तक देकर आज खरीदेंगे हम ज्वाला!

मस्तक देकर आज खरीदेंगे हम ज्वाला!

फूलों में जिसकी लाली है, धरती में जो हरियाली है,
जिससे तप-तप कर सागर-जल, बनता श्याम घटाओं वाला!
मस्तक देकर आज खरीदेंगे हम ज्वाला!
कृष्ण जिसे वंशी में गाते, रामधनुष-टंकार बनाते,
जिसे बुद्ध ने आँखों में भर, बाँटी थी अमृत की हाला!
मस्तक देकर आज खरीदेंगे हम ज्वाला!
जब ज्वाला से प्राण तपेंगे, तभी मुक्ति के स्वप्र ढलेंगे,
उसको छूकर मृत साँसें भी, होंगी चिनगारी की माला!
मस्तक देकर आज खरीदेंगे हम ज्वाला!

Invoking the masses to prepare to be ready to sacrifice their heads for freedom, Mahadevi exhorts for a fiery zeal to cross all limits in a selfless homage to a nation and secure independence and strive for highest glory for India

पूछता क्यों शेष कितनी रात?

पूछता क्यों शेष कितनी रात
छू नखों की क्रांति चिर संकेत पर जिनके जलातू
स्निग्ध सुधि जिनकी लिये कज्जल-दिशा में हँस चला तू
परिधि बन घेरे तुझे, वे उँगलियाँ अवदात!
व्यंग्यमय है क्षितिज-चेरा
प्रश्नमय हर क्षण निठुर पूछता सा परिचय बसेरा;
आज उत्तर हो सभी का ज्वाल वाही श्वास तेरा!
छीजता है इधर तू, उस ओर बढता प्रात!
प्रणय लौ की आरती ले, धूम लेखा स्वर्ण-अक्षतनील-कुमकुमवारतीले
मूक प्राणों में व्यथा की स्नेह-उज्जवल भारती ले
मिल, अरे बढ़ रहे यदि प्रलय झंझावात।
कौन भय की बात,
पूछता क्यों कितनी रात?

Mahadevi, in one of her stimulating couplets, exhorts the people to prod along working and toiling hard, wading through the storms, as that is how the dark and long night will change over with the first shimmer of morning sunlight.

मधुर-मधुरमेरे दीपक जल!

मधुर-मधुर मेरे दीपक जल!, युग-युग प्रतिदिन प्रतिक्षण प्रतिपल
प्रियतम का पथ आलोकित कर!
सौरभ फैला विपुल धूप बन, मृदुल मोम-साघुलरे, मृदु-तन!
दे प्रकाश का सिन्धु अपरिमित, तेरे जीवन का अणुगल-गल

पुलक-पुलक मेरे दीपक जल!
तारे शीतल कोमल नूत, न माँग रहे तुझसे ज्वालाकण;
विश्व-शलभ सिर धुन कहता मैं, हाय, न जल पाया तुझमें मिल!
सिहर-सिहर मेरे दीपक जल!
मेरे निस्वासों से द्रुततर, सुभग न तू बुझने का भयकर।
मैं अंचल की ओटकिये हूँ! अपनी मृदु पलकों से चंचल
सहज-सहज मेरे दीपक जल!
सीमा ही लघुता का बन्धन, है अनादि तू मत घड़ियाँगिन
मैं दृग के अक्षय कोषों से, -तुझमें भरती हूँ आँसू-जल!
सहज-सहज मेरे दीपकजल!

मैं नीर भरी दुख की बदली!
मैं नीर भरी दुख की बदली!
स्पन्दन में चिरनिस्पन्द बसा, क्रन्दन में आहत विश्व हँसा
नयनों में दीपक से जलते, पलकों में निर्झारिणी मचली!

मेरा पग-पग संगीत भरा, श्वासों से स्वप्न-पराग झरा
नभ के नवरंग बुनते दुकूल, छाया में मलय-बयार पली।
पथ को न मलिन करता आना, पथ-चिह्न दे जाता जाना;
सुधि मेरे आगन की जगमें, सुख की सिहर नहो अन्त खिली!

विस्तृत नभ का कोई कोना, मेरा नक भी अपना होना,
परिचय इतना, इतिहास यही-,उमड़ी कल थी, मिट आज चली!

फूल

मधुरिमा के, मधु के अवतार
मधुरिमा के, मधु के अवतार, सुधासे, सुषमासे, छविमान,
आंसुओं में सहमे अभिराम, तारकों से हे मूकअजान!
सीखकर मुस्काने की बान, कहां आऐ हो कोमल प्राण!

स्निग्ध रजनी से लेकर हास, रूप से भर कर सारे अंग,
नये पल्लव का घूंघट डाल, अछूता ले अपना मकरंद,
ढूढं पाया कैसे यह देश? स्वर्ग के हे मोहक संदेश!

रजत किरणों से नैन पखार, अनोखा ले सौरभ का भार,
छलकता ले कर मधु का कोष, चले आऐ एकाकी पार;
उषा के छू आरक्तक पोल, किलक पडता तेरा उन्माद,
देख तारों के बुझते प्राण, न जाने क्या आ जाता याद?

चांदनी का श्रृंगार समेट, अधखुली आंखों की यह कोर,
लुटा अपना यौवन अनमोल, ताकती किस अतीत कीओर?
कौन है वह सम्मोहन राग, खींच लाया तुमको सुकुमार?
तुम्हें भेजा जिसने इस देश, कौन वह है निष्ठुर करतार?
हंसो पहनो कांटों के हार,
मधुर भोलेपन का संसार!

She could be very simple often while writing on a simple flower or moments of anguish and the culminating tears, expressing the languish and the beauty in the simplest of words.

JAISHANKAR PRASAD:

Pt Jai Shankar Prasad, established himself as a thespian with one of the marvels of long hindi poetry- *Kamayani,* besides other famous compilations including *"Aansoo...".* Largely a nationalist and a motivational poet, he directed lot of his work to glory of India and nationalism, as clearly evident in the *"Bharat Mahima....."*, *"Arun, yeh madhumah desh hamara..."*. He was one of the pillars of the concept of *Chhayavaad* or neo romanticism in hindi poetry with Mahadevi Verma, Suryakant nirala and Sumitranandann Pant.

((xii) Reference picture on page 153)

जयशंकर प्रसाद

कामायनी, आँसू, झरना, कानन-कुसुम, लहर

भारत महिमा

हिमालय के आँगन में उसे, प्रथम किरणों का दे उपहार
उषा ने हँस अभिनंदन किया और पहनाया हीरक-हार

जगे हम, लगे जगाने विश्व, लोक में फैला फिर आलोक
व्योम-तमपुँज हुआ तब नष्ट, अखिल संसृति हो उठी अशोक
विमल वाणी ने वीणा ली, कमल कोमल कर में सप्रीत
सप्तस्वर सप्तसिंधु में उठे, छिड़ा तब मधुर साम-संगीत

धर्म का ले ले कर जो नाम, हुआ करती बलि कर दी बंद
हमीं ने दिया शांति-संदेश, सुखी होते दे करआनंद
विजय केवल लोहे की नहीं, धर्म की रही धरा पर धूम
भिक्षु हो कर रहते सम्राट, दया दिखलाते घर-घर घूम

यवन को दिया दया का दान, चीन को मिली धर्म की दृष्टि
मिला था स्वर्ण-भूमि को रत्न, शील की सिंहल को भी सृष्टि
....

हमारे संचय में था दान, अतिथि थे सदा हमारे देव
....

जियें तो सदा इसी के लिए, यही अभिमान रहे यह हर्ष
निछावर कर दें हम सर्वस्व, हमारा प्यारा भारत वर्ष

Jai Shankar Prasad and his poems show outstanding love for the motherland, India, and it comes out through each of the lines he expresses, whether recounting India's contribution to the world in peaceful coexistence through Buddha, who established his faith of peace far and wide in China, and in other countries, and also through the exemplary king Ashoka, who set up an example in modesty renouncing all worldly gains. He also revels in the geographical diversity with ice laden Himalayas, basking in sunlight on one side acting as harbinger of light for the world and Ganges as the purifying meandering river washing away all that is superfluous, impure or reduntant.

धर्मवीर भारती

Dharmveer Bharti was another poet who witnessed the Indian independence in his twenties and had his own imagination of a free India, a place of opportunity for everyone. Born, brought up and completing his Ph D in hindi literature in the creative city of Prayag, he enthusiastically set out to contribute in his own way for social imorovrmrnt, reform and contributions through plays, poems and writings and created some of the masterpieces of social reflection in post independence India, as under, many of which have been hosted as immensely popular stage and theatre plays stretching to full houses for many weeks in major metros in Idia in the 1970s and 1980s, the era which produced many great actors, directors and technicians. His major compilations include

देशान्तर, ठण्डा लोहा तथा भारती की अन्य कविताएँ, सपना अभी भी, आद्यन्त, अन्धा युग, कुछ लम्बी कविताएँ, कनुप्रिया, मेरी वाणी गैरिक वासना!!

He was hugely admired as a long time editor of Dharmayug, the magazine. He also contributed with small writings and poems in the form of,

नवम्बर की दोपहर,धर्मवीर भारती, कविता की मौत, टूटा पहिया,एक वाक्य,उपलब्धि, उत्तर नहीं हूँ

((xiii) Reference picture on page 153)

Kaifi Azmi

A stupendous writer who could comment on the social and communal harmony through hisstimulating and thought provoking poem.............., wherein he reflects pensively,

अब तमद्दुन की हो जीत के हार
मेरा माज़ी है अभी तक मेरे काँधे पर सवार

His reflections very well expressed the emotions of people post partition, wherein he repented the animosity between the people generated through the process and culmination of partition, and the barbaric violence through which the countries and its people finaly settled down loosing many of their own as their gravest animies. These memories are evident as permanent scars in his writings.

पड़ता रहता है मेरे माज़ी का साया मुझ पर
दौर-ए-ख़ूंख़्वारी से गुज़रा हूँ छिपाऊँ क्यों पर
जिनसे मेरा न कोई बैर न प्यार
उनपे करता हूँ मैं वार
उनका करता हूँ शिकार
मल लिया माथे पे तहज़ीब का ग़ाज़ा लेकिन
बरबरियत का जो है दाग़ वोह छूटा ही नहीं
गाँव आबाद किए शहर बसाए हमने
रिश्ता जंगल से जो अपना है वो टूटा ही नहीं

He could also connect effortlessly with great pathos to the boil and steam of a speeding rail engine to the emotions of past association and separations, stepping out into a lonely dawn through the stark silence of early wee hours, after prolonged pangs of a dark night through the jungles and their isolation.

These poets made the day for millions of lower, lower middle, middle and even upper class Indians as they got something to relish upon through their long days. Those were the days!

वो सर्द रात जबकि सफ़र कर रहा था मैं
रंगीनियों से ज़र्फ़-ए-नज़र भर रहा था मैं...
तेज़ी से जंगलों में उड़ी जा रही थी रेल
ख़्वाबीदा काएनात को चौंका रही थी रेल....

पहुँची जिधर ज़मीं का कलेजा हिला दिया
दामन में तीरगी केगरेबाँ बना दिया....
धोके से छू गईं जो कहीं सर्द उँगलियाँ
बिच्छू सा डंक मारने लगती थीं खिड़कियाँ....
पिछले पहर का नर्म धुँदलका था पुर-फ़िशाँ
मायूसियों में जैसे उमीदों का कारवाँ....
बे-नूर हो के डूबने वाला था माहताब
कोहरे में खुप गई थी सितारों की आब-ओ-ताब....

In an era of no mobile, no internet and even no television, these lines and poems by him and many others infact were an industry in themselves, providing emotional succor and support to many people, even stabilizing them on and off their daily work. They provided a medium for self reflection, catharsis and then a sense of let go and move.

क़ब्ज़े से तीरगी के सहर छूटने को थी
. . . .

. . . .
याद आ रहा था किससे बिछड़ना न पूछिए.....
दिल में कुछ ऐसे घाव थे तीर-ए-मलाल के
रो-रो दिया था खिड़की से गर्दन निकाल के.....

Or he could be out and out romantic and optimistic in his next two...... "Doshija malan and Tasavvur", as under, imagining the beauty of early morning, as the star lit night gives way to a chirpy dawn, with the plants and the thorns in the garden yearning for a romantic satin brush with the beautiful gardner's drape........Or dreaming of a romantic interlude with his pristine, sculpted, fairy lady love in "tasavvur".....

दोशीज़ा मालन

लो पौ फटी वो छुप गई तारों की अंजुमन
लो जाम-ए-महर से वो छलकने लगी किरन...
खिंचने लगा निगाह में फ़ितरत का बाँकपन
जल्वे ज़मीं पे बरसे ज़मीं बन गई दुल्हन.....
गूँजे तराने सुब्ह का इक शोर हो गया
आलममय-ए-बक़ा में शराबोर हो गया.....
झोंके चले हवा के शजर झूमने लगे
मस्ती में फूल काँटों का मुँह चूमने लगे....

दोशीज़ा एक ख़ुश-क़द ओ ख़ुश-रंग-ओ-ख़ूब-रू
मालन की नूर-दीदागुलिस्ताँ की आबरू...
ज़ुल्फ़ों में ताब-ए-सुम्बुल-ए-पेचाँ लिए हुए
आरिज़ में शोख़ रंग-ए-गुलिस्ताँ लिए हुए...
ऐहुर-ए-बाग़ इतनी ख़ुदी से न काम ले
उड़कर शमीम-ए-गुल कहीं आँचल न थाम ले...
शाएर का दिल है मुफ़्त में क्यूँ दर्द-मन्द हो
इक गुल इधर भी नज़्म अगर ये पसन्द हो!

तसव्वुर

ये किस तरह याद आ रही हो ये ख़्वाब कैसा दिखा रही हो
कि जैसे सचमुच निगाह के सामने खड़ी मुस्कुरा रही हो...
ये जिस्म-ए-नाज़ुक, ये नर्म बाहें, हसीन गर्दन, सिडौल बाज़ू

शगुफ़्ता चेहरा, सलोनी रंगत, घनेरा जूड़ा, सियाह गेसू
नशीली आँखें, रसीली चितवन, दराज़ पलकें, महीन अबरू
तमाम शोख़ी, तमाम बिजली, तमाम मस्ती, तमाम जादू....
लचक लचक गुनगुना रही हो
ये ख़्वाब कैसा दिखा रही हो....
तो क्या मुझे तुम जला ही लोगी
गले से अपने लगा ही लोगी

....

ये ख़्वाब कैसा दिखा रही हो.......

These poets infact corrected social interactions and conduct
by their writing pointing out rights, wrongs, possibilities and the
way forward by of their expressions, which they accumulated
through what they saw and felt and then came out with at
appropriate moment. Thus, they could also be deeply dismissive,
pessimistic and sad about the way society was seemingly shaping
into.....as in his next- "Talash" where he delves deep into dark
rooms of depression, with no ray of hope, with fear all around.

तलाश

ये बुझी सी शाम ये सहमी हुई परछाइयाँ
ख़ून-ए-दिल भी इस फ़ज़ा में रंग भर सकता नहीं.....
आ उतर आ काँपते होंटों पे ऐ मायूस आह.....
सक्फ़-ए-ज़िन्दाँ पर कोई परवाज़ कर सकता नहीं.....
झिलमिलाए मेरी पलकों पे मह-ओ-ख़ुर भी तो क्या?....
इस अन्धेरे घर में इक तारा उतर सकता नहीं.....

हैं इसी ऐवान-ए-बे-दर में यक़ीन न रहनुमा......
आ के क्यूँ दीवार तक नक़्श-ए-क़दम गुम हो गए....
देखऐ जोश-ए-अमल वोसक्फ़ ये दीवार है....
एक रौज़न खोल देना भी कोई दुश्वार है!!

207

दाएरा

रोज़ बढ़ता हूँ जहाँ से आगे....
फिर वहीं लौट के आ जाता हूँ.....
बारहा तोड़ चुका हूँ जिनको....
उन्हीं दीवारों से टकराता हूँ......
....
अपने हाथों को पढ़ा करता हूँ.....
कभी कुरआँ कभी गीता की तरह...

Faiz Ahmed Faiz
फ़ैज़ अहमद फ़ैज़

Faiz Ahmed Faiz, was a poet who earned tremendous following for his poems which were very vocal with fervor of nationalism and society and humanity. He was also to the point and very soulful even in other genres. He impressed, affected and actuated a great mass to think about doing right when it came to national and social duties and express human touch in whatever way possible with the pathos in his poems. He garnered respect in undivided India and also across the border even after partition, and was even known for his writings in Punjabi. The following lines from his poem by the same title, has been the central theme of many a plays, theatrical and television plays portraying deep sense and need for social service and doing good, raising the hands in prayer, and raising hopes in many a hearts.

आइए हाथ उठाएँ हम भी

आइए हाथ उठाएँ हम भी
हम जिन्हें रस्मे-दुआ याद नहीं

हम जिन्हें सोज़े-मुहब्बत के सिवा
कोई बुत, कोई ख़ुदा याद नहीं

जिनकी आँखों को रुख़े-सुब्हे का यारा भी नहीं
उनकी रातों में कोई शम्म' अमुनव्वर कर दे
जिनके क़दमों को किसी रह का सहारा भी नहीं
उनकी नज़रों पे कोई राह उजागर कर दे

इश्क़ का सर्रे-निहाँ जान-तपाँ है जिससे
आज इक़रार करें और तपिश मिट जाए
हर्फ़े-हक़ दिल में खटकता है जो काँटे की तरह
आज इज़हार करें और ख़लिश मिट जाए

*In "rabba sacchiya", he questions God (rabba), that
although He promised that post independence, man would be
the lord of his own destiny, on the contrary, the terror of police
and corruption by the collector has turned the system upside
down, and it is not the lordship that the citizen wants, but a
life with self esteem that is lot better............. a crisp slap on the
faulty administrative system........*

रब्बा सच्चिया

रब्बा सच्चिया तूँ ते आखियासी
जा ओए बंदिया जग दा शाह हैं तूँ
साडियाँ नेहमताँ तेरियाँ दौलताँ ने
साडा नैबते आली जाह है तूँ

किते धौंस पुलिस सरकार दीए
किते धान्दली माल पटवार दीए
ऐंवेंह डडाँ चकल्पे जान मेरी
जिवें फाहीच' कूंज कुर लावन्दीए

209

चंगा शाह बनाया ईर बसाइयाँ
पोले खान्दे याँ वारन आंवदी ए

मैनूँ शाही नईं चाही दी रब मेरे
मैं ते इज़्ज़त दा टुक्कड़ मंगनाँहाँ
मैनूँ ताँ हगनई, महलाँ माड़ीयाँ दी
मैं ते जीवीं दी नग्गर मंगनाँ हाँ

He was known for a number of marvelous collection of poems, nazms and shayari including

नक़्शे-फ़रियादी,

दस्ते-सबा,

दस्ते-तहे-संग

He could also be intensely emotive about romance and longing as in the following immensly popular nazm, also making to the top of the charts by its music and rendition as a part of a famous hindi film. The following *nazm.... aapki yaad aati rahee....* makes the listner sit up and take note whenever played on the All India Radio stations at night as a lilting start to the the often haunting and melancholic Chhaya Geet at 10 PM on Vividh Bharti, and just revel in the masterly rendition and soul of the music. These were the creations which set them as leaders apart, influencing social behaviour, helping maintain huamane touch in the day to day interactions. They were leaders who preferred remaining behind the curtains, who preferred remaining away from the lime light and stage. They had the power to frame the thinking of the masses and subdue them into dwelling on the pains and still revell on them, bear with them..... Other two compositions *Shakh par......* and , *yoon bahar...* also show his versatality.

आपकी याद आती रही रात भर

"आपकी याद आती रही रात-भर"
चाँदनी दिल दुखाती रही रात-भर
गाह जलती हुई, गाह बुझती हुई
शम-ए-ग़म झिलमिलाती रही रात-भर
कोई ख़ुशबू बदलती रही पैरहन
कोई तस्वीर गाती रही रात-भर
एक उमीद से दिल बहलता रहा
इक तमन्ना सताती रही रात-भर

1978

शाख़ पर ख़ूने-गुल रवाँ है वही

शाख़ पर ख़ूने-गुल रवाँ है वही
शोख़ी-ए-रंगे-गुलसिताँ है वही
अब जहाँ मेहरबाँ नहीं कोई
कूचः-ए-यारे-मेहरबाँ है वही
बर्क़ सौ बार गिर के ख़ाक हुई
रौनक़े-ख़ाके-आशियाँ है वही
चाँद-तारे इधर नहीं आते
वरना ज़िंदाँ में आसमाँ है वही

यूँ बहार आई है

यूँ बहार आई है इस बार कि जैसे क़ासिद
कूचा-ए-यार से बे-नैलो-मराम आता है
हर कोई शहर में फिरता है सलामत-दामन
रिंद मयख़ाने से शाइस्ता-ख़राम आता है
....
दाग़े-दिल कर के फ़रोज़ाँ सरे-शाम आता है

211

Mirza Ghalib

While discussing literature, be it any language, if there is no reference to Mirza Ghalib (Mirza Asadullah Baig Khan, Asad or najm-ud Daula, as referred by his names and honorifics showered at him by the King Bahadur Shah Zafar II and others), the poetic expression of the last era of the falling Mughal Empire and the rising British sun in India in the 1860s, is failed and not given its due. **((xiv) Reference picture on page 154)**

Starting to write as early as at the age of 11 in Urdu in the 1810s, getting married at 13, experiencing a bitter experience of loosing all kids in early infancy, Ghalib wrote with a flourish not possessed by any in Urdu or Persian, and became a legend posthumously. Thus while his travails of a married life are reflected in his early ghazals or shairy, the deep sorrow of seeing all the glory, regality and habitation of moghul residencies get vanished, and loss of known friends during establishment of British rule between 1850-1860s, inspired some of his ghazals, and a famous ghazal where he relished is later years style of alcoholism, and a uninhibited life, where he mocks a poet who wants to write without having indulged in alcohol, women, love or not being castigated for the same during one's lifetime.

Thus while one of his famous line was

क़ैद-ए-हयात-ओ-बंद-ए-ग़म,
अस्ल में दोनों एक हैं,
मौत से पहले आदमी ग़म से निजात पाए क्यूँ?

Translated in English, it implies, there is no escape, either from the ironies and angst of life, just like one cant escape from death or end of life, and you have to realize that you are a prisoner, of either of the two, at some point of life, and its ironies, and then of death.

Later on, he became more worldwise and let his life take its own direction, through wine, women and wanderings. Thus he wrote;

अगर न ज़ोहरा-जबीनों के दरमियाँ गुज़रे
तो फिर ये कैसे कटे ज़िन्दगी कहाँ गुज़रे

जो तेरे आरिज़ ओ गेसू के दरमियाँ गुज़रे
कभी-कभी वही लम्हे बता-ए-जाँ गुज़रे

मुझे ये वहम रहा मुद्दतों कि जुर्अत-ए-शौक़
कहीं न ख़ातिर-ए-मासूम पर गिराँ गुज़रे

उसी को कहते हैं जन्नत उसी को दोज़ख़ भी
वो ज़िन्दगी जो हसीनों के दरमियाँ गुज़रे

वो जिनके साए से भी बिजलियाँ तरजती थीं
मिरी नज़र से कुछ ऐसे भी आशियाँ गुज़रे

बहुत हसीन सही सोहबतें गुलों की मगर
वो ज़िन्दगी है जो काँटों के दरमियाँ गुज़रे

बहुत अज़ीज़ हैं मुझको उन्हें क्या याद 'जिगर'
वो हादसात-ए-मोहब्बत जो ना-गहाँ गुज़रे

दिल ही तो है.....

दिल ही तो है, न संग-ओ-ख़िश्त', दर्द से भर न आये क्यों
रोयेंगे हम हज़ार बार, कोई हमें सताये क्यों

दैर नहीं, हरम नहीं, दर नहीं, आस्ताँ नहीं
बैठे हैं रहगुज़र पे हम, कोई हमें उठाये क्यों

जब वह जमाल-ए-दिल फ़रोज़ सूरत-ए-मेहर-ए-नीमरोज़
आप ही हो नज़ारा-सोज़, पर्दे में मुँह छुपाये क्यों

दश्ना-ए-ग़मज़ा' जाँसिताँ, नावक-ए-नाज़ बे पनाह
तेरा ही अक्स-ए-रुख़ रही, सामने तेरे आये क्यों

क़ैद-ए-हयात-ओ-बन्द-ए-ग़म, अस्ल में दोनों एक हैं
मौत से पहले, आदमी ग़म से निजात पाये क्यों

हाँ वो नहीं ख़ुदा परस्त, जाओ वो बेवफ़ा सही
जिस को हो दीन-ओ-दिल अज़ीज़, उसकी गली में जाये क्यों

"ग़ालिब"-ए-ख़स्ता के बग़ैर कौन से काम बंद हैं
रोइये ज़ार-ज़ार क्या, कीजिये हाय-हाय क्यों

...If the life is not under the shadow of the lover's mane, then it stands no use, although company of roses is a comfortable one, but the time spent amongst thorns is something that stands out.

Another of his couplet compilation that became immensely popular as a ghazal was

Dil hi to hai.......

And, of course...*Bazeecha-e-atfal hai.....*

Bazeecha-e-itfal hai duniya meray aage
Hota hai shab-o-roz tamasha meray aage

The world is a children's playground before me
Night and Day, this theatre is enacted before me

Ek khel hai aurang-e-Suleman meray nazdeek
Ek baat hai aijaz-e-Masiha meray aage

For me the flying throne of Solomon is a game
And only talk, the miracles of Christ before me

Ghalib earned his immense popularity in the 19th Century
and much later after his death in the 20th Century and beyond by
his easy expression, a touch of satire in the most serious of the
thoughts, and ability to rake up contemporary issues, as well as
simply putting and relishng own follies including alcoholism etc.

Mazrooh Sultanpuri

A man with immense gift of words, a very adaptive style, a flair
for classical urdu rendition as well as for flamboyant hindi film
songs, he surprised Indian generations with his variety and ease
of lyrics between 1950s to start of the 21st century and left behind
such a legacy of nazms, shayari and hindi film songs, which have
been leaders in their own sense in shaping the society, reflecting
its mood, portraying social change as well as makig Stars and
superstars out of the heroes. But for them could we imagine our
soldiers, postmen, farmers, clerks, doctors, engineers, officers,
housewives deliver on the given duties. The range of songs he
wrote, depicted message, vision, ideology, the way forward and
poise which was well taken up by a ricksaw puller and by an Officer
as well. These compositions even set the tone for cross country
relations and revelry through cultural exchange. The following
four nazms, *ham hain mataye...., liye baitha hai dil..., jal ke......,*
and, ham ko junoon kya...., are a testimony to his skills.

((xv) Reference picture on page 154)

मजरूह सुल्तानपुरी

हम है मता-ए-कूचा-ओ-बज़ार की तरह

हम हैं मता-ए-कूचा-ओ-बाज़ार की तरह
उठती है हर निगाह ख़रीदार की तरह
इसकू-ए-तिश्नगी में बहुत है के एक जाम
हाथ आ गया है दौलत-ए-बेदार की तरह
वो तो हैं कहीं और मगर दिल के आसपास
फिरती है कोई शयनिगाह-ए-यार की तरह
सीधी है राह-ए-शौक़ प यूँ ही कभी कभी
ख़म हो गैइ है गेसू-ए-दिलदार की तरह
अब जा के कुच खुला हुनर-ए-नाख़ून-ए-जुनून
ज़ख़्म-ए-जिगर हुए लब-ओ-रुख़्सार की तरह
'मजरूह' लिख रहे हैं वो अहल-ए-वफ़ा का नाम
हम भी खड़े हुए हैं गुनहगार की तरह

लिए बैठा है दिल इक अज़्मे-बेबाकाना बरसों

लिए बैठा है दिल इकअज़्मे-बेबाकाना बरसों से
कि इसकी राह में हैं काबा-ओ बुतख़ाना बरसों से

दिले-सादा न समझा, मासिवा-ए-पाकदामानी
निगाहे-यार करती है कोई अफ़साना बरसों से
गुरेज़ा तो नहीं तुझसे मगर तेरे सिवा दिल को
कई ग़म और भी हैं ऐ ग़मे-जानाना बरसों से

. . . .

वही 'मजरूह', समझे सब जिसे आवारा-ए-ज़ुल्मत
वही है एक शमए-सुर्ख़ का परवाना बरसों से

हमको जुनूँ क्या सिखलाते हो
हमको जुनूँ क्या सिखलाते हो हम थे परेशाँ तुमसे ज़ियादा
चाक किये हैं हमने अज़ीज़ों चार गरेबाँ तुमसे ज़ियादा
. . . .
. . . .

हम भी हमेशा क़त्ल हुए अन्द तुमने भी देखा दूर से लेकिन
ये न समझे हमको हुआ है जान का नुक़साँ तुम से ज़ियादा
ज़ंजीर-ओ-दीवार ही देखी तुमने तो "मजरूह" मगरहम
कूचा-कूचा देख रहे हैं आलम-ए-ज़िंदाँ तुम से ज़ियादा

जला के मशाल-ए-जान

जला के मशाल-ए-जान हम जुनूँ सिफात चले
जो घर को आग लगाए हमारे साथ चले

दयार-ए-शाम नहीं, मंजिल-ए-सहर भी नहीं
अजब नगर है यहाँ दिन चले न रात चले
सुतून-ए-दार पे रखते चलो सरों के चिराग
जहाँ तलक ये सितम की सियाह रात चले
. . . .
बुला ही बैठे जब अहल-ए-हरमतो ऐ मजरूह
बगल मैं हम भी लिए एक सनम का हाथ चले

Innumerable of his songs have been reverberating off the radio into the hearts of young, old, men and women across the borders and oceans and stoking the same passion, positiveness and liveliness since ages, and include:

इन बहारों में अकेले न फिरो..., इतना हुस्न पे हुज़ूर न ग़ुरूर कीजिए..., उठेगी तुम्हारी नज़र धीरे-धीरे..., चलो सजना, जहाँ तक घटा चले... ,छलकाएँ जाम, आइए आप की आँखों के नाम..., छोड़ दो आँचल जमाना क्या कहेगा...,चुरा लिया है तुमने जो दिल को..., दिल का भँवर करे पुकार..., प्यार का राग सुनो, दिल पुकारे, आरे आरे आरे...,दिलबर दिल से प्यारे..., इक दिन बिक जाएगा, माटी के मोल...., हम हैं राही प्यार के..., होठों में ऐसी बात मैं दबा के चली आई...., इक लड़की भीगी भागी सी...., इन्हीं लोगों ने ले लीन्हा दुपट्टा मेरा...., जब तक रहे तन में जिया...., ख़्वाब हो तुम या कोई हकीकत...., कोई जब राह न पाए..., मेरे सँग आए...., क्या हुआ तेरा वादा...., लेके पहला पहला प्यार..., माना जनाब ने पुकारा नहीं..., मेरी भीगी भीगे सी, पलकों पे रह गए...., मीत ना मिला रे मनका....,ओ हसीना जुल्फ़ों वाली जाने जहाँ..., ओ मेरे दिल के चैन....., ओ मेरे सोनारे, सोनारे, सोना..., पापा कहते हैं बड़ा नामकरेगा..., पत्थर के सनम....,पुकारता चला हूँ मैं, राही मनवा दुख की चिंता क्यूँ सताती है, रात कली इक ख़्वाब में आई, रहें न रहें हम, महका करेंगे, रुला के गया सपना मेरा !!

Mazrooh Sultanpuri was one of the stalwart trio, the other two being Kaifi Azmi and Sahir Ludhianwi, who contributed literary jewels as situational film songsfrequently backed with a marvelous musical track by musical greats in the Indian film industry, including S D Burman, Roshan, Ravi, Gulam Mohammed, Shankar jaikishan, Laxmikant Pyarelal, R D Burman, Jaidev, Khayyam, O P naiyyar, Madan Mohan and many others. The stand alone feature of his composition was often classic urdu shayari, presented in an easier, soulful composition and rendition.

The Leading Pop, Music and Rock Icons: 1900-2000

The 20ᵗʰ Century, the period between 1900 to 2000, can be wisely called as the era of soul stirring, eccelestial and awe inspiring compositions and music, which can be felt, remembered and revered with a deep sense of greatness to the magical heroes behind them. Imagine human pathos, affection, comic momments, love, sensuality, social comments, political expressions, protest, anger, deep sorrow or pain, evry emotion could be identified expressed in the most astonishing and beautiful fashion in one or the other composition, song, play, ballad or theatrical expression.

The Century also stands paradoxical to this great era of human exptression of highest echelons, as against the brutality, enmity, rage, force and destruction witnessed by the world in the form of the two World Wars. Naturally attribution may be done to as many of factors and causes as possible to the reasons behind the global conflicts, but one thing can be said for certain and that is-musical creations must have been the major force that helped people withstand this onslaught of destruction, rally behind each other, and rise again from the bed every next day with same human enthusiasm and passion expecting a better world.

From ballads to vaudeville to Broadway to jazz to blues to rock and roll to rock, people were regaled with different styles of music, giving them the best of their times, whether, deprived, well off or the the ones who ruled and governed.

After the initial phases of evolving performing arts with music as a strong component, including the minstrel shows, the blackface performances in the 19ᵗʰ Century, followed by the more bolder Extravaganzas, inviting songs with implicit contents, and then to the toned down Vaudeville performances, decent enough for ladies and children to sit through and watch at the beginning of 20th Century, all these ultimately paved the way for the larger landscaped theatrical performances with substantial musical content, viz., the Broadways theatres, which attracted a huge pool of successful talent of musicians, song writers and production houses, including the biggest of them all, the Gilbert and Sullivan, the British Operas which were immensely popular as compared to American operas. Songwriters like George Gershwin, Vincent Youmans, Irving Berlin, Porter, Kern and others, and producers including Cohan, Cook, Europe and Johnson, made a mark.

((xvi) Reference picture on page 155, 156)

Ragtime, a notably black ethnic music followed, with stars like Scott Joplin becoming immensely popular, giving way ultimately to the waves of other music including Blues and Classic Female Blues, helped with Thomas Edison's recording phonographs, making the music available to a large population. Female blues era had some great singers including Bessie Smith, Mamie Smith, Ma Rainey, Sophie Tuckers & others with popular tracks including *"Some of these days"* and *"Crazy Blues"*.

The Popular jazz period after 1920s was notable for many styles, including Swing, Blue notes, Syncopation and others to mark the jazz medleys with Paul Whiteman as the most popular of them all. The Blues diversified into the faster Rhythm and Blues and also the Country music, mixed with Anglo Celtic songs, and finaly emerging as Rock and Roll wirgh R and B mixed with country music by the 1960s. Then started the true Pop era helped by the gramophone records and their sales, giving rise to Italian-American singers including Perry Como, Tony Bennett, Dean Martin and the biggest of them all-Frank Sinatra.

Music as a money making industry got a further, and a major push with emergence of the star- Elvis Presley, bringing Rock and Roll back with a tremendous success with Philips of Memphis Tennesse and Sun Records bringing out the songs. *The era of teenage stars had begun!!*

Frank Sinatra and Elvis Presley: Pioneers in the Pop and Rock industry

Finaly the era of Rock and hard Rock started with bands like Surf, The Beach Boys, individuals like Bob Dylan, The Doors, and others. The final mega stars were the English groups, The Beatles, The Rolling Stone, The Moody Blues and The Zombie which marked the English invasion of American music.

((xvii) Reference picture on page 157)

Beatles were in fact a cultural phenomenon during 1960s

Counterculture rock or the psychedelic rock made into the mainstream with performers like Timothy Leary and the Band – The Greatful Dead, which then merged with other forms of

Rock including punk rock, heavy metal and other forms which originated from near San Fransisco, and popularized further by bands like Chicago. Disco or the dance songs of the underground dance clubs caught the fancy of the people between 1970 and further, represented by the immensely popular band Bee Gees and the soundtrack of Saturday Night Fever

The Beatles and Bob Dyllan Rocked the world, truly ....

Dona Summers, American song writer and singer, ruled the Disco wave in the 1970s with hits like *"This time I know its for Real", "Love to love you baby", I feel love", Hot Stuff", "Dim all the nights", Last Dance", "No more tears"* and many more which were a rage in dance clubs. A frequent Grammy winner included in the Rock and Roll Hall of Fame and labeled by Billboard as the 6th most successful dance artist, Dona Summers constantly hit top 20 and top 10 on the UK and US charts. George Michael, Celione Dione, Barbara Striesand, Venessa Williams and even .... made the people groove with soft melodious souns of disco, rhythm and blues in the 1980s and 1990s. The era could well be remembered for the mystic feeling of sweet, innocent and chirpy romance in the air, everywhere around.

((xviii) Reference picture on page 157)

Hard rock or metallic rock also referred to as psychedelic rock further gained in prominence by the end of 1970s with bands like *Eagles (Hotel California, Desperado, Witchy Woman, take it easy), Dire Straits (Dire Straits, Sultans of Swing, Private Investigation, Brothers in Arms, Money for Nothing), Police (outlands de Amor, Ghost in the machine, Every breath You Take, Reggatta de blanc), Men at Work (Down under, Business as Usual, Two Hearts)* doling out these tremendous hits, most of which topped in both British and US charts and also bagged frequent Grammy and Brit awards. Most of these bands have made it to the Rock and Roll Hall of Fame, Rolling Stones top 500 and also in World's best selling artistes of all time lists.

((xix) Reference picture on page 158)

Lead vocalists and guitarists from the above bands and their team made a huge impact on the youth through the decades in the 20th Century, both with their music and composition and style and fashion as well. Thus Sting, Summers, Copeland (Police), Mark Knopfler, David knopfler, Illsley, Withers (Dire Straits), Hay, Ham, Speiser (Men at Work), Rhodes, Roger Taylor, John Taylor, Andy taylor (Duran Duran) became style statements themselves in the 1970-1980s.

Mark Knopfler, with his tall brooding persona and heavy baritone became a rage as a lead vocalist and guitarist in the metallic genre.

((xx) Reference picture on page 158)

By the 1990s different groups chose their own style of composition, music, content, story, mood and presentation. While some retained the purose of presenting good instrumental music on stage and live performances, including Boyz II Men, who rather retained the '70s R and B style presenting soulful songs *(Coolyhighharmony, End of the Road, Motownphily, Its so hard to say Goodbye)*, Bryan Adams, earning a crazy following more as an individual lead vocalist with a baritone that incited hysteria in live shows, but with compositions and songs as mellow and soft as could be *(Run to You, Summer of 69, You Want it You get It, Straight from the Heart, All For Love, Have You ever loved a Woman and many more).* Others expanded their horizon, to focus on the presentation, by adding excellent team members in picturisation and editing, and a storyline as a parallel video with the song, or rather the story told through the song. Madonna, in 1990s and 2000 became a rage with often soft and agonising compositions, melodious rhythm and a sensational video to tell the storyline (Take a bow!!).

((xxi) Reference picture on page - 159,160)

Others took to instrumental in a big way, including Eric Clapton, rated in top ranks in the Rollingstones and ranked many a time in Rock and Roll Hall of Fame, and conferred many a Grammys, besides being rated in the top 50 global guitarists of all time, and remained a loyal hard metallic rock instrumentalist, inspiring many others. Many next generation Groups including Guns and Roses kept the ardent fans of hard metallic alive with their heady mix of metallic tunes.

((xxii) Reference picture on page 161, 162)

The young girl brigades in the late 1990s, 2000 and in recent years have taken a leaf out of their predecesssors, added their personal flair, style, passion and panache and meade a great statement with their works including Britney Spears, *Christina Aguilira (Reflections, Geanie in a bottle, All I want is You, What a Girl Wants) and lately Katty Perry (One of the boys, I kissed a Girl, Hot and cold, California Girls, Teenage Dreams, The One that Got Away, Wide Awake, Ur so Gay.... for which even Madonna expressed her fondness)and Lady Gaga (The Fame, Just Dance, Poker Face, The Fame Monster, Bad Romance, Telephone, Alejandro, Born This Way, The Edge of Glory, You and I),* who have taken forward the charisma of melody, beats and visuals that Madonna was capable of and have been a rage amongst the young generations.

((xxiii) Reference picture on page 163, 164)

All woman bands like En Vogue *(Hold on, Born to sing, You don't have to worry, Free Your mind),* and others including Bangles (gave some beautiful tracks in between) underlining the point that they were no less when it came to making great, feet tapping and melodious compositions which could last for eternity.

((xxiv) Reference picture on page 165)

Of late, the music industry, has been experimenting with lots of sounds, genres and styles, and singers including Enrique Iglesias have had a stunning impact using faster tenured, tempered sounds and beats from spanish and continental music and compositions which have fired the imagination and sensuality of the Generation X and others to come.

((xxv) Reference picture on page 166)

Many others in the 20th Century and of the recent leading musicians have come out with songs that are contemporary, soulful, thoughtful as well as reflective of the general, and sometimes collective mood of people, or even countries, putting them on adifferent pedestial. These include Sir Elton John, Pink Floyd, Stevie Wonder, Mariah Carey and more recently Rehana, who have been recognished for the finesse they allocate to their compositions.

19.

GANDHI: The Mercurial, Innovative Mass Leader

…. The leader who defeated the British with love, truth and without violence

CONTEXT:

Emergence of Gandhian philosophy in leadership of Indian masses taking a stand against the authoritarian and exploitative British rule became evident through his personal stamp of non violence and satyagraha (urging the truth through a mass protest) on protests like Civil Disobedience in the 1925 and later the Dandi March in 1930s. Gandhiji could well exemplify the best management principles relevant today, adopting the philosophy of "Learn, Unlearn and Relearn" to the hilt, when he came back from South Africa as a modern, well educated well off barrister having adapted the western sartorial style and living, and then deciding to take an all India travel to decipher and learn the indian culture and psyche in the vast rural India, and finaly taking on a lifestyle that could help him make an immediate connect with the masses and mobilize the public anguish against the British en masse, to bring forth issues and create the desired impact of nationalist movements. Gandhian philosophy explicitly demonstrates an indepth understanding of local and larger nationalistic issues of a rural India of that time and the long-term peaceful struggle that was the way forward to achieve the goal of swaraj.

Although various factors between 1910 to 1947 made great impact on the freedom struggle and its outcome, including the World Wars and their impact on global British empirialism, the labour strife, communism and movements in different countries and their impact on Indian psyche, the contribution by the relatively radical thoughts and freedom fighters who believed in the impact of a forceful response to a subversive and sometimes violent British rule over the masses, Gandhian philosophy became instrumental in making the British understand by 1945 that it was impossible to govern subsequently and things were out of their control, by a string of movements in which Gandhiji emerged as the main leader the British tried to engage with to manage and communicate with the masses, with their hands full with World War II and Japanese crisis. In the later stages of his movements, even Gandhiji, specifically in the "Quit India movement" in the 1940s and the violent subversive British response to it and a subconscious realization that it was now or never, had to subscribe to the thaught of "Do or Die", the call for resorting to all means to give the last major push to gain independence.

Gandhian philosophy, though seemingly in contrast to British industrialization, can be in fact interpreted as very much a philosophy supportive of pro rural small scale enterprises very relevant to a rural India at that time.

Moahndas karamchand Gandhi, started as a barrister, and after an international stint at South Africa, suffering racist humiliation, came back stronger to India with a first hand experience and the feel of social discrimination, privileges of the ruling and the plight of the ruled. After handling typical civil, land and other legal disputes of the masses, he realized that there was more to India and Indians than just serving the British with humiliation. On the basis of his wisdom, he collated the situation into his philosophy, which on one hand identified the facets of Indian citizen and society which could be improved upon for changing the mindset from a subservient to a self confident one and from a fragmented diaspora into a nationalistic, coherent group, and on the other hand, initiated and gradually developed upon a series of social patterns which were effective in communicating to the British, as a ruler, that they were unwanted and no more held in the highest esteem if they did not reciprocate the same gestures to the common Indian citizen.

It was the first instance of a nationalist spirit, which aimed at dethroning the rulers by making them self realize their undoing to the society. Undoubtedly, the parallel coercive protests by the other freedom fighters including Bhagat Singh, Azad and others and the burden of World War II, helped seriously divert and deplete the British administration and army, but Gandhian philosophy had left its deep impression on the British, as they had never seen, faced or fought before, and there was a sense of appreciation to the same amongst quite a bulk of the administrators within India and in Britain at that time, which finally helped culmination of the prolonged events of freedom struggle into the British withdrawal and Indian independence, which was although marred by the unpleasant division, which even Gandhiji could not help.

The Facets of Character That Gandhiji Emphasized to Build Upon:

Satya (Truth): Gandhiji emphasised on truthfulness in thought, speech and action as the cornerstone for a meaningful life. He

227

stressed on the aspect to make people in India wake up to the fact that they could bond with each other only through this common thread of truthfulness, which could be an opening or start of meaningful communication between people and sharing of unbridled thoughts through the confidence that the other person would be honest in his opinion. This would in turn bolster the confidence and harmony within the community, which he emphasized as the force that could stand up to the larger cause of satyagraha. Various writings on same are available in back volumes of *"Yeravada Mandir" and "Diary of Mahadev" Bhai.*

Ahimsa: Gandhiji, realizing the uselessness of destructive or violent protests against the authoritarian and exploitative British regime, being sure that it would only cause a ripple, which could be overawed by an immediate British administrative backlash, emphasized on the concept of Ahimsa, wherein one should not harbor major feeling of vengeance against others and rather just have a strong opinion on an issue and express the same with full conviction. This he believed would guarantee a better hearing by the power to be in the British regime and also not attract an immediate brutal retaliatory crushing action, and thus could sustain longer and build up to create a magnificient impact for demand for sovereignity. In various contemporary issues of *Young India* in the preindependence days, he preached on acquiring the trait of ahimsa to restrain the public anger so that it could be manifested as a common concern and cause for representing the greater idea of sovereignity with a magnitude and thrust that could create an impact. Thus he admired the trait of ahimsa as that possessed by the brave and even proposed love for the enemies, and compared it to the strength to face death without flinching.

Asteya (Non-stealing): Gandhiji wanted the public to develop the capability to be in full control of their needs as this could temper the trait of asteya, a desire for stealing in the true sense, which could be manifested as a desire to acquire beyond one's capabilities and capacity, causing disruption and violence in harmonious community bonding. He mentioned the same in various articles in *Yeravada Mandir and Bapu ke Ashirwad*. Gandhiji wanted people to control their greed so that they could curb the habit of looking upto and expecting from the British regime for their privilages and could say no to their largesse whatever there were and claim for sovereignity.

Aswada (Control of the Palate): Gandhiji tried to bring down the divide between the haves and have nots and very poor Indian citizens by propogating philosophy of rationalization and avoiding over indulgence. The more he could bring homogeneity amongst people, the more he could unite them for the bigger cause. Thus he propogated the concept of *aswada*, or feeding one's body only for the maintenance of physical health and remaining in a state of being healthy and well balanced, and not for treatment of body as a refuse bin indulging in unwanted food. He mentions many such issues in *"My Philosophy of Life"*, and they also find mention in *"Speeches and Writings of Mahatma Gandhi"*

Brahmcharya was another way Gandhiji exhorted Indians to come together in abstinence and and refraining from consumerism and putting pressure on the British Trading company and regime by not using the goods promoted by them. In Bapu's letters to Mira, he urges people to refrain from indulgence in all senses, with the principle aim of creating a common conviction of uniting for a common cause against the British regime. He set an extraordinary example of leading people aginst consumerism and market at that time and for the same he showed an outstanding style of leading by example, wherein he himself had to act as a religious preacher. He often thus forbade people from indulgence in suggestive pictures, stimulating food and thus burning their fingers in fire.

Aparigraha (Non-possession):Parallel to the above values, he promoted *aparigrah,* or the willingness to have bare minimum possession of things as required for daily life and not falling prey to hoarding or over possession. He exhorted values of service to fellow beings as a source of joy and not looking around for pleasure in things, as mentioned in *Bapu ke Ashirwad and Mahatma.* He was thus creating the first sense of being content and managing within the available resources.

((xxvi) Reference picture on page 166)

Sharirshrama (Bread Labour): Gandhiji understood the empirialistic psyche of British very early and wanted the concept of ruling and the ruled immediately obliterated from the Indian thoughts, and so he relied on this principle of sharirshram or body labour, where he convinced even the well off to engage in body labour every day to carry out their various tasks and even achieve livelihood through some self efforts, however opulent they were. This was a distinct way to make people develop a love for physical work and develop compassion for the labourers and workers, again a big effort in unifying the masses irrespective of their class, for the larger aim of initiating nationalistic movements. In *Harijan and Young India* he has clearly made many refrences to physical work, not just for the sake of it but to develop a selnse of service to mankind.

Sarvatra Bhayavarjana (Fearlessness): As a great leader, he needed people, who had settled down as poor, downtrodden subservient masses to the British rule, to rise and take a stand, and this could not be done without instilling a sense of fearlessness or *bhayavarjana,* a sense of fear against, injury, hunger, insult, death, ghosts and other's anger. At the same time he wanted the masses to not be arrogant or over aggressive and be restrained for the larger aim and the longer struggle that he was about to take up. Many of his speeches, as in *"Harijan" and "Bapu ke Ashirwad"* mention the same.

Sarva Dharma Samantva (Equality of the religions): Gandhiji had another herculean task at his hand, before he coud lead the masses in droves against the British regime; that of uniting the people following different religious thoughts. It was relevant that the people could understand that all the religions followed the same fundamental truth of being subservient to the greater power known by different names and practicity social harmony in day-to-day life causing minimum harm to others. Thus a thought that all religious philosophies have some basics in agreement and no basic fundamental running counter to each other, gandhiji preached the principle of *sarva dharma samantva* in all his community meetings and writings too, as evident through such writings mentioned in *"Harijanbandhu" and "Harijan"* in various issues. He was also aware of the British tacftics of ruling through well thought divisive practices over the years and this thought was supreme in his scheme of things to help masses present a united face for a prolonged struggle for independence or *swaraj*.

Swadeshi (Use Locally Made Goods): Another major realization, that the British regime was exploiting the local resources to make their own national interests and industry stronger by bringing back goods from their country and popularizing amongst the Indian masses, and making them opt for American wheat or Cloth brands like Regent Street, led Gandhiji to further define his thoughts for initiating a movement he called as *"swadeshi"*. He defined it as a concern for one's most near or proximal neighbor and environment or the so called first care, to make sure that we satisfy all our daily needs by a way of general or business interaction with these neighbours, so that they grow along with us and are clothed and fed by the resources generated through these mutual transactions, taking the nation as a whole to a path of growth and glory. Although we are not binded in respect to what and from where we procure the things for our use from distand or remote places, but this will definitely not be a service to humanity whereby the near ones will be neglected, as mentioned in vaious issues of *"Young India"*.

Sparshbhavna (Untouchability): Another issue that plagued the Indian society at that time was a divide by the principle of untouchability or *sparshbhavna*, wherein a person, by way of his birth in a particular family or state was labeled untouchable, creating barriers in communication, human bonding and love and harmony towards each other. This principle causes rifts in the society, which Gandhiji thought was another major stumbling block in uniting the people against the oppressive British rule. Gandhiji propogated removal of this practice as mentioned in various issues of *Yeravada Mandir and Young India,* whereby love and service could be done to mankind.

Thus Gandhian philosophy and its interpretation reveal deeper sense of astute management principles Gandhiji used in creating a cohesive society focused and ready to work towards the same goal of achieving independence. The philosophy thus entails all tenets of proactiveness, effective communication and well laid out goals.

20.

The American and the Indian story: receptive and all encompassing

…..The parallel and the paradox

CONTEXT:

Although starting in a similar fashion after gaining independence, and with a similar inherent receptive and all encompassing nature, US has been able to draw more constructive contribution from diverse diaspora towards industrialization, technical advancements, national growth and development of the nation and the original settlers or citizens. India on the other hand, till independence, and understandably only since the last seventy odd years has been able to define a national identity after having been severed, plundered and traumatised by various foreign invasions and settlements. Both nations are not typically fanatic about their racial origin and are respectful to other races, religions and thoughts, but there is a visible difference in how the national interests have been defined, developed, ingrained, protected and taken care of by the masses and the state.

The Indian culture, with roots in grand and inspirational preachings of the Ramayana, Gita, Mahabharata, vedas and Puranas, developed as a system of value based social and administrative norms, wherein the public interest at large was taken care of by the rulers who exhibited highest practice of just and compassionate conduct, as mentioned in the Ramayana, with great lessons on the human and interpersonal fallacies and aspirational confrontations between communities, as in the Mahabharata, and the associated philosophical and the greatest preachings on the value of unattached and devoted work, as in *The Holy Geeta*. The society thus drew inspiration from the high moral conduct of the exemplary idols and developed as a philosophical society, which tried to be religious to their duties and deeds (*the karma*), being receptive and compassionate to others and yet striving for the best of efforts and thoughts. Thus, the focus being more on inner development, material and physical gains being not the primary focus, Indian society invited wide contribution from diverse thinkers and philosophers including, Kabir, Ravidas, Guru nanak, Mahaveer, Gautam Buddha and even welcomed the philosophy of human bonding as brought in by traders and conquerers, including the thoughts and vision of the Holy kuran and Holy Bibel. It also welcomed literature and other creative compositions including *Suphi, Shayari, Ghazal* and many diverse writing styles, growing rich in the tradition of human evolution. Thus the Indian story is that of receptivity and all encompassing nature, but with a folly that after the golden age of Chandragupta Maurya and Gupta dynasties, the vast Indian diversity was subjected to loot and plunder by conquerers and traders from outside, taking some advantage of this harmlessness.

American culture, after declaring independence from the colonial era, drew lessons from the gains of labour and openness to ideas, thus basing its policy on diversity and plurality, reflected in a similar all encompassing and receptive version as in India, but with a rider that diversity was welcome if it could contribute to national growth of United States. The diversity became more and more evident in the 20th Century, as the requirement for industrial advancements through discoveries and innovation gained ground. Thus after an initial phase of agricultural economy, US made good use of its diaspora in providing them an atmosphere where in exploration, innovation, contribution and entrepreneurship were given due recognistion and business opportunities, thereby also stimulating the process of national development at a faster pace. Thus oil exploration, oil based economy, industrialization, machineries and then communication and technology industries flourished mainly as individual entrepreneurship soared.

There is a contrast though in how the two countries managed the visitors at different times. The Indian subcontinent through the period 1000 AD to the time of becoming a full fledged British Colony, comprised of different kingdoms spread across different regions and states, who had their own conflicts of interests and somewhere this set the tone for foreign invaders and rulers to enter, establish base, spread out and plunder, and even settle for long time, taking initial help from one or more of the Indian rulers. Thus initialy the Mughal empires and Sultanets, and later the East India Trading Company and the British Empire established their rule across major parts and harnessed the geographical and human resources to the benefit of their own countries for a long period.

The Indian culture imbibed different habits, customs, rituals, dressing styles, arts and music from these settlers and became more and more heterogeneous. The things thus being out of control, India was in a sense mainly exploited and not contributed to by the foreign visitors till independence, in contrast to America, who had been able to establish a clear foreign policy which took appropriate measures through the years to guard its sovereignity and the interest of the original citizens.

India has been able to generate some technological advancements from foreign visitors,viz., courtesy the British rule, including the extensive railways and railways management system, which has very well helped the Indian growth post independence, the Administrative Services infrastructure which has helped maintain and grow vastly segregated areas by ensuring systematic flow of resources to and fro these areas to the governments at the state and central level, although acquiring its own stigma of corruption on the way years after independence. However, more relevant, fruitful foreign collaborations have happened through the 20th and in the 21st Century, as the focus of the world is changing from conflicts to issues management in the interest of business promotion, financial stability and increasing quality of life. Both, The United States of America and India, have been fortunate to have the advice, counsel and contribution by eminent industrialists in their gorowing years. While America saw a greast surge in Oil exploration entrepreneurs, Indian counterparts, prominently the TATAs and the Birlas were instrumental in entrepreneural expansion in the minerals exploration industry as well as the agro industrial produce and related industries. It can be seen that, the early industrialists in both America, be it Rockfellar in Petroleum industry, Andrew Carnegie in Coal and Iron industry, or Henry Fordin automotive industry, and those in India, including TATAs, Birlas, Mathais, Thakurdas, Singhanias, Chinoys, Goenkas, Kirloskars, kotharis, Modis, Bajajs, Poddars, Amins and Lodhas and others, worked on the principle of philanthropy guided capitalism, well reflected by the statement by Andrew Carnegi;

This, then, is held to be the duty of the man of wealth: First, to set an example of modest, unostentatious living, shunning display or extravagance; ... and, after doing so, to consider all surplus revenues which come to him simply as trust funds, which he is called upon to administer... to produce the most beneficial results for the community—the man of wealth thus becoming the mere trustee and agent for his poorer brethren, bringing to their service his superior wisdom, experience and ability to administer, doing for them better than they would or could do for themselves."

Somewhere down the line, with increasing competition there have been phases of dilution of philanthropist values in both countries, as represented by the statement by Vanderbilt as follows, but have been countered in acts and spirits by giants such as Bill Gates Foundation, Infosys and others in both countries: *Law? Who cares about the law. Hain't I got the power?"* — Comment alleged to have been made by Cornelius Vanderbilt, when warned that he might be violating the law

Another paradox in USA and Indian development is a clear understanding in US of the importance of infrastructure by way of a magnificient and integrated system of lake and river water transport system much early in the 18th and 19th Century along with the road and rail road systems which gave immense speed and fillip to the industrialization process, reducing movement hurdles for business. India has been witness to an integrated road and highway system development only of late by the turn of 20th Century, and in a typical fact that industrialization has proceeded unbridled despite movement hurdles & poor infrastructure over the years and private entrepreneurs have excelled despite this setback over the years to at least keep India in the reckoning in many industrial segments like agriculture, chemicals, pharmaceuticals, IT and others. The matter for river connectivity and transport has caught the fancy now and may see developments in near future. Two nations with great entrepreneurs, private players, but different perspectives in development, which seemingly stand out, due to the difference in period of independent existence without external rule, and also in some way to the differences in approach to the developmental issues. Still India seems to be catching up, having started late.

Paradoxically, India and its IT professionals took to IT developments in the last decade of 20th Century and in early years of 21st Century, quite seriously, and with a proactive government policy on the telecommunication and information technology, coupled with greater Technology education options available, these professionals steered miles ahead and have been a prominent part of the US Silicon Valley IT industries, as also in many other places in the globe, apart from making a big impact in the Indian industrial economy.

Both countries are presently being steered by governments with more postured views on nationalism, welfare of the citizens and jobs for native professionals as against the migrant professionals, and flair for protectonist trade policies, in favour of domestic business houses.

21.

India through the Ages

....The mammoth elephant moves on

CONTEXT:

The amazing, simple, rustic yet charming post independence Indian growth story. The post independent majorly rural India has patiently toiled in the sun, silently supporting the governments, abiding by the constitution and sending their sons and daughters in the service of the nation and community as nurses, transport, army and other employees, always believing in the virtues of honesty, simplicity and compliance. The incumbent governments led by tall leaders from Pandit Nehru to Shastri to Ms Indira Gandhi, to Morarji Bhai to Rajiv Gandhi to I K Gujral to Atal Biharijee to Manmohan Singh and Sh Narendra Modithrough the years, steered India and its masses with stringent budgets, establishing basic institutions in agriculture, industrial, education, health, rural and urban development, basic and advanced research and technology, also trying to ensure that the basic needs of the poorest of poor were taken care of. It has been a tightrope walk, very delicate one for the initial leaders, more so the same for later ones as the priorities for global standing and development and standards of living have drastically changed and have been a tough task to match to as a state leader.

Taking a leaf out of the global incidents including World Wars, the Iron curtain and periods of Cold war, India was

239

taken forward by leaders retaining the rural simplistic ethos, establishing higher institutes of research including agriculture, astronomy and later IT & telecommunication, to ensure that India could gradualy match steps with what was current and relevant and contribute to building a better world. The country has transformed itself from dulcet and sleepy villages to bustling towns and districts and aspiring Cities with a generation that wants to contribute in the development in many ways and rake in the benefits for a much better living in more ways than one. Thus, the Indian story is akin to that of the mammoth elephantthat moves on taking bulky steps lurching side by side, but still managing a fine balance and moving at a suitable pace with a formidable and competitive aura.

Yes, India, as a country, has been moving along like a mammoth elephant, carrying the heterogenous social mass in a very curious sloppy and sometimes amazingly swift pattern, as an elephant coming into its own and in action, but has never lost the sense of direction and speed as desired!!

India After Independence: looking For Leadership: PART I

Long back, after independence, the aspirations from the newfound freedom goaded the people to look upto the political class to show them the way forward. The population expected India to catch up with the world progress, viz., mission to the moon, atomic explosion and its pros and cons, science and space and television and cinematic technology and modern agricultural technology.

The Indian population even then consisted of groups of people with different thinking caps. The smart middle aged or septuagenarian *TAUUS* of Haryana, of the "Seen all and Been there" types, who engaged in discussions on all matters above often on, but in a limited fashion, focusing more on the job in hand and relying on their rustic wisdom for all matters related to agricultural produce and distribution and economy and their own circle of friends.

Then there was the other class who gave a deeper thought to what was about to happen nationally and globally, and even listened to advise from younger generation and adopted an all encompassing approach.

Then there was the grand Indian middle class of *BABOOS*, left behind by the British Empire in all administration Depts. The class itself consisted of different groups. The honest, positive and patriotic *baboos*, who followed a disciplined life, spending time with their families in the evening after work, and motivating their kids to work hard and become part of a forward looking independent India. The other group of *Baboos* got busy in the administration with Senior Executives in the Administrative Services, and with mutual suggestions, scheming, and selfish temperament, created their own happy world in India, reveling in making best use of rules, which could be tweeked.

The Indian Cinema made big use of these two diverse groups of *Baboos* often as pivotal characters in their cinemas and developed screenplay centered around these diametrically and dramatically opposite characters and interplay of emotions and melodrama ultimately ending in a patriotic massage. Prem Chopra, Manoj Kumar, Madan Puri, Pran, Raaj Kapoor, all together made such characters legendry with their panache and brilliant screenplay ideas, viz., *Aawara, Shri 420, Roti, Roti kapda aur makaan* and many more.

Another class consisted of *Baniyas* or the entrepreneurs, a smart class never dependent for survival even on the British Empire or even on the *Sultanat,* and rather making the best by selling their goodies at a commanding price to the kings, the

Viceroys, and the Sultans. Although not directly affected by what direction the country could move, they had their own strong sense of patriotic thinking and vision for their motherland. Although a majority of the class kept themselves busy making money, luring people with their business sense and sweetness into purchasing the goodies at skewed prices, counting their money at the end of the day and dozing off to sleep. Some of them however showed great sense of politically correct wisdom and influenced the masses during the elections regarding the choice of leaders.

The Focussed and Subdued Charismatic family Leaders and Entrepreneurs

Then there were the visionary *Lalas*, who defined the term entrepreneurship in India. The class was represented by the legendary Jamshedjee Tata, Birla, Modi, Kirloskars, and others, who put their ancestral acquisitions into judicious use and business to generate resources and wealth for themselves and at the same time generated employment for the masses and took India forward.

Leadership in Defence Services: Everchanging Paradigm:

Yet another class, the men in the Services-Army, Navy and Air Force, watched India and themselves move forward. The class was trained in discipline and integrity and sacrifice and meant to shoulder India's souverenity, and for the same always compensated with ample service benefits as per policy on job security and posthumous compensations to families including free residential help, food, canteen and other benefits during and post retirement. Many of the Servicemen remained true patriots, showing their mettle and sacrifice during the wars in 1962, 1971 and in other assignments.

Indian Military and air Force Leaders: The Param Veer Chakra Awadees

Param Veer Chakra awrdees include officers from different ranks across the Indian Defense Services. Lt Colonel Ardeshir Tarapore was one of those, who joined the Hyderabad army after commissioning in Jan 1942, served during World War II and the Middle East, and after training in the Centurian Tank in the UK, he was involved in the Indo Pak War in 1965 in Sialkot sector as a leader of Tank regiment and got martyred in September 1965, achieving the feat that out of the 69 tanks destroyed in the battle, 60 were of Pakistan and only nine were from India, for which he was awarded the highest honour.

Second Lt Arun Khetarpal, after schooling from Sanawar School, graduated from the NDA and then the IMA dehradoon in 1971 and was give the charge as a Tank Officer in Squadron B in the 47th Brigade in the Battle of Basantar against Pakistan in 1971. As the Squadron A asked for cover up during the task of buiding bridge head on Basantar river, the Squadron B including Arun Khetarpal and his team rushed to the spot, and during the retaliation by the Pakistani imported Patton Tank regiment, lost his life ensuring that he had destroyed 10 enemy tanks before death, for which he was awarded the highest honour.

Pilot Officer Nirmaljeet Singh Sekhon got commissioned into the Indian Air Force in 1967 and was in the Squadron 18 Folland Gnat Aircraftfleet at Srinagar in 1971 Indo Pak war, when 3 Sabre pairs from Squadron 26 of Pakistan Air Force attacked aboard F86 jets, when Sekhon lost no time in getting on with the task and bringing down a pair before he was himself hit and could not eject while the aircraft nosed dive, for which he was awarded the highest honour.

Other Param Veer Chakra awardees included, Banna Singh, Lance Naik Albert Ekka (IV Corps, Brigade of Guards, battle of Gangasagar, North East), Captain Gurbachan Singh Salaria (Alumnus first batch NDA, member of United Nations Peace keeping Force at Congo against secessionist State of Katanga in 1961), Colonel Hoshiar Singh (Part of the 3rd Grenadiers Regiment and carried out counter attacks against the Pakistani Army at battle of Basantar in north east in 1971 war), Naik Jadu Nath Singh (Indo Pak War 1948), Subedar Joginder Singh (Sino Indian war 1962, Sikh Regiment, Battle of Bum La Pass, North East), Subedar and Hon Captain karam Singh (Sikh Regiment, Battle of Burma World wat II, Indo Pak War 1948, Kashmir), Captain Manoj Kumar Pandey (Gurkha Rifles, employed in Kargill War at batalik Section in 1999), Havildar Piru Singh (Rajputana Regiment, Indo Pak War 1948, kashmir), Major Rama Raghoba Rane (Engineer's Corpse, 4th Dogra Regiment, Indo Pak War 1948 Rajouri, Kashmir), Major Ramaswamy Parameswaran (Indian Peace Keeping Force at Srilanka, 1987), Major Shaitan Singh(Kumaon Regiment, 1962 Sino Indian War, Battle of Rezang La), Major Som nath Sharma (Kumaon regiment, Indo Pak War 1948, Battle of Badgam, Shrinagar airport), Dhan Singh thapa, Vikram Batra and Yogendra Singh Yadav.

((xxvii) Reference picture on page 167)

Army generals over the years have displayed a steely mettle, integrity and sense of service to the nation, which has been exemplary for the forces and made a mark globally. General Kumarmangalam (World War II veteran, also held captive by Italian and German Army for some time, awarded DSO, MBE, was 7th Chief of Army Staff from 1967-70 after serving as Chief of DSS College and Deputy and Vice Chief of Army Staff), contributed greatly with inputs on reorganization, upgradationn and training and tacticts after the 1965 war and was awarded Padma Vibhushan.

Gen Sam Manekshaw (8th COAS 1969-1973, Padma Bhushan, Padma Vibhushan, served as Chief of DSS College, a great hand at Military planning and administration as part of MO and awarded Miltary Cross for his extreme valour in World War II against Royal Japanese Army in the Battle of Pagoda, where despite a life threatening multiple bullet injuries in lungs and intestine, he miraculously survived), was later awarded the first designation of Field Marshal, which perfectly recognized the extremes that he witnessed in his personal, professional and army life (having been subjected to supercession and enquiries), coming back with equal force and designated to command and organize the forces after the Sino Indian War debacle, ultimately drafting effective strategies to defeat Pak army and create Bangladesh with strategic training and support of Bangladeshi troops and Guerrillas. He was earlier also instrumental in ensuring that Indian army was effectively employed in Kashmir post independence, after King Hari Singh agreed to get it annexed to India with the impending fear of attack by Pak army, which was effectively taken care.

General Krishnaswami Sunderji (PVSM), is widely recognized as the General who vouched for greater mechanization and automation and being instrumental in the formation of The Mechanised Infantry Regiment, and also redesigning the Army manual laying great emphasis on mobility and speed. Having been part of the Royal British Army and then the Sino Indian and both Indo Pak Wars, he developed a great vision for transforming the army through integration of forces for speed and mobility, envisioning Operation Brasstacks for greater integration exercise of Forces, and also during the formation of nuclear deterrence vision. He was involved in various prominent operations including the successful Operation Falcon during Sino Indian War in 1965 at Hathung La bridge, and other operations, which were discussed at length for their political outcomes including Operation Blue Star and the IPKF operations at SriLanka.

General V P Mallik (PVSM, AVSM) was the COAS between 1997-2000 during the kargill War, which again demanded an instant response on a tough terrain with very high altitude, where even the Air Force could not be used to a great amount to give strategic support to the army units, and even after a mass mobilization of about 200000 troops, effectively 30000 soldiers were utilized on the kargil Batalik sectors on Srinagar Leh Highway. Due to the successful completion of Pakistani Army eviction and resultant global and specifically American pressure on Pakistan, Gen Mallik is remembered for having succesfuly led the operations with all the complexities of the terrain.

Other Generals who have kept the Army flag and spirits flying soaring high, include Gen R S Jadeja (DSO, COAS 1955), Gen S M Shrinagesh (COAS 1955-57), Gen K S Thimayya (DSO, ADC, COAS 1957-1961), Gen P N Thapar (COAS 1961-1962), Gen J N Chaudhary (PVSM, DSO, COAS 1962-1966), Gen G G Bewoor (PVSM, COAS 1973-1975), Gen T N Raina (Padma Bhushan, MVC, COAS 1975-1978), Gen O P Malhotra (PVSM, COAS 1978-1981), Gen K V Krishna Rao (PVSM, COAS 1981-1983) Gen A S vaidya (Padma Vibhushan, PVSM, MVC, AVSM, COAS 1983-1985), Gen V N Sharma (PVSM, AVSM, ADC, COAS 1988-1990), Gen S F Rodrigues (PVSM, VSM, COAS 1990-1993), Gen B C Joshi (PVSM, AVSM, ADC, COAS (1993-1994), Gen S R Chowdhary (PVSM, ADC, COAS 1994-1997), Gen Suderarajan Padmanabhan (ADC, COAS 2000-2002), Gen Nirmalchandra Vij (PVSM, UYSM, AVSM, ADC, COAS 2003-2005), Gen J J Singh (PVSM, AVSM, VSM, ADC, COAS 2005-2007), Gen Deepak Kapoor (PVSM, AVSM, SM, VSM, ADC, COAS 2007-2010), Gen V K Singh (PVSM, AVSM, YSM, ADC, COAS 2010-2012), Gen Bikram Singh (PVSM, UYSM, AVSM, SM, VSM, ADC, COAS 2012-2014), Gen Dalbir Singh (PVSM, UYSM, AVSM, VSM, ADC, COAS 2014-2016), Gen Bipin Rawat (PVSM, UYSM, AVSM, YSM, SM, VSM, ADC, COAS 2016-Incumbent).

The various Indian Chief of Air Staff over the years have also played a crucial role in strategic national matters and proved their mettle as great leaders in all strategic defence and security policy implementation be it the post independence organization of the Air Force, Indo Pak War, Sino Indian war, Kargill war or other incidents. What they did can be cited as exemplary leadership model, as it was a period which saw continuous changes and evolution in the fighter aeroplanes, their models, working and spares, with each day presenting new issues. Thus, discipline, adaptation and capacity for incessant skill upgradation, problem solving were the differentiating leadership traits desired of all of them. At an administrative level and with constant geographical threats in the form of a formidable and troublesome neighbor Pakistan, they had to be constantly on their toes, and strategicalyy on the same discussion page with the political, executive and the the other defence service elites. Thus they also needed to be outstanding in the matters of communication, team readiness, policy formation and execution.

Air Marshal Subroto Mikherjee (OBE, King George Medal, Queen Elizabeth Medal, Indian Service Medal, War Medal, IGSM and many others, CAS 1955-1960, titled "Father of Indian Force") had many firsts in his illustrious carrier, the first batch of Indians to join the Royal Air Force College, Cranewell, England, the first batch of Indian pilots at the Royal Air Force, the first to fly as an Indian Air Force pilot, the first IAF pilot to airdrop material to army, the first Squadron Leader and finaly the first Indian Commander in Chief and then the first Indian Air Marshal. He was oinstrumental in managing the North West Frontier rebellions in undivided India, fought in World War II and later instrumental in structuring the IAF as such.

Air Chief Marshal Arjan Singh (PVSM, GSM, Samar Seva Star, Raksha Medal, Distinguished Flying Cross, War Medal, India Service Medal, CAS 1964-69, first Air Chief Marshal), earned a 5 star Marshal status as the only IAF officer to get so and being on service for life, having earned great laurels during the Arakan campaign against Japan in Burma in 1944 and later during 1965 Sino Indian War. He contributed to the Indian forces in the form of strategy and organization and later as a civil servant as high Commisssioner to Kenya, Ambassador to Switzerland and even Lt Gov for Delhi.

Air Chief Marshal O P Mehra (PVSM, Padma Vibhushan, CAS 1973-1976), later Chairman HAL, Bangalore, Governer Maharashtra and Rajasthan, Air Chief Marshal Hrushikesh Moolgavkar (PVSM, MVC, CAS 1976-1978), Air Chief Marshal Idris Latif (PVSM, CAS 1978-1981) also served as Governer of Maharshtra and Ambassador to France, Air Chief Marshal Dilbagh Singh (PVSM, AVSM, VM, CAS 1981-1984), known for introduction of MIG 21 and also the supersonic Mystere IV in IAF, later served as Ambassador Brazil, Air Chief Marshal L M Katre (PVSM, AVSM, CAS 1984-1985), Air Chief Marshal Denis La Fontaine (PVSM, AVSM, VM, CAS, 1985-1988), oversaw the introduction of Mirage 2000 and MIG 29 in the IAF, Air Chief Marshal S K Mehra (PVSM, AVSM, VM, CAS 1988-1991), Air Chief Marshal N C Suri (PVSM, AVSM, VM, ADC, CAS 1991-1993), instrumental in introduction of Women Air Force Officers in ground and later in Flying duties, Air Chief Marshal (PVSM, VM, CAS 1993-1995) is remembered for innumerable assessment sorties over Bangladesh in 1971 Indo Pak War, Air Chief Marshal Satish Sareen (PVSM, AVSM, VM, ADC, CAS 1998-1998), Air Chief Marshal A Y Tipnis (PVSM, AVSM, VM, ADC, CAS 1998-2001), oversaw the critical Kargil high altitude support operations, Air Chief Marshal S Krishnaswami (PVSM, AVSM, VM, ADC, CAS 2001-2004), oversaw introduction of electronic warfare Command in IAF and indigenization, Air Chief Marshal F H Major (PVSM, AVSM, VM, ADC, CAS 2007-2009), served as Chief of Integrated Defence Staff and oversaw joint exercises with US and Singapore.

Patriotism: an invisible leadership Model

Post independence, a pleasant taste of freedom lingered on till the seventies, where people felt proud taking the names of great national leaders including Rajendra Prasad, Sardar Patel, Lal Bahadur Shastri, Maulana Azad, Ambedkar, Sarojini Naidu, with the Mahatma always revered as the guiding father figure. Honesty, simplicity and sense of duty were considered as the virtues that were most sought after and the meaning of independence and its actual implications were discussed and understood even in day-to-day affairs. This sense of independence was the source of sense of nationality and that made people work and toil in the day and come back to their houses in the evening with a proud sense of satisfaction even with a meager salaries/earnings, and continue again on the next day.

It was a common sight to see families make both the ends meet and at the same time bring up their kids despite severe scarcity of resources, where clothes of elder brother/sister in a typical lower middle class family would necessarily be preserved for later use by the younger one (whether he/she liked it or not due to the miserable feeling of having to wear used clothes every time), and the fruits, milk and breads being items of luxury and hard to earn being divided judiciously amongst siblings. But it was still not so difficult as the sense of nationality had still prevented malices like black marketing, hoarding etc to take roots at that time.

The Nehruvian era gave India a solid govt administrative setup, the instrumental Indian and Agricultural universities, the CSIR institutes and the Arts and Films and other Institutes. India was however low on consumerism with average Indian family leading a slow and laid back life everyday with father leaving for office by 10:30 AM after a hearty night's sleep and a heavy meal, and the kids often missing their 10-3 PM school, for which neither the mother nor the teachers cared too much. There being no aggressive focus on health, fitness and personality, it was irrelevant as to what was being eaten at what time, although their remains a good food pattern uniformity in all families. Still consumerism was very low or absent as an attitude

By the turn of the eighties, Indira Gandhi had given India that strong sense of confidence that inspired all sections of the society-men, women, boys, girls, young and old alike. Be it her sartorial style, her elegance, her interactions with world leaders, her flair to mix and dance with the farmers and tribes and the masses across Indian landscape, and her personal charisma spread across newspapers almost everyday, made the day for all people--the peons, the *Saahibs,* the scientists, the clerks, the *baniyaas* and the farmers alike. Her acts and decisiveness displayed amply during Bangladesh and other wars made a strong impact on men and women across all classes and ages, and it was common to see many families in all the strata of the society having their daughters named after and even groomed in a similar way with a ready to go and very strong aptitude.

Whether there was a social meet or a club party or chowpal, there was a pep, a positive pep, when people talked about Indira, India as such and the resultant global presence that India could make feel due to Indira, and everyone tried to soak in some of that sense of pride.

With the available resources and technology, Indira Gandhi and the former Prime Ministers had understood the importance of global interaction and investments required to fund the growth in various sectors in the country. By this time, maladies of hoarding, blackmarketing and corruption had hit India real time hard, coupled with the travails of natural disasters, like famines, floods and others making it worse at many places.

Leadership through Planning and Governence:

India starts making efforts to self govern post independence by way of Five Year plans

1951-56: 1st Plan allocated the budget so that Agriculture and farming land and resource development got the major fillip with 55%, budget on support to development of Industries stood at 10%, increasing public support for Transport was also decided as a key area, and got 25%, and further allocations done in various social development schemes. Growth happened at a meager 2% GDP, as expected of country low on reserves and also low on consumerism to drive the growth. Still far sightedness was amply visible with imagination and development of concepts of IITs, GGC, Steel Plant and other major infrastructural decisions. Total outlay in the budget proposed was atound 2000cr.

1956-61: IInd Plan: The Second plan saw the ideation and further expansion of of Public Sector institutions, including 6 major Steel Plants, establishment of Premiere institutes of Fundamental Research as Public Private model or Private model, including Tata Inst of Funda Res and others, which laid the foundation for higher thinking in different areas of science, humanities and social sciences, laying the foundation for exemplary higher education institutes and centres of learning, excellence and thinking. The phase saw mproved Growth pegged at 4.5% GHDP, with increase in Import of capital goods, still better infrastructure support in Transport and Social development. Agriculture got a push with heavy plan of investment in infrastructure for Irrigation along with power generation, to increase basic illumination across towns and villages. The plan outlay touched 48000 crore.

1961-66: IIIrd Plan; The 3rd plan continued on development of Irrigation canals and systems for ensuring better agricultural facility and output, which was mainly targeted at procuring bumper Wheat crops. With growing concern over neighbouhood movements across the border, Army was allocated major investents for upgradation, along with thrust on development of major bridges across strategic locations and rivers. Cement was identified as an important element for infrastructure, and fillip was given to setting up of cement plants to produce the planned capacity. Formation of Public Works Department (PWD) to maintain upkeep of town and city structures was an important aspect with upgradation of Secondary Education and associated Secondary Education Boards in all states.

1966-69: The period 1966-69 was marked as Plan Holidays, with no disturbance being done to plan expenditures over the next three years. The GDP progressed at 5% (Actual 2%)

1969-74: The IVth plan has been famous for bringing about nationalization of Banks, thus trying to bring about homogeneity in the savings and credit processes across the nation, in an effort to rectify the existing maladies. It is also prominent for redrafting out plans for greater agricultural productivity and taking giant steps towards the Green Revolution. Also prominent decision during the plan was to go ahead with acquiring nuclear deterrence through the Smiling Buddha underground Nuclear Test to deter 7th fleet by USA. The set Target GDP was 5-6%, however, the actual achievement was around 3.3%.

1974-79: The Vth Plan laid emphasis on Employement, powerty alleviation, and promulgation of the Central Electrical Power Supply Act (NTPC) to bring about integration and management of power generation and distribution across the states. It also laid out visionary plan for creation of Indian National Highway networks, to facilitate interstate transport management. The Target GDP, as a cross over from earlier plan was 4.4%, and the actual performance was better than expected at 5%.

Rolling Plans:1978-80: Rolling plans were put in place between these periods.

1980-85: The VIth Plan saw the beginning of greater Economic Liberalisation, Elimination of Price Control, and other measures to promote industrial functioning and efficacy. The target growth was pinned at 5.2%, however the actual growth was 5.4%.

1985-90: In the VIIth Plan, emphasis was laid on improvrmrnt in policies and implementation of Social justice through various enactments and provisions. Development of modern technology across various industries and specifically for Agricultural Development was one of the key areas. Poverty alleviation through various schemes, including supply of food, shelter, clothes, and other measures was allocated sufficiently in the plan. Measures to develop an independent economy were put in place. Trade promotioms policies were given enough emphasis to ensure aachievement of a reasonable Trade Deficit (200-300).

1990-92: Interim plans were put in place in this period.

1992-97: The VIIIth plan is well remembered as the Rao and Manmohan era, with great measures to further open the economy for Privatisation, Liberalisation, and modernization. India ensured that it was able to develop close working relations with WTO and similar organisations to further the efficiency of trade and business. Heavy budget outlays were planned for increased infrastructural improvements, establishment of institutions of repute at national level, and a greater fillip to human resource and increased tourism. A prominent development that took place was the effort to give the local village administration in the hands of the people through the Panchayat Raj and Nagar Palika systems. NGOs were encouraged to provide social inputs in various forms. Energy was given another big push in the form of a strong budget outlay of 26%, for conventional and nonconventional energy research and output.

1997-02: The IXth plan was put in place with Bajpayee government in power, and comprised of various Special Action Plans (SAPs), with great emphasis on Social Infrastructure, agriculture, and a well thought out Water policy, foreseeing the global changes. The targrt GDP was 7.1%, and it was reasonably monitored with actual being at 6.8%.

2002-07: The Xth plan had a GDP growth target of 8.1% and a reasonable actual achievement of 7.7%.

2007-12: The XIth Plan rolled for the period 2007-12 envisioned greater access to higher education for age groups 18-23 and converges of all formal and nonformal, IT and distant education. It envisaged a growth rate of 4% for agriculture, 10% for industry and 9% for services with environmental sustainability and reduction in gender inequality.

2012-17 (12th): The XIIth Plan envisaged reduction of poverty by 10% by various measures along with reduction in social and gender gap in school education and also ensuring high enrolment in higher education and reduction in malnutrition prevelance in age group 0-3. It also aimed at attracting private investment for Infrastructure development upto the tune of 1 trillion dollars and ensuring electricity in every village. It also envisaged availability of drinking water to 50% of village population and banking services to 90% of population.

The constitution was regularly referred to and qualitatively added upon through various important enactments which were reflected in official Gazette, Some specific examples include The nationalised Bank management and Miscellaneous Provisions Act, 1970, Indian Medicine Central Council Act 1970, IMC PG Dip Course Regulations 2010, 16 specialisations, MD Ayur,

Scheduled Area order 2003 MP, Indian Patents Act 1970, FCI
Staff Regulations Act 1971 (Amendment 2008) and others.

India, the Elephant catches speed in the '80s and '90s

India, the country, then saw the rise of the industrial phase, as
happened globally and suddenly what all sons and daughters
wanted to become was Engineers or doctors. With the advent
of the 80s, need for engineers grew in all major govt, public
and existing private sectors with mechanical engineers getting
in great demand in the agricultural, defense, assembly and
other equipments. Other sectors too started acquiring various
new branches namely, electronics, instrumentation, and
automation. Apparel industry saw a meteoric change along with
steady growth in pharma industry and electrical and electronic
appliances. A positive hope thus became available for the kids
of the literate middle-income employed families. The defence
continued to charm young generations across all income and
educated classes of the society.

Then the idea of promoting Indian youth in international
sports and tapping and promoting rural talent was fructified
as 1982 Asian Games with expected foreign investment
in infrastructure and facilities and overall upgradation and
enhancement of skill pool of India in the area of sports and
related infrastructural facilities. Industrial impetus was also
provided in some measures to the industrial sectors as per the
scenario existing at that time. Maruti being the mascot for the
aspirations of upper middle class families.

Along with Asian Games, Indian traditions and Cultural
Folk dances got an exposure to world stage and thus the art and
culture scenario was reinvigorated with governments allocating
good amount of the budget on interstate cultural interactions and

theatre establishments along with various other impetus in the form of Apna Utsav, Annual SAARC festival as promoted by the then Prime Minister Rajiv Gandhi etc. The economics associated with these fests and their live sponsored coverage on Television gave smile and taste of commercisl success to all stakeholders involved including the artists, performers, technicians, aponsors, telecasters, advertisers and even the government.

Cooperatisation and the economics as propounded by Dr Kurien, brought the white revolution, industrialization of milk production and marketing. Television and satellite advancements brought a sense of positiveness and associated increase in employement in the form of content writer, artists, technicians and other job opportunities. Advent of televised education programs and establishment of open universities like IGNOU motivated people across ages to take up to education in big way which were further bolstered by expansion of computer and networking technologies later in the rajiv Gandhi era.

India, the Mammoth Elephant, just moved on through the Ups and Downs!!

The political churning brought out a breed of political class, who differed from the Congress and distanced themselves from the party and its administrative style highlighting the rampant maladies and branding the Congress as extremely anti poor and not in the know of the ground realities. Janata Party, Vinoba Bhave, Ram Manohar Lohiya, Jai Prakash Narayan represented movements, which wanted to represent the things going wrong at various places and wanted a shift towards a better socialistic arrangement that could offer some support to the various strata of the society.

In a brief interlude between 1975-78, India had brief exposure to a biparty political system with Janta Party taking over the reins after emergency. However for various reasons, the

Govt could not sustain and fulfill the aspirations of the people and during the next elections, the reins of Govt went agin into the hands of Congress.

Apart from this, other events affected destiny of India, including operation Bluestar and massacre of Indira Gandhi, which again had a bearing on the inspiration, mood and activities of the average Indian citizens. The spirit of nationalism got a hit with people being wrongly goaded into ideas of factionalism, separatism etc. India on the roll had slightly gone on the backfoot with problems in Punjab, North East and other places. A lot of writings have already been published on all these problems. In Punjab and Assam the problems were taken to their peaks and then gradualy sorted out by a will for nationality, a conscientious administration and some political parties coming above board to join hands in the spirit of national interests and diffusing the contentious issues.

With a shot in the arm by the Rajiv Gandhi government, India's telecommunication and information technology got kickstarted and flowered into a formidable sector in the period starting mid 80s and became a major source for FDI. Parallely, the country saw a great spurt in technical education with the people realizing that a technical degree in Engineering in the core branches and even in the new IT and communication branches would take them far and guarantee a fledgling career and plenty of money. Topping a technical degree with an MBA degree also caught on the fad of the children and parents, and was taken as a bridge to assure a corporate position much early in the career and helping a candidate rise from the initial field, operational or workshop position. Education sector in India also saw a great rise since then with many educational institutes coming up in various states and other parts of country. With education becoming commercial, activities like books and stationery manufacture, transport services, educational accommodation, educational loans, educational construction also gained lots of ground.

Opening up of economy in the 1990s by Narsimha Rao and Manmohan Singh Governments, helped bring more foreign money and players and funds for development, typicaly in automobiles, hospitality, food, IT, Telecommunication, Insurance and Banking. The aggressive work culture and attractive salary packages offered by these companies turned the young generation consumer behavior upside down or rather completely on the head. Docile Indian customers got the taste of consumerism with foreign labels and brands being available in India in the sectors of clothing, suitings, styling, and even fitness and body health and physique management.

Post independence India: The flip side, the rule benders and the menace of corrution

Post independence, Indian economy, as well as the common man seemed to be too much in awe of lawyers as a profession owing to the massive role played by so many eminent personalities from the profession in Indian independence. It was also reflected in many Hindi movies where lot of protagonists played the role of a social or civil or criminal lawyer, and by the fact that every parent wanted their son or daughter to become a lawyer. This in a way played a negative role too in the development with so many people gradually interpreting the laws in their own nefarious ways trying to bend around the rules in a way to effect a wrong judgment, thereby gradually decreasing the quality of social justice and thereby eroding the sense of a nation bound by rule.

Gradually over the 70s and 80s and in the 90s, it became fashionable to have legal counselors who were experts in showing the way out of a self made crisis and subverting the law of the land. These troubleshooters earned a formidable name and also an increasing clout even within the political fraternity, with many of them gaining political posts as a member of one or the other political group. This gradually created a trend in the Indian cinema and theatre where the rule of law was severely scoffed and scorned at, viz., *Aakhiri Rasta, Andha Kanoon, Aaj Ki Awaaz* and many more, and sometimes hilariously riled and joked at as in *Jaane bhi do yaron.* As police works hand in hand with the legal system, its degradation and presence of sinister officers amongst the upright ones and the system being eaten away by its own keepers became a versatile topic for screenplay development in many Hindi Films as evident in *Khakee, Sarfarosh, Ghayal* and many more. India went through a phase where a particular section of society wanted to get ther sons attached in anyway to the police system, where it was expected that with the inspection and enforcement authority attached with the posts, whether at the constable or high up at the SP or still higher level, it could be possible to milk the authority by using and bending the rules to mutual benefits.

Yet, like everywhere else, here too exceptions could be found during many incidents including the seaside terrorist attack on Mumbai Central Taj Hotel in Mumbai. Yet the flip side to the police face got murkier during the phase, which showed exceptional rise of the underworld kingpins and the understated role of many personnel in the growth of land and other mafia. The positive side has always been that the realization of the pending doom happens just in time, initiating recovery and repair just before it is too late, thanks to some sudden political necessity and also again to some different and bold personnel who like doing the things differently, just because of the love and passion to do so. Thus somehow we are able to maintain some semblance of social order and balance, although we are *dangerously low* in guaranteeing an assurance to the general public about personal safety and that is why people still prefer to avoid unsavory *places, time and people* as golden rules for themselves and their family members to be on the safe side and maintain their self respect. Thankfully smaller towns have been lucky enough to having witnessed less of theses malaise. However small villages and hamlets have been bearing the brunt of planned political atrocities to affect desired political outcomes, causing major atrocities to the poor and the downtrodden in the process in the form of murder, rapes and communal violence.

Some people in the defence, however developed their own thought process, getting themselves busy more in the administration, climbing up the ladder, and in the process getting lured more by the perks offered by the services rather than sticking to the task and sacrifice expected of them. Thus incidences of misuse, including the free canteen doll outs and other facilities started being heard, gradually turning into cycle of corruption in larger things even concerned with defence purchases with lot of shady angles attached, earlier restricted to the lower and middle ranks, but later becoming exposed higher up too.

Incidences of intermittent misuse of military powers and positions in the form of Defence (in most cases military) excesses sometimes in J and K and sometimes in North East states as misuse of AFPOSA and other acts, appointments, transfers and promotions being influenced in one way or the other and not being on the basis of merit alone became visible sporadically in services, although being earlier restricted to lower levels but later afflicting the middle and top levels too, indicating a clear sense of loss of aura in the phrase "Service to the Nation", wherein the defense forces seemed to have blindly incorporated social and other patterns, borrowed from the west and incorporated them in their own working and life routine, and in the process these have been evident in the form of some incidents viz., peer abuse, suicides and even peer shootouts.

These matters have come up as issues, but were largely due to individual cases on indescrete actions, and the Indian army has stood the test of times as a strong, cohesive unit with myriad colours represented by armymen from diverse geographical locations, bringing with them their own level of passion and sense of service to nation.

The Indian Schyooling System: Evolution over the years, and the strain of Giving in to Societal Compulsions: The Vicious circle of Society guiding Schools

The earliest government schools in India, started as a place meant to instill a responsible sense of new found independence and ability to comply with social norms and create some skills for the typical clerical government jobs that were available in the categories Class to Class I, with children from educated and well of families generaly being lucky to have a grooming for Class I jobs.

Still in many villages, with proper rustic innocence prevalent in the kids, the Schools and class rooms meant places where a vagabond boy or a slippery girl would be sent to learn the ropes, get lessons in self discipline, self control, change to a thinking personality and learn the basics of education. This started with a father or a mother and sometimes a grandparent, pulling and dragging a relentless crying boy to the class doorstep and thereonthe master catching hold of the kid and making sure that the kid was buried deep in the scary surroundings of the classroom walls and resolved to not trouble her mother with his tantrums once allowed to reach home (However the story continued in the same vain next day). Gradually with some improvement in financial conditions, images of father dropping a happy child by a bicycle at schools also started becoming prominent, and further changed in later years to a drop by a scooter.

Thus Guptaji would be coaxed out of bed at 8 AM to take out his Vespa scooter to drop *"Pappu"* to the nearby Balniketan where he would join his friends in class III. Pappu's mother would be so anxious to get him ready with the correct pleat on the knickers and correct amount of oil on the hair neatly combed to one side. Dada and Dadi would wish him good luck and ward off demons hanging around him with measures to cast off evil eyes that would harm him.

At the same time they would be happy that *Pappu* was sent off to school and they could now escape from his tricks on them that included hiding their sticks, teeth set, spectacles and even the newspapers or clothes to dingy and dirty hide outs that left them miserable, and pestered.

Mothers would leave a sign of relief, having packed off *Pappu* to the school early in the day having escaped his million trips to the kitchen and million questions. Questions that would be basic, others that would demand an esoteric explanation, still others that would question simple logics and matters as to why a spade was a spade.

Same would the case be with *Guriya*, the tiny girl next door, who would lay hands on all kitchen items and spread out her own imaginary feast in her room making Dadi, booa (Father's sister) and mother go wild looking for the tiny spoon or the fork. In the school, however pappu and guriya would have to face *masterjee* (Sir/male Teacher) or *masterneejee* (Lady teacher) normaly a pentagenarian, struggling to cope up with the professional and personal life and just making both ends meet and being at the school, more to find answers for himself or herself, rather than for the kids handed over by their parents.

Thus the routine would start with an assembly round, with kids trotting off half asleep to the assembly area, some teachers talking and walking by the sides while others arriving just in time and trying to escape the tearing eyes of the headmaster.

The assembly would start with national song and then end, or continue with another school song (As came in practice later), a social or disciplinary or life message by the principal, and then some announcements, and then end with the rows of kids being sent back to classes, with some getting in their elements by that time, while others still dazed enough to get on, and on the verge of breaking out having to miss the comfortable environs of the home and having to cope up with the rigours of the school routine.

The earliest govt schools typically had some discussion on the preachings of Mahatma Gandhi, Lal Bahadur Shastri or Jawahar Lal Nehru. Later on, the schools run by Christian missions and NGOs initiated the practice of using Assembly as a morning platform for general discussion on various topics including the current political and international situations. Later on discussion in quotes, sports scheme and even films formed a part of the assembly discussion and then the practice of having a complete band play out the sequence of anthems, prayers and motivational songs with music.

Talking again of the earliest schools (mostly government owned), called the *"Paathshaala" or "Niketan",* the class teachers or subject teachers were earlier retained on the basis of mutual recommendations (with very few graduates available around that time to man the various schools) and later on the recruitment process was changed and done via state administered UGT (Undergraduate Teacher), PGT (Postgraduate Teacher) and other tests including SSC (State Service Commission) based recruitments which tried to select the candidates on the basis of academic merit and some other rationale which tried to calibrate teachers on the basis of teaching and other aptitude. Thus the earliest schools had a variegated diaspora of teachers available in the schools ranging from the extremely pensive, to the point, learned, didactic but strict disciplinarian creating terror in the mind, to learned but flexible and supportive ones, who helped the prospective talents bloom, to the average street smart one's who took teaching as an oral art regaling the audience with petty incidence and some lessons *some times and many a time or rather most of the time using the position to earn favourable* benefits from the students, their parents as relatives and society.

The non teaching staff of a school behaved in a way that was symbolic of the tilt of the balance between the different category of teaching members and completed the ambience either making it a *"Temple of Learning"* or rotting it from within to a *"Workshop of machinations"* producing students who added to the miseries of the society once out.

Then there was another category of teachers, who neither were fully conversant with the subject themselves nor the significance of mentorship responsibility desired of a teacher, nor were apt at managing their own personal issues making them butt of jokes of the student as well as colleagues who destroyed the learning fabrics still to a greater length, producing pupils with that *innate lack of sense of appropriateness, ethics, goodness, usefulness and productiveness* that became a damaging force when they entered society at some point with that incomplete sense of duty and a *dangerous and callous disregard for ethics.* Thus it was left to the individual brilliance of the student or his parental guidance that guided some of these students, along with the mentorial brilliance of some teachers, into this world armed with the *correct mix of knowledge, poise, ethics and sense of duty.* However some schools administered with a true mentoral, nurturing, educative and Indian cultural vision stood out amongst all for their good work and professionalism in delivering education.

Gradually, more and more mission schools run by Christian missionaries took over the task of teaching from the Govt.

schools at most places and established their branches at many places. They had a sense of service and application.

They indulged in education as a service to humanity. They could see an uneducated child as a problem to the society and also as a problem to himself/herself, a component of the society, who would pose lot of questions but no answer.

They brought about the initial thoughts and sense of professionalism in almost everything related to education. The sisters and nuns would make sure that the child was made to imitate the mannerism, the dapper look and pronunciation to the letter- T. They also made sure that subjects that dealt with social, geographical and biological sciences were aptly and smartly dealt with. The maths teacher, essentially a father or brother, would be good at his calculation and so would be a physics teacher, also a brother in most cases.

The sports teacher, again a brother, would take his task so seriously that within the allotted games hours and the available confines of the outdoor playing arena in the school compound, he would motivate a hundred little hearts into as diverse physical activities as sprinting, long and high jump, volleyball, badminton and even cricket, and some of them even shining later on at different levels.

Many mission schools in the far off small towns ant outskirt peripheral villages specially focused on identifying and honing such boy and girl talents in various sports and were able to make them shine at state, national and international levels. P.T Usha, Shiny Abraham, Wilson, all hailed from such small town academics somewhere patronized by some mission or a principled Hindu society, involved in education.

Schooling became a properly monitored activity with set targets in the form of home and classwork after the classroom demonstrations and teaching. Students started enjoying each other's company attired in the uniform, took a liking for the disciplined glances of the teachers and also started responding back to the questions posed in the class in a foreign language. Thus Savita, Mohan, Rajan, Mohammad and Naseer started becoming comfortable with a foreign way of behavior and interaction.

The prominent mission schools at various locations were:

1   St. Marry School, Patiala

2. The Lady Fatima School, at various locations

3. Holy Angels School, at various locations

4. Holy Cross Schools at various locations

5. Caramel Convent Schools at various locations

6. St Joseph's Schools at various locations

7. St Peter's Schools at various locations

8. Christchurch Schools at various locations

9. St Joseph's School, Darjeeling, India

10. St Bishop's School, Darjeeling, India

11. BishopCotton School, Shimla, India

12. La Martiniere, Calcutta

13. La Martiniere, Lucknow,

By the 1980's and 1990's however these Missionery schools also had some change in their style of conduct with a new generation taking over with a different outlook. The mission schools also started hiring teachers from within the Indian population who were graduates and postgraduates in education and after a period of training started utilizing them. Also many

Indian communities particularly those that belonged to down south, who belonged to lower strata of the Indian caste system, went for conversions took over the robes of brothers and sisters, fulfilling at the same time the manpower requirements of teachers in such school.

The trend offered some advantages as well as disadvantages. While to an average lower and middle class Indian men and women, slightly well off in studies, it opened the door for a respectable career opportunity, with some upper middle class and upper class women toaking to teaching for the sake of passion, self-satisfaction and as a means of creative use of time that provided a satisfaction of social contribution.

It was another matter that many of them gradually got lost in the mid way, transforming themselves to chatterbox when free and exchanging food and homely tips with each other and overdoing it to a point that the enthusiasm of teaching was taken over by the enthusiasm to meet fellow teachers.

However some schools realized the issues and opted for a professional conduct where in evaluation and continuation of services was based on productive teaching involvement and output.

Some schools developed based on the concept of grooming of princes, sons and daughters of elite and regal govt. servants and businessmen as in Britain. They ensured that a student who joined the school at an early age, around 8-10, went through a disciplined and planned scheduled that included physical exercises, a sumptuous breakfast, a tough selective sports activity, a rigorous academic schedule that included a strong emphasis on soft skills, communication and personality and then evening sessions on social behaviors, unwinding and highlighting comfortable evening relaxation before going to bed.

The prominent schools that came up during the period were

- Bishop Cotton School, Shimla, India
- The Doon School, Dehradun, India
- The Scindia School, Gwalior
- Mayo College, Ajmer
- Welham Girls School, Dehradun, India
- Mayo College Girls School, Ajmer
- Sahyadri School, Pune, India
- Rishi Valley School, Chittoor, India
- Lawrence School, Sanawar, india
- Rajghat Besant School, Varanasi
- The Assam valley School, balipara, India
- Jain International Residential School, Bangalore, india
- Mussourie International School, Mussoorie, Indoia
- Mody School, Lakshmangarh, India
- Shri Satya Sai School, Puttaparthi
- St Joseph's School, Darjeeling, India
- Sarala Birla Academy, Bangalore, India
- Army Public School Solan, India
- Vidya Devi Jindal School, Hissar, India
- G D Goenka Public School, Delhi, India
- Belgaum Military School, India
- Bangalore Military School, India
- La Martiniere, Lucknow,
- La Martiniere, Calcutta

- St Bishop's School, Darjeeling, India
- Aga Khan Academy Hyderabad
- Apollo International School Panipat
- Anubhuti School Jalgaon
- The Aryan School Dehradun
- Atmiya Vidya Mandir Gujarat
- Baldwin Boys High School Bangalore
- Gen B C Joshi Army Public School, Pithoragarh
- Birla Sr Secondary School, Pilani
- Birla Balika Vidya peeth pilani

Some schools started adopting a SWOT approach analyzing their strengths and weaknesses and developing on their core strengths. Thus some of them promised a great sports environment providing academy facilities for cricket, table tennis, badminton and other sports. Others promised a great academic environment in the high school with excellent teaching in Maths/science and other subjects, while some prided themselves with excellence in general awareness and related streams.

Also schools started focusing on overall development of a child and his/her personality and started including activities ranging from drama, drama, debate and other competitions. The teaches were made to plan, organize and motivate participation of student in various co curricular activities. Somewhere the focus on such activities overshadowed achievements and performance in academics and even at some stages, the rankers were labeled as boors and duds and bookworms, thus more children were diverted towards this extra academic performance rather than studies.

This led to over involvement of teachers in such activities and gradual blurring of teacher- taught relation, and of a distant aura about the teachers that mesmerized the students. Some teachers were able to maintain a respect and decorum; whereas others were just pulled into this too comfortable a relation with the students, which made them, loose their sheen and dignity as a teacher.

Many prominent teachers and mentors and sports specialist and personality trainers made a name for themselves and their wards and have been recognized for their selfless devotion to education, mentoring and bringing up the new generation. The prominent ones to be awarded through National Teacher/ Principal Awards by MHRD, Govt of India through Central Board of Secondary Education (CBSE) and its regional offices at N Delhi, Ajmer, Allahabad, Patna, Bhubaneshwar, Panchkula, Chennai, Guahati and in the category of Principal at Indian School in other country were, Sh. Vikram Sonba Adsul, Dr. Rameshappa G, Dr Gopal Jee, Sh. Arvind Raj Jajware, Dr Usha Khare, Ms. Pragya Nopany, Ms. Meka Susatya Rek, Sh. GS Zaithantluanga (All 2017) Sh. Ashok Kumar Tangri, Principal, The Indian High School, Dubai, United Arab Emirates (2002). Sh. Ainesley Leonard Edgar, Principal, Ideal Indian School, Doha, Qatar (2003), Sh. V. Gopalan, Principal, The New Indian School, Bahrain (2004), Smt. Asha Sharma, Principal, Indian Educational School, Kuwait (2007), Dr. Mohammed Shaffe E.K. Principal, International Indian School, Kingdom of Saudhi Arabi (2009), (All awarded in the category "Principal at Indian School in Foreign country"), Mrs. Adarash Kohli, Principal, Darbari Lal DAV Model School, N Delhi (1999), Ms. Manju Gupta, Principal, Navrachna High Sec. School, Baroda (1999), Sh. Salam Anil Kumar Singh, Manipur Public School, Imphal (1999), Smt. Usha Ram, Principal, Laxman Public School, New Delhi (2001), Mrs. A. Shastri, Principal, Bhavan's B.P. Vidyamandir, Nagpur (2001), Dr. (Mrs.) Hemlata S. Mohan, Principal, Delhi Public School, Bokaro Steel City (2004), Smt. Meenu Goswami, Principal, K.R. Mangalam World School, New Delhi (2007), Smt. Neera Mathur, Principal, Maharaja Sawai Man Singh Vidyalaya, Jaipur (2007),

Sh. A. Rengaswamy, SBOA School and Junior College, Anna Nagar, Chennai (2008), Dr. Dharam Veer Singh, Principal, Sri Guru Harkrishan Senior Secondary, Amritsar (2008), Sh. Pradeep Kumar Pandey, Principal, Vivekananda Kendra Vidyalaya, Lohit, Arunachal Pradesh (2010)

Many other leading personalities have been role models for all the above award winning teachers, including Bharat ratna Dr S Radhakrishnan, Former President of India, who was once a Professor, the acclaimed author R K Narayan, who was once a teacher at a school at Chennapatna at Mysore, Mr Nissim Ezekiel, starting as a Professor in English at Univ of Mumbai, becing adjunct Professor at Leeds and also later winning the Padma Shri in 2004 with his feats in poetry, Bharat Ratna Dr APJ Abdul Kalam, a great teacher, philosopher and scientist before turning a full time ISRO Head and later the President of India, Savitribai Fule was the first lady instructor in the first school for young ladies starting at Pune in 1948, and other schools that opened after that, thus making sure that she and her husband had started a movement and change in the society that brought about a sea change in the society.

Students have also evolved over the years, with the change in the perception of a smart student. The only thing that needs to be taken care of is whether in the quest for making the upcoming generation worldwise and globaly proactive, the basic tenets of life, viz., thoughtful actions, perseverance, balance and social compatibility are being compromised, and whether the changing social norms, in the garb of modernity, are helping the cause of a sustainable, compatible and harmonious society with appropriate amount of peace and happiness factored in at evry level from individuals, to families as the basic uniyt to society and nation at large. Thus schooling and the sytem and stakeholders in education need to be again and again sensitized to their crucial role in a cohesive society and nation building.

Emergence of Technology as the Prime word in Global Industrial Vocabulary and parallel emergence of Focus on Technical Education

Somewhere by the 1990's, the social trends forced the parents to direct the students to technical education, rather than military and other administrative jobs as that also did not involve a high cost of education in such costly schools.

Setting up of technical Education Boards, Ministry of Tech Education, AICTE was an important step in the direction of coordinating Technical education, its quality and uniformity in delivery across various institutes, giving them uniform norms of infrastructure, academic and output delivery.

Liberation by Way of Ability to Cross Boundaries to Developed Countries for Financial Freedom:

Over the years Indian parents have invested in education of their kids, in the positive hope of getting the taste of progress and good life that seemed to be offered by the swanky, tranquil and clean cities and towns in the US and Europe.Thankfully, these countries valued skilled and professional working hands that contributed to the progress of the country with an intelligent acceptance of the outsider with some restrictions and criteria that they kept on adjusting at different times in the form of work, professional or permanent visas. Some were lucky being backed by appropriate finance for shifting to their mental heavens or havens. Thus with period many settled in New Jersey, New Orleans, Kentucky, Colorado, London, Birmingham, Montreal...and many other places, and got themselves gelled with the locals, acquiring their lingo, lifestyle and even habits reveling in the foods, Inherited financial freedom offered by the countries to realise their dreams of comfortable house and life style. Thus Montek singh christened himself Monty, Harpreet singh Happy and Jaspreet became Jassi.

During the period highly engineers, doctors and other professionals shifted to these countries. Punjab has benefitted and progressed dramatically thanks to the FDI pumped in by NRI relatives of various local Punjabi families who had settled abroad. Punjab has been witness to meteoric rise in rich spending, swanky marriages, palatial houses, imported car and farmhouses and offices de extraordinaire.

An affected accent came easily and even kids were uncomfortable with their mother tongue when they returned to India for a short while. Thus with a reasonable family, the kids would still call their grandparents as Dada Dadi when in India and not to forget to touch their feet and give them a hug, where as with others who got almost completely uprooted, it was mostly grandpa and grandma and a distance that could never be bridged. Comfort of the video games and parlors and for the teenagers, a new culture of soft and hard drink, initiated a new trend that helped them looking advanced and different from the earlier generation.

Many such families that drifted between India and these countries lost their and their kids connect to culture during the growing up years and were left with no one to depend upon to stick to their roots. Still other families were able to strike a balance and keep a hold on their identities and roots. They realized the ideological differences between the societies in the two countries and were able to pick up the best from one society while retaining the best for their native and do the ditto for their kids.

Thus a Rajat Gupta or Rajeev aggarwal would still walk out of his home in the morning to take a car to the office after a heavy breakfast of Aaloo ke paranthe, poori sabzi and taking a tiffin with 10 idlis to his office with his wife warning him off from the house door with daughter in tow.

Even purists and musicians including Ravi Shankar, Jagjit Singh, Amjad Ali Khan, Zakir Hussain, Sabri Brothers, Pt. Hari Prasad and santoor maestro Pt. Shiv Kumar Sharma have earned name, fame, repute and dividends by having one of their feet firmly in place in a foreign city in America or European country. With their purist talent, they have been able to establish a clout for themselves in their respective fields to such an extent that they became a formidable force to reckon with in India too. It may however be a point worth discussion whether they earned a wide respect more out of the impact of their Indian or NRI audience. Same is the case with many other musicians, viz., Peenaz Masani, Pankaj Udhas, Manbhar Udhas, Meetali and Bhupinder, Anup Jalota, Rajan and Sajan Mishra and so on.

Even film stars have tried to reach a wider audience by worldwide concerts and shows. *Amitabh, Shahrukh, Rishi, Parveen, Kalyanji Anandji, Biddoo, Laxmikant Pyarelal, Asha Bhosle, Adnan Sami, Sonu nigam, Alka, Kishore, Lata, Rafi* and many more have at one point or the others struck on worldwide tours.

The trend has settled down to a more reasonable attrition and brain, talent and skill drain offshore, with Indian economy having picked up and the opportunities available in diverse areas offering greater chance for creative, monetary and social satisfaction to people from different walks, strata and skill areas. Thus, over the last decade, sufficient entrepreneurial and industrial growth has ensured that those ready to invest their brains, efforts, knowledge and skill are comfortably taken care by good entrepreneur houses in terms of money, facilities and perks.

22.

The New Bullish India of the '80s and '90s

CONTEXT:

Playing or toying with money was earlier the favourite escapade for the elite. But with the opening of the economy and equity based capitalism, people took to stock investments with a vengeance in the '80s and '90s, which has still continued, but has become more systematic and mature with people learning the ropes after glaring examples of disastrous enthusiastic misadventure by many stock players and fall of major giants including Harshad Mehta in the 1990s lured into the fallacy of instant gains by manipulative innovations.

As entrepreneurship gained momentum, so did hunger for inviting investments and budgetary provisions for setting up, expansion or diversification of business, resulting in stock equities. The idea of stock equity and shares initiates with rise of mega trading companies like East India Company, which traded across diferent continents and travelled across various oceans, sending shiploads of consumer goods and utilities. With possibilities of pirate attackes, sea calamities and plunder, the idea of sharing possible losses emerged, wherein different trading companies chipped in definite value of goods on particular ships, so that loss due to calamities or piretes could be minimal and not extensive.. Other Trading companies followed suit and thus emerged the idea of minimizing risk through common sharing.

This idea of sharing of trade risk diversified into shared investment, during setting up and establishing a large enterprise. Thus companies started inviting investments from other business houses, and this started occurring at specific places, which later turned into official stock trading areas or exchanges. Thus the initial stock exchanges emerged at Antwerp as Beurzen markets, after the influential business family Buerze, and later changed to Bourses. London stock market soon followed in 1801, but strted trading in company stocks only by 1825, with New York Stock exchange, NYSE having been formed earlier at 1817, followed by exchanges in various countries in Europe and Japan, with Canadian Stock exchange coming up as TSX by 1861.

Investment Heroes: Chandrakant Sampat, Raamdeo aggarwal, Jhoonjhun wala, Sunil Singhania, Aswath Damodaran, Bharat Shah, Samir Arora and many others

India has had its own standout leaders in investment, whio have shaped investing strategies over the decades for others and at least 20 of them have been named in Forbes India's inaugural Wealth Wizards package, having seen the markets through the rough and in good times, and survived to give the tips. "Invest in equities for the long term and you will eventually make money" has been a uniform refrain by all these experts, be it Chandrakant Sampat, the FMCG man by way of investment preference, Bharat Shah and Samir Arora, the dotcom specialists of the '90s, the infrastructure man, Sunil Singhania, Motilal Oswal's Raamdeo Agrawal, known for his Hero Honda fancy,or Professor Aswath Damodaran, at the Stern School of Business in New York University, whose every comment and analysis is lapped up by the fund managers across the world. Though all have crossed failures in between, they are quintessential optimists in equity investing, and have their own set of golden tenets to go by, and for a general investor, these are as good as Standard Operating Procedures.

After dominating the world economy for nearly three centuries, the New York Stock Exchange faced its first legitimate challenger in the 1970s,in the form of NASDAQ Stock exchang-the National Association of Securities Dealers and Financial Industry Regulatory Authority, being different in the fact that trading was completely online and electronic, pushing the NYSE to innovate and collaborate with Euronext and form NYSE-Euronext.

Parallely, the Stock market indices started indicating the approximate standing of top business houses across various countries, led by the Dow Jones Index and the Dow Jones Industrial Average-DJIA- created by Wall Street Journal Editor Charles Dow and Investor Edward Jones, to indicate the total wealth of top industrial houses playing major role in country's economy, mainly heavy industries earlier, but now represented by many others including American Express, 3M, Goldman Sachs, General Electric, DuPont, Coca-Cola, IBM for USA.Other major stock market indices include the Nasdaq Composite, the S&P 500, and the Russell 2000. Thus primarily, the Blue Chip stocks, High in demand and highly priced make the DJIA top 30 and make about one fifth of the total market value, and offer moderate dividends, which are definite to keep growing over the years with low volutility. Income stocks offer a similar but stble and sustained dividend over many years and are supposed to be safest stock investments, offered by big established companies, and investors who want to avoid risk, normaly invest in income stocks.

In contrast, the penny stocks, the low priced speculative stocks of relatively new companies, show extreme volutility, involve risk of failures or in exceptional cases huge gains, and consequently are termed more speculative stocks. A value stock also offers a similar speculative option, represented by companies and stock having good earnings and growth potential, currently selling at a low price, which is not reflective of the actual standing of company. Speculative and calculative investors, who are sure that it is a temporary phase are attracted towards these two types. Defensive stocks are those whose prices stay stable when the market declines and are issued by industries that naturally do well during recessions.

Various players help, interact, invest and support individuals and organisations in the investment market, parallel to the playing rules and guidelines given by SEBI and other regulators. Thus India has had its own leaders in the above areas including Individual Institutional Investors, IIIs, which may be DIIs, the Domestic or Indian Institutional Investors or FIIs, the Foreign Institutional Investors, all of the above being represented bysingle individuals or by Corporations. Typical representative IIIs and DIIs who have stimulated Indian investment market over the years include theInsurance Companies, with LIC being the largest player, Mutual Fund organisations, Commodity advisors and private investment stalwarts including the likes of Rakesh Jhunjhunwala.

The IIIs and DIIs trade in high value shares of established businesses in high amounts and qualify for preferential treatments by the companies and are allowed to do so at lover commissions. FIIs, like Bridgewater Associates, Quantum Funds, Berkshire Hathaway and others play their part withgin the rules framed by SEBI and others and are limited in the investment allowance in the Indian Companies. Ambani, Premji Invest and Nathan and Company represent the Indian Family Offices, who provide wealth management services including budgeting, insurance, charitable giving, family owned businesses, wealth transfer and tax services, onturnkey basis to high net worth investors.

Ramdeo Aggarwal, Jt MD and cofounder, Motilal Oswal Financial Services, is a leading name in investment and stock trading in India, and he is a strong advocate of the principle of Quality, Growth, Longevity, and Bargaining-QGLB and a staunch supporter of value stocks and even income stocks, stressing that even if the present value of a company may not be as promising or strong, but if the Company shows the four parameters of QGLB, investors should take a decision for it. That is how, he made a critically acclaimed decision of investin in Hero Honda Corp, standing today at 50000 crores, in 1997, when it was just 1000 crores.

Parag Parikh, 60, Chairmann and CEO Parag Parikh Financial Advisory Services, PPFAS, is also an old school vocalist in investments, with a strong coniction in the principle of farms "You can not sow something today and reap tomorrow", a conviction that made him think and prevent being very enthusiastic about many dotcom companies during the period of the dotcom bubble, a very difficult and even a questioned stance, which later however proved to be very right. So he propogates the simple old school thought of investing in firms with long term possibilities.

Ashish Dhawan, 45, founder of Chrys Capital Investments Ltd, is again a staunch proponent of value stocks, stressing the importance of a deep understanding of risk aversion, diversification, growth rate, market share and historical perspective of a company, before investing-all the principles that made him take a stron decision of a major investment of 100 million in HCL Technologies in 2008 and offload 2% of this investment to earn 500 million in 2018, when others were not too sure about the stock.

Saurabh Mukherjee, 38, CEO, Institutional Equities and Ambit Capital, has a habit of going against the tide, based on strong research based analysis of management functioning of a company, which made him decide that Infosys was not adapting to the new requirements and would soon loose its ground, making him advise people that the stocks, priced at Rs 3200 at the time, could be considered for sell off, and the same intuitive peep into a company's strategic decisions made him realize TVS as a right opportunity for investment against Hero and Bajaj, when it revitalized itself with partnership with BMW and other efforts.

Another leader in individual invetments, Chandrakant Sampat, 87, is a stalwart and a marathoner in Indian stock investments, starting way back in1950s at the Bombay Stock exchange with pen and scribble pad and cheque book, and is also a strong proponent of value and income stock and consumer goods companies like Uniiver, Colgate Palmolive and others, which are likely to have low capital expenditure, and outlines his master strategy of small investment portfolio only in 6-7 companies which are sure to offer at least 25% return on investments and have the capacity for continuous high dividends.

Sanjay Bakshi, 48, Managing Partner, Value Quest Capital, a graduate of London School of Economics and great admirer of Warren Buffet, learnt to question the market responses, as per Buffet's philosophy, and developed a habit of relying on investment action based on the competency and honesty of a company's management and clarity of growth thoughts, based on which he made a handsome gain out of investing on Relaxo footwears, with initial shares priced at Rs 100, which soared to Rs 400, with the management charting out a clear growth strategy of initialy starting at a small capital in slippers and then diversifying into a broad range of footwears.

Samir Arora, 52, Founder Helios Capital, elaborates on experience gained during his days at Allianz capital and his philosophy of identifying the opportuniyies of investments in upcoming trends, before many others start doing, based on which he identified PSUs and Banks as a major investment areas durin the 1990, when these organisations were flung open for privatization, making huge gains from HDFC Banks investments. He further propogates an eye for new businesses based on which he made investment gains in retail, multiplex and food chains.

Rakes Jhunjhunwala, 53, Founder rare Enterprises, and India's own answer to Warren Buffet, Jhunjhunwala likes to be out and out invested, and is labeled as master blaster in investments with his capabilities to ready deep, fast and comprehend and invest and deinvest even mush faster. His investing tenets include-Trends as Friends while investing, critically assessing a company's fundamentals before investment and not falling prey to an analysis paralysis downhill, thus having made huge gains from low lying businesses like Sessa Goa/Sessa Sterlite, TITAN and other companies, when others could not spot the potential.

Ridham Desai, 46, MD, Morgan Stanley India, is a charmed man when it comes to Indian investment market and likens it to his favourite hobby, Formula one, often citing efficiency of government poilicies to ensure a smooth drive, at the same time being gung ho about the fact that Foreign investors have been more understanding of the Indian investment scenario with FIIs in last five years being many times higher even as compared to the boom period between 2003- 2007. S naganath, 46, MD and CIO of DSP BalckRock MFs, believes in keeping it simple while anyone makes an investment decision, whrein, the success depends upon one's ability to decide on his/her idea of amount of returns and his/her capacity to take risks, which he calls as the prime tenet to make an investment count.

((xxviii) Reference picture on page 168, 169)

Ridham Desai, 46, MD, Morgan Stanley India, is a charmed man when it comes to Indian investment market and likens it to his favourite hobby, Formula one, often citing efficiency of government poilicies to ensure a smooth drive, at the same time being gung ho about the fact that Foreign investors have been more understanding of the Indian investment scenario with FIIs in last five years being many times higher even as compared to the boom period between 2003- 2007.S naganath, 46, MD and CIO of DSP BalckRock MFs, believes in keeping it simple while anyone makes an investment decision, whrein, the success depends upon one's ability to decide on his/her idea of amount of returns and his/her capacity to take risks, which he calls as the prime tenet to make an investment count.

There have been stalwarts who have tasted drastic failures too, as in the case of Bharat Shah, 53, Exec Director, ASK Group, who relied heavily on big businewsses and high net worth companies for investing andnadvising investments, including the Tech and IT majors, Infosys and Wipro, having seen about 130 times increase in invested worth, he had to bear the brunt due to major Tech setbacks in the phase og Tech bubble burst, which he attributed to his inability to read between the linesand failure to realize the fact that the businesses had got too much expensive to mange in case of sudden collapse. Thus, Shah would rather advise on betting on mixed portfolios, with a fair component of counted risks on possible new dark horses, keeping an eye on good and well-managed houses, not paying too extravagant a price, after having checked certainity of earning and growth.

S Naren, 48, CIO ICICIC Prudential also advises people to be able to be contrarion to what is happening in the market and make their decisions after extensive written exercises themselves. He cites his personal example aboy Bharti, wherein he invested when the market value was down by 40%, but later made a huge return as times changed.

((xxix) Reference picture on page 170)

Ramesh danani, 57, Founder Ramesh Danani Finance Pvt Ltd, is another man, who worked by identifying big businesses and stocks including major investments in Infosys in 1990s and getting a 100 fold increase in his investment in 6 years by 1999. Ha also mixes up with investments in companies like Bharat Electronics Ltd and Bharat Earthmovers and favours appropriate investment when markets are down, as in 2008.

Many investors indulge in a variety of other options too, including, Gold of gold-mining companies, which moves up or down with the price of gold, treasury stocks, that has been bought back by the company that issued it, when they believe it is underpriced on the market, setting it aside the stock for future uses such as debt payment or the awarding of stock options. Cyclical stocks show cyclical variations with the business cycle, including the housing industry and industrial equipment companies stocks, and are preferred by investors who do not mind buying and selling as the market fluctuates.

With such huge investments and trading, a single etiological event starts a apiralling cascade of events that make huge withdrawals, making the markets crash disastrously in a hurry, with many not able to see it and being left with unuseful scrips that do not have a significant value, and their money making dreams shattered, exposing the uncertainities of the investments and stocks, the concept of market equilibrium, efficient market hypothesis, theory of rational human conduct and other basics. 1929 was a milestone crash christened as Black Thursday or Terrible Thursday of 1929, and later there have beenthe Black Monday and the Black Tuesday, represented by theStock Market Crash of 1973-1974, Black Monday of 1987, Dot-com Bubble of 2000, Stock Market Crash of 2008, with drastic reductions in stocks, values, siphoning followed by economic depression and other spiraling events, as evidenced by major losses to major stock markets and indices, viz., the Dow Jones Industrial Average loosing 50% of its value, Hong kong market having gone down as much as 45%, Australian market 42%, Us and Canada going down upto 25%.

23.

The IT Boom and the Indian Summer

The leadership trait that all IT entrepreneurs have shown as a common one, is that of looking into the future, rather creating the future, a great dejavu for development in information technology, and providing solutions with the standout advantages of speed, precision, replication, design, innovation and quantum of work supported and facilitated. Another trait that stands out is the ability to create user market for technology in existing business, in a sense creating the need in the existing business. This certainly stands out aginst satisfying an existing demand. This is visible in the diverse areas in which Information technology has made inroads and made impact inclusing Business process outsourcing, ERP, advanced analytics, managed innovation, embedded system, business intelligence and others.

Major Business Housesin India, including TATA, WIPRO, BIRLA, Infosys and others, and those outside including HP, Mphasis, have initiated specific business arm related to products and services based on information technology at the most suitable time, initialy as an in house need and later on as specialized commercial products.

What these companies look out for as leadership traits are application & intuitive skills, problem solving aptitude, eye for creativity and solutions for society.

Zoho, started by the name Advent Net by Shridhar Vembu and Tony Thomas in 1996 in California, offering web based business tools, IT solutions IOT management platform, finally spread out to 7 countries, renaming itself Zoho in 2009 with headquarter at Chennai, with divisions and products including Zoho CRM, Creator and Sheet, Zoho doccs, Zoho meeting, Zoho one and others.

Zensar, a software development company, has been formed after renaming the parent Company ICIM (International Computers Indian Manufacturers), set up by a British group at Pune way back in 1963, and which itself was born out of the British counterpart ICL, and is now being steered by Ganesh Natrajan as CEO since 2001, providing software solution to more than 500 companies with 7000 employees, as a 500 million dollar company, listed in NSE, BSE, NIFT 500, S & PBSE 500.

Xansa strted by Shirley in UK in 1962 as Freelance Programmers, offering software development services, the prominent client being Concorde for its Black Box programming, changed to F international in 1974, where F included Freelancer, promoting women and dependents, Free and Flexible, with inclusion of equal number of men and women, and finaly changed to FI Group in 1987-88, with Shirley quitting to let Hillary Cropper take over as CEO. Finaly by 2000 it expanded to include Indian subsidiary IIS infotech Computer services Company at N Delhi, London based OSI, a business consulting firm, and Druid, an IT consulting firm, and renamed itself to Xansa in 2001, finaly operating across various business sectors including, banking, finance, insurance, telecoms, transport, logistics, utilities and a partnership with Renault for F1.

WNS Global is a business Process Management (BPM) company, starting as in house unit of British Airways in 1996, presently employing 38000 people in two arms WNS BPM and WNS Autoclaims BPM, with Adrian Dillon as Chairman and Keshav Murugesh as CEO, operating in China, Russia and Baltic countries, Europe, UK, USA for top Fortune 500 companies, including Air Canada, Iceland Air, British Airways, Virgin Atlantic Airlines, Indy Mac Bank, Tesco, Travelocity, First Mangus Financial, Sabre Holdings and others in healthcare, utilities, retail and consumer products, with delivery centres, knowledge services, with proprietory platform including WNS Verifare, WNS Jade, WNS Dynamic Discount manager, WNS ProClaim, and WNS Analytical Decision Engine, WADE. The major projects handled include end-to end insurance project for Suncorp and Genpact in Australia, a back office Bank project for Mashreq bank in UAE. Its acquisitions include, Town and Country Assistance Ltd, UK, Greensnow Health Claim Management Business, Trinity Services offering BPO services to financial institutions, PRG airlines fare audit system, GHS holding financial accounting business, offshore analytics business of Marketics, AHA accidents Happen Assistance Ltd, AVIVA global Services, Fusion outsourcing services, Denali Outsourcing services and Health Help, a leader in Healthcare management.

UST Global is a software outsourcing company, initiated in 1990 at Califonia by Stephen Ross and having spread its operations, extensively in India, Mexico, Spain, Poland, Sinmgapore and other countries, offering a range of outsourcing services for Digital and IT solution areas including Banking, healthcare, retail, and others, having won prestigious awards like, best software outsourcing company in 2012, and having collaborate with majors such as GE to for GenShare and with Fox Centre at Mexico. Headed by Sajan Pillai as the CEO, it offers a range of services including Consulting, managed innovation, human centred design, tech build, advanced analytics, embedded system development (ESD), e-commerce, business intelligence (BI) and others. It has state of the art offices and innovation labs at Coimbatore, Kochi, Bhopal, Gurgaon, Pune and other places and is reognised as a the best innovation based company awarded with "Most Innovative Emerging Corporation" at Business Awards 2012, and rated very highy by NASSCOM and Forester Research reports, offering its employees extra time and space for innovation ideation and development through labs such as "Infinity Labs, Innovation Hub and Open Minds".

Thoughtworks started as Singham Business Solutions, initiated by Roy Singham in 1980, and renamed itself in 1993 as tHoughtwork, expanding its software development from C++ to Java, Foryte 4GL, and others and drafting the "Agile Manifesto" to intiate Agile Technologies as its niche division, and launching agile products including Mingle, Gauge, Snap CI, GoCD, Talisman, Brahmni, and have been outstanding on Continuous development and integration platforms like Cruise Control, which has even motivated companies like GE to move towards agile technologies and others with active contributions by Mathew Foemmel, Martin Fowler Rebecca Parsons, Randy Stafford and others through Thoughtwork Studios. Many outstanding developers including Dr David Watson, Trevor Mather, Ken Collier Aaron Swartz and Jim Highsmith, have associated with Thoughtwork with Rebecca having been named the "Most influential Women Technologist", and Thoughtwork, as an organization having been recognized as Top Company for Women Technologists by Anita Borg Institute.

Thirdware is an Information Technology Services Company offering Enterprise application services (EAS), ERP, Customer Relationship management (CRM) solutions, BI/DW services and served various clients including Ford, Pfizer, Ingersol Rand, L and T, Coca Cola and many others. It has been created by Pradeep Erinjery, Mohan Kirane, Bhavesh Shah, Manish Sharma and Satish Menon in Mumbai in 1993, and recognsed, appreciated and awarded by QUAD Inc, SEEPZ and other Associations in Ireland and other countries, and has collaborated with Oracle, HelpGo China, Hyperion APAC, Ford and others with extensive offices in India at Chennai and other places. In the Transaction solutions and services it provides solutions based on SAP, QAD, Oracle and Infor FMS, and for Analytics, on Hyperion, Informatica and SAS.

ThinkPalm based at Kochi and initiated in 2010, offers various apps including QAud (for quality and audit), Palm BI (Business Intelligence), Astra (GPS based fleet tracking), netShack (network management system) and an app for Self-breast cancer assessment for women under its charity arm ThinkLife and its initiative "Save your mother 2015.

TIS (TATA Interactive Services), initiated in 1990s and later taken over by MPS, offers a range of interactive learning products mainly for Corporate houses, and also for schools on eLearning, virtual Labs, Special needs education portal and mathematical learning (SPARKMath), with main products on Business Simulations, Learning Portals and content management systems. With over 3000 hours of e Learning content created every year with about 800 employees for approximately 50 Fortune 500 companies, it has been awarded by various agencies including BIMA, ASTD, IT Training, World-NID Excellence Awards, Brandon hall excellence Awards, APEX and BETT and has a huge Calcutta operations office. It is now a conglomerate of companies including Skill Soft, EI Design, Swat Rush Lernnovators, UpsideLearning, SkillUp.com and others.

TCS, TATA Consultancy Services, a Group Company of TATA group, became the first IT company in Inda to cross the 100 billion mark, also being the second Indian company to do so after Reliance Group, accounting for 70% of profits for rhe TATA group, employing abour 3.8 lakhs employees, the highest by a private corporate house after Indian railways, Indian posts etc,with Collabnet, Cassatt, IITs, Stanford, MIT, Carnegie Mellon and Sequoia as collaborators, and a stste of the art research centre at Pune, the TATA Research Development and Design Centre

TRDDC focusing on software engineering, process engineering, and a suite MasterCraft for digitization, and having Hoffman La Roche and EliLillly as clientys for medical writing, data management and biostatistics services and solutions.

Wipro started as Western India vegetable products as a vegetable oil company (Sunflower oil) in 1940, also venturing into consumer products, talcum, toiletries and related products, changing to Wipro Products Lts by 1980s, also venturing into heavy duty industrial cyliners and mobile hydraulic cylinders, and diagnosting imaging products as Wipro GE alliance. and then to Wipro Ltd, with Azeem Premjee initiating the IT business, initiating Wipro Odyssey overseas Design Lab, integrating other arms including Wipro Systems, Wipro Infotech, Wipro Acer and also tying up with Wipro KPN for internet technology and tying up later with LockHead Martin and later forming Wipro Eco Energy Systems. Other partnerships include that with Oki Techno Centre Singapore and R and D contracts with Nokia Siemens Network in Germany, eShiksha wiyh Intel, also collaborating on consumer, oil and gas and other segments with Australian Trade Promotion Management Group, the Promax Application Group and with Science Application Internayional Corporation (SAIC) for gas and refinery IT solutions, a contract with ATCO, the Canadian Energy and Utilities company. It is now operating with well established subsidiaries, including Western India Products Ltd, Wipro Consumer Care and Lightening, Wipro Infrastructure Engineering, Wipro GE Medical Systems, and has won laurels including the Most Ethical Company by Etisphere Institute, Gold Award for Intehgrated Security Assurance Services, being on Forbes Global 2000 list, India's most trusted Brand by Brand Trust Report and others.

((xxx) Reference picture on page 171, 172, 173, 174)

HCL Technologies started as Hindustan Computers Ltd Enterprise in 1976 with telecdigital calculators by Shiv Nadar and 5 others, and by 1991 first changed to HCL overseas Ltd, hen to HCL Consulting Ltd and finaly to HCL Technologies Ltd, specializing in software development and IT solutions, ultimately ranking in Forbes Global 2000, providing services to major Fortune 500 companies in aerospace, defense, automotive banking, capital market, chemicals, consumer goods, energy, utilities, healthcare, high tech, industrial manufacturing, insurance, life sciences, media and entertainment, mining and natural resources, oil and gas, retail, telecom, travel, transport, logistics, hospitality. It has further diversified into HCL Corporation with four companies HCL Infosystems, HCL Healthcare, HCL TalentCare and HCL Technologies, and has done major acquistions, notable amongst them being Stream Inc, Liberata, Control Point Solutions, Axon Group, UCS Group, Concept 2 Silicon Solutions, Geometric Ltd, Power objects, Butler America aerospace, ETL, H & D Group and others.

Oracle Financial Services Software Ltd, came into existence in 2005 after Oracle acquired CITIL (also called as i-flex Solutions I Ltd), the CitiCorp Information Technology Industries Ltd, a subsidiary of CitiCorp formed after changing CitiCorp Overseas Ltd in 1990, which provided internal software solutions only to CitiBank financial and Banking Functions, whereas CITIL was promulgated to provide financial software solutions to other Banking institutions too, offering products like Finware, FlexCube and MicroBanker, with top notch leaders including Shankar enkatachalam, Chet Kamat, harinderjeet Singh, Richard Jackson and others at helm of affairs.

Mphasis started by merger of US based IT Technology company Mphasis Corporation and Indian IT services company, BFL Software in 1998, being taken over by EDS (Electronic Data Systems) in 2006 and subsequently by HP systems in 2008, to be renamed Mphasis, an HP Enterprise, and later as it started providing IT services to outside companies also, it was rechristened Mphasis, Unleash the Next, by 2015, till HP decided to sell its stake in 2016, when it was taken over by Blackstone competing with Apollo and Tech Mahindra, with Nitin Rakesh taking over soon as CEO Based at Bangalore with a major office, and about 30 units in about 16 countries, Mphasis provides BPO, Infrastructure Technology, application development and maintenance and support services to Insurance, Healthcare, manufacturing, retail, financial, transport and communication sectors, and has acquired Navion Software, China, Kshema Tech, Onida Infotech Services, Mumbai, Princeton Consulting, UK, AIG system Solutions, Stelligent US, and others.

While Infosys and Tech Mahindra need no introduction, other IT companies which have put India on the global IT map include MindTree, a company formed in 1999 at Mauritius by 10 IT professionals with venture capital infusion from Franklin and other sources and by 2006, gaining its place under the sun by listing at NSE, followed by massive expansion in 17 countries with about 40 offices, diversifying into a development lab at Bengaluru, the Digital Pumpkin, providing services in application development, maintenance, Data Analytics, Digital Services, BPM and Infrastructure management Services and products like MindTest, MWatch, Atlas, SAP insurance and Omni Channel for media, entertainment, electronics, consumer goods, insurance, banking, capital, semiconductors, travel and hospitality sectors, having acquired ASAP solutions, Linc Software Services, CoSystems, Tes Purple

SOCIAL MEDIA AS THE NEW COMPONENT OF LEADERSHIP

CONTEXT:

Social media has given an alternate platform in connectivity for professional, social and personal application, but, are we assuming that we are "Ordained with technological freedom to mock one and all? or "Overinformed and overorganised to be chaotically overconversant and dischordant!!"

Social media emerged as a lousy pass time activity for the young and chirpy generation, converted into a serious online connectivity, that has fired the imagination of the young, the professionals and the business class alike, wherein the platform is being reinvented at breakneck speed before the dawn of next day to add features to make it competent for specific purpose. The purpose are wide ranging- as a social platform for hanging around, showing off, business introduction, expanding reach of business, the often discussed official communications, documents transfer, information and news sharing, group sharing and even advertising. Social media can be of different types including social networking sites, including facebook, linkedin, google+, blogs, micronetworks including twitter, instagram etc, forums and aggregators, instant messengers like skype, whatsapp etc, content communities including Youtube, slideshare, podcasts etc, social knowledge and wikis, and all of these are rented medias. The users may be conversationalist, aggregators, researchers, marketeers, learners and lurkers.

By the end of the first decade of 21st Century, these platforms, paired with the highly technical software driven smart phones, have changed the behavioural, interactive and communication patterns of the society. To some they have come up as a brilliant source of information by virtue of the content community media, which if professionaly used yields high dividend in knowledge enhancement, qualification upgradation or technical advancements. To others they may be tools of instant group interaction and enjoyement. To official users they have become tools of instant official communications.

There is although a flip side to this, that of instant reaction. The lurking angers and going overboard in all matters, professional, personal or social makes this media particularly sensitive to abuse, as in the following comment, based on some national incidents in 2017-18 which invited instant interaction through the social media.

The incident of surgical strikes by India on PoK terror camps has incited various responses with people taking freedom to speak with reference to data procured through net/internet or reliable sources using all possible methods, internet of things and what have you not, to prove that they have the most reliable source of information. Heavens have fallen and hell has broken loose on an action that was being first fiercely exhorted for from all corners with everyone taking postures to show what they could do if they were let off the hook.

Progress is important and so is development, as it provides better life to the ever-growing population, which is getting mature, professional and raring to go at a much early age. Thus we see more opportunities, faster incremental status and associated glamour or aura. Progress, also amply exemplified as more savvy handhelds and multifunctional sets that are incessantly displaying more and more updated information. Progress also in the form of more liberty backed by more stronger legal provisions to make sure no one can interrupt you when you are speaking your mind, whether tested for the veracity of facts to the last point or not. Progress, also as having more spare time to sit down and see, talk and discuss so much over sumptuous food at leisure time. Progress by way of having liberty to doubt everything, and liberty to own everything by way of 'likes' or "texts."

And so we see as many news channels with as many anchors as you may count trying to overshadow as many invited respectful panelists with their own astuteness, know-hows and expertise on the subject.

Overawed by the facilities at hand and inebriated with the self-fascination, we seek explanations that we never should make an attempt at as a responsible respectful and respected citizen. Sitting at a comfortable studio we try to imagine actions, which can be performed only by single dedicated professionals. "How deep the soldiers went, what did they achieve, how did they blow up, how did they escape the enemy, how did they finish it off?" these are things worth discussing to an extent that does not deify the extreme dangers taken by, and on the spot decisions and camaraderie of the team, that executed the operations, and to be left for post operational analysis by experts to improve upon any possible minor details or lapses.

Armed defense force is created to ensure safety for the nation on all corners, by way of all possible methods and actions required, as entailed in the oath administered during commission, that puts individual life not above the pride of the nation. As the defense strategies have evolved over the years, secrecy of operations before it is concluded has become a major strategic point, as the world is getting more and more informed or rather over informed by way of information through net, internet of things and by all other methods. A minor loss of information prior to the operations can lead to major disaster by way of preemptive action by the opponent.

Covert operations have been carried out since the ages of the Byzantine Roman armed forces, the Ottomans, Asoka, World wars, and later by organized unified NATO and other forces, with intentional nondisclosure of prior and post information for the purpose of not handing over the opponents opportunities of critical retaliatory strikes on a platter.

As a nation, all components of the society, the ordinary citizens, the media, the political parties and the executives need to understand the responsibility that comes with the advanced technology increasingly available at hand to get information, data, technology for facilitating work, performance or day to day mundane chores and making life comfortable. Being smart and doing smart is one thing, and being outsmarted enough by technology to be thrown into pompous self arrogance belittling everything else and everyone else by some tits and bits gathered from here and a bit from there, ultimately takes the sheen out of the brilliance that is purported to be projected by show of the high intelligence quotient, and rather comes out as an immature, dangerous blunder that is placid, distasteful and demeaning, and which makes relevant and important things look incredible and make everyone, collectively as a society, incredulous of each other. It is an intentionally created loss of credibility by way of vain repeated questioning by one and all on all matters irrespective of whether the opinions are asked for or not, in the process making even the significant matters look as trifle, insignificant and useless.

This may be compared to the action by soldiers, sneaking forward on foot, climbing trees, using surveillance to a limit, and then taking physical action with mental steel and resolve and coming out all trumps, without keeping on harping on technology, with more of a decisive mental resolve, decisive will for action, mental focus, and then a do or die physical action.

Internationaly, issues like Brexit, Americal Presidential election and Russian role, Egyptian crisis and coup, Chinese aggression, have become topics which have been served critiques right and left from all quarters even from those in no or very little know of things, or rather, from those who just wanted to sound their own trumpet in between and add to the cacophony. This has only helped complicate the matters. Somewhere a distinct line has to be drawn, wherein the trend of creating self styled sensation is checked.

Projection of additional knowhow and being technologically savvy may serve a momentary purpose but should not demystify human and individual inherent strengths, character and astuteness, that are called for in tasks that demand on the spot decisions and innate human traits and uniqueness that machines can not copy and paste and create.

This should be the point parallely ingrained in all assigned duties, roles and in applied trainings and education in technology, to make sure that society as a whole progresses and contributes to evolution, and does not take itself to self created revolutions which eat at its own roots.

24.

India: 21st Century: Leadership by the Boys from Small Towns

The Hands that Keep India Safe and Rocking

COMMENT: SOCIAL ANALYSIS AND CHANGING ATTITUDES

With passage of time the cultural divide between urban and rural India is becoming evident as never before. This time it is not the elitist, rich and educated abroad urban youth who scored earlier for having the knowhows to do things that appeared to look like making the country run. It is the other way round, when the people from the second strata of life across India are doing their bit in a big way to pull out massive achievements that have really dwarfed the upper strata in the society in the big way.

It is a matter of serious concern that, while we have excellent facilities coming up in the form of private, corporate, public and individual level

While the "Haves" revel in their prized possessions (Swanky mobile sets as smart phones and big i-pads, flashy wrist watches, elegant and colourful T shirts, with out of the world captions), the "HAVE NOTS" from the farlands in Bihar, Haryana, Kerala and Sikkim, thank God for the small things, dingy houses, parents and relatives bestowed on them, and that they have as their possession and go to sweat it out over their determined goals. Thus we have a Marry komm, shining apart just because of gritty determination, despite responsibility of two kids to look after, a Mohammed Shami from Jammu and Kashmir, giving a deaf ear to divisive calls and excelling internationally through India, a P.T. Usha making best use of the least available natural facilities, and so on...

These extraordinary persons have some things in common: They are unperturbed by the disturbing noises of mobiles, TV or the ipads and other smart gadgets, and have an inherent stability of mind that helps them overlook, or rather, avoid the meaningless din of unnecessary glitz and power show and ego clashes and focus upon work in hand.

Thus Saina Nehwal, would rather revel in sweating her T shirt out on a badminton court, rather than keeping herself engrossed in front of a mundane TV show like many others through the day. It is as if all these people are in a constant trance, murmuring silent prayers to an innate GOD, and piling up loads of strength in the process to scale up enormous and dizzying targets that they have set for themselves. Thus they are more seen doing things rather than heard boasting meaningless bravado and expletives.

It is a pity that the "HAVES" have totally bowed down their heads in complete surrender to the western culture, that boasts of immoral indulgence in useless exchange of sms, MMS, Facebook, Whatsapp and Skype informations and messages that serve no purpose other than exchange of mostly polluting thoughts and ideas that initiate a vicious cycle of ego boosts at the cost of riling a third person or party and keeping oneself destructively and continuouisly amused till one looses all enthusiasm for any positive thinking and positive contribution to society.

Facebook has become a malady in society in itself, with people starting their day off with a bang by clicking a "SELFIE"

NAMO style and posting it on FACEBOOK, SKYPE, WHATS APP and WHATNOT....etc. The "SELFIE" may range from things as mundane as;

- *Lazying around and stretching while getting up in the morning..*
- *Seeing the Toothpaste Foam in one's own mouth in the mirror in the morning...*
- *Hanging around in Towels...*
- *Trying a new pant or shirt...*
- *Saying cheers to a mundane cup of Tea...*
- *Smooching one's doggy...*
- *Poking one's doggy...*

Stretching out on a double bed with a big Teddy Bear Soft Toy or Dalmatian soft toy with an equally Dalmatian night suit...

A SELFIE" while leaping up in the air (For nothing, but having tasted love -and sleeze- time)

Swinging a badminton or Tennis racket (Not in the Courts but in the bathrooms and in the kitchen and keeping it later in Garage for years without use).

- *Stepping out of the house...*
- *Waving to an Auto rickshaw to stop...*
- *Stepping up in a bus or local...*
- *Peeping out of the bus...*
- *Having a mouthful of Pizzah with a thumbs up (A great achievement being symbolized)...*

- *Arriving at the office/workplace/college/even school kids are not far behind...*

- *1 or 2 selfie during work with or without colleagues (Till the actual work pressures down the seriousness in the mind and brings some soberness ...*

- The same things start agin in the evening with;

- *SELFIE while stepping out of the Office/College/ other places...*

- *Buying vegetables...*

- *Buying groceries...*

- *Pumping it out in the Gym...*

- *Saying cheers to a cup of evening coffee...*

- *Visiting a Mall with Girlfriend or wife (Even boyfriends get together to pose a big Victory "V" SELFIE just to celebrate some thing....)*

- *Discussing politics with friendly neighbourhood Guptajee...*

- *Watering the lawn and plants...*

And so it goes on…. Till the "HAVES call it a day with a bit of ego boost (By ego bashing of opponents), lots of tit bits to guzzle down the intestine, *loads of sleazy thoughts, and some completed work and targets achieved (The achievements may wary from person to person and his/her vicinity).*

What we all Indians should be thankful to is that we see such composed and strong minds nurtured with great pains in far off small towns by a gritty mother, father, coach, guardian or mentor, sometimes lucky enough to catch the eye of a corporate sponsor and sometimes not. Be it the extremes of cold conditions in Punjab, Haryana, Himachal or J and K and even in far off

Uttar Pradesh, a bunch of determined souls set upon their task early in the morning, motivated by either the good wishes and blessings of their near and dear ones, and working each day to upgrade their skills in a definite area to a level just for the sake that it ensures that it may bring laurels to them in their respective field and mores a great sense of pride to their near and dear ones.

Is it this strong sense of attachment and human bonding that brings out such stupendous efforts and marvelous rewards, which still exists in rural and small towns of India and is getting extinct in cities and larger towns? It has been discussed at lengths that Emotional Quotient (EQ) is a more productive force than the Intelligence Quotient (IQ) and this applies well to the possible role of strong human bonding as the driving force behind super achievers from small towns.

This gives rise to another question. In a larger city, we normally assume that higher levels of education and skills grooming and associated facilities are available to the aspirants. But where is the driving force amongst the urban youth?

Rather it is a common observation now that city adolescents, youth and now even kids are showing more deviant patterns of behavior, showing a typical sense of sarcasm, and lack of respect and attachment to almost all things, including communication gap with parents (which is more an affected or peer influenced or cinematic lack, influenced by Indian cinema), vanishing respect for teachers, even such disregard sometimes so as to openly taking swipes at them in such a wicked manner that could bring professional eveteasers to shame sometimes, and then even sarcastic lack of mutual bonding and confidence amongst the friends or mates with discussions getting centered mainly on style, fashion (That includes which Coaching institute or tutor in town is in fashion), the opposite sex and food. And why should boys have all the fun?? This is a question that is a poser to almost everyone and leaves him or her clueless. A great display of inquisitiveness indeed!!

Some leading news makers from small towns and their backup supports include-Saina Nehwal, Vinod kambli, Vrijender Singh, Sushil Kumar, Mahendra Dhoni, Sir jadeja, Md Shami, Mary Komm, The Pathan Brothers, Sarita devi, CAPTAIN RATHORE and countless small town people who serve and rise to appropriate positions in the railways, army, civil services, medical colleges, public works, highway authority, media, entertainment, films, theatre, police, security and paramilitary forces, nursing, paramedical, transport authority, construction and architecture, trading and commerce chain, and retail-sales. Many of them are faceless, having not reached the pinnacle of popularity like actor Ranveer Singh, Ashutosh from Aaj Tak, Kumar Vishwas from AAP, Dr Chella Kumar, INC, Sh Gaurav gogoi, INC, Sh Jitendra Singh, INC, Sh Sachin Rao, INC, Dr Ampareen Lyngdoh, INC, Sh Anil Chaudhary, INC, Sh Gokul Butail, INC, Sh Bhupendra Yadav, BJP, Sh Prabhat Jha, BJP, Smt D Purandheshwari, BJP,Ms B chandraka, IPS, Sh ajit Doval, IPS, Sh Satyendra Dubey, IES NHAI, Sh Armstrong Pame, IAS Manipur, Shivdeep Waman Lande, IPS Bihar, V V laxminarayana, JD, CBI, Kiran Bedi, Archana Ramsundaram, Snajukta Parashar, Meera borwankar, all womwn IPS of mettle and steel, or others, but silently they are devoted to the task assigned to them making sure that they stand up to the principle of "Duty First", and that is what is actualy making the world go around for Indian economy as a whole and giving the chance to prime time panelists to discuss changing patterns of GDP, WPI, Trade Deficit and inflation. Not going far away at all, example of Narendra Modi, christening himself a Chaiwala and going on to become the Prime Minister of India itself is a model in motivation. Though many have been unhappy about his radical past with a flair for giving away to public emotions and allowing himself to be won away by casteist and religious influences, no body denies the efforts that he has put up to administer good governance in Gujarat.

What stands out for most of the names mentioned above as leaders in their own way, is the inner grit, sense of duty and confirmation to the system, intense desire to maintain the integrity of the system, borne out of great reverence and regards for the system, and the hunger for adding their own touch to the existing way of things and leave a mark. It may not be an entrepreneurial leadership example in any way, but it stands out as exemplary model in making sure that the public aspirations do not face hinderence or injustice or prejudice and malpractices in any way, and are falicitated to work conveniently, making sure that they even work behind the curtains, so that others can shine in fame, glory and lime light. The sportspersons, in their own way show the innate desire to exceed the expected limits and go beyond in their quest for standing out to earn laurels for their motherland, a desire that is different in intensity and passion than anyone else in that arena.

II

Emerging Leadership Styles

(Between the Ears..........!!)

25.

The "don't give a hoot" and the Casual Bermuda Clan: Leading ads Making the Business Happen

CONTEXT

Lifestyle, communication revolution, Facebook and relevant effect on all matters including media and content and projections.

Lifestyle and style have steered the human and social behaviours through the decades, more so since the era of coloured talkies in Hollywood and in all other countries too including Bollywood in India. Post World War II. The world has seen emergence of varied style statements including those of country leaders, viz., Roosevelt, Eisenhower, Stalin, Nehru, to military Generalsin flamboyant uniforms, and also from leading sports, music and art icons.

for the commons, as well as for the leaders, was assumed earlier to mean, a state of being fit, groomed, well oiled, well healed, morally and socially correct and smart, that included well read, well mannered and sober. Years ago, with social habitation of humans taking full shape, the bards and poets defined styles with their thoughtful looks, sorrowful eyes and long flowing robes that seemed continuous with their pensive natures. Back home it was Mirza Ghalib, Khusro and the likes defining style.

Late in the 20th century, as you said style, images of James Bond, be it -----or a recent----- flashed before the eyes. Or so it meant a Morlin Monroe in a swashbuckling pose, or to some in India, it meant Madhubala besides a Ford Model. It even meant, Indira Gandhi and American president John F Kennedy to some, not to forget Pt Jaweahar Lal Nehru. To many it meant Gregory Peck, and to some in India Dev Anand and Raj Kapoor in a three piece suit, all in black, with Manoj Kumar and Dilip Kumar in good company. As times changed it were Robert De Neiro, Elton John and to some -----and Shammi Kapoor, Pataudi and even Ajit to some in India.

Then came the World of Disney, Chaplin and Johny Walker/s in between and garrulousness and gawkiness made the people forget about style for some time for sake of a full laughter. Still definitions changed with Sylvester Stallone, Jacki Shroff, Anil Kapoor or a Jean Claude Van Damme redefining style quotient along with a Hema, Zeenat or Madonna and others to represent that oomph style quotient in between.

Jackie Chan, and Govinda at home led the absurd but still lovable and street smart style period, emoting, joking, laughing, jumping, fighting at the same time. The others to join in were Karishma, Raveena and alikes with Sandra Bullok as counterparts in Hollywood. George Bush Junior completed the christening of this new style by taking on the mantle of American President twice after his father's glorious years with Clinton in between. He had his own free for all, least bothered, cheaky grin and style that at once declared war on Saddam and alikes to highlight America's no nonsense attitude. At home Lalu was not too far behind giving the best of Comedy Circus and Laughter Challenge heroes a run for their mill apart from running a state as chief minister or helping Rabri do it for him. All style role model in themselves to their fans.

Style still is the buzz word around everywhere. The import of the word *"style"* seems to have taken up on a different latitude altogether. The saari gave way first to safari for women (remember Ranjeeta in mid 70s bollywood or others), then to salwar kameez (in vogue till last few years), and now to jeans and top, noodle strap and what not and also pant and shirts for women, and to the latest, vibrant coloured shorts and even shorter T shirts and shoes which are vibrant and coloured in absolute contrast with a goggle in contrast too. For men it has changed from 3 piece suit to safari to jeans and T shirt to the latest *"Dark Blazer against a light pant with contrasting dark vibrant shirt with that devil may care open first two buttons and a gelled and spiked hair to match, and the shoes with that long nose that just cant be resisted.............."*.

Well, things have definitely changed and... of course, for the better, and no one is complaining if a CEO comes to an Executive meet attired as above, as party has to immediately roll on after the short meeting and proceed into late night (That is a must).

Even at the school and College level, the shy girl and impish boys paved way for either the outspoken girl or the smart guy, and now to a mixed breed which is a boy or a girl next door, coy and also outspoken (and what not...........) in the same go (or turn by turn......) both taking digs at each other, or being cozy a minute later to having moved on a minute later................!!. This definitely requires a different set of style to match and so it is lazy pyjamas (Or our very own Bermuda) and lousy T shirts for women and that casual slipper to match. For boys, it is that unkempt look with that lazy shirt half tucked in and half out (It may be any which way, that should be guessed), in that rough and *smartly dirty jeans* and our very own chappals to match (A coloured goggle or Gandhian spectacles may best fit in). (You may have to juggle in and out of that intellectual and happy go lucky attitude a million times, then this attire is the best that suits).

The crux of the matter is that you should be on your toes for that party that may be any time on …..(God knows when….??). Catch any IT leader on a foreign official business tripo, relaxing in the hotel in the evening, ands you would mistake him for a boarding degree undergrad chilling out in pyjamas.

Apart from the attires the gadgets are becoming coloured and flashy too with the Apple phone (Now I- phone or smart phone) looking flashy pink or yellow or orange with a similar look for that *MY-laptop.* Accordingly it is Kareena with that mean and smart attitude and a dress to match in colours, who is on the ads throwing the gadgets around, in contrast to the earlier men with executive looks who were made to speak at length about the technical nuances of the gadgets with that stiff upper lips, to the more dapper customers. And mind you, these gadgets have to match our very own Bermudas in gaudiness (Some/most even provide a touch screen which can change colours to match).

The crux of the matter is that, a leader who is not flashy, colourful and casual at the same time is definitely not a happening one!!

Even Amitabh Bachchan, has changed and dons looks and attire that has a mix of all above ingredients, but amazingly, and not surprisingly for him, carries it off with great élan as he always does in all the roles he sets his hands on (The stand up people may note the mental homework he does and just not the swagger that has to be again and again paraded for applauds).

The parallel style codes that are making the world go round for the elitist or the intellectuals or the addabaz in India either on newhours or at other places are a NaMo kurta, a Rahul pyjama kurta or even a tailored crossed Kejriwal shirts with that simple babu pant and chappals.

But somewhere, it can be sensed that it is the restlessness of the Bermuda clan, which is affecting the jantar mantar rallys, the newshours or even the KBC sets and of course undoubtedly our own Ekta Kapoor sets for the soap operas. Whether the rub off is positive, cohesive, indiscrete or meaningless and rowdy or elitist, that remains to be judged.

Hail my Bermuda!!

26.

Leadership: The "GIVE ME FIVE"!! Style

Humour

CONTEXT:

Often, as the world gets more competitive, either in consumer selling, innovation, sports, administration or even political leadership of the masses, it is widely observed that small groups form in the larger organization and try to prove being more better and efficient than the others within or even outside. Herein lies the action that makes such scuffles and skirmishes enjoyable and game, and even give tongue in cheek moments to those involved and even those observing the battle first hand. Sports are naturally witness to such happenings where some groups have to outsmart the other, but when it happens against the expected mandate or rule of thumb or clandestinely or out of an overt desire to derail the progress of the opposite camp, as in politics or films or other areas, it may become hilarious or amazing and "Give Me Five"!!

As expected build up to such "Give Me Five" events requires a ring leader, who brings the team around, goads and accentuates the performance so that the desired purpose is achieved in a resounding fashion and the opposite camp is left to pick up the remains after the symbolical mortal thrashing received, to the proudest, loudest and most vicarious grins and gaffes of the other camp.

BACKGROUND: 2012-2014; Impending elections in 2014, and the BJP versus Congress stand off has naturally goaded members in both camps, and hectic parleys are the order of the day as pre rally or post rally annexures, meant to iron out, sort out and ease out a lot many things, remotely, distantly, covertly or overtly likely to affect the outcomes or the harmonious balance within and in the opposite camp. In context to the same, many Give Me Five events happen cutting across party lines and grab the lime lights for various reasons. Sports and other professions also take on this leadership skill with a vengeance, and many groups settle many a scores with one or more such "Give Me Five" momments.

June 2013

Mr Narendra Modi's rise in BJP hierarchy, Sh Lalkrishna Advani's stance and parallel political, social and sports goings on and sense of déjà vu at sudden achievements and sense of exhilaration.

Goa Chief Minister Mr Manohar Parikkar almost jumped out of his seat on stage, and thumped the palm of Chhatisgarh Chief Minister Raman Singh at the National Convention of BJP in June 2013 at Goa. *"GIVE ME FIVE!!"* he was almosct about to yell having sensed that the two of them had almost made it to the Central rank and top elite leadership in BJP by their performance at the respective state level and now at the national scheme of things.

Suddenly their eyes exchanged a mischievous glance and they cut short their celebrations and slumped into their chairs with the most somber faces.

Day Two of the BJP Conclave:

Advaniji is supposed to get on board the plane to Goa from Ahmedabad to attend the Conclave and all news channels are stationed strategically with cameras focused on the door of Advaniji's house. Gradually by 2 PM sweat and dust settle down on the foreheads and whispers get in circulation in a tongue tied fashion.

Finally it was 4 PM and Advaniji was still not indicating any movement towards the airport, let alone being on stage at the Goa Conclave, and it was the turn of Congress Core group in Delhi jumping up with gay abandone and there it was, Mr Singhvi shouting to Mr Digvijay Singh *"GIVE ME FIVE!!"* Sh Rahul and Ms Sonia ji however let no sign of voyeurism escape their facesand wore the nonchalant look to perfection with Sh Manmohan Singh standing in complete acceptance.

Day Three of the BJP Conclave:

It was the third day of the Conclave and after lots of speculations and brainstorming, Sh Narendra Modi was finally anointed the Chairman of National Campaign Committee for BJP in the coming elections for 2014, and there it was; the majority of second rung BJP leadership leaped in air with a loud and thunderous *"GIVE ME FIVE!!"*

Day after the BJP Conclave:

Amid speculations of being sidelined and branded a forgotten patriarch, Advaniji comes up with a trump card; resignation from the BJP Executive Committee, and there it was; the Congress Head Office went gung-ho and berserk expecting *BJP bandwagon* to come to a grinding halt, giving some breathing space to the *sinking ship* Congress, and there seemed to be an all pervasive*"GIVE ME FIVE!!"* mood in the party with many leaders lookingdebonair and bearing *"I told you so"* look to perfection during prime time debates on News channels.

Thus political class across party lines today is taken over by the *"GIVE ME FIVE!!"* phenomenon. Not long ago Sh Narendra Modi had gone tweeting about Shashi Tharoor's girl friend being a million dollar friend, to which Mr Shashi Tharoor had retorted tweeting "To me my friend is invaluable". It was indeed a *"GIVE ME FIVE!!"* moment for all those believing in Page 3 romantic bonding on social network.

Also, it was not long ago that Sh Arvind Kejriwal, Sh Prashant Bhushan and Ms kiran Bedi had started a series of "Reveal all" press conferences and public gathering, christening it "Anna Hazare Jantar mantar Krantees". With Mr kejriwal needing no proding efforts, it was *"GIVE ME FIVE!!"*moment for the media almost every day. Mr Kejriwal would come up with new trump cards and aces up his sleeves and give them their joyous moments every other day, be it the revelations on the Coalgate Scam, CWG scam, Food scam, oil scam, 2G scam,........and it seemed to go on with no parties being spared, leaving his own team mates Bedi and Bhushan puzzled. There he was either pulling the Congress down or tearing the BJP apart while the parties sat with their fingers crossed and the media jumped with joy for the print and visual content it got to keep themselves alive and kicking every day, with all, including the reporters, cameramen, editors, newsreaders across all newspapers and channels making hay while the sun shone, and the new entrants getting a chance to hoan their yellow journalistic skills through all the melee and drama helping them sail through their "on the job" graduation in journalism with plenty of fun, tea rounds and smoke to make it attractive with plenty of sting practices, right or wrong, being thrown in as good ingredients (remember Jindal group and Zee News).

The same voyeuristic *"GIVE ME FIVE!!"* moments were also reflected on field recently in Indian Cricket team with some insinuations in the media, as to how Sehwag teaming up with Gambhir in creating their own "Give Me Five" moment against the charisma of M S Dhoni and team (Virat included) by planned display of wonderful destructive batting that left the Indian fans in awe as Indian batting line up came crashing down so often. How much substance was there in the insinuations or allegations, is however a matter of individual discretion, but it definitely gave "Give Me Five" moment to many a journalism and media team, in the form of thousands of ways the same could be analysed on air with lots of slow motion videos and commercial breaks being merrily put in between, with repeated melodramatic scream of the debate or analysis theme, which would often go like….*Kya kar rahee hai Ganmbhir Sehwag kee Jodi??……………*

Bollywood has its own give me five moments with rival camps biting and chewing off their nails with every new release, anticipating that the hero or heroine concerned bites the dust and the film gets labeled damp squib. Ramgopal Verma wears a glee on his face with every Karan Johar release, as also Ajay Devgan of a Yash Chopra banner release, and Salman too with every SRK release and vice versa. They have their own *"GIVE ME FIVE!!"* moments in RA-one, Veer, Jhoom Barabar Jhoom, Ramgarh ke Sholay *et al.*

The corporate circle is often abuzz with *"GIVE ME FIVE!!"* moments with incidences where a reputed name fails to save the day, as in the case of Vijay Mallya and his Kingfisher and Subroto Roy and his Sahara loosing some steam in between. They are however constructive even in such moments as the follies of others are taken as a lesson in business by the others.

Navjyot Singh Siddhu is often riled for his on screen "jump off the chair" guffaws and fists thumping antiques. But he only represents the expressive and joyous mood all around town and the pervasive *"GIVE ME FIVE!!"*moments that are also stimulating the citizens to jump to the TV channels and celebrating taking dig at each othermay it be Big Boss or Rakhi ka Swayamvar.

It seems that the phrase has come out of the football stadium, rubbed off on school kids and the public at large and has been interpreted in thousand ways to make it most efficient to mark the most vicious team spirit in most bizarre of situations for the rivals, devoid of anything to mark as personal achievement by the individual or its team.

Amen and Give me Five!!

27.

The in The Face Leadership Style

COMMENT:

Leadership styles have drastically evolved over the years with reference to the visible differences in the Socio cultural behavior and communication patterns evident in the form of things as big as US presidential election, India Australia Test series, upfront election campaigning in India, Consumer goods positioning by rival FMCG majors in India, or the famous Bollywood heroines' envy parade and cat fight against each other Trump was loud, inflammatory, no holds barred and hoarse during campaign against Obama, and same is the case during elections in India. This change in global leadership is neglected precisely through a parallel clearly visible change. Change from the soft, soulful musical film style to a raunchy dance number style over the years)

Not long ago the Indian Film industry, fondly christened Bollywood, mesmerized us with its soul touching renditions of equally soulful composition by great masters that included musicians and poets like Ram Lal, Faiz Ahmed Faiz, Mazrooh Sultanpuri, Neeraj, Raja Mehandi Ali Khan, Naushad, Salil Chowdhary, Ravi, Jaidev, Khayyam, Ravindra Jain, Madan Mohan, Shankar Jaikishan, Rajendra Krishna, Roshan, S D Burman, Bade Ghulam Ali Khan and many other stalwarts, who did not come out with a composition unless they found it worth a second look and of some soulful content worth its salt to be able to express the desired emotion in a balanced way.

Films, Theatre plays and stage shows were once made laying great emphasis on the relevance to situation and incorporate a variety of genres of dance and music while portraying a story with lot of pathos depending on the total emotional content or flavours to be added to the story.

Accordingly the films may incorporate a classical dance and song sequence, a folk dance, a romantic randes-vouse number, a situation with hero or heroine being too morose to do anything but just coming out with a melancholic song. A cabaret would always be performed by a Helen, Jayshree T, a Padma Khanna and their ilk only, while the bhajans and devotional songs would go to the heroines.

The doyens of the Public Centre entreprises becoming operational in these years thus showed a very philosophical leadership style typical of Vimal Roy or V Shantaram cinema, imbibing all that was there in the films of that era. Thus they would stick to an innate value of ethics and morality in public dealing, bear a down to earth demeaneaur in interactions, and display social equality in their leadership by way of referring even to peons as *Madanjee or Gopaljee,* and also displaying a sense of support for equal opportunity for both gendres by acknowledging the presence of female subordinates and secretaries as *"Meenajee" or "Kusumjee"* .

Gradually the films shifted from social message as the driver to entertainment as the central idea. Thus the Vimal Roys and the V Shantarams were replaced gradually by the Chopras, Hussains, Sagars, Raviprasad and other southern stalwarts with connoissures of art, namely K Abbas, Rahi Masum Raza and Gulzars and many others thrown in. The stress came to be on the thrill in the contents in the form of suspense, romance or romantic triangle, comedy and celebrations with a pinch of story, a social message with some gallantry and love for once country thrown in as some additional ingredients.

This marked another change in leadership style with Bosses acquiring Club manners with most of the babus, either senior or juniors starting to spend evening time in clubs playing cards and many also enjoying a sip too much which caused some definite turbulence at home later. *Meenajee* was thus many a times referred to as *Meena* and *namastejee* changed to *Hello* in most cases, and cigarette on the lips became an official statement and a mark of intense involvement in the daily official proceedings, a la Dev Anand, Ajeet or even a Shatrughan in many films.

A stage reached in Indian cinema, where the hero was followed by the heroine who crooned love songs to woo him whereas he would act coy or sullen keeping in mind that he had to still get a good job for himself let alone maintaining a wife too. Thus we could hear Mala Sinha wooing Dharmendra in Aankhen with "MILTI HAI ZINDAGI MEIN MUHABBAT..............". The trend continued with other songs and combinations too, viz., *"Jaiye aap kahan jayenge, yeh nazar laut ke aayegi"* with Aasha crooning for Aasha parekh who would follow.............. Also other numbers, viz., *Dil mein tujhe bitha ke, kar loon main band aankhein"*, the sweetly composed song by Ravindra Jain and very soulfuly sung by Lataji made the day for listeners across all ages and groups. The Indian heroine was further given liberty to express herself with some very melodious songs, like, *"Ankhiyon ko rehne de akhiyon ke as paas, door se dil kee bujhatee rahe pyaas"*, wherein Latijee sings for a very somber and melancholic Dimple in Bobby, or the *"Jab bhi jee chahe nayee duniyaan basa lete hain log"*, sung by Lataji for the Yashraaj love triangle.

Years later, the heroine was allowed more space and freedom to dance to pacy numbers while announcing her undying love for the protagonist, as in *"Saat samundar paar main tere peechhe peechhe aa gayee"* . Then came the stage wherein, the heroine could carry off a raunchy mechanised love song and make the audience go wild about the dance steps at the same time, as in Madhuri's "Ek do teen chaar panch chhe saat........................ The song and then many such numbers performed by Madhuri, set the stage for many following actresses to break the mould, come into their own and express their love and passion unabashedly as a very fast paced dance number rather than through a soul stirring song. Thus Madhuri continued with *Bada dukh deena, tere lakhan ne ", Paalki mein ho ke sawar chali re ",* or *"O tere pyaar ko salam o sanam"* by Alka Yagnik for Sridevi in Chaal Baaz.

Then came the twist in the tale with new starlets and even lead female singers coyingly agreeing to mouth or sing double meaning compositions and sway to body and hip movements that were later termed as liberation of women's sexuality. It started with some subtly worded and beautifuly composed songs earlier including "Raat nashilee hai bujh gaye deeye" sung by a lead female protagonist but later on being restricted to sidekicks and wimps till 80s when songs including "Doctor babu sui laga do, ...uiee" and later "Cholee ke peechhe kya hai" opened the flood gates and all composers showed their been there done that attitude with songs having lots of titillation and seductiveness. Gradually it became a stamp of success and producers asking composers to pen down and compose a mix of songs, which could help audience vent, all sorts of emotions. Thus followed "Chhat par soys tha...", "dil waalon ke dil kaa karaar lootne....", "shaam hai dhuwaan dhuwaan....", and many others with lead heroines letting themselves loose on the screen with either Saroj Khan, or other choreographers directing them to swoon their audiences.

Then came the era of item numbers with choreographing becoming the buzzword and many female choreographers entering the stage namely Faarah Khan, and with the lead heroine belting out a loud and raunchy item number hitting straight under the belt with no holds barred vengeance.

These numbers, if studied closely, reveal a peculiar path to composition. The urge for the song being the need of the film, making the screen play writer to add a song sequence at such a point that was totally irrelevant to the story and unwanted and out of nowhere the heroine would emerge and gyrate such violently to the song that even the most sizzling and notorious of a courtesan in a sultan's darbar would be put to shame. Thus, while a Madhuri will make mischievous glances at the camera and count numerals inviting her bueau towards her in the sensational dance number "Ek do teen chaar panch chhe sat aath....," in Tezaab, a Sridevi would sizzle in a wet blue saari near a pond on a rainy day and announce in no uncertain terms that she was hardly able to keep herself in that wet weather or pass her time in day nor at night and would like to say the magical words "I Love You" in the song "Kaate nahin katte yeh din yeh raat....." to theinvisible protagonist, Mr Anil Kapoor. Gradually the item song has become a neccessty with producers bullyuing the screenplay writer to have provision for such a song. Every heroine had to bow down to such demand be it even the super elegant Diya Mirza when she had to gyrate in rain to impress Emran Hashmi in the song......... Raveena Tandon was compelled to do a hardcore bar striptease in the name of the outstanding script demand in Aks apart from some other rather sobre numbers like "Pichhoo pade re mere pichhoo pade....". Karishma almost went into the alley of such numbers with "Sexy sexy sexy mujhe log bolein..." which was later rephrased to "Baby baby baby mujhe log bolein...." The famous Anu Malik - Alisha combination, which gave much news for a long time by means of long and continuous spat between Alisha and Anu on how Anu had evil designs on Alisha or otherwise. Matter however ended with good sense prevailing on both for professional reasons. Similarly Aysha Jhulka condescended to dance to some numbers in which later turned into a mutual public spat between all stakeholders dangerous and calculated risk and incorporating western liberal behavior patterns into Indian senses which naturally affected in the persons involved in filming such scenes in more ways than one, definitely more in a negative way.persons involved taking. Shilpa Shetty danced to a rustic number "Dilwalon ke dil ka karrar lootne...." But thankfuly it was perceived as a more positive and light rustic expression of simplicity of enjoyment and time pass and revelry and not taken as a lecherous hardcore item number. However Shilpa and Shamita Shetty had to move their legs in rain to a rather hot number together "Baras jaa baras jaa ae badal..." for the male protagonist.

Kareena has been smart enough to carry many of such borderline numbers with elan and aesthetics without getting labeled or involved in controversies over songs such as "

As the trend goes, all leading heroines, including Deepika Padukone, Katreena Kaif, and others had to bow down to such demands and dance to "Sheela kee jawani..." and "................".

The point to be noted however is that most of the leading ladies have somewhere concluded that now it is eminent that an item number is a job assigned for sure for the leading lady of a film, and so it is discussed with some sense of aesthetics and technical soundness to project it as a technical work of art (Whatever it may sound like, as art and Technology demand different set of thought processes, but still we have to listen to such things as "It was most aesthetically done".... and so on)

The item number has become a sort of illusionary image, which one would crave to possess at the same time look at the other doing the same, with lot of sarcasm. Thus we see a lot of heroines indulging in give and take banters regarding each other's item numbers, washing their dirty linen in public, and then washing their hands off...........(Period!!).

The itch for an item number has conquered the psyche of modern day Bollywood wannabee heroines to such an extent that it is considered a great addition of another colour stripe in one's robe and something to boast about.

Things really have come a full circle, with mujras being once looked down upon for being derogatory to women's respect for showing one women being lusted upon and used as an object of use by a largely male crowd, to this day when an item number is taken as a great creation of art with no misgivings about the loss of respect, or being lusted upon by ogling eyes and rowdy comments and verbal assaults during the making.

Parallel "in the face" leadership changes

As time progressed, the melancholic and pensive style of Manoj kumar became hit even with leaders, with senior corporate and public sector leaders, taking care of a dapper sartorial attire matched with a parallel khadi west coat often projecting Indian values even at public places. There was a strange connectivity between the elite and the working class with an understanding of mutual hardships of day-to-day life and the emotional pangs of the elite. Thus the workers could relate to the elite and vice versa. It all came to the realization that every one was trying to earn their basic Roti, Kapda aur makan in their own way. Thus, it was sort of way in real life, with to an officer calling Ramlal as Ramlaljee with respect and Savitri as Savitri devi, with leadership style meanng going to the shopfloor and sharing the tiffin with a worker. With films like Namakharam and Rajesh Khanna making definite social statement underlining the strength of the working class, the leadership style again acquired a social hue with public sector leaders showing more affection towards their assistants and secretaries.

With more films focusing on workers and the strength of their unions (namak haram, kala patthar…), the leadership style got variegated colours with some leaders adopting a stubborn, obstinate and reprimanding style against the unions. Others still going on with the soft glove approach, while still others working in an intriguing way, trying to setup informers within the worker unions and playing as per divide and rule policy, so well reflected in many films.

A stage reached where both the workers as well as the leadership styles were juxtaposed to each other and were *In the face, or with an itch for conflicts.* Thus the arrogance and straight face attitudes became more and more prominent with women members in the leadership team showing either a filmy vampish consonance with the stubborn and spoiled corporate brats and sons, or breaking away from the villanish and scheming management to side with the defiant, honest, hard working workers (and thereby woo the hero in films). The working places by this time could witness lot of overtures, covert or overt, impish grins, glances and suggesting remarks combined with songs which became more and more open, a far cry for workplace modesty that once happened to be. The Bombay or the metropolitan culture remained mostly in the metropolitan cities, but started spreading across to smaller towns and work cultures largely through the films (which no doubt exaggerated on all counts). Thus be it public sector enterprises like the state power boards, their generation units or distribution offices, agriculture universities and their farms, transport corporation or public sector banks, the undercurrent to some extent was the possibility of misuse of power by the incumbent operational heads which united the clerical and 4th class employee to some extent. This union generated a sense of belonging further strengthened by the.

Thoughts portrayed in Indian cinema. Further down the line, with corporations and limited forums gaining in number and formal and HR, personal norms and regulations coming into place, the style has again under gone a metamorphosis. Time has actually become money and every body seems to be short on time. Thus communication starts with informal short names and end often with a pat on the back or with an appreciating "Great." Recently it is more through encrypted whatsapp messages. retorted with more encrypted work completion messages, world is changing!

28.

Leadership, the Bang Bang style

(It is Diwali!!: And no one knows where it will Bang-Bang)!!

Period and Context: 2013 Indian continent and the neighbours

The world and the global citizen is on a fast track; it is action in everything and everywhere! Gone are the days of cautious steps, calculated moves and tight lipped utterances without much of an eyebrow movement and the most stiff of the upper lips, giving nothing away. Gone are the days of being diplomatic, savyy and affable! From cricket to basketball to politics to diplomacy to films to life as an ordinary citizen, things are definitely on fast track, and every body wants to make it large. Large by way of doing, projecting or creating something that carries a grandeaur, an aura and an impact, and that too an instant impact!!

After missiles, and now the drone assisted seek and destroye prowess, and the instant outreach of media taking news to all corners on the globe ina minute, everybody wants to make the world sit up and take notice. Militaries want to assert themselves across the borders by sound of bullets and bombs and countries negotiate with each other after an initial round of bombastic rhetoric bringing the roof down and the associated melodrama. Elections in India as well as across the globe also heighten and set the tone for hyperboles from all quarters, tearing apart the opposition.

It is Indian politics and imminent 2014 elections, and all political parties including stalwartsSh Narendra Modiji for BJP, Soniajee, rahuljee, Yadavjee, Yechurijee, Nabi Azadjee, Shivraj jee, Mamtadee, and othersare on a rally speeches spree, going all bang bang. Globally Central Asia and Afghanistan are as usual abuzz with Bang Bang activities leaving no dull moment for this part of the world. India Pak relations are also taking shape or loosing shape with a lots of bang bang. and the IPL Cricket India BangBang parties

It is Diwali time again and this year definitely things are going *kitty kitty, bang-bang* for many at the state, national or international stage. Though Diwali in India signifies a time to go all out in celebration of RAMA's win over evil and his return back to Ayodhya, also, a period of joyous celebration of business productivity and invoking of Goddess Laxmi for year round success, the period marks differently to different people and to some it is *bang bang* on a different note.

Modijee seems to be on a year round Diwali spree, shooting off his lips, hips and whatsoever, and going *bang bang* over Shehzada, Maharani, RJD and all. But for his kurta pyjama dress, he would have looked real debonair in a Mexican hat with a Mexican officer attire to match sitting atop a horse and commandeering his army of Shah and others to trailblazing campaigns in UP, Bihar, Karnataka, Orissa etc, shooting all and sundry who dare come in between his race to Delhi Darbar.

Rahuljee too seems to be riding on a cracker of an inspiration as an orator, mouthing proverbs, phrases and all, that even his colleagues and seniors up there in the Congress echelons would like to eat it all up themselves or make him do so. There he is either putting his own house on fire courtesy the *"........All Nonsense"* media briefing, or evoking that emotional or cross country terrorrockets that are expected to bring down the Modi balloon, but misfire making politicians play judging games about his intent.

Across the border, Pakistan seems to have come to a state where it seems to be at war with itself or its own people. The numbers of hardcore Islamic outfits that try to influence the political process with their maulanas spitting fire at various places is best left to guessing. The Pakistan Police seems to have reached a state where they appear tangled in their own web hardly knowing where the next explosion will kill their own women and kids, Lahore, Karachi,……..??. Further, USA is shooting off Drones targeted at one or the other Laden cloans or Al Quaida chieftain, which fall on Pak cities and outskirts just like an Indian kid cynically letting his Diwali rocket take its own course towards a neighborhood window. It is definitely *Bang Bang* but no body has a clue as to where and how.

The leaders, and the Taliban Heads too, in Afghanistan seems to be in a constant Diwali cracker mode with Taliban refusing to accept any loss of face againstruling government, or the residual allied forces, whatever remaining after US, UK and other troop withdrawals. Afghan kids seem to be growing up with rockets flying all helter skelter, with all groups and leaders trying to prove or score a point in a Bang Bang way.

Egypt too seems to have discovered a taste for mass hysteria and coups with people going all guns in bringing down the high and mighty with a loud bang (It is a classic case of a protest without a sole leader but possessing a leadership essence, Bang Bang). Mubarak could never imagine that he would be subject to such a show of massive crowd surge after having laid siege to the country, its population, its resources and its wealth for so many years with such a Bang Bang style for so many years.

Rupee seems to be tumbling and coming down against the Dollar taking a beating everyday- *Bang bang, thud-thud* and……………... What could be the style of leadership attributed to this phenomenon is open for discussion.

Naxals are having a hey day as they ambush and *bang bang* CRPF, state Police or Politicians at their will and score decibel points over the governments regarding their technical savvy in using latest gadgets to tramck, force or maraud and ambush. The leaders thus rely only on the Bang Bang way of making point to the local population as to what opinion they hold for local governance and how they plan to administer welfare.

Gen V K Singh has decided to go all out and light up a thousand lights every day throwing caution or sundry defence protocols to a hit out of the window (in a true sense across the boundary where the Musharrafs and Quayanis and all are all just too happy to lap it all up and shout "How's that??"

US FDA is hell bent on playing police thug games with Indian Pharma companies, trying to catch them off guard either in Patent infringement, noncompliance of Good manufacturing or quality policies and bundle them off to moon with a *bang*, making sure they are banned to manufacture or market for US thus protecting its own manufacturers. The leadership style here as shown by Pharma bigwig MNCs sitting at US is to arm-twist US FDA for the various favours into doing the same with Indian Companies trying to establish a hold in US in any way. Bang comes a ban on one Indian Pharma and bang on the other with bangon infringment charges or noncompliance to Quality charges.

T 20 matches have become sound and light affair with bowlers going for long sixes with Gayle, Dwayne, Virat, Rohit, Morkel or Dinesh Kartik charging up and having a blast hitting the ball into the space. The stadia are on fire as these players come chasing down the pitch towards theballers. Thus the captains too have to be Bang on in either winning a close one or even chilled out bang on while losing one.

Shikhar Dhawan has initiated his test and ODI carrier with a *bang* and so has Rohit Sharma come back in form with a *bang* and Virat and Dhoni have always been there playing their part and carrying the team on their shoulders with a *bang*.

President elect Trump has been bang on in laying out all his priorities for the country, as far as he has calculated with his team, inciting many to start thinking the way he does, taking along as many people he can sway along towards his right wing and Pro American thought. By the time this goes into publishing, he might have proved his acceptability bang on for sometimes to come.

29.

Chapter: Leadership: Transition From an over the top, to stingy Bosses

(From Get, Set and Splurge! To: Get, Set and save!)

Period and Background: (2011-14) It is all going on too merrily for the world in the first decade of the 21st century with economic activity proceeding decently globaly, and then suddenly, one after the other the economies start snapping and suddenly the buzz word changes across the globe from splurge to save to the last penny. How the societies adapt to the ill gotten habits of heavy spending, amidst changing scenario and the trends,and how the leaders and Bosses change their colours and their leadership styles, sets the context for the commentary.

The first decade of 21st Century is witness to some dramatic shifts and emerging global economic patterns, including formation of a more wide and inclusive G 20, the EU becoming more inclusive with countries like Latvia, Lithuania, Estonia, Poland, Hungary, Romania, Czeck Republik, Slovakia, Slovania and Bulgaria coming out of Russian shadow and entering the EU, Brazil being able to cast aside its image for decades as a promising but irresponsible, crime ridden economy, steered by leaders such as Cardoso and Lula, Japan and China signaling some thawing of relations, and a massive cellphone penetration boosting economic activity in the far off small towns even in third world countries. The formation of G 20, taking away some of the monopoly and economic clout from G7, considered the locus of economic power with 22% GDP of world being contributed by 7% of global population primarily from Europe and US has stimulated a larger global economic dynamism with involvement of much larger conglomerate of countries.

Despite such shaking transformations, the world saw a major economic crisis in the first decade of 21st Century, evident through major crisis, including the Russian crisis, the Argentina Crisis and the US Crisis. Argentina, experienced a sudden downgrade of its currency Peso as against the US $ sending shock waves in major investing activities, followed by Russian crisis induced by sudden nose diving of oil and natural gas global prices while Russia was increasingly getting habitual of basing its economic activity on sale of oil and natural gas. Finally the Amercican crisis resulted from the overleveraged banks, which mainly operated through MBS- Mortagage based securities for the housing sector, when the housing prices sudden collapsed with the collapse of housing sector bubble, bursting the MBS based financial standing of most of the major investing banks including Lehman Brothers, AIG, Bear Stearns, Countrywide Financials, Wachovia and Washington Mutual.

The financial crisis in 2008 has left global footprints of tremors in all major continents. The jilted, perplexed, knee jerk and irritated response by the executives from top to bottom, has shown a cascading effect on spending patterns, with major temperament changing from "devil may care" to "cautious, judicious and more miser", leaving behind an economic inertia shock in organisations, which is even evident in private lives.

A paradoxical state seems to have set across the world with economy playing snake and ladders since the last decade. Everything and every market and economy seemed so astoundingly bullish not very long ago at the turn of the century. The US paranoia of retail therapy and bizarre shopping seemed to have caught on with all and sundry in major cities across the world, and there you could see people splurging on stylish attires, extravagant lifestyle and sumptuous food and eateries from across the world and you had Mallyas and Bransons flying and showing off their chartered plains and spicy calendars. Thus Bosses became flashy and relished their *"Get Set and Splurge"*attitude.

Not long ago we saw people and leaders in various areas, upgrading from a landline to a handset and then to a sleeker one and then finally to a smart phone or I- phone and then a tablet. Even kids and wives made life miserable for their fathers or husbands if such demands were unmet with. The parties of the rich became more eventful with more on the platter, more music, more splash and lots of other things thrown in.

The eateries gradually transformed themselves to places of hanging out, drooling on and finding a global platter with a wide range of delicacies to gorge upon. The marketing team under the stewardship of the Zonal or Country Head could many a times be found laughing out boisterously in a premium restaurant in the evening with the Boss spending and splurging to generate a motivated group. The style of the Boss reflected in the work when you could see business houses splurging heavens on location and shooting for organizational marketing Calenders at beaches.

Keeping in tune with the splurging sense of the leaders, the restaurants" Bosses too started laying out a splurge menu, wherein you could start from the sizzling starters, simmering stews and soups and then dip your fingers in luscious curries, oriental, occidental or Italian delicacies, finally cooling yourself with Sundays and icecream mixes. Gone were the days when you entered a restaurant in India to find only Dum aaloo, chicken curries and kadhai paneer as the only solace for the stomach.

Younger generation took up beer as an alternate healthy soft drink labeling those sticking to Limca and Cola as dumb and juvenile. To top it, many urban pockets viz., Bangalore boasted of a female population, which had names of wine mixes on their fingertips. IT leaders working late in the night, often engaged in a style statements with glasses of bears in their hands. To add on, the hotel industry introduced lavish Kitty party, Bachelor's party, theme marriages and executive meet packages providing grand options to splurge upon. Thus Leadership style in all the cases was *Get Set and Splurge*, whether it was organizing a modeling event, leading a Fashion show, holding or mediating a business decisionmeeting or even the influential wives into social leadership roles hosting their contemporaries.

The same trend could be observed in all spheres of life. There you started having grand houses and complexes with lavish interiors, spacious and expanded 4 bedroom flats with extra large living room with a golf course view. Wives would settle for nothing less than a royale residential park colony with all the above and a special area to let women have their kitty parties be accommodated. With IT boom and an open economy advantage, many a young families found such suitable havens as home for themselves in cities as crowded as Mumbai and Bangalore.The hunger to have the old car exchanged for a brand new sedan, or even a resale giving the sedan MUV sensation, could be found all pervasive from men to their wives, sons or daughters.

However things seem to have taken a U turn in the last few years of the decade. America has suddenly developed cold feet over the expenses incurred in maintaining status quo in Afghanistan and Iraq and has gradually pulled out but not before the senate and Congress have been assigned the task to bring an economy in doldrums to a reassuring shape. With the Bush era having become a past and Obama having taken charge, the offensive, *take it head on* and *"have it so splurge it"* attitude (whether it is about splurging its might and intelligence here and there or other things) has given way to the pensive cautious, minimalistic and *" have it yet save it"* approach in all aspects (assuring that hands are not burnt in far off and irrelevant fires) of life from top to bottom leadership, even affecting the lifestyle spending. European economies have followed suit with some exceptions like French and German, which have shown some resilience. The Dragon also seems to be in a stage where it has lost some shine off the open and galloping economy tag but still retained the status of being a global challenge to others in spending.

World over the booming middle class has found the turf under their feet being swept away by the rapidly vanishing FDIs and henceforth stalling of vital developmental projects and consequent dwindling projects offering jobs and livings to millions who have come to streets atop local issues, be it Egypt, Taiwan or other countries. The rest of the middle class who have retained their profiles have reoriented their life styles in tune with the times and that is evident in the global decrease in spending and slowed economies heralding the current mantra *"Get set and SAVE"*.

The British stiff upper lip indicated intent on judicious use of phonetics to produce and portraythe required and actual intent of the spoken word. In a way it was very symbolic of the virtue of saving at the right places and still making the most of it. Many European societies monitor loudnesss of the spoken and communicated word and the resultant social comfort levels stressing on judicious and frugal communication.

Indian mythology is replete with calculated use of words, summons etc wherein balanced communication took place, between the Gods, general public and the *asuras*. Thus the sentences started with respectful or patronizing sermons like *"Arya", "Aryaman", "Dev", "Prabhu", "Tat",* and expressed the content in a terse and refined manner, which expressed all that was to be conveyed.

The defense force anywhere tries to be terse and very precise in all its communications (must have taken a leaf straight out from mythological communications) between the hierarchy and that is how the leadership ensures flow of command from top to bottom or flow of inputs back It is all about *Get, Set and Save....,* save on words, save on redundant expressions, save on energy for other good things, save on time and save on focus that should be on enemy movements and coordination.

The Hindu calendar still reminds people of various days coinciding with the moon cycle on which one can save upon eating habit by following a particular fasting pattern, which is also supposed to provide a rejuvenating effect on the body. Thus we have *Ekadashi Vrat, Pradosh Vrat,* and son.... The Jains follow the practice of Paryushan Parv, which reminds everybody to purify the body of toxins at least once a year by use of this *"Save on What You Eat"* practice by way of a serial fasting method, lasting for a specific number of days.

Some leaders whether on the shop floor, or in technology transfer or in promotion, are not the ones to shy away from using the phrases *"Economise where you can, Cut the costs, low inventory, wasteful expenditures, inventory management overheads"* and so on, so frequently that the people down the order are always on the toes and on the *Get, Set and Save....* mode as soon as they site them or are supposed to have an interaction. This style is seen to become more and more prominent as a person goes higher up the hierarchy. It seems to be a straight extension of the Hindu calendar and the fasting tradition "fast whenever you can".

A penny saved is a penny earned was the idiom, which represented golden wisdom for many years. It was adopted with reasonable logical approach by people ensuring saving but not being labeled miserly, and at the same time not loosing out on social competitions ion the form of good looks, physique, personality, style and fashion. Consumerism has affected global health and disease pattern, making a whole industry out of it. Thus obesity and the fight against it is a burgeoning industry in western parts of the globe with monitoring, equipments, food substitutes, lifestyle clinics, physical trainers, and antiobesity and cardiac drugs providing career to millions, as researcher, producer, distributor etc. Globalization is a real as well as virtual process with people across different nations picking up food, lifestyle, cultural habits of another country via satellite communication based technology, television, internet, telephone and mobile based tele audio video communications. Larger than life images have set the people's imagination wild in all spheres. Thus a young boy had learnt the tricks to massive spending on restaurant food. A young girl had learnt the tricks to sport flashy eyeliner, nail polish and oomph appeal that is way above her age. A teenager could recount the numbers of her girlfriends on his fingers and also the delicacies that her girlfriend would agree to have at his request. Another must strut his new sedan on the streets with stereo in full blaze. The earning young hardly cared for the world and made sure he spends a bulk of his salary and saved only the minimum. All this has received a major blow.

Even countries under right wing leaders are showing leadership intent and decisions which can be clearly categorized as not openminded, markedly miser, so far as the variety of diaspora they are meant to take care of, and against a culture of openness for a free global economy and work place for outsiders. Thus you feel US, UK and many other countries are on a Get, Set and save mode, as evident from pulling out of Agreements, Brexit and other landmark events. Once a leading proponent of free global trade and order, UK is in a hurry to exit from EU as Brexit looms large. Pakistan is severely hit by this mindset, where the patrons, US, UK, France et al have woken up to the perils of supporting indirect terror, and are suddenly on the Get, Set and Save mode as far as financial support to countries like Pakistan is concerned.

Israel and Palestine stand out by still being in the Splurge mode, as far as the firing of missiles and bombing each other is concerned-No holds barred. So is Syria aflush with bombings and destruction.

III.
Afterthoughts

30.

21st Century Leadership: Misleading Leadership through misinformation

CONTEXT:

In the past recent years, the charisma of social media, the bizzare Peter and indrani Mukerjee saga, Marathwada drought, Shashi Tharur and his blistering similies and metaphors, whatsapp and its astounding, amazing and many a times, devastating outreach….. have all unfolded in a peculiar fashion, wherein all the protagonists, the associated characters, and even the media and the people have discussed and behaved in a most outlandish way without well defined scripts, faultlines or limits. At many a time, the scripts have strayed down into being false, made up and inciting rather than bemusing. How they have touched, split open and laid bare the socio-politico and economical fabrics at many a times, is something to be sensed and felt through these situations…………….wherein, someone, somewhere seems to have lost it……………….., or jumped the gun, or taken things too far and damaged the spirit of humanity.

They have lost it

When they create a storm, out of a small ripple,

That starts from a matter trifle,

You realize,

They have lost it!!

When you see them
Exploit a body dead and still,
Shouting and sloganeering and going for the kill,
You realize,
They have lost it!!
When you see a personality change to a persona nongrata
Profiles changing to grey and shady, from black and white
All over the place are mediators, operating fly by night
You realize,
They have lost it!!

When you see people creating disasters of their own,
With small crackers turning into infernos,
With the bigwigs weighing down upon the ordinary
To make sure their will is carried out as mandatory,
You realize,
They have lost it!!

When you see parched lands in plenty,
With people down deep dry wells going trekking,
And on conservation & water harvesting others are
conferencing,
You realize,
They have lost it!!

When you see a bottle gourd overnight changing size,
And cows injected and milked twice and thrice,

Adulteration, making oncology thrive,
You realize,
They have lost it!!

When you see the society changing,
In the name of modernism and trendiness,
With thoughts giving way to compulsion for flashiness
Being smart Alek, becoming every dull nerd's business,
People on media oversocialising,
Then charging friends with loot, murder, blasphemy and,
Personalities taking downsizing,
You realize,
They have lost it

31.

Urbanization and loss of rustic innocence Cost of unrooted leadership

India is changing, and changing fast at that. Citys are bursting at seems and spreading out or rather anastomosing or proliferating out in all directions deep into the nearby towns, uprooting the rustic peace of vilages and their blissful distance from the modernization façade of a big city. In the process some of the innocence, some of the mutual connectivity is being lost. There is gradual loss of some traits which leave a void which gets wider by the day and a smartness which lacks the tint of sincerity, compassion and innocence between people of the same ilk, race or habitat. It is this bustle which is approaching, ...and poaching as well...........................

The approaching bustle of the town

A village sleeps merrily after a hard day's work,
With GOD in heart and prayler on lips.
Fathers have done it all, ploughed, planted,
Irrigated& protected,
Mothers have been there right behind,
Chopping, baking, roasting and frying,
While sons and daughters have ran around with songs on lips.
Elders exchange pleasantries and blessings to kids

Grandmas making a chorus with a campfire in their midst.
Rising aroma of the roast makes the meetings merry
Young and old spread on cots,
Under the open sky blue and starry.
Lilt of the violin and cusp of the *dholak*
Match the ghungroos and their ring
And so do the danceaurs and their zing.
Celebrations run daily late in the wee
Till all dance in twos and three.

Mornings have been early and aesthetic,
With cattle being attended, milk and butter collected,
Carts decking up and leaving for the fields
Oxes heaving and the rhyming neck bells, creating an aura
charismatic.
Men sweat it out in the backyard,
Shaping up for the tough day out
Getting ready then with a simple cold splash
And a colourful attire that runs riot.

Far away from the bustling city,
The small village is biding its time in bliss,
While the city runs amock from dusk to dawn,
The village never had its satisfying day and fulfilling sleep
amiss.

But change is life and nothing escapes it,
So does the fortune of the village and its people,
Gradually the farms get sold and multiplexes replace it.

One by one the tide of development approaches and engulfs,
The farms, the trees, the huts and the pavements,
And replaces them with shops, eateries and settlements.
The morning rumble of the cattle is going din,
The smoke and fire fresh from the earthen hearth is falling dim,
Wives forget the fresh buttermilk and paratha and talk more
about the SIM.
The evening cheer of togetherness is slowly giving space to
stubborn youth banters and riles
Matters close to heart are giving way to bikes and their miles,
The wise old men seldom seem to be sitting together
Seeing their families revel,
The youth, unruly, stubborn and sometimes wise
occupy the space and dwell,
Matters of commerce and money take over,
With interaction on cars, and means to achieve, the prime
mover.
Along come the roars of the cars and their horn,
And gradually the ring of the ghungroos in the bullock carts
is silent and forlorn.
The vibrant and loud colours of ghagras and chooridars
Are lost in the lane,
Making way for the jaded jeans and the pale shirts
And the elegant turbans give way to the unkempt mane.
The village well is slowly given the slip by
Small vends of cokes and cans.
Marriage palaces and banquets stand tall
Added to the revelries are cyber café and cinema hall.
Deenu has a mobile and Salim a smart phone

Together they roam, all over the place,

With schemish style, geeky attire and affected tone.

Girls too, don't want to be left behind,

Holding back is no more the in thing,

Reveling with a vengeance, is the priority in mind.

Hardly do we have the time to see,

The beauty of the azure of the sky through dawn to dusk,

The isolated quirks and the chirps of the small birds

Do no more entice us into a mango grove or atop a mound of husk.

Something has struck the innate sense of life,

Taken away the slow and pleasant pace of rustic emotion,

In the effort to fly high, there one goes down,

The approaching Bustle of the Town,

Seems more of a Commotion, more of a Commotion!!

32.

eBooks and the missing pleasure of reading a Sherlock Homes: revisiting the Classics

In the 20th Century, one thing that the world leaders that emerged had in common was a great and diverse reading habit. Books, which presented with a diverse range of context, situations and information to an inquisitive mind, made the day for such leaders. Great authors of intense fiction, hard hitting biographies, descriptions, war stories, drama, science, mystery and the ethereal world, made this world a beautiful place with their flair with language, adding quality in all spheres of life. From the biblical Psalms or the holy Quran or Ramayana or Gurugranth, to the later day fictions and mysteries making Aladdin, Phantom and Sherlok Holmes legendary characters, to the intensly literary period of English Classics to painstakingly romantic novels, the legendary authors gave a lot to feed and assimilate from.

As the world has progressed into the higher echelons of technical progress, the contents are becoming digital, hands on and available at the push of a button as ebooks. But the impact that suchon the go reading makes and the impression that it creates, whether transitional or eternal, is an open question, and looked at in a different way. Definitely, the amount of content that is available has multiplied beyond imagination, and it is upto a good leader, to make sure that s/he reads voraciously, and assimilates the best for him/her.

A good book can fire a reader's imagination beyond limit. A book may be a text book, a course book, a manual, a fiction book, a book on a science fiction, a biography, an autobiography, a book on sports, a book on history of a region, or a country or a book on culture, music, arts, local lifestyle, topography, food, geography or climate. It may also be a prose or a drama, a thriller, an action book or on technology.

A fiction or a thriller in any language, were the earliest pills for making a person unwind and then gradually get engrossed in the story and novel in the series of events that unfolded, living every moment as the protagonist or any other character fabricated into the stories. Thus not in a distant past we had a Sherlock Homes novel, building up a situation very high on intrigue, suspense, thrill, scheming, pace and machinations, and a fascinating, quirky personality with an aura, going about setting things right in a most surgical manner trying to find out a clue on the pathology of the situation, the symptoms, and then the leads that could help crack the suspense.

The reader meanwhile gets into the skin of the protagonist Sherlock Homes and vicariously sniffs around the site of crime and elaborates his musings about the crime to an imaginary Watson in all attention. Like Sherlock, gradually he manners all his activity all through the day, -intense, pensive, even a large hat dropping on the eyes, as if to have a view of everything without anyone coming to know. He pauses, a pensive pause, after almost every word, with wife, kids, relatives, all in attention, a bit bemused, and a little cautious-as if the fish he is smelling may just sneak out of their pockets and make them feel as the sinister villains.

Then there was the James Bond Series and its own set of admirers across a very wide age group ranging from 16 to 60 years, who wanted an adrenalin rush each time they would immerse themselves in reading a novel. A James Bond series actually does this by way of setting the whole drama at a very fast pace and developing situations which take the protagonist into either a well laid trap or to a mission which demands extraordinary heroism.

It also happened that books of individual poets were launched amidst great fanfare and show inviting elite people from all walks of life to celibrate and decipher the written letter in their own way at leisure time. Compilations of *couplets, nazms, and ghazals by Nida Fazli, Neeraj, Sahir Ludhianwi, Faiz, Aazmi*or those of great authors including Brown, Grante, Byron, Shakespeare, and other stalwarts generated such fiery passion that they made their readers thrive on reading and analysis of their works for years at a stretch.

Men would woo their wives in the evening with a prose out of the books. College students would plan and rehearse recital of works of specific writers to impress and attract the opposite sex, and any show of collection of such books ensured that popularity amongst peers was instantly obtained. Special meetings would be arranged amongst family friends or colleagues based on discussions and celebrations of the literary work of specific writers. Audiences would generally throng to theaters on release of musical films with the protagonist playing a famous writer or a composer. It is easy to recall*Rajesh Khanna in Mere jeewansaathi and other films, Sanjeev Kumar in Anamika, Amitabh in Abhiman and Yaarana, and Mukerjee in Ek Baar Muskura do, and Rishi Kapoor and Rajinder Kumar in many more or whio can forget Raj Babbar in Premgeet and Nikaah.* The success of such films was bolstered by the very strong literary content in dialogues as well as in lyrical compositions.

A major section of society grew upon a variety of magazines in local, regional or national language, namely Sarita, Manorama, Dharmyug, Illustrated Weekly, Grihshobha. The magazines offered a variety of content including an editorial themed on contemporary issues, current political analysis, tourism location profile, a section on delicacies and their preparation, a large kid section, a section on hindi films, reviews and interviews, sufficient number of stories on human relations, intrigue, social message and ideas which also vetted the diverse taste of readers. The magazines were lapped up the moment they were distributed at homes by hawkers either fortnightly or monthly and sometimes even caused arguments amongst readers in the same family to get first hand on the magazine.

The magazines connected various writers on one hand with a diverse age group of readers on the other. They provided entertainment, spread awareness, as well as were great source of information and personality grooming by way of such articles.

However content of such magazines showed gradual shift with focus increasing on glossiness and appeal to selective audiences and readership. But the fact that hit the popularity hard was the availability of online content on gossips, film celebrities, tourist places and all the matters under the sky. But the fact can not be denied that a whole generation grew upon such magazines with cartoon strips "Dabboojee," "Shreematijee" or a cartoon sketche by James Thurber, Bill Gallo, Stan Lee, Mort Walker or Milton Caniff in the western world,and many others, making the day for young and old alike (rather days together) and leaving a sweet tingling taste that left people smiling and pleasant faced.

These magazines were also at many a time silent solicitors and marriage counselors with many a stories hitting there right on the spot and striking a chord in a husband or a wife making him or her realize his or her follies and making them get up and patch up. The same held true for the saas –bahus and dada-dadi and potas.

Another section of the society was hooked upon religious books and periodicals. Still another section savoured biographies and memoirs and classified data books. Over the years many biography books have been lapped up by the voracious reader, most of them during train or air travel, prominent amongst them being on Eisenhour, Churchill, Napolean, Jawahar Lal Nehru, Gandhijee, Indira Gandhi, Sardar Patel, Zakir Hussain, R M Lohiya, J P Narayan, Jagjeewan Ram, Morarjee Desai, Abul Kalam, Sam Manekshaw, Ramanujam, Amjad Ali khan, Viv Richards, Ian Bothom, Sunil Gawaskar, Kapil Dev and many more from sports, culture and social life. The biographies offered a happy reading time as well as insight into the grit, determination and the thought process of the personality from which reader could gather some points and traits to learn from. The positive pointabout the books was that the reader could return back to the books for as many times as possible for inspiration at convenient time of the day, either early morning with bed tea, at the breakfast table, in the office, at dinner table, before dozing off to sleep with the bedlamp on, or sometimes in the comforts of loo areamaking it possible to leave a lasting impression on the mind of the reader.

((xxxi) Reference picture on page 175)

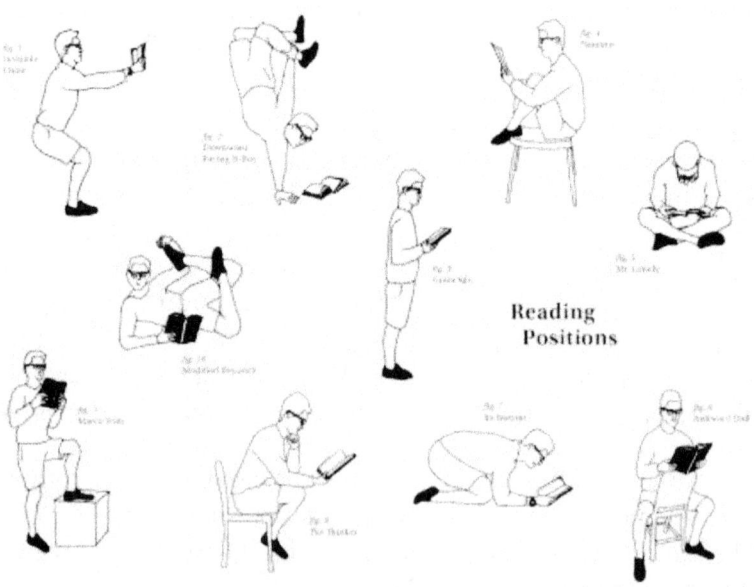

Reading
Positions

There is no denying the fact that ebooks provide an opportunity to have vast content handy and at a convenience to the readers, but the fact that the digital content needs to be adjusted in size and clarity and has to be constantly rolled on, appeals to some and does not to others although the younger and upcoming generations are more apt at the thing and ebooks come naturally to them, as compared to the hardback.

Reader's Digest has been an old time favourite with the readers who have a flair for reading English text. Some of the stories based on real life incidances have been phenomenally motivating and inspirational to the readers by their edge of the seat and chilling portrayal of headstrong characters, gritt and drive shown by the protagonist to overcome extreme handicaps or adverse situtations and hitting back almost rising from the ashes. Stories of men/women getting body parts amputated in major accidents, calamities at work place or in wilderness, and stories of women physicaly, mentaly and emotionaly coming out strong through a major physical or sexual assault, that left them physicaly and mentaly shattered.

The stories proved to be major turning points for innumerable readers across all ages, be it a young man trying for an army recruitment, a budding doctor, an official trying for a promotion, a college teacher learning the ropes of student handling, and even inspired kids to think beyond the fear of fatality.

Mills and Boon novels had their own loyalists. Teenage girls and boys under the watchful eyes of their mothers and fathers were goaded into good English literary and contemporary reading and Mills and Boon Series, by default formed one of the components of the reading mix. Girls would be so engrossed reading it that they would slip their daily chores and would have to be coaxed and cajoled and sometimes harangued by their mothers into doing their things. The novels had a very inebriating effect and the girls would surreptitiously drool over the pages that elaborated romantic interlude between dozing off with novels in their hands with their imaginations running wild with themselves playing as the female protagonist. The soft and gentle romance provided a halcyon escape from the daily humdrum of textbook, homework and mother's chiding and other's intrusion, into an imaginary and very private world where no one else was allowed (By orders!!).

The novels infact played a role in getting the daughters detatched from their mothers and get swooned by the protagonist off their feet into the clouds where love, and only love encompassed everything and there was need for nothing else, not even best friends. Thought process has changed today and the next generation has, as always, come up with contemporary definitions of love and romance and relations, and is connected to real as well as virtual world of friendship through facebook and other social sites. But people of the Mills and Boon generations still cant get over the awesomeness of the effect that these books had on them, and their first and then unending tryst with romance and friendship through the novels.

The same generation that fed on such vide array of romance, thrill, detective and other readings, however by virtue of the realization of the competitiveness the times demanded, had to pull their sons and daughters away from the leisurely readings and make them go through the grinds of competitive exams, coaching and preparatory books, which have become reading passion for the generation and the speed at which texts from various text books are recited by the generation, even leaves their fathers open mouthed and star struck.

Anyway they are reading and everyone else too!!

Bibliography and References

1. Ali Sami (1956). Pasargadae: the oldest imperial capital. Musavi Printing Office. pp. 90–94.

2. Baden, Joel (2014-07-29). The Historical David: The Real Life of an Invented Hero. HarperCollins Publishers. ISBN 9780062188373

3. Birla, Krishna Kumar (17 April 2009). *"Brushes With History". Penguin UK.* Retrieved 9 July 2017 – *via Google Books.*

4. Brass, Paul R. The Politics of India since Independence (1980)

5. Chandler, David (2003). The Oxford history of the British Army. Oxford University Press. p. xv. ISBN 978-0-19-280311-5.

6. Ch'ien Tuan-Sheng (Qian Duansheng)The Government and Politics of China, 1912-1949. (Cambridge, MA: Harvard University Press, 1950).

7. Gandhi, Rajmohan (2006). Mohandas: A True Story of a Man, His People, and an Empire By Gandhi. p. 5. ISBN 9780143104117.

8. "Improving Our World – IEEE Annual Report (page 4)" (PDF). *IEEE. 2005.*

9. Khan, Yasmin (2007). The Great Partition: The Making of India and Pakistan. Yale University Press. p. 18. ISBN 978-0-300-12078-3. Archived from the original on 12 October 2013. Retrieved 1 September 2013

11. Louis, William Roger; Low, Alaine M.; Porter, Andrew (1 January 2001). The Oxford History of the British Empire: The nineteenth century. Oxford University Press. p. 332. ISBN 978-0-19-924678-6.

12. Rothermund, Indira (1969). "The Individual and Society in Gandhi's Political Thought". The Journal of Asian Studies. Cambridge University Press. 28 (2): 313–320. doi:10.2307/2943005.

13. Solomon Alexander Nigosian (1993). The Zoroastrian faith: tradition and modern research. McGill-Queen's Press. pp. 47–48.

14. Sng, Tuan-Hwee. "Size and Dynastic Decline: The Principal-Agent Problem in Late Imperial China, 1700–1850." Explorations in Economic History 54 (2014): 107–27

15. Tewari, S. M. (1971). "The Concept of Democracy in the Political Thought of Mahatma Gandhi". Indian Political Science Review. 6 (2): 225–51.

16. *Corporate History – www.TechMahindra.com*